Charlotte Mary

Beechcroft at Rockstone

Outlook

Charlotte Mary Yonge

Beechcroft at Rockstone

1. Auflage | ISBN: 978-3-73261-888-0

Erscheinungsort: Paderborn, Deutschland

Erscheinungsjahr: 2018

Outlook Verlag GmbH, Paderborn.

BEECHCROFT AT ROCKSTONE

By Charlotte M Yonge

CONTENTS

AND THE DRAGON

CHAPTER I. — A DISPERSION

'A telegram! Make haste and open it, Jane; they always make me so nervous! I believe that is the reason Reginald always *will* telegraph when he is coming,' said Miss Adeline Mohun, a very pretty, well preserved, though delicate-looking lady of some age about forty, as her elder sister, brisk and lively and some years older, came into the room.

'No, it is not Reggie. It is from Lily. Poor Lily! Jasper—accident—Come.'

'Poor dear Lily! Is it young Jasper or old Jasper, I wonder?'

'If it were young Jasper she would have put Japs. I am afraid it is her husband. If so, she will be going off to him. I must catch the 11.20 train. Will you come, Ada?'

'Oh no; I should be knocked up, and on your hands. The suspense is bad enough at home.'

'If it is old Jasper, we shall see in the paper to-day. I will send it down to you from the station. Supposing it is Sir Jasper, and she wants to go out to him, we must take in some of the children.'

'Oh! Dear little Primrose would be nice enough, but what should we do with that Halfpenny woman? If we had the other girls, I suppose they would be at school all day; but surely some might go to Beechcroft. And mind, Jane, I will not have you overtasking yourself! Do not take any of them without having Gillian to help you. That I stipulate.'

Jane Mohun seemed as if she did not hear as these sentences were uttered at intervals, while she stood dashing off postcards at her davenport. Then she said, on her way to the door—

'Don't expect me to-night. I will send Fanny to ask one of the Wellands to come in to you, and telegraph if I bring any one home with me.'

'But, Jane dear—'

However, the door was shut, and by the time Miss Adeline had reached her sister's room, the ever-ready bag was nearly packed.

'I only wanted to say, dear Jane, that you must give my love to dear Lily. I am grieved—grieved for her; but indeed you must not undertake anything rash.' (A shake of the head, as the shoes went into their neat bag.) 'Do not let her persuade you to stay at Silverfold in her absence. You cannot give up everything here.'

'Yes, yes, Ada, I know it does not suit you. Never fear.'

'It is not that, but you are much too useful here to drop everything, especially now every one is away. I would willingly sacrifice myself, but—'

'Yes, I know, Ada dear. Now, good-bye, and take care of yourself, and don't be nervous. It may mean only that young Japs has twisted his little finger.'

And with a kiss, Miss Mohun ran downstairs as fast and lightly as if her years had been half their amount, and accomplished her orders to Fanny—otherwise Mrs. Mount—a Beechcroft native, who, on being left a widow, had returned to her former mistresses, bringing with her a daughter, who had grown up into an efficient housemaid. After a few words with her, Miss Mohun sped on, finding time at the station to purchase a morning paper just come down, and to read among the telegrams—

'COLOMBO, Sept. 3rd.

'Lieutenant-General Sir Jasper Merrifield, G.C.B., has been thrown from his horse, and received severe injuries.'

She despatched this paper to her sister by a special messenger, whom she had captured by the way, and was soon after in the train, knitting and pondering.

At Silverton station she saw the pony carriage, and in it her niece Gillian, a girl not quite seventeen, with brown eyes showing traces of tears.

'Mamma knew you would come,' she said.

'You have heard direct, of course.'

'Yes; Claude telegraphed. The horse fell over a precipice. Papa's leg and three ribs are broken. Not dangerous. That is all it says; and mamma is going out to him directly.'

'I was quite sure she would. Well, Gillian, we must do the best we can. Has she any plans?'

'I think she waited for you to settle them. Hal is come; he wanted to go with her, but she says it will cost too much, and besides, there is his Ordination in Advent.'

'Has she telegraphed to your uncles?'

'To Beechcroft and to Stokesley; but we don't quite know where Uncle Reginald is. Perhaps he will see the paper.'

Gillian's tears were flowing again, and her aunt said—

'Come, my dear, you must not give way; you must do all you can to make it better for your mother.'

'I know,' she answered. 'Indeed, I didn't cry till I sat waiting, and it all came over me. Poor papa! and what a journey mamma will have, and how dreadful it will be without her! But I know that it is horrid of me, when papa and my sisters must want her so much more.'

'That's right—quite right to keep up before her. It does not sound to me so bad, after all; perhaps they will telegraph again to stop her. Did Claude ask her to come out?'

'Oh no! There were only those few words.'

No more could be learnt till the pony stopped at the door, and Hal ran out to hand out his aunt, and beg her privately to persuade his mother to take him, or, if she would not consent to that, at least to have Macrae, the old soldier-servant, with her—it was not fit for her to travel alone.

Lady Merrifield looked very pale, and squeezed her sister close in her arms as she said—

'You are my great help, Jenny.'

'And must you go?'

'Yes, certainly.'

'Without waiting to hear more?'

'There is no use in losing time. I cannot cross from Folkestone till the day after to-morrow, at night. I must go to London to-morrow, and sleep at Mrs. Merrifield's.'

'But this does not seem to me so very bad.'

'Oh, no, no! but when I get there in three weeks' time, it will be just when I shall be most wanted. The nursing will have told on the girls, and Jasper will be feeling weary of being laid up, and wanting to take liberties.'

'And what will you be after such a journey?'

'Just up to keeping him in order. Come, you have too much sense to expostulate, Jenny.'

'No; you would wear yourself to fiddle-strings if you stayed at home. I only want you to take Hal, or Macrae.'

'Hal is out of the question, I would not interfere with his preparation on any account. Macrae would be a very costly article; and, moreover, I want him to act major-domo here, unless you would, and that I don't dare to hope for.'

'No, you must not, Lily; Ada never feels well here, nor always at Brighton, and Emily would be too nervous to have her without me. But we will take as many children as you please, or we have room for.'

'That is like you, Jenny. I know William will offer to take them in at home, but I cannot send them without Miss Vincent; and she cannot leave her mother, who has had a sort of stroke. Otherwise I should try leaving them here while I am away, but the poor old lady is in no state for it—in fact, I doubt her living long.'

'I know; you have been governess by yourself these last weeks; it will be well to relieve her. The best way will be for us to take Mysie and Valetta, and let them go to the High School; and there is a capital day-school for little boys, close to St. Andrew's, for Fergus, and Gillian can go there too, or join classes in whatever she pleases.'

'My Brownie! Have you really room for all those?'

'Oh yes! The three girls in the spare room and dressing-room, and Fergus in the little room over the porch. I will write to Fanny; I gave her a hint.'

'And I have no doubt that Primrose will be a delight to her aunt Alethea, poor little dear! Yes, that makes it all easy, for in the holidays I know the boys are sure of a welcome at the dear old home, or Hal might have one or two of them at his Curacy.'

The gong sounded for the melancholy dinner that had to go on all the same, and in the midst all were startled by the arrival of a telegram, which Macrae, looking awestruck, actually delivered to Harry instead of to his mistress; but it was not from Ceylon. It was from Colonel Mohun, from Beechcroft: 'Coming 6.30. Going with you. Send children here.'

Never were twenty words, including addresses, more satisfactory. The tears came, for the first time, to Lady Merrifield's eyes at the kindness of her brothers, and Harry was quite satisfied that his uncle would be a far better escort than himself or Macrae. Aunt Jane went off to send her telegram home and write some needful letters, and Lady Merrifield announced her arrangements to those whom they concerned.

'Oh! mamma, don't,' exclaimed Valetta; 'all the guinea-pigs will die.'

'I thought,' said Gillian, 'that we might stay here with Miss Vincent to look after us.'

'That will not do in her mother's state. Mrs. Vincent cannot be moved up here, and I could not lay such a burthen on them.'

'We would be very good,' said Val.

'That, I hope, you will be any way; but I think it will be easier at Rockstone, and I am quite sure that papa and I shall be better satisfied about you.'

'Mayn't we take Quiz!' asked Fergus.

'And Rigdum Funnidos?' cried Valetta.

'And Ruff and Ring?' chimed in Mysie.

'My dear children, I don't see how Aunt Jane can be troubled with any more animals than your four selves. You must ask her, only do not be surprised or put out if she refuses, for I don't believe you can keep anything there.'

Off the three younger ones went, Gillian observing, 'I don't see how they can, unless it was Quiz; but, mamma, don't you think I might go to Beechcroft with Primrose? I should be so much quieter working for the examination there, and I could send my exercises to Miss Vincent; and then I should keep up Prim's lessons.'

'Your aunt Alethea will, I know, like doing that, my dear; and I am afraid to turn those creatures loose on the aunts without some one to look after them and their clothes. Fanny will be very helpful; but it will not do to throw too much on her.'

'Oh! I thought they would have Lois—'

'There would not be room for her; besides that, I don't think it would suit your aunts. You and Mysie ought to do all the mending for yourselves and Fergus, and what Valetta cannot manage. I know you would rather be at Beechcroft, my dear; but in this distress and difficulty, some individual likings must be given up.'

'Yes, mamma.'

Lady Merrifield looked rather dubiously at her daughter. She had very little time, and did not want to have an argument, nor to elicit murmurs, yet it might be better to see what was in Gillian's mind before it was too late. Mothers, very fond of their own sisters, cannot always understand why it is not the same with their daughters, who inherit another element of inherited character, and of another generation, and who have not been welded together with the aunts in childhood. 'My dear,' she said, 'you know I am quite ready to hear if you have any real reasonable objection to this arrangement.'

'No, mamma, I don't think I have,' said Gillian thoughtfully. 'The not liking always meeting a lot of strangers, nor the general bustle, is all nonsense, I know quite well. I see it is best for the children, but I should like to know exactly who is to be in authority over them.'

'Certainly Aunt Jane,' replied Lady Merrifield. 'She must be the ultimate authority. Of course you will check the younger ones in anything going wrong, as you would here, and very likely there will be more restrictions. Aunt Ada has to be considered, and it will be a town life; but remember that your aunt is mistress of the house, and that even if you do think her arrangements uncalled for, it is your duty to help the others to submit cheerfully. Say anything you please fully and freely in your letters to me, but don't let there be any collisions of authority. Jane will listen kindly, I know, in private to any representation you may like to make, but to say before the children, "Mamma always lets them," would be most mischievous.'

'I see,' said Gillian. 'Indeed, I will do my best, mamma, and it will not be for very long.'

'I hope and trust not, my dear child. Perhaps we shall all meet by Easter—papa, and all; but you must not make too sure. There may be delays. Now I must see Halfpenny. I cannot talk to you any more, my Gillyflower, though I am leaving volumes unsaid.

Gillian found Aunt Jane emerging from her room, and beset by her three future guests.

'Aunt Jane, may we bring Quiz?'

'And Rigdum Funnidos and Lady Rigdum?'

'And Ruff and Ring? They are the sweetest doves in the world.'

'Doves! Oh, Mysie, they would drive your aunt Ada distracted, with coo-roo-roo at four o'clock in the morning, just as she goes off to sleep.'

'The Rigdums make no noise but a dear little chirp,' triumphantly exclaimed Valetta.

'Do you mean the kittens? We have a vacancy for one cat, you know.'

Oh yes, we want you to choose between Artaxerxes and the Sofy. But the Rigdums are the eldest pair of guinea-pigs. They are so fond of me, that I know poor old Funnidos will die of grief if I go away and leave him.'

'I sincerely hope not, Valetta, for, indeed, there is no place to put him in.'

'I don't think he would mind living in the cellar if he only saw me once a day,' piteously pleaded Valetta.

'Indeed, Val, the dark and damp would surely kill the poor thing, in spite of your attentions. You must make up your mind to separation from your pets, excepting the kitten.'

Valetta burst out crying at this last drop that made the bucket overflow, but Fergus exclaimed: 'Quiz! Aunt Jane! He always goes about with us, and always behaves like a gentleman, don't you, Quizzy?' and the little Maltese, who perfectly well understood that there was trouble in the air, sat straight up, crossed his paws, and looked touchingly wistful.

'Poor dear little fellow!' said Aunt Jane; 'yes, I knew he would be good, but Kunz would be horribly, jealous, you see; he is an only dog, and can't bear to have his premises invaded.'

'He ought to be taught better,' said Fergus gravely.

'So he ought,' Aunt Jane confessed; 'but he is too old to begin learning, and Aunt Ada and Mrs. Mount would never bear to see him disturbed. Besides, I really do not think Quiz would be half so well off there as among his own friends and places here, with Macrae to take care of him.' Then as Fergus began to pucker his face, she added, 'I am really very sorry to be so disagreeable.'

'The children must not be unreasonable,' said Gillian sagely, as she came up.

'And I am to choose between Xerxes and Artaxerxes, is it?' said Aunt Jane.

'No, the Sofy,' said Mysie. 'A Sofy is a Persian philosopher, and this kitten has got the wisest face.'

'Run and fetch them,' suggested her aunt, 'and then we can choose. Oh,' she added, with some relief at the thought, 'if it is an object to dispose of Cockie, we could manage him.'

The two younger ones were gratified, but Gillian and Mysie both exclaimed that Cockie's exclusive affections were devoted to Macrae, and that they could not answer for his temper under the separation. To break up such a household was decidedly the Goose, Fox, and Cabbage problem. As Mysie observed, in the course of the search for the kittens, in the make-the- best-of-it tone, 'It was not so bad as the former moves, when they were leaving a place for good and all.'

'Ah, but no place was ever so good as this,' said poor Valetta.

'Don't be such a little donkey,' said Fergus consequentially. 'Don't you know we are going to school, and I am three years younger than Wilfred was?'

'It is only a petticoat school,' said Val, 'kept by ladies.'

'It isn't.'

'It is; I heard Harry say so.'

'And yours is all butchers and bakers and candlestick makers.'

On which they fell on each other, each with a howl of defiance. Fergus grabbed at Val's pigtail, and she was buffeting him vehemently when Harry came out, held them apart, and demanded if this were the way to make their mother easy in leaving them.

'She said it was a pet-pet-petticoat school,' sobbed Fergus.

'And so it ought to be, for boys that fight with girls.'

'And he said mine was all butchers and bakers and candlestick makers,' whined Valetta.

'Then you'd better learn manners, or they'll take you for a tramp,' observed Harry; but at that moment Mysie broke in with a shout at having discovered the kittens making a plaything of the best library pen-wiper, their mother, the sleek Begum, abetting them, and they were borne off to display the coming glories of their deep fur to Aunt Jane.

Her choice fell upon the Sofy, as much because of the convenience of the name as because of the preternatural wisdom of expression imparted by the sweep of the black lines on the gray visage. Mr. Pollock's landlady was to be the happy possessor of Artaxerxes, and the turbulent portion of the Household was disposed of to bear him thither, and to beg Miss Hacket to give Buff and Ring the run of her cage, whence they had originally come, also to deliver various messages and notes.

By the time they returned, Colonel Mohun was met in the hall by his sister. 'Oh, Reggie, it is too good in you!' were the words that came with her fervent kiss. 'Remember how many years I have been seasoned to being "cockit up on a baggage waggon." Ought not such an old soldier as I to be able to take care of myself?'

'And what would your husband say to you when you got there? And should not I catch it from William? Well, are you packing up the youthful family for Beechcroft, except that at Rotherwood they are shrieking for Mysie?'

'I know how good William and Alethea would be. This child,' pointing to Primrose, who had been hanging on her all day in silence, 'is to go to them; but as I can't send Miss Vincent, educational advantages, as the advertisements say, lie on the side of Rockstone; so Jenny here undertakes to be troubled with the rabble.'

'But Mysie? Rotherwood met me at the station and begged me to obtain her from you. They really wish it.'

'He does, I have no doubt.'

'So does Madame la Marquise. They have been anxious about little Phyllis all the summer. She was languid and off her feed in London, and did not pick up at home as they expected. My belief is that it is too much governess and too little play, and that a fortnight here would set her up again. Rotherwood himself thinks so, and Victoria has some such inkling. At any rate, they are urgent to have Mysie with the child, as the next best thing.'

'Poor dear little Fly!' ejaculated Lady Merrifield; 'but I am afraid Mysie was not very happy there last year.'

'And what would be the effect of all the overdoing?' said Miss Mohun.

'Mysie is tougher than that sprite, and I suppose there is some relaxation,' said Lady Merrifield.

'Yes; the doctors have frightened them sufficiently for the present.

'I suppose Mysie is a prescription, poor child,' said her aunt, in a tone that evoked from her brother—

'Jealous, Jenny?'

'Well, Jane,' said Lady Merrifield, 'you know how thankful I am to you and Ada, but I am inclined to let it depend on the letters I get to-morrow, and the way Victoria takes it. If it is really an earnest wish on that dear little Fly's account, I could not withstand old Rotherwood, and though Mysie might be less happy than she would be with you, I do not think any harm will be done. Everything there is sound and conscientious, and if she picks up a little polish, it won't hurt her.'

'Shall you give her the choice?'

'I see no good in rending the poor child's mind between two affections, especially as there will be a very short time to decide in, for I shall certainly not send her if Victoria's is a mere duty letter.'

'You are quite right there, Lily,' said the Colonel. 'The less choice the greater comfort.'

'Well done, sir soldier,' said his sister Jane. 'I say quite right too; only, for my own sake, I wish it had been Valetta.'

'So no doubt does she,' said the mother; 'but unluckily it isn't. And, indeed, I don't think I wish it. Val is safer with you. As Gillian expressed it the other day, "Val does right when she likes it; Mysie does right when she knows it."'

'You have the compliment after all, Jane,' said the Colonel. 'Lily trusts you with the child she doesn't trust!'

There was no doubt the next morning, for Lady Rotherwood wrote an earnest, affectionate letter, begging for Mysie, who, she said, had won such golden opinions in her former visit that it would be a real benefit to Phyllis, as much morally as physically, to have her companionship. It was the tenderest letter that either of the sisters had ever seen from the judicious and excellent Marchioness, full of warm sympathy for Lady Merrifield's anxiety for her husband, and betraying much solicitude for her little girl.

'It has done her good,' said Jane Mohun. 'I did not think she had such a soft spot.'

'Poor Victoria,' said Lady Merrifield, 'that is a shame. You know she is an excellent mother.'

'Too excellent, that's the very thing,' muttered Aunt Jane. 'Well, Mysie's fate is settled, and I dare say it will turn out for the best.'

So Mysie was to go with Mrs. Halfpenny and Primrose to Beechcroft, whence the Rotherwoods would fetch her. If the lady's letter had been much less urgent, who could have withstood her lord's postscript: 'If you could see the little pale face light up at the bare notion of seeing Mysie, you would know how grateful we shall be for her.'

Mysie herself heard her destiny without much elation, though she was very fond of Lady Phyllis, and the tears came into her eyes at the thought of her being unwell and wanting her.

'Mamma said we must not grumble,' she said to Gillian; 'but I shall feel so lost without you and Val. It is so unhomish, and there's that dreadful German Fraulein, who was not at home last time.'

'If you told mamma, perhaps she would let you stay,' returned Gillian. 'I know I should hate it, worse than I do going to Rockstone and without you.'

'That would be unkind to poor Fly,' said Mysie. 'Besides, mamma said she could not have settling and unsettling for ever. And I shall see Primrose sometimes; besides, I do love Fly. It's marching orders, you know.'

It was Valetta who made the most objection. She declared that it was not fair that Mysie, who had been to the ball at Rotherwood, should go again to live with lords and ladies, while she went to a nasty day-school with butchers' and bakers' daughters. She hoped she should grow horridly vulgar, and if mamma did not like it, it would be her own fault!

Mrs. Halfpenny, who did not like to have to separate Mysie's clothes from the rest after they were packed, rather favoured this naughtiness by observing:

'The old blue merino might stay at home. Miss Mysie would be too set up to wear that among her fine folk. Set her up, that she should have all the treats, while her own Miss Gillian was turned over to the auld aunties!'

'Nonsense, nurse,' said Gillian. 'I'm much better pleased to go and be of some use! Val, you naughty child, how dare you make such a fuss?' for Valetta was crying again.

'I hate school, and I hate Rockstone, and I don't see why Mysie should always go everywhere, and wear new frocks, and I go to the butchers and bakers and wear horrid old ones.'

'I wish you could come too,' said Mysie; 'but indeed old frocks are the nicest, because one is not bothered to take so much care of them; and lords and ladies aren't a bit better to play with than, other people. In fact, Ivy is what Japs calls a muff and a stick.'

Valetta, however, cried on, and Mysie went the length of repairing to her mother, in the midst of her last notes and packings, to entreat to change with Val, who followed on tip-toe.

'Certainly not,' was the answer from Lady Merrifield, who was being worried on all sides, 'Valetta is not asked, and she is not behaving so that I could accept for her if she were.'

And Val had to turn away in floods of tears, which redoubled on being told by the united voices of her brothers and sisters that they were ashamed of her for being so selfish as to cry for herself when all were in so much trouble about papa.

Lady Merrifield caught some of the last words. 'No, my dear,' she said. 'That is not quite just or kind. It is being unhappy that makes poor Val so ready to cry about her own grievances. Only, Val, come here, and remember that fretting is not the way to meet such things. There is a better way, my child, and I think you know what I mean. Now, to help you through the time in an outer way, suppose you each set yourself some one thing to improve in while I am away. Don't tell me what it is, but let me find out when I come home.' With that she obeyed an urgent summons to speak to the gardener.

'I shall! I shall,' cried little Primrose, 'write a whole copy-book in single lines! And won't mamma be pleased? What shall you do, Fergus? and Val? and Mysie?'

'I shall get to spin my peg-top so as it will never tumble down, and will turn an engine for drawing water,' was the prompt answer of Fergus.

'What nonsense!' said Val; 'you'd better settle to get your long division sums right.'

'That s girls' stuff,' replied Fergus; 'you'd better settle to leave off crying for nothing.'

'That you had!' said several voices, and Val very nearly cried again as she exclaimed: 'Don't be all so tiresome. I shall make mamma a beautiful crewel cushion, with all the battles in history on it. And won't she be surprised!'

'I think mamma meant more than that,' said Mysie.

'Oh, Mysie, what shall you do?' asked Primrose.

'I did think of getting to translate one of mamma's favourite German stories quite through to her without wanting the dictionary or stumbling one bit,' said Mysie; 'but I am sure she meant something better and better, and I'm thinking what it is—Perhaps it is making all little Flossie Maddin's clothes, a whole suit all oneself—Or perhaps it is manners. What do you think, Gill?'

'I should say most likely it was manners for you,' volunteered Harry, 'and the extra you are most likely to acquire at Rotherwood.'

'I'm so glad,' said Mysie.

'And you, Gill,' inquired Primrose, 'what will you do? Mine is a copy- book, and Fergus's is the spinning-top-engines, and rule of three; and Val's is a crewel battle cushion and not crying; and Mysie's is German stories and manners; and what's yours, Gill?'

'Gill is so grown up, she is too good to want an inside thing' announced Primrose.

'Oh, Prim, you dear little thing,' cried both elder brother and sister, as they thought with a sort of pang of the child's opinion of grown-up impeccability.

'Harry is grown up more,' put in Fergus; 'why don't you ask him?'

'Because I know,' said Primrose, with a pretty shyness, and as they pressed her, she whispered, 'He is going to be a clergyman.'

There was a call for Mysie and Val from upstairs, and as the younger population scampered off, Gillian said to her brother—

'Is not it like "occupy till I come"?'

'So I was thinking,' said Harry gravely. 'But one must be as young as Mysie to throw one's "inside things" into the general stock of resolutions.'

'Yes,' said Gillian, with uplifted eyes. 'I do—I do hope to do something.'

Some great thing was her unspoken thought—some great and excellent achievement to be laid before her mother on her return. There was a tale begun in imitation of Bessie Merrifield, called "Hilda's Experiences". Suppose that was finished, printed, published, splendidly reviewed. Would not that be a great thing? But alas, she was under a tacit engagement never to touch it in the hours of study.

CHAPTER II. — ROCKQUAY

The actual moment of a parting is often softened by the confusion of departure. That of the Merrifield family took place at the junction, where Lady Merrifield with her brother remained in the train, to be carried on to London.

Gillian, Valetta, and Fergus, with their aunt, changed into a train for Rockstone, and Harry was to return to his theological college, after seeing Mysie and Primrose off with nurse on their way to the ancestral Beechcroft, whence Mysie was to be fetched to Rotherwood. The last thing that met Lady Merrifield's eyes was Mrs. Halfpenny gesticulating wildly, under the impression that Mysie's box was going off to London.

And Gillian's tears were choked in the scurry to avoid a smoking-carriage, while Harry could not help thinking—half blaming himself for so doing—that Mysie expended more feeling in parting with Sofy, the kitten, than with her sisters, not perceiving that pussy was the safety-valve for the poor child's demonstrations of all the sorrow that was oppressing her.

Gillian, in the corner of a Rockstone carriage, had time for the full heart-sickness and tumult of fear that causes such acute suffering to young hearts. It is quite a mistake to say that youth suffers less from apprehension than does age; indeed, the very inexperience and novelty add to the alarms, where there is no background of anxieties that have ended happily, only a crowd of examples of other people's misfortunes. The difference is in the greater elasticity and power of being distracted by outward circumstances; and thus lookers-on never guess at the terrific possibilities that have scared the imagination, and the secret ejaculations that have met them. How many times on that brief journey had not Gillian seen her father dying, her sisters in despair, her mother crushed in the train, wrecked in the steamer, perishing of the climate, or arriving to find all over and dying of the shock; yet all was varied by speculations on the great thing that was to offer itself to be done, and the delight it would give, and when the train slackened, anxieties were merged in the care for bags, baskets, and umbrellas.

Rockstone and Rockquay had once been separate places—a little village perched on a cliff of a promontory, and a small fishing hamlet within the bay, but these had become merged in one, since fashion had chosen them as a winter resort. Speculators blasted away such of the rocks as they had not covered with lodging-houses and desirable residences. The inhabitants of the two places had their separate churches, and knew their own bounds perfectly well; but to the casual observer, the chief distinction between them was that Rockstone was the more fashionable, Rockquay the more commercial, although the one had its shops, the other its handsome crescents and villas. The station was at Rockquay, and there was an uphill drive to reach Rockstone, where the two Miss Mohuns had been early inhabitants—had named their cottage Beechcroft after their native home, and, to justify the title, had flanked the gate with two copper beeches, which had attained a fair growth, in spite of sea winds, perhaps because sheltered by the house on the other side.

The garden reached out to the verge of the cliff, or rather to a low wall, with iron rails and spikes at the top, and a narrow, rather giddy path beyond. There was a gate in the wall, the key of which Aunt Jane kept in her own pocket, as it gave near access to certain rocky steps, about one hundred and thirty in number, by which, when in haste, the inhabitants of Rockstone could descend to the lower regions of the Quay.

There was a most beautiful sea-view from the house, which compensated for difficulties in gardening in such a situation, though a very slight slope inwards from the verge of the cliff gave some protection to the flower-beds; and there was not only a little conservatory attached to the drawing-room at the end, but the verandah had glass shutters, which served the purpose of protecting tender plants, and also the windows, from the full blast of the winter storms. Miss Mohun was very proud of these shutters, which made a winter garden of the verandah for Miss Adeline to take exercise in. The house was their own, and, though it aimed at no particular beauty, had grown pleasant and pretty looking by force of being lived in and made comfortable.

It was a contrast to its neighbours on either side of its pink and gray limestone wall. On one side began the grounds of the Great Rockstone Hotel; on the other was Cliff House, the big and seldom-inhabited house of one of the chief partners in the marble works, which went on on the other side of the promontory, and some people said would one day consume Rockstone altogether. It was a very fine house, and the gardens were reported to be beautifully kept up, but the owner was almost always in Italy, and had so seldom been at Rockstone that it was understood that all this was the ostentation of a man who did not know what to do with his money.

Aunt Adeline met the travellers at the door with her charming welcome. Kunz, all snowy white, wagged his tight-curled tail amid his barks, at sight of Aunt Jane, but capered wildly about the Sofy's basket, much to Valetta's agony; while growls, as thunderous as a small kitten could produce, proceeded therefrom.

'Kunz, be quiet,' said Aunt Jane, in a solemn, to-be-minded voice, and he crouched, blinking up with his dark eye.

'Give me the basket. Now, Kunz, this is our cat. Do you hear? You are not to meddle with her.'

Did Kunz really wink assent—a very unwilling assent?

'Oh, Aunt Jane!' from Val, as her aunt's fingers undid the cover of the basket.

'Once for all!' said Aunt Jane.

'M-m-m-m-ps-pss-psss!' from the Sofy, two screams from Val and Fergus, a buffeting of paws, a couple of wild bounds, first on a chair-back, then on the mantelpiece, where, between the bronze candlestick and the vase, the Persian philosopher stood hissing and swearing, while Kunz danced about and barked.

'Take her down, Gillian,' said Aunt Jane; and Gillian, who had some presence of mind, accomplished it with soothing words, and, thanks to her gloves, only one scratch.

Meantime Miss Mohun caught up Kunz, held up her finger to him, stopped his barks; and then, in spite of the 'Oh, don'ts,' and even the tears of Valetta, the two were held up—black nose to pink nose, with a resolute 'Now, you are to behave well to each other, from Aunt Jane.

Kunz sniffed, the Sofy hissed; but her claws were captive. The dog was the elder and more rational, and when set down again took no more notice of his enemy, whom Valetta was advised to carry into Mrs. Mount's quarters to be comforted and made at home there; the united voice of the household declaring that the honour of the Spitz was as spotless as his coat!

Such was the first arrival at Rockstone, preceding even Aunt Adeline's inquiries after Mysie, and the full explanation of the particulars of the family dispersion. Aunt Ada's welcome was not at all like that of Kunz. She was very tender and caressing, and rejoiced that her sister could trust her children to her. They should all get on most happily together, she had no doubt.

True-hearted as Gillian was, there was something hopeful and refreshing in the sight of that fair, smiling face, and the touch of the soft hand, in the room that was by no means unfamiliar, though she had never slept in the house before. It was growing dark, and the little fire lighted it up in a friendly manner. Wherever Aunt Jane was, everything was neat; wherever Aunt Adeline was, everything was graceful. Gillian was old enough to like the general prettiness; but it somewhat awed Val and Fergus, who stood straight and shy till they were taken upstairs. The two girls had a very pretty room and dressing-room—the guest chamber, in fact; and Fergus was not far off, in a small apartment which, as Val said, 'stood on legs,' and formed the shelter of the porch.

'But, oh dear! oh dear!' sighed Val, as Gillian unpacked their evening garments, 'Isn't there any nice place at all where one can make a mess?'

'I don't know whether the aunts will ever let us make a mess,' said Gillian; 'they don't look like it.'

At which Valetta's face puckered up in the way only too familiar to her friends.

'Come, don't be silly, Val. You won't have much time, you know; you will go to school, and get some friends to play with, and not want to make messes here.'

'I hate friends!'

'Oh, Val!'

'All but Fly, and Mysie is gone to her. I want Mysie.'

So in truth did Gillian, almost as much as her mother. Her heart sank as she thought of having Val and Fergus to save from scrapes without Mysie's readiness and good humour. If Mysie were but there she should be free for her 'great thing.' And oh! above all, Val's hair—the brown bush that Val had a delusion that she 'did' herself, but which her 'doing' left looking rather worse than it did before, and which was not permitted in public to be in the convenient tail. Gillian advanced on her with the brush, but she tossed it and declared it all right!

However, at that moment there was a knock. Mrs. Mount's kindly face and stout form appeared. She had dressed Miss Ada and came to see what she could do for the young people, being of that delightful class of old servants who are charmed to have anything young in the house, especially a boy. She took Valetta's refractory mane in hand, tied her sash, inspected Fergus's hands, which had succeeded in getting dirty in their inevitable fashion, and undertook all the unpacking and arranging. To Val's inquiry whether there was any place for making 'a dear delightful mess' she replied with a curious little friendly smile, and wonder that a young lady should want such a thing.

'I'm afraid we are all rather strange specimens of young ladies,' replied Gillian; 'very untidy, I mean.'

'And I'm sure I don't know what Miss Mohun and Miss Ada will say' said good Mrs. Mount.

'What's that? What am I to say?' asked Aunt Jane, coming into the room.

21

But, after all, Aunt Jane proved to have more sympathy with 'messes' than any of the others. She knew very well that the children would be far less troublesome if they had a place to themselves, and she said, 'Well, Val, you shall have the boxroom in the attics. And mind, you must keep all your goods there, both of you. If I find them about the house, I shall—'

'Oh, what, Aunt Jane?'

'Confiscate them,' was the reply, in a very awful voice, which impressed Fergus the more because he did not understand the word.

'You need not look so much alarmed, Fergus,' said Gillian; 'you are not at all the likely one to transgress.'

'No,' said Valetta gravely. 'Fergus is what Lois calls a regular old battledore.'

'I won't be called names,' exclaimed Fergus.

'Well, Lois said so—when you were so cross because the poker had got on the same side as the tongs! She said she never saw such an old battledore, and you know how all the others took it up.'

'Shuttlecock yourself then!' angrily responded Fergus, while both aunt and sister were laughing too much to interfere.

'I shall call you a little Uncle Maurice instead,' said Aunt Jane. 'How things come round! Perhaps you would not believe, Gill, that Aunt Ada was once in a scrape, when she was our Mrs. Malaprop, for applying that same epithet on hearsay to Maurice.'

This laugh made Gillian feel more at home with her aunt, and they went up happily together for the introduction to the lumber-room, not a very spacious place, and with a window leading out to the leads. Aunt Jane proceeded to put the children on their word of honour not to attempt to make an exit thereby, which Gillian thought unnecessary, since this pair were not enterprising.

The evening went off happily. Aunt Jane produced one of the old games which had been played at the elder Beechcroft, and had a certain historic character in the eyes of the young people. It was one of those variations of the Game of the Goose that were once held to be improving, and their mother had often told them how the family had agreed to prove whether honesty is really the best policy, and how it had been agreed that all should cheat as desperately as possible, except 'honest Phyl,' who *couldn't*; and how, by some extraordinary combination, good for their morals, she actually was the winner. It was immensely interesting to see the identical much-worn sheet of dilapidated pictures with the padlock, almost close to the goal, sending the counter back almost to the beginning in search of the key. Still more interesting was the imitation, in very wonderful drawing, devised by mamma, of the career of a true knight—from pagedom upwards—in pale watery Prussian-blue armour, a crimson scarf, vermilion plume, gamboge spurs, and very peculiar arms and legs. But, as Valetta observed, it must have been much more interesting to draw such things as that than stupid freehand lines and twists with no sense at all in them.

Aunt Ada, being subject to asthmatic nights, never came down to breakfast, and, indeed, it was at an hour that Gillian thought fearfully early; but her Aunt Jane was used to making every hour of the day available, and later rising would have prevented the two children from being in time for the schools, to which they were to go on the Monday. Some of Aunt Jane's many occupations on Saturday consisted in arranging with the two heads of their respective schools, and likewise for the mathematical class Gillian was to join at the High School two mornings in the week, and for her lessons on the organ, which were to be at St. Andrew's Church. Somehow Gillian felt as if she were as entirely in her aunt's hands as Kunz and the Sofy had been!

After the early dinner, which suited the invalid's health, Aunt Jane said she would take Valetta and Fergus to go down to the beach with the little Varleys, while she went to her district, leaving Gillian to read to Aunt Ada for half an hour, and then to walk with her for a quiet turn on the beach.

It was an amusing article in a review that Gillian was set to read, and she did it so pleasantly that her aunt declared that she looked forward to many such afternoon pastimes, and then, by an easier way than the hundred and a half steps, they proceeded down the hill, the aunt explaining a great deal to the niece in a manner very gratifying to a girl beginning to be admitted to an equality with grown-up people.

'There is our old church,' said Aunt Ada, as they had a glimpse of a gray tower with a curious dumpy steeple.

'Do you go to church there!'

'I do—always. I could not undertake the hill on Sundays; but Jane takes the school-children to the St. Andrew's service in the afternoon.'

'But which is the parish church?'

'In point of fact, my dear; it is all one parish. Good morning, Mr. Hablot. My niece, Miss Gillian Merrifield. Yes, my sister is come home. I think she will be at the High School. He is the vicar of St. Andrew's,' as the clergyman went off in the direction of the steps.

'I thought you said it was all one parish.'

'St. Andrew's is only a district. Ah, it was all before your time, my dear.'

'I know dear Uncle Claude was the clergyman here, and got St. Andrew's built.'

'Yes, my dear. It was the great work and thought with him and Lord Rotherwood in those days that look so bright now,' said Aunt Ada. 'Yes, and with us all.'

'Do tell me all about it,' entreated Gillian; and her aunt, nothing loth, went on.

'Dear Claude was only five-and-twenty when he had the living. Nobody would take it, it was such a neglected place. All Rockquay down there had grown up with only the old church, and nobody going to it. It was a great deal through Rotherwood. Some property here came to him, and he was shocked at the state of things. Then we all thought the climate might be good for dear Claude, and Jane came to live with him and help him, and look after him. You see there were a great many of us, and Jane—well, she didn't quite get on with Alethea, and Claude thought she wanted a sphere of her own, and that is the way she comes to have more influence than any one else here. And as I am always better in this air than anywhere else, I came soon after—even before my dear fathers death. And oh! what an eager, hopeful time it was, setting everything going, and making St. Andrew's all we could wish! We were obliged to be cautious at the old church, you know, because of not alarming the old-fashioned people. And so we are still—'

'Is that St. Andrew's? Oh, it is beautiful. May I look in?'

'Not now, my dear. You will see it another time.'

'I wish it were our church.'

'You will find the convenience of having one so near. And our services are very nice with our present rector, Mr. Ellesmere, an excellent active man, but his wife is such an invalid that all the work falls on Jane. I am so glad you are here to help her a little. St. Andrew's has a separate district, and Mr. Hablot is the vicar; but as it is very poor, we keep the charities all in one. Rotherwood built splendid schools, so we only have an infant school for the Rockstone children. On Sunday, Jane assembles the older children there and takes them to church; but in the afternoon they all go to the National Schools, and then to a children's service at St. Andrew's. She gets on so well with Mr. Hablot—he was dear Claude's curate, you see, and little Mrs. Hablot was quite a pupil of ours. What do you think little Gerald Hablot said—he is only five—"Isn't Miss Mohun the most consultedest woman in Rockquay?"'

'I suppose it is true,' said Gillian, laughing, but rather awestruck.

24

'I declare it makes me quite giddy to count up all she has on her hands. Nobody can do anything without her. There are so few permanent inhabitants, and when people begin good works, they go away, or marry, or grow tired, and then we can't let them drop!'

'Oh! what's that pretty spire, on the rise of the other hill?'

'My dear, that was the Kennel Mission Chapel, a horrid little hideous iron thing, but Lady Flight mistook and called it St. Kenelm's, and St. Kenelm's it will be to the end of the chapter.' And as she exchanged bows with a personage in a carriage, 'There she is, my dear.'

'Who? Did she build that church?'

'It is not consecrated. It really is only a mission chapel, and he is nothing but a curate of Mr. Hablot's,' said Aunt Ada, Gillian thought a little venomously.

She asked, 'Who?'

'The Reverend Augustine Flight, my dear. I ought not to say anything against them, I am sure, for they mean to be very good; but she is some City man's widow, and he is an only son, and they have more money than their brains can carry. They have made that little place very beautiful, quite oppressed with ornament—City taste, you know, and they have all manner of odd doings there, which Mr. Hablot allows, because he says he does not like to crush zeal, and he thinks interference would do more harm than good. Jane thinks he ought not to stand so much, but—'

Gillian somehow felt a certain amusement and satisfaction in finding that Aunt Jane had one disobedient subject, but they were interrupted by two ladies eagerly asking where to find Miss Mohun, and a few steps farther on a young clergyman accosted them, and begged that Miss Mohun might be told the hour of some meeting. Also that 'the Bellevue Church people would not co-operate in the coal club.'

Then it was explained that Bellevue Church was within the bounds of another parish, and had been built by, and for, people who did not like the doctrine at the services of St. Andrew's.

By this time aunt and niece had descended to the Marine esplanade, a broad road, on one side of which there was a low sea wall, and then the sands and rocks stretched out to the sea, on the other a broad space of short grass, where there was a cricket ground, and a lawn-tennis ground, and the volunteers could exercise, and the band played twice a week round a Russian gun that stood by the flagstaff.

The band was playing now, and the notes seemed to work on Gillian's feet, and yet to bring her heart into her throat, for the last time she had heard that march was from the band of her father's old regiment, when they were all together!

Her aunt was very kind, and talked to her affectionately and encouragingly of the hopes that her mother would find her father recovering, and that it would turn out after all quite an expedition of pleasure and refreshment. Then she said how much she rejoiced to have Gillian with her, as a companion to herself, while her sister was so busy, and she was necessarily so much left alone.

'We will read together, and draw, and play duets, and have quite a good account of our employment to give,' she said, smiling.

'I shall like it very much,' said Gillian heartily.

'Dear child, the only difficulty will be that you will spoil me, and I shall never be able to part with you. Besides, you will be such a help to my dear Jane. She never spares herself, you know, and no one ever spares her, and I can do so little to help her, except with my head.'

'Surely here are plenty of people,' said Gillian, for they were in the midst of well-dressed folks, and Aunt Ada had more than once exchanged nods and greetings.

'Quite true, my dear; but when there is anything to be done, then there is a sifting! But now we have you, with all our own Lily's spirit, I shall be happy about Jane for this winter at least.

They were again interrupted by meeting a gentleman and lady, to whom Gillian was introduced, and who walked on with her aunt conversing. They had been often in India, and made so light of the journey that Gillian was much cheered. Moreover, she presently came in sight of Val and Fergus supremely happy over a castle on the beach, and evidently indoctrinating the two little Varleys with some of the dramatic sports of Silverfold.

Aunt Ada found another acquaintance, a white moustached old gentleman, who rose from a green bench in a sunny corner, saying, 'Ah, Miss Mohun, I have been guarding your seat for you.'

'Thank you, Major Dennis. My niece, Miss Merrifield.'

He seemed to be a very courteous old gentleman, for he bowed, and made some polite speech about Sir Jasper, and, as he was military, Gillian hoped to have heard some more about the journey when they sat down, and room was made for her; but instead of that he and her aunt began a discussion of the comings and goings of people she had never heard of, and the letting or not letting of half the villas in Rockstone; and she found it so dull that she had a great mind to go and join the siege of Sandcastle. Only her shoes and her dress were fitter for the esplanade than the shore with the tide coming in; and when one has just begun to buy one's own clothes, that is a consideration.

At last she saw Aunt Jane's trim little figure come out on the sands and make as straight for the children as she could, amid greetings and consultations, so with an exclamation, she jumped up and went over the shingle to meet them, finding an endeavour going on to make them tolerably respectable for the walk home, by shaking off the sand, and advising Val to give up her intention of dragging home a broad brown ribbon of weed with a frilled edge, all polished and shiny with wet. She was not likely to regard it as such a curiosity after a few days' experience of Rockquay, as her new friends told her.

Kitty Varley went to the High School, which greatly modified Valetta's disgust to it, for the little girls had already vowed to be the greatest chums in the world, and would have gone home with arms entwined, if Aunt Jane had not declared that such things could not be done in the street, and Clem Varley, with still more effect, threatened that if they were such a pair of ninnies, he should squirt at them with the dirtiest water he could find.

Valetta had declared that she infinitely preferred Kitty to Fly, and Kitty was so flattered at being adopted by the second cousin of a Lady Phyllis, and the daughter of a knight, that she exalted Val above all the Popsys and Mopsys of her present acquaintance, and at parting bestowed on her a chocolate cream, which tasted about equally of salt water and hot hand—at least if one did not feel it a testimonial of ardent friendship.

Fergus and Clement had, on the contrary, been so much inclined to punch and buffet one another, that Miss Mohun had to make them walk before her to keep the peace, and was by no means sorry when the gate of 'The Tamarisks' was reached, and the Varleys could be disposed of.

However, the battery must have been amicable, for Fergus was crazy to go in and see Clement's little pump, which he declared 'would do it'—an enigmatical phrase supposed to refer to the great peg-top-perpetual-motion invention. He was dragged away with difficulty on the plea of its being too late by Aunt Jane, who could not quite turn two unexpected children in on Mrs. Varley, and had to effect a cruel severance of Val and Kitty in the midst of their kisses.

'Sudden friendships,' said Gillian, from the superiority of her age.

'I do not think you are given that way,' said Aunt Jane.

'Does the large family suffice for all of you? People are so different,' added Aunt Ada.

'Yes,' said Gillian. 'We have never been in the way of caring for any outsider. I don't reckon Bessie Merrifield so—nor Fly Devereux, nor Dolores, because they are cousins.'

'Cousins may be everything or nothing,' asserted Miss Mohun. 'You have been about so much that you have hardly had time to form intimacies. But had you no friends in the officers' families?'

'People always retired before their children grew up to be companionable,' said Gillian. 'There was nobody except the Whites. And that wasn't exactly friendship.'

'Who were they?' said Aunt Jane, who always liked to know all about everybody.

'He rose from the ranks,' said Gillian. 'He was very much respected, and nobody would have known that he was not a gentleman to begin with. But his wife was half a Greek. Papa said she had been very pretty; but, oh! she had grown so awfully fat. We used to call her the Queen of the White Ants. Then Kally—her name was really Kalliope—was very nice, and mamma got them to send her to a good day-school at Dublin, and Alethea and Phyllis used to have her in to try to make a lady of her. There used to be a great deal of fun about their Muse, I remember; Claude thought her very pretty, and always stood up for her, and Alethea was very fond of her. But soon after we went to Belfast, Mr. White was made to retire with the rank of captain. I think papa tried to get something for him to do; but I am not sure whether he succeeded, and I don't know any more about them.'

'Not exactly friendship, certainly,' said Aunt Jane, smiling. 'After all, Gillian, in your short life, you have had wider experiences than have befallen your old aunts!'

'Wider, perhaps, not deeper, Jane,' suggested Miss Adeline.

And Gillian thought—though she felt it would be too sentimental to say— that in her life, persons and scenes outside her own family had seemed to 'come like shadows and so depart'; and there was a general sense of depression at the partings, the anxiety, and the being unsettled again when she was just beginning to have a home.

CHAPTER III. — PERPETUAL MOTION

If Fergus had not yet discovered the secret of perpetual motion, Gillian felt as if Aunt Jane had done so, and moreover that the greater proportion of parish matters were one vast machine, of which she was the moving power.

As she was a small spare woman, able to do with a very moderate amount of sleep, her day lasted from 6 A.M. to some unnamed time after midnight; and as she was also very methodical, she got through an appalling amount of business, and with such regularity that those who knew her habits could tell with tolerable certainty, within reasonable limits, where she would be found and what she would be doing at any hour of the seven days of the week. Everything she influenced seemed to recur as regularly as the motions of the great ruthless-looking engines that Gillian had seen at work at Belfast; the only loose cog being apparently her sister Adeline, who quietly took her own way, seldom came downstairs before eleven o'clock, went out and came in, made visits or received them, wrote letters, read and worked at her own sweet will. Only two undertakings seemed to belong to her—a mission working party, and an Italian class of young ladies; and even the presidency of these often lapsed upon her sister, when she had had one of those 'bad nights' of asthma, which were equally sleepless to both sisters. She was principally useful by her exquisite needlework, both in church embroidery and for sales; and likewise as the recipient of all the messages left for Miss Mohun, which she never forgot, besides that, having a clear sensible head, she was useful in consultation.

She was thoroughly interested in all her sister's doings, and always spoke of herself as the invalid, precluded from all service except that of being a pivot for Jane, the stationary leg of the compasses, as she sometimes called herself. This repose, together with her prettiness and sweetness of manner, was very attractive; especially to Gillian, who had begun to feel herself in the grip of the great engine which bore her along without power of independent volition, and with very little time for 'Hilda's Experiences'.

At home she had gone on harmoniously in full acquiescence with household arrangements; but before the end of the week the very same sensations came over her which had impelled her and Jasper into rebellion and disgrace, during the brief reign of a very strict daily governess, long ago at Dublin. Her reason and sense approved of all that was set before her, and much of it was pleasant and amusing; but this was the more provoking by depriving her of the chance of resistance or the solace of complaint. Moreover, with all her time at Aunt Jane's disposal, how was she to do her great thing? Valetta's crewel battle cushion had been reduced to a delicious design of the battle of the frogs and mice, drawn by Aunt Ada, and which she delighted in calling at full length 'the Batrachyomachia,' sparing none of the syllables which was to work below. And it was to be worked at regularly for half an hour before bed-time. Trust Aunt Jane for seeing that any one under her dominion did what had been undertaken! Only thus the spontaneity seemed to have departed, and the work became a task. Fergus meanwhile had set his affections on a big Japanese top he had seen in a window, and was eagerly awaiting his weekly threepence, to be able to complete the purchase, though no one but Valetta was supposed to understand what it had to do with his 'great thing.'

It was quite pleasant to Gillian to have a legitimate cause of opposition when Miss Mohun made known that she intended Gillian to take a class at the afternoon Sunday-school, while the two children went to Mrs. Hablot's drawing-room class at St. Andrew's Vicarage, all meeting afterwards at church.

'Did mamma wish it?' asked Gillian.

'There was no time to mention it, but I knew she would.'

'I don't think so,' said Gillian. 'We don't teach on Sundays, unless some regular person fails. Mamma likes to have us all at home to do our Sunday work with her.'

'Alas, I am not mamma! Nor could I give you the time.'

'I have brought the books to go on with Val and Ferg. I always do some of their work with them, and I am sure mamma would not wish them to be turned over to a stranger.'

'The fact is, that young ladies have got beyond Sunday-schools!'

'No, no, Jane,' said her sister; 'Gillian is quite willing to help you; but it is very nice in her to wish to take charge of the children.'

'They would be much better with Mrs. Hablot than dawdling about here and amusing themselves in the new Sunday fashion. Mind, I am not going to have them racketing about the house and garden, disturbing you, and worrying the maids.'

'Aunt Jane!' cried Gillian indignantly, 'you don't think that is the way mamma brought us up to spend Sunday?'

'We shall see,' said Aunt Jane; then more kindly, 'My dear, you are right to use your best judgment, and you are welcome to do so, as long as the children are orderly and learn what they ought.'

It was more of a concession than Gillian expected, though she little knew the effort it cost, since Miss Mohun had been at much pains to set Mrs. Hablot's class on foot, and felt it a slight and a bad example that her niece and nephew should be defaulters. The motive might have worked on Gillian, but it was a lower one, therefore mentioned.

She had seen Mrs. Hablot at the Italian class, and thought her a mere girl, and an absolute subject of Aunt Jane's stumbling pitifully, moreover, in a speech of Adelchi's; therefore evidently not at all likely to teach Sunday subjects half so well as herself!

Nor was there anything amiss on that first Sunday. The lessons were as well and quietly gone through as if with mamma, and there was a pleasant little walk on the esplanade before the children's service at St. Andrew's; after which there was a delightful introduction to some of the old books mamma had told them of.

They were all rather subdued by the strangeness and newness of their surroundings, as well as by anxiety. If the younger ones were less anxious about their parents than was their sister, each had a plunge to make on the morrow into a very new world, and the Varleys' information had not been altogether reassuring. Valetta had learnt how many marks might be lost by whispering or bad spelling, and how ferociously cross Fraulein Adler looked at a mistake in a German verb; while Fergus had heard a dreadful account of the ordeals to which Burfield and Stebbing made new boys submit, and which would be all the worse for him, because he had a 'rum' Christian name, and his father was a swell.

Gillian had some experience through her elder brothers, and suspected Master Varley of being guilty of heightening the horrors; so she assured Fergus that most boys had the same sort of Christian names, but were afraid to confess them to one another, and so called each other Bill and Jack. She advised him to call himself by his surname, not to mention his father's title if he could help it, and, above all, not to seem to mind anything.

Her own spirits were much exhilarated the next morning by a note from Harry, the recipient of all telegrams, with tidings that the doctors were quite satisfied with Sir Jasper, and that Lady Merrifield had reached Brindisi.

There was great excitement at sight of a wet morning, for it appeared that an omnibus came round on such occasions to pick up the scholars; and Valetta thought this so delightful that she danced about exclaiming, 'What fun!' and only wishing for Mysie to share it. She would have rushed down to the gate umbrellaless if Aunt Jane had not caught and conducted her, while Gillian followed with Fergus. Aunt Jane looked down the vista of young faces—five girls and three boys—nodding to them, and saying to the senior, a tall damsel of fifteen,

'Here are my children, Emma. You will take care of them, please. You are keeping order here, I suppose?'

There was a smile and bow in answer as the door closed, and the omnibus jerked away its ponderous length.

'I'm sorry to see that Stebbing there,' observed the aunt, as she went back; 'but Emma Norton ought to be able to keep him in order. It is well you have no lessons out of the house to-day, Gillian.'

'Are you going out then?'

'Oh yes!' said Miss Mohun, running upstairs, and presently coming back with a school-bag and a crackling waterproof cloak, but pausing as she saw Gillian at the window, nursing the Sofy, and gazing at the gray cloud over the gray sea. 'You are not at a loss for something to do,' she said, 'you said you meant to write to your mother.'

'Oh yes!' said Gillian, suddenly fretted, and with a sense of being hunted, 'I have plenty to do.'

'I see,' said Miss Mohun, turning over the books that lay on the little table that had been appropriated to her niece, in a way that, unreasonably or not, unspeakably worried the girl, 'Brachet's French Grammar—that's right. Colenso's Algebra—I don't think they use that at the High School. Julius Caesar—you should read that up in Merivale.'

'I did,' said Gillian, in a voice that very nearly said, 'Do let them alone.'

'Well, you have materials for a very useful, sensible morning's work, and when Ada comes down, very likely she will like to be read to.'

Off went the aunt, leaving the niece stirred into an absolute desire, instead of spending the sensible morning, to take up 'Near Neighbours', and throw herself into an easy-chair; and when she had conscientiously resisted that temptation, her pen would hover over 'Hilda's Experiences', even when she had actually written 'Dearest Mamma.' She found she was in no frame to write such a letter as would be a comfort to her mother, so she gave that up, and made her sole assertion of liberty the working out of a tough double equation in Colenso, which actually came right, and put her in such good humour that she was no longer afraid of drumming the poor piano to death and Aunt Ada upstairs to distraction, but ventured on learning one of the Lieder ohne Worte; and when her Aunt Ada came down and complimented her on the sounds that had ascended, she was complacent enough to write a very cheerful letter, whilst her aunt was busied with her own. She described the Sunday-school question that had arisen, and felt sure that her father would pronounce his Gill to be a sensible young woman. Afterwards Miss Adeline betook herself to a beautiful lily of church embroidery, observing, as Gillian sat down to read to her Alphonse Karr's Voyage autour de mon Jardin, that it was a real pleasure to listen to such prettily-pronounced French. Kunz lay at her feet, the Sofy nestled in Gillian's lap, and there was a general sense of being rubbed down the right way.

By and by there loomed through the rain two dripping shiny forms under umbrellas strongly inclined to fly away from them—Miss Mohun and Mr. Grant, the junior curate, whom she had brought home to luncheon. Both were full of the irregularities of the two churches of Bellevue and St. Kenelm's on the recent harvest-thanksgiving Sunday. It was hard to tell which was most reprobated, what St. Kenelm's did or what Bellevue did not do. If the one blew trumpets in procession, the other collected the offertory in a warming- pan. Gillian had already begun to find that these misdoings supplied much conversation at Beechcroft Cottage, and began to get half weary, half curious to judge for herself of all these enormities; nor did she feel more interested in the discussion of who had missed church or school, and who needed tickets for meat, or to be stirred up to pay for their coal club.

At last she heard, 'Well, I think you might read to her, Gillian! Oh! were not you listening? A very nice girl near here, a pupil teacher, who has developed a hip complaint, poor child. She will enjoy having visits from you, a young thing like herself.'

Gillian did not like it at all, but she knew that it would be wrong to refuse, and answered, 'Very well,' with no alacrity—hoping that it was not an immediate matter, and that something might happen to prevent it. But at that moment the sun came out, the rain had ceased, and there were glistening drops all over the garden; the weather quarter was clear, and after half an hours rest after dinner Aunt Jane jumped up, decreeing that it was time to go out, and that she would introduce Gillian to Lilian Giles before going on to the rest of her district.

She gathered a few delicate flowers in the little conservatory, and put them in a basket with a peach from the dessert, then took down a couple of books from the shelf. Gillian could not but acquiesce, though she was surprised to find that the one given to her was a translation of Undine.

'The child is not badly off,' explained Miss Mohun. 'Her father is a superior workman. She does not exactly want comforts, but she is sadly depressed and disappointed at not being able to go on with her work, and the great need is to keep her from fretting over her troubles, and interested in something.'

Gillian began to think of one of the graceful hectic invalids of whom she had read, and to grow more interested as she followed Aunt Jane past the old church with the stout square steeple, constructed to hold, on a small side turret window, a light for the benefit of ships at sea. Then the street descended towards the marble works. There was a great quarry, all red and raw with recent blasting, and above, below, and around, rows of new little stuccoed, slated houses, for the work-people, and a large range of workshops and offices fronting the sea. This was Miss Mohun's district, and at a better- looking house she stopped and used the knocker.

That was no distinction; all had doors with knockers and sash windows, but this was a little larger, and the tiny strip of garden was well kept, while a beautiful myrtle and pelargonium peeped over the muslin blind; and it was a very nice-looking woman who opened the door, though she might have been the better for a cap. Aunt Jane shook hands with her, rather to Gillian's surprise, and heard that Lily was much the same.

'It is her spirits are so bad, you see, Miss Mohun,' she added, as she ushered them into a somewhat stuffy little parlour, carpeted and bedecked with all manner of knick-knacks, photographs, and framed certificates of various societies of temperance and providence on the gaily-papered walls. The girl lay on a couch near the fire, a sallow creature, with a big overhanging brow, made heavier by a dark fringe, and an expression that Gillian not unjustly decided was fretful, though she smiled, and lighted up a little when she saw Miss Mohun.

There was a good deal said about her bad nights, and her appetite, and how the doctor wanted her to take as much as she could, and how everything went against her—even lardy cake and roly-poly pudding with bacon in it!

Miss Mohun put the flowers on the little table near the girl, who smiled a little, and thanked her in a languid dreary manner. Finding that she had freshly been visited by the rector, Miss Mohun would not stop for any serious reading, but would leave Miss Merrifield to read a story to her.

'And you ought to get on together,' she said, smiling. 'You are just about the same age, and your names rhyme—Gillian and Lilian. And Gillians mother is a Lily too.'

This the young lady lid not like, for she was already feeling it a sort of presumption in the girl to bear a name so nearly resembling her mother's. She had seen a little cottage poverty, and had had a class of little maidservants; but this level of life which is in no want, keeps a best parlour, and does not say ma'am, was quite new to her, and she did not fancy it. When the girls were left together, while Mrs. Giles returned to her ironing, Gillian was the shyer of the two, and began rather awkwardly and reluctantly—

'Miss Mohun thought you would like to hear this. It is a sort of German fairy tale.'

Lilian said, 'Yes, Miss Merrifield' in a short dry tone, completing Gillian's distaste, and she began to read, not quite at her best, and was heartily glad when at the end of half an hour Mrs. Giles was heard in parley with another visitor, so that she had an excuse for going away without attempting conversation. She was overtaken by the children on their way home from their schools, where they had dined. They rushed upon her, together with the two Varleys, who wanted to take them home to tea; and Gillian giving her ready consent, Fergus dashed home to fetch his beloved humming-top, which was to be introduced to Clement Varley's pump, and in a few minutes they were off, hardly vouchsafing an answer to such comparatively trifling inquiries as how they were placed at their schools.

Gillian found, however, that neither of her aunts was pleased at her having consented to the children's going out without reference to their authority. How did she suppose they were to come home?

'I did not think, can't they be fetched?' said Gillian, startled.

'It is not far,' said Adeline, pitying her. 'One of the maids—'

'My dear Ada!' exclaimed Aunt Jane. 'You know that Fanny cannot go out at night with her throat, and I never will send out those young girls on any account.'

'Can't I go?' said Gillian desperately.

'Are not you a young girl? I must go myself.'

And go she did at a quarter to eight, and brought home the children, looking much injured. Gillian went upstairs with them, and there was an outburst.

'It was horrid to be fetched home so soon, just as there was a chance of something nice; when all the tiresome big ones had gone to dress, and we could have had some real fun,' said Valetta.

'Real fun! Real sense!' said Fergus.

'But what had you been about all this time?'

'Why, their sisters and a man that was there *would* come and drink tea in the nursery, where nobody wanted them, and make us play their play.

'Wasn't that nice? You are always crying out for Harry and me to come and play with you.'

'Oh, it wasn't like that,' said Val, 'you play with us, and they only pretended, and played with each other. It wasn't nice.'

'Clem said it was—forking,' said Fergus.

'No, spooning,' said Val. 'The dish ran after the spoon, you know.'

'Well, but you haven't told me about the schools,' said Gillian, in elder sisterly propriety, thinking the subject had better be abandoned.

'Jolly, jolly, scrumptious!' cried Fergus.

'Oh! Fergus, mamma doesn't like slang words. Jasper doesn't say them.'

'Not at home, but men say what they like at school, and the 'bus was scrumptious and splendiferous!'

'I'm sure it wasn't,' said Valetta; 'I can't bear being boxed up with horrid rude boys.'

'Because you are only a girl!'

'Now, Gill, they shot with—'

'Val, if you tell—'

'Telling Gill isn't telling. Is it, Gill?'

She assented.

'They did, Gill. They shot at us with pea-shooters,' sighed the girl.

'Oh! it was jolly, jolly, jolly!' cried the boy. 'Stebbing hit the girl who made the sour face on her cheeks, and they all squealed, and the cad looked in and tried to jaw us.'

'But that dreadful boy shot right into his mouth,' said Val, while Fergus went into an ecstasy of laughter. 'Wasn't it a shame, Gill?'

'Indeed it was' said Gillian. 'Such ungentlemanly boys ought not to be allowed in the omnibus.'

'Girls shouldn't be allowed in the 'bus, they are so stupid,' said Fergus. 'That one—as cross as old Halfpenny—who was she, Val?'

'Emma Norton! Up in the highest form!'

'Well, she is a prig, and a tell-tale-tit besides; only Stebbing said if she did, her junior would catch it.'

'What a dreadful bully he must be!' exclaimed Gillian.

'I'll tell you what,' said Fergus, in a tone of profound admiration, 'no one can hold a candle to him at batting! He snowballed all the Kennel choir into fits, and he can brosier old Tilly's stall, and go on just the same.'

'What a greedy boy!' exclaimed Val.

'Disgusting,' added Gillian.

'You're girls,' responded Fergus, lengthening the syllable with infinite contempt; but Valetta had spirit enough to reply, 'Much better be a girl than rude and greedy.'

'Exactly,' said Gillian; 'it is only little silly boys who think such things fine. Claude doesn't, nor Harry, nor Japs.'

'You know nothing about it,' said Fergus.

'Well, but you've never told me about school—how you are placed, and whom you are under.'

'Oh! I'm in middle form, under Miss Edgar. Disgusting! It's only the third form that go up to Smiler. She knows it is no use to try to take Stebbing and Burfield.'

'And, Gill,' added Val, 'I'm in second class too, and I took three places for knowing where Teheran was, and got above Kitty Varley and a girl there two years older than I am, and her name is Maura.'

'Maura, how very odd! I never heard of any one called Maura but one of the Whites,' said Gillian. 'What was her surname?'

This Valetta could not tell, and at the moment Mrs. Mount came up with intent to brush Miss Valetta's hair, and to expedite the going to bed.

Gillian, not very happy about the revelations she had heard, went downstairs, and found her younger aunt alone, Miss Mohun having been summoned to a conference with one of her clients in the parish room. In her absence Gillian always felt more free and communicative, and she had soon told whatever she did not feel as a sort of confidence, including Valetta's derivation of spooning, and when Miss Mohun returned it was repeated to her.

'Yes,' was her comment, 'children's play is a convenient cover to the present form of flirtation. No doubt Bee Varley and Mr. Marlowe believe themselves to have been most good-natured.'

'Who is he, and will it come to anything?' asked Aunt Ada, taking her sister's information for granted.

'Oh no, it is nothing. A civil service man, second cousin's brother-in-law's stepson. That's quite enough in these days to justify fraternal romping.'

'I thought Beatrice Varley a nice girl.'

'So she is, my dear. It is only the spirit of the age, and, after all, this deponent saith not which was the dish and which was the spoon. Have the children made any other acquaintances, I wonder? And how did George Stebbing comport himself in the omnibus? I was sorry to see him there; I don't trust that boy.'

'I wonder they didn't send him in solitary grandeur in the brougham,' said Miss Ada.

Gillian held the history of the pea-shooting as a confidence, even though Aunt Jane seemed to have been able to see through the omnibus, so she contented herself with asking who George Stebbing was.

'The son of the manager of the marble works; partner, I believe.'

'Yes,' said Aunt Ada. 'the Co. means Stebbing primarily.'

'Is he a gentleman?'

'Well, as much as old Mr. White himself, I suppose. He is come up here— more's the pity—to the aristocratic quarter, if you please,' said Aunt Jane, smiling, 'and if garden parties are not over, Mr. Stebbing may show you what they can be.'

'That boy ought to be at a public school,' said her sister. 'I hope he doesn't bully poor little Fergus.'

'I don't think he does,' said Gillian. 'Fergus seemed rather to admire him.'

'I had rather hear of bullying than patronage in that quarter,' said Miss Mohun. 'But, Gillian, we must impress on the children that they are to go to no one's house without express leave. That will avoid offence, and I should prefer their enjoying the society of even the Varleys in this house.'

Did Aunt Jane repent of her decision on the Thursday half-holiday granted to Mrs. Edgar's pupils, when, in the midst of the working party round the dining-room table, in a pause of the reading, some one said, 'What's that!'— and a humming, accompanied by a drip, drop, drip, drop, became audible?

Up jumped Miss Mohun, and so did Gillian, half in consternation, half to shield the boy from her wrath. In a few moments they beheld a puddle on the mat at the bottom of the oak stairs, while a stream was descending somewhat as the water comes down at Lodore, while Fergus's voice could be heard above—

'Don't, Varley! You see how it will act. The string of the humming-top moves the pump handle, and that spins. Oh!'

'Master Fergus! Oh—h, you bad boy!'

The shriek was caused by the avenging furies who had rushed up the back stairs just as Miss Mohun had darted up the front, so as to behold, on the landing between the two, the boys, one spinning the top, the other working the pump which stood in its own trough of water, receiving a reckless supply from the tap in the passage. The maid's scream of 'What will your aunt say?' was answered by her appearance, and rush to turn the cock.

'Don't, don't, Aunt Jane,' shouted Fergus; 'I've almost done it! Perpetual motion.' He seemed quite unconscious that the motion was kept up by his own hands, and even dismay could not turn him from being triumphant.

'Oh! Miss Jane,' cried Mrs. Mount, 'if I had thought what they boys was after.'

'Mop it up, Alice,' said Aunt Jane to the younger girl. 'No don't come up, Ada; it is too wet for you. It is only a misdirected experiment in hydraulics.'

'I told him not,' said Clement Varley, thinking affairs serious.

'Fergus, I am shocked at you,' said Gillian sternly. 'You are frightfully wet. You must be sent to bed.'

'You must go and change,' said Aunt Jane, preventing the howl about to break forth. 'My dear boy, that tap must be let alone. We can't have cataracts on the stairs.'

'I didn't mean it, Aunt Jane; I thought it was an invention,' said Fergus.

'I know; but another time come and ask me where to try your experiments. Go and take off those clothes; and you, Clement, you are soaking too. Run home at once.'

Gillian, much scandalised, broke out—

'It is very naughty. At home, he would be sent to bed at once.'

'I am not Mrs. Halfpenny, Gillian,' said Aunt Jane coldly.

'Jane has a soft spot for inventions, for Maurice's sake,' said her sister.

'I can't confound ingenuity and enterprise with wanton mischief, or crush it out for want of sympathy,' said Miss Mohun. 'Come, we must return to our needles.'

If Aunt Jane had gone into the state of wrath to be naturally expected, Gillian would have risen in arms on her brother's behalf, and that would have been much pleasanter than the leniency which made her views of justice appear like unkindness.

This did not dispose her to be the better pleased at an entreaty from the two children to be allowed to join Mrs. Hablot's class on Sunday. It appeared that they had asked Aunt Jane, and she had told them that their sister knew what their mother would like.

'But I am sure she would not mind,' said Valetta. 'Only think, she has got a portfolio with pictures of everything all through the Bible!'

'Yes,' added Fergus, 'Clem told me. There are the dogs eating Jezebel, and such a jolly picture of the lion killing the prophet. I do want to see them! Varley told me!'

'And Kitty told me,' added Valetta. 'She is reading such a book to them. It is called The Beautiful Face, and is all about two children in a wood, and a horrid old grandmother and a dear old hermit, and a wicked baron in a castle! Do let us go, Gillyflower.

'Yes,' said Fergus; 'it would be ever so much better fun than poking here.'

'You don't want fun on Sunday.'

'Not fun exactly, but it is nicer.'

'To leave me, the last bit of home, and mamma's own lessons.'

'They ain't mamma's,' protested Fergus; but Valetta was touched by the tears in Gillian's eyes, kissed her, and declared, 'Not that.'

Whether it were on purpose or not, the next Sunday was eminently unsuccessful; the Collects were imperfect, the answers in the Catechism recurred to disused babyish blunders; Fergus twisted himself into preternatural attitudes, and Valetta teased the Sofy to scratching point, they yawned ferociously at The Birthday, and would not be interested even in the pony's death. Then when they went out walking, they would not hear of the sober Rockstone lane, but insisted on the esplanade, where they fell in with the redoubtable Stebbing, who chose to patronise instead of bullying 'little Merry'—and took him off to the tide mark—to the agony of his sisters, when they heard the St. Andrew's bell.

At last, when the tempter had gone off to higher game, Fergus's Sunday boots and stockings were such a mass of black mud that Gillian had to drag him home in disgrace, sending Valetta into church alone. She would have put him to bed on her own responsibility, but she could not master him; he tumbled about the room, declaring Aunt Jane would do no such thing, rolled up his stockings in a ball, and threw them in his sister's face.

Gillian retired in tears, which she let no one see, not even Aunt Ada, and proceeded to record in her letter to India that those dreadful boys were quite ruining Fergus, and Aunt Jane was spoiling him.

However, Aunt Jane, having heard what had become of the youth, met him in no spoiling mood; and though she never knew of his tussle with Gillian, she spoke to him very seriously, shut him into his own room, to learn thoroughly what he had neglected in the morning, and allowed him no jam at tea. She said nothing to Gillian, but there were inferences.

The lessons went no better on the following Sunday; Gillian could neither enforce her authority nor interest the children. She avoided the esplanade, thinking she had found a nice country walk to the common beyond the marble works; but, behold, there was an outbreak of drums and trumpets and wild singing. The Salvation Army was marching that way, and, what was worse, yells and cat-calls behind showed that the Skeleton Army was on its way to meet them. Gillian, frightened almost out of her wits, managed to fly over an impracticable-looking gate into a field with her children, but Fergus wanted to follow the drum. After that she gave in. The children went to Mrs. Hablot, and Gillian thought she saw 'I told you so' in the corners of Aunt Jane's eyes.

It was a further offence that her aunt strongly recommended her going regularly to the High School instead of only attending certain classes. It would give her far more chance of success at the examination to work with others and her presence would be good for Valetta. But to reduce her to a schoolgirl was to be resented on Miss Vincent's account as well as her own.

CHAPTER IV. — THE QUEEN OF THE WHITE ANTS

The High School was very large. It stood at present at the end of a budding branch of Rockquay, where the managers, assisted by the funds advanced by Lord Rotherwood and that great invisible potentate, the head of the marble works, had secured and adapted a suitable house, and a space round it well walled in.

The various classes of students did not see much of each other, except those who were day boarders and spent the midday recreation time together. Even those in the same form were only together in school, as the dressing-room of those who dined there was separate from that of the others, and they did not come in and out at the same time. Valetta had thus only really made friends with two or three more Rockstone girls of about her own age besides Kitty Yarley, with whom she went backwards and forwards every day, under the escort provided in turn by the families of the young ladies.

Gillian's studies were for three hours in the week at the High School, and on two afternoons she learnt from the old organist at Rockstone Church. She went and came alone, except when Miss Mohun happened to join her, and that was not often, 'For,' said that lady to her sister, 'Gillian always looks as if she thought I was acting spy upon her. I wish I could get on with that girl; I begin to feel almost as poor Lily did with Dolores.'

'She is a very good girl,' said Miss Adeline.

'So she is; and that makes it all the more trying to be treated like the Grand Inquisitor.'

'Shall I speak to her? She is always as pleasant as possible with me.'

'Oh no, don't. It would only make it worse, and prevent you from having her confidence.'

'Ah, Jane, I have often thought your one want was gentleness,' said Miss Ada, with the gesture of her childhood—her head a little on one side. 'And, besides, don't you know what Reggie used to call your ferret look? Well, I suppose you can't help it, but when you want to know a thing and are refraining from asking questions, you always have it more or less.'

'Thank you, Ada. There's nothing like brothers and sisters for telling one home-truths. I suppose it is the penalty of having been a regular Paul Pry in my childhood, in spite of poor Eleanor making me learn "Meddlesome

Matty" as soon as I could speak. I always *do* and always *shall* have ringing in my ears—

```
'"Oh! what a pretty box is this,
        I'll open it," said little Miss.'
```

'Well, you know you always do know or find out everything about everybody, and it is very useful.'

'Useful as a bloodhound is, eh?'

'Oh no, not that, Jenny.'

'As a ferret, or a terrier, perhaps. I suppose I cannot help that, though,' she added, rather sadly. 'I have tried hard to cure the slander and gossip that goes with curiosity. I am sorry it results in repulsion with that girl; but I suppose I can only go on and let her find out that my bark, or my eye, is worse than my bite.'

'You are so good, so everything, Jenny,' said Adeline, 'that I am sure you will have her confidence in time, if only you won't poke after it.'

Which made Miss Mohun laugh, though her heart was heavy, for she had looked forward to having a friend and companion in the young generation.

Gillian meantime went her way.

One morning, after her mathematical class was over, she was delayed for about ten minutes by the head mistress, to whom she had brought a message from her aunt, and thus did not come out at noon at the same time as the day scholars. On issuing into the street, where as yet there was hardly any traffic, except what was connected with the two schools, she perceived that a party of boys were besetting a little girl who was trying to turn down the cross road to Bellevue, barring her way, and executing a derisive war-dance around her, and when she, almost crying, made an attempt to dash by, pulling at her plaited tail, with derisive shouts, even Gillian's call, 'Boys, boys, how can you be so disgraceful!' did not check them. One made a face and put his tongue out, while the biggest called out, 'Thank you, teacher,' and Gillian perceived to her horror, that they were no street boys, but Mrs. Edgar's, and that Fergus was one of them. That he cried in dismay, 'Don't, Stebbing! It's my sister,' was no consolation, as she charged in among them, catching hold of her brother, as she said,

'I could not believe that you could behave in such a disgraceful manner!'

All the other tormentors rushed away headlong, except Stebbing, who, in some compunction, said—

'I beg your pardon, Miss Merrifield, I had no notion it was you.'

'You are making it no better,' said Gillian. 'The gentlemen I am used to know how to behave properly to any woman or girl. My father would be very sorry that my brother has been thrown into such company.'

And she walked away with her head extremely high, having certainly given Master Stebbing a good lesson. Fergus ran after her. 'Gill, Gill, you won't tell.'

'I don't think I ever was more shocked in my life,' returned Gillian.

'But, Gill, she's a nasty, stuck-up, conceited little ape, that Maura White, or whatever her ridiculous name is. They pretend her father was an officer, but he was really a bad cousin of old Mr. White's that ran away; and her mother is not a lady—a great fat disgusting woman, half a nigger; and Mr. White let her brother and sister be in the marble works out of charity, because they have no father, and she hasn't any business to be at the High School.'

'White, did you say? Maura White!' exclaimed Gillian. 'Captain White dead! Oh, Fergus! it must be Captain White. He was in the dear old Royal Wardours, and papa thought so much of him! To think of your going and treating his daughter in that shocking way!'

'It was what Stebbing said,' gruffly answered Fergus.

'If you let yourself be led by these horrid cads—'

'He is no such thing! He is the crack bat of Edgar's—'

'A boy is a cad who can't behave himself to a girl because she is poor. I really think the apology to me was the worst part or the matter. He only treats people well when he sees they can take care of themselves.'

'I'll tell him about Captain White,' said Fergus, a little abashed.

'Yes. And I will get the aunts to call on Mrs. White, and that may help them to a better level among these vulgar folk.'

'But you won't—' said Fergus, with an expressive pause.

'I won't get you into trouble, for I think you are sorry you treated one of our own in such a manner.'

'I wouldn't, indeed, if I had known.'

'I shall only explain that I have found out whom Maura belongs to. I should go and see them at once, only I must make Val find out where she lives.'

So Gillian returned home, communicating the intelligence with some excitement that she had discovered that Valetta's schoolmate, Maura White, was none other than the daughter of her father's old fellow-soldier, whose death shocked her greatly, and she requested to go and call on Mrs. White as soon as she could learn her abode.

However, it seemed to be impossible that any one should live in Rockstone unknown to Aunt Jane.

'White?' she said. 'It can't be the Whites down by Cliffside. No; there's a father there, though he generally only comes down for Sunday.'

'I am sure there are some Whites on the Library list,' said Miss Ada.

'Oh yes; but she washes! I know who they must be. I know in Bellevue there are some; but they go to the Kennel Church. Didn't you come home, Ada, from that function you went to with Florence, raving about the handsome youth in the choir?'

'Oh yes, we thought it such an uncommon, foreign face, and he looked quite inspired when he was singing his solo.'

'Yes; I found out that his name was White, a clerk or something in the marble works, and that he had a mother and sister living at Bellevue. I did see the sister when I went to get the marble girls into the G.F.S., but she said something foolish about her mother not liking it.'

'Yes; nobody under the St. Kenelm influence ever will come into the G.F.S.'

'But what is she doing?' asked Gillian. 'Do you mean Kalliope?'

'I suppose I do. I saw a rather nice-looking young woman in the department where they make Florentine mosaic, and I believe they said she was Miss White, but she cut me off very short with her mother, so I had no more to do with her.'

'I am sure mamma would wish me to call on Mrs. White,' said Gillian.

'There's no reason against it,' said Aunt Jane. 'I will go with you the first day I can.'

When would that be, wondered Gillian. She told Valetta to talk to Maura and learn the name of the house; and this was ascertained to be 3 Ivinghoe Terrace, Bellevue Road, but Val had very little opportunity of cultivating the acquaintance of town girls, who did not stay to dinner, as she had to go home immediately after school, under Emma Norton's escort, and perhaps she was not very ardent in the cause, for Kitty Varley and her other friends did not like the child, and she was more swayed by them than perhaps she liked to confess to her sister.

Each morning at breakfast Gillian hoped that Aunt Jane would lay out her day so as to call on Mrs. White; but first there was the working party, then came the mothers' meeting, followed by afternoon tea at Mrs. Hablot's for some parish council. On the third day, which might have been clear, 'a miserable creature,' as Gillian mentally called her, wrote to beg the Misses Mohun to bring themselves and her niece to make up a lawn-tennis set, since some one had failed. Gillian vainly protested that she did not care about lawn tennis, and could not play unless Jasper was her partner; and Aunt Jane so far sided with her as to say it was very inconvenient, and on such short notice they ought not to be expected. But Aunt Ada clearly wanted to go; and so they went. It was a beautiful place, but Gillian could not enjoy herself, partly because she knew so few of the people, but more because she was vexed and displeased about the Whites. She played very badly; but Aunt Jane, when pressed into the service, skipped about with her little light figure and proved herself such a splendid player, doing it so entirely con amore, that Gillian could not but say to herself, 'She was bent on going; it was all humbug her pretending to want to refuse.'

That afternoon's dissipation had made it needful to do double work the next day, and Gillian was again disappointed. Then came Saturday, when Miss Mohun was never available, nor was she on Monday; and when it appeared that she had to go to a meeting at the Cathedral town on Tuesday, Gillian grew desperate, and at her tete-a-tete meal with Aunt Ada, related the whole history of the Whites, and her great desire to show kindness to her father's old brother-officer's family, and how much she was disappointed.

Miss Adeline was touched, and indeed, fond as she was of her sister, she could not help being flattered by Gillian's preference and confidence.

'Well, my deal, this is a nice day, not too hot or too cold; I do not see why I should not walk down with you and call. If I find it too far, we can take a cab to go back.'

'Oh, thank you, Aunt Ada; it is very very kind of you, and there is no knowing when Aunt Jane may be able to go. I don't like to close up my Indian letter till I can say I have seen them.'

Gillian fidgeted a good deal lest, before her aunt's postprandial repose was over, visitors should come and put a stop to everything, and she looked ready to cut the throat of a poor lady in a mushroom hat, who came up to leave a message for Miss Mohun about a possible situation for one of her class of boys.

However, at last they started, Kunz and all, Miss Adeline quite infected by Gillian's excitement.

'So your father and mother were very fond of them.'

'Papa thought very highly of him, and was very sorry he had to return,' said Gillian.

'And she was a beautiful Greek.'

Gillian began to be quite afraid of what she might have said.

'I don't think she is more than half Greek,' she said. 'I believe her mother was a Gorfiote, but her father was English or Irish. I believe he kept a shop in Malta.'

'Quite a mixture of nationalities then, and no wonder she is beautiful. That youth had a very striking profile; it quite reminded me of a gem as I saw it against the dark pillar.'

'I did not say she was very beautiful now,' said Gillian, feeling a qualm as she recollected the Queen of the White Ants, and rather oddly divided between truthfulness, fear of alarming her aunt into turning back, and desire of giving her a little preparation.

'Ah! those southern beauties soon go on. Some one told me that Lord Byron's "Maid of Athens," whose portrait I used to think the loveliest thing in the world, became a great stout woman, but was quite a mother to all the young Englishmen about. I remember I used to try to hold my head and keep my eyelids down like the engraving in an old book that had been my mother's.'

'Oh! I think I have seen it at Beechcroft,' said Gillian, very much amused, for she now perceived whence arose Aunt Ada's peculiar turn of the head and droop of the eyelashes, and how the conscious affectation of childhood had become unconsciously crystallised.

She grew more and more anxious as they found some difficulty in making out Ivinghoe Terrace, and found it at last to be a row of rather dilapidated little houses, apparently built of lath and stucco, and of that peculiar meanness only attained by the modern suburb. Aunt Ada evidently did not like it at all, and owned herself almost ready to turn back, being sure that Valetta must have made some mistake. Gillian repeated that she had always said the Whites were very poor, but she began to feel that her impatience had misled her, and that she would have been better off with the aunt who was used to such places, and whose trim browns and crimsons were always appropriate everywhere, rather than this dainty figure in delicate hues that looked only fit for the Esplanade or the kettledrum, and who was becoming seriously uneasy, as Kunz, in his fresh snowiness, was disposed to make researches among vulgar remains of crabs and hakes, and was with difficulty restrained from disputing them with a very ignoble and spiteful yellow cur of low degree.

No. 3, with its blistered wall and rusty rail, was attained, Kunz was brought within the enclosure, and Gillian knocked as sharply and fast as she could, in the fear that her aunt might yet turn about and escape.

The door was opened with a rapidity that gave the impression that they had been watched, but it was by a very untidy-looking small maid, and the parlour into which they were turned had most manifestly been lately used as the family dining-room, and was redolent of a mixture of onion, cabbage, and other indescribable odours.

Nobody was there, except a black and white cat, who showed symptoms of flying at Kunz, but thought better of it, and escaped by the window, which fortunately was open, though the little maid would have shut it, but for Miss Adeline's gasping and peremptory entreaty to the contrary. She sat on the faded sofa, looking as if she just existed by the help of her fan and scent- bottle, and when Gillian directed her attention to the case of clasps and medals and the photograph of the fine-looking officer, she could only sigh out, 'Oh, my dear!'

There was a certain air of taste in the arrangement of the few chimney- piece ornaments, and Gillian was pleased to see the two large photographs of her father and mother which Captain White had so much valued as parting gifts. A few drawings reminded her of the School of Art at Belfast, and there was a vase of wild flowers and ferns prettily arranged, but otherwise everything was wretchedly faded and dreary.

Then came the opening of the door, and into the room rolled, rather than advanced, something of stupendous breadth, which almost took Gillian's breath away, as she durst not look to see the effect on her aunt. If the Queen of the White Ants had been stout before, what was she now? Whatever her appearance had been in the days of comparative prosperity, with a husband to keep her up to the mark, and a desire to rank with the officers' wives, she had let everything go in widowhood, poverty, and neglect; and as she stood panting in her old shiny black alpaca, the only thing Gillian recalled about her like old times was the black lace veil thrown mantilla fashion over her head; but now it was over a widow's cap, and a great deal rustier than of old. Of the lovely foreigner nothing else remained except the dark eyes, and that sort of pasty sallow whiteness that looks at if for generations past cold water and fresh air had been unknown. There was no accent more interesting in her voice than a soupcon of her Irish father as she began, 'I am sorry to have kept the lady so long waiting. Was it about the girl's character that you came?'

'Oh no, Mrs. White, interrupted Gillian, her shyness overpowered by the necessity of throwing herself into the breach. 'Don't you remember me? I am Gillian Merrifield, and this is my aunt, Miss Adeline Mohun.'

The puffy features lighted up into warmth. 'Little Miss Gillian! And I am proud to see you! My little Maura did tell me that Miss Valetta was in her class at the High School; but I thought there was no one now who would come near the poor widow. And is your dear mamma here, Miss Gillian, and are she and your papa quite well?'

Gillian could hardly believe in such dense remoteness that her father's accident should be unknown, but she explained all, and met with abundant sympathy, the dark eyes filled with tears, and the voice broke into sobs, as Mrs. White declared that Sir Jasper and Lady Merrifield had been the best friends she ever had in her life.

But oh! that the handkerchief had been less grimy with which she mopped her eyes, as she spoke of the happy days that were gone! Gillian saw that poor Aunt Ada was in an agony to get away, and hurried out her questions for fear of being stopped. 'How was Kalliope—was she at home?'

'Oh no, poor Kally, she is the best girl in the world. I always say that, with all my sorrows, no one ever was more blest in their children than poor little me. Richard, my eldest, is in a lawyer's office at Leeds. Kally is employed in the art department, just as a compliment to her relation, Mr. White. Quite genteel, superior work, though I must say he does not do as much for us as he might. Such a youth as my Alexis now was surely worthy of the position of a gentleman.'

The good lady was quite disposed to talk; but there was no making out, through her cloud of confused complaints, what her son and daughter were actually doing; and Aunt Ada, while preserving her courtesy, was very anxious to be gone, and rose to take leave at the first moment possible, though after she was on her feet Mrs. White detained her for some time with apologies about not returning her visit. She was in such weak health, so unequal to walking up the cliff, that she was sure Miss Mohun would excuse her, though Alexis and Kally would be perfectly delighted to hear of Miss Gillian's kindness.

Gillian had not made out half what she wanted to know, nor effected any arrangement for seeing Kalliope, when she found herself out in the street, and her aunt panting with relief. 'My dear, that woman! You don't mean that your mother was fond of her.'

'I never said mamma was fond of her.'

'My dear, excuse me. It was the only reason for letting you drag me here. I was almost stifled. What a night I shall have!'

'I am very sorry, Aunt Ada, but, indeed, I never said that mamma was fond of her, only that papa thought very highly of her husband, and wished us to be kind to her.'

'Well, you gave me that impression, whether you wished it or not! Such a hole; and I'm sure she drinks gin!'

'Oh no, aunt!'

'I can't be mistaken! I really was afraid she was going to kiss you!'

'I do wish I could have made out about Alexis and Kalliope.'

'Oh, my dear, just working like all the lot, though she shuffled about it. I see what they are like, and the less you see of them the better. I declare I am more tired than if I had walked a mile. How am I ever to get up the hill again?'

'I am sorry, aunt,' said Gillian. 'Will you take my arm? Perhaps we may meet Kalliope, if the marble people come out at four or five. What's that bell?' as a little tinkle was heard.

'That's St. Kenelm's! Oh! you would like to go there, and it would rest me; only there's Kunz.'

'I should like to see it very much,' said Gillian.

'Well,' said Aunt Ada, who certainly seemed to have something of the 'cat's away' feeling about her, and, moreover, trusted to avoid meeting Kalliope. 'Just round the corner here is Mrs. Webb's, who used to live with us before she married, Kunz will be happy with her. Won't he, my doggie, like to go and see his old Jessie?'

So Kunz was disposed of with a very pleasant, neat-looking woman, who begged Miss Adeline to come and have some tea after the service.

It was really a beautiful little church—'a little gem' was exactly the term that suggested itself—very ornate, and the chief lack being of repose, for there seemed not an inch devoid of colour or carving. There was a choir of boys in short surplices and blue cassocks, and a very musical service, in the course of which it was discovered to be the Feast of St. Remigius, for after the Lesson a short discourse was given on the Conversion of Clovis, not forgetting the sacred ampulla.

There were about five ladies present and six old women, belonging to a home maintained by Lady Flight. The young priest, her son, had a beautiful voice, and Gillian enjoyed all very much, and thought the St. Andrew's people very hard and unjust; but all this went out of her head in the porch, for while Lady Flight was greeting Miss Mohun with empressement, and inviting her to come in to tea, Gillian had seen a young woman who had come in late and had been kneeling behind them.

Turning back and holding out her hands, she exclaimed—

'Kalliope! I so wanted to see you.'

'Miss Gillian Merrifield,' was the response. 'Maura told me you were here, but I hardly hoped to see you.'

'How can I see you? Where are you? Busy?'

'I am at the marble works all day—in the mosaic department. Oh, Miss Gillian, I owe it all to Miss Merrifield's encouraging me to go to the School of Art. How is she? And I hope you have good accounts of Sir Jasper?'

'He is better, and I hope my mother is just arriving. That's why we are here; and Alethea and Phyllis are out there. They will want to know all about you.'

At that moment Aunt Adeline looked round, having succeeded in persuading Lady Flight that she had another engagement. She saw a young woman in a shabby black dress, with a bag in her hand, and a dark fringe over a complexion of clear brown, straight features, to whom Gillian was eagerly talking.

'Ah!' she said, as Mr. Flight now came up from the vestry; 'do you know anything of that girl?'

'Second-rate people, somewhere in Bellevue,' said the lady.

'The brother is my best tenor,' said Mr. Flight. 'She is very often at St. Kenelm's, but I do not know any more of her. The mother either goes to Bellevue or nowhere. They are in Bellevue Parish.'

This was quite sufficient answer, for any interference with parochial visiting in the Bellevue district was forbidden.

Aunt Ada called to Gillian, and when she eagerly said, 'This is Kalliope, aunt,' only responded with a stiff bow.

'I do not know what these people might have been, Gillian,' she said, as they pursued their way to Mrs. Webb's; 'but—they must have sunk so low that I do not think your mother can wish you to have anything to do with them.'

'Oh, Aunt Ada! Kalliope was always such a good girl!'

'She has a fringe. And she would not belong to the G.F.S.,' said Aunt Ada. 'No, my dear, I see exactly the sort of people they are. Your aunt Jane might be useful to them, if they would let her, but they are not at all fit for you to associate with.'

Gillian chafed inwardly, but she was beginning to learn that Aunt Ada was more impenetrable than Aunt Jane, and, what was worse, Aunt Jane always stood by her sister's decision, whether she would have herself originated it or not.

When the elder aunt came home, and heard the history of their day, and Gillian tried to put in a word, she said—

'My dear, we all know that rising from the ranks puts a man's family in a false position, and they generally fall back again. All this is unlucky, for they do not seem to be people it is possible to get at, and now you have paid your kind act of attention, there is no more to be done till you can hear from Ceylon about them.'

Gillian was silenced by the united forces of the aunts.

'It really was a horrid place,' said Aunt Ada, when alone with her sister; 'and such a porpoise of a woman! Gillian should not have represented her as a favourite.'

'I do not remember that she did so,' returned Aunt Jane. 'I wish she had waited for me. I have seen more of the kind of thing than you have, Ada.'

'I am sure I wish she had. I don't know when I shall get over the stifling of that den; but it was just as if they were her dearest friends.'

'Girls will be silly! And there's a feeling about the old regiment too. I can excuse her, though I wish she had not been so impatient. I fancy that eldest daughter is really a good girl and the mainstay of the family.'

'But she would have nothing to do with you or the G.F.S.'

'If I had known that her father had been an officer, I might have approached her differently. However, I will ask Lily about their antecedents, and in six weeks we shall know what is to be done about them.'

CHAPTER V. — MARBLES

Six weeks seem a great deal longer to sixteen than to six-and-forty, and Gillian groaned and sighed to herself as she wrote her letters, and assured herself that so far from her having done enough in the way of attention to the old soldier's family, she had simply done enough to mark her neglect and disdain.

'Grizzling' (to use an effective family phrase) under opposition is a grand magnifier; and it was not difficult to erect poor Captain White into a hero, his wife into a patient sufferer, and Alethea's kindness to his daughter into a bosom friendship; while the aunts seemed to be absurdly fastidious and prejudiced. 'I don't wonder at Aunt Ada,' she said to herself; 'I know she has always been kept under a glass case; but I thought better things of Aunt Jane. It is all because Kalliope goes to St. Kenelm's, and won't be in the G.F.S.'

And all the time Gillian was perfectly unaware of her own family likeness to Dolores. Other matters conduced to a certain spirit of opposition to Aunt Jane. That the children should have to use the back instead of the front stair when coming in with dusty or muddy shoes, and that their possessions should be confiscated for the rest of the day when left about in the sitting-rooms and hall, were contingencies she could accept as natural, though they irritated her; but she agreed with Valetta that it was hard to insist on half an hour's regular work at the cushion, which was not a lesson, but play. She was angered when Aunt Jane put a stop to some sportive passes and chatter on the stairs between Valetta and Alice Mount, and still more so when her aunt took away Adam Bede from the former, as not desirable reading at eleven years old.

It was only the remembrance of her mother's positive orders that withheld Gillian from the declaration that mamma always let them read George Eliot; and in a cooler moment of reflection she was glad she had abstained, for she recollected that *always* was limited to mamma's having read most of Romola aloud to her and Mysie, and to her having had Silas Marner to read when she was unwell in lodgings, and there was a scarcity of books.

Such miffs about her little sister were in the natural order of things, and really it was the 'all pervadingness,' as she called it in her own mind, of Aunt Jane that chiefly worried her, the way that the little lady knew everything that was done, and everything that was touched in the house; but as long as Valetta took refuge with herself, and grumbled to her, it was bearable.

It was different with Fergus. There had been offences certainly; Aunt Jane had routed him out of preparing his lessons in Mrs. Mount's room, where he diversified them with teaching the Sofy to beg, and inventing new modes of tying down jam pots. Moreover, she had declared that Gillian's exemplary patience was wasted and harmful when she found that they had taken three-quarters of an hour over three tenses of a Greek verb, and that he said it worse on the seventh repetition than on the first. After an evening, when Gillian had gone to a musical party with Aunt Ada, and Fergus did his lessons under Aunt Jane's superintendence, he utterly cast off his sister's aid. There was something in Miss Mohun's briskness that he found inspiring, and she put in apt words or illustrations, instead of only rousing herself from a book to listen, prompt, and sigh. He found that he did his tasks more thoroughly in half the time, and rose in his class; and busy as his aunt was, she made the time not only for this, but for looking over with him those plates of mechanics in the Encyclopaedia, which were a mere maze to Gillian, but of which she knew every detail, from ancient studies with her brother Maurice. As Fergus wrote to his mother, 'Aunt Jane is the only woman who has any natural *scence*.'

Gillian could not but see this as she prepared the letters for the post, and whatever the ambiguous word might be meant for, she had rather not have seen it, for she really was ashamed of her secret annoyance at Fergus's devotion to Aunt Jane, knowing how well it was that Stebbing should have a rival in his affections. Yet she could not help being provoked when the boy followed his aunt to the doors of her cottages like a little dog, and waited outside whenever she would let him, for the sake of holding forth to her about something which wheels and plugs and screws were to do. Was it possible that Miss Mohun followed it all? His great desire was to go over the marble works, and she had promised to take him when it could be done; but, unfortunately, his half-holiday was on Saturday, when the workmen struck off early, and when also Aunt Jane always had the pupil-teachers for something between instruction and amusement.

Gillian felt lonely, for though she got on better with her younger than her elder aunt, and had plenty of surface intercourse of a pleasant kind with both, it was a very poor substitute for her mother, or her elder sisters, and Valetta was very far from being a Mysie.

The worst time was Sunday, when the children had deserted her for Mrs. Hablot, and Aunt Ada was always lying down in her own room to rest after morning service. She might have been at the Sunday-school, but she did not love teaching, nor do it well, and she did not fancy the town children, or else there was something of opposition to Aunt Jane.

It was a beautiful afternoon, of the first Sunday in October, and she betook herself to the garden with the 'Lyra Innocentium' in her hand, meaning to learn the poem for the day. She wandered up to the rail above the cliff, looking out to the sea. Here, beyond the belt of tamarisks and other hardy low-growing shrubs which gave a little protection from the winds, the wall dividing the garden of Beechcroft Cottage from that of Cliff House became low, with only the iron-spiked railing on the top, as perhaps there was a desire not to overload the cliff. The sea was of a lovely colour that day, soft blue, and with exquisite purple shadows of clouds, with ripples of golden sparkles here and there near the sun, and Gillian stood leaning against the rail, gazing out on it, with a longing, yearning feeling towards the dear ones who had gone out upon it, when she became conscious that some one was in the other garden, which she had hitherto thought quite deserted, and looking round, she saw a figure in black near the rail. Their eyes met, and both together exclaimed—

'Kalliope!'—'Miss Gillian! Oh, I beg your pardon!'

'How did you come here? I thought nobody did!'

'Mr. White's gardener lets us walk here. It is so nice and quiet. Alexis has taken the younger ones for a walk, but I was too much tired. But I will not disturb you—'

'Oh! don't go away. Nobody will disturb us, and I do so want to know about you all. I had no notion, nor mamma either, that you were living here, or—'

'Or of my dear father's death!' said Kalliope, as Gillian stopped short, confused. 'I did write to Miss Merrifield, but the letter was returned.'

'But where did you write?'

'To Swanage, where she had written to me last.'

'Oh! we were only there for six weeks, while we were looking for houses; I suppose it was just as the Wardours were gone to Natal too?'

'Yes, we knew they were out of reach.'

'But do tell me about it, if you do not mind. My father will want to hear.'

Kalliope told all in a calm, matter-of-fact way, but with a strain of deep suppressed feeling. She was about twenty-three, a girl with a fine outline of features, beautiful dark eyes, and a clear brown skin, who would have been very handsome if she had looked better fed and less hardworked. Her Sunday dress showed wear and adaptation, but she was altogether ladylike, and even the fringe that had startled Aunt Ada only consisted of little wavy curls on the temples, increasing her classical look.

'It was fever—at Leeds. My father was just going into a situation in the police that we had been waiting for ever so long, and there were good schools, and Richard had got into a lawyer's office, when there began a terrible fever in our street—the drains were to blame, they said—and every one of us had it, except mother and Richard, who did not sleep at home. We lost poor little Mary first, and then papa seemed to be getting better; but he was anxious about expense, and there was no persuading him to take nourishment enough. I do believe it was that. And he had a relapse—and—'

'Oh, poor Kalliope! And we never heard of it!'

'I did feel broken down when the letter to Miss Merrifield came back,' said Kalliope. 'But my father had made me write to Mr. James White—not that we had any idea that he had grown so rich. He and my father were first cousins, sons of two brothers who were builders; but there was some dispute, and it ended by my father going away and enlisting. There was nobody nearer to him, and he never heard any more of his home; but when he was so ill, he thought he would like to be reconciled to "Jem," as he said, so he made me write from his dictation. Such a beautiful letter it was, and he added a line at the end himself. Then at last, when it was almost too late, Mr. White answered. I believe it was a mere chance—or rather Providence—that he ever knew it was meant for him, but there were kind words enough to cheer up my father at the last. I believe then the clergyman wrote to him.'

'Did not he come near you?'

'No, I have never seen him; but there was a correspondence between him and Mr. Moore, the clergyman, and Richard, and he said he was willing to put us in the way of working for ourselves, if—if—we were not too proud.'

'Then he did it in an unkind way,' said Gillian.

'I try to think he did not mean to be otherwise than good to us. I told Mr. Moore that I was not fit to be a governess, and I did not think they could get on without me at home, but that I could draw better than I would do anything else, and perhaps I might get Christmas cards to do, or something like that. Mr. Moore sent a card or two of my designing, and then Mr. White said he could find work for me in the mosaic department here; and something for my brothers, if we did not give ourselves airs. So we came.'

'Not Richard?' said Gillian, who remembered dimly that Richard had not been held in great esteem by her own brothers.

'No; Richard is in a good situation, so it was settled that he should stay on there.'

'And you—'

'I am in the mosaic department. Oh, Miss Gillian, I am so grateful to Miss Merrifield. Don't you remember her looking at my little attempts, and persuading Lady Merrifield to get mother to let me go to the School of Art? I began only as the girls do who are mere hands, and now I have to prepare all the designs for them, and have a nice little office of my own for it. Sometimes I get one of my own designs taken, and then I am paid extra.'

'Then do you maintain them all?'

'Oh no; we have lodgers, the organist and his wife,' said Kalliope, laughing, 'and Alexis is in the telegraph office, at the works; besides, it turned out that this house and two more belong to us, and we do very well when the tenants pay their rents.'

'But Maura is not the youngest of you,' said Gillian, who was rather hazy about the family.

'No, there are the two little boys. We let them go to the National School for the present. It is a great trial to my poor mother, but they do learn well there, and we may be able to do something better for them by the time they are old enough for further education.'

Just then the sound of a bell coming up from the town below was a warning to both that the conversation must be broken off. A few words—'I am so glad to have seen you,' and 'It has been such a pleasure'—passed, and then each hastened down her separate garden path.

'Must I tell of this meeting?' Gillian asked herself. 'I shall write it all to mamma and Alethea, of course. How delightful that those lessons that Kalliope had have come to be of so much use! How pleased Alethea will be! Poor dear thing! How much she has gone through! But can there be any need to tell the aunts? Would it not just make Aunt Ada nervous about any one looking through her sweet and lovely wall? And as to Aunt Jane, I really don't see that I am bound to gratify her passion for knowing everything. I am not accountable to her, but to my own mother. My people know all about Kalliope, and she is prejudiced. Why should I be unkind and neglectful of an old fellow-soldier's family, because she cannot or will not understand what they really are? It would not be the slightest use to tell her the real story. Mrs. White is fat, and Kalliope has a fringe, goes to St. Kenelm's, and won't be in the G.F.S., and that's enough to make her say she does not believe a word of it, or else to make it a fresh ground for poking and prying, in the way that drives one distracted! It really is quite a satis-faction to have something that she can't find out, and it is not underhand while I write every word of it to mamma.'

So Gillian made her conscience easy, and she did write a long and full account of the Whites and their troubles, and of her conversation with Kalliope.

In the course of that week Fergus had a holiday, asked for by some good-natured visitor of Mrs. Edgar's. He rushed home on the previous day with the news, to claim Aunt Jane's promise; and she undertook so to arrange matters as to be ready to go with him to the marble works at three o'clock. Valetta could not go, as she had her music lesson at that time, and she did not regret it, for she had an idea that blasting with powder or dynamite was always going on there. Gillian was not quite happy about the dynamite, but she did not like to forego the chance of seeing what the work of Kalliope and Alexis really was, so she expressed her willingness to join the party, and in the meantime did her best to prevent Aunt Ada from being driven distracted by Fergus's impatience, which began at half-past two.

Miss Mohun had darted out as soon as dinner was over, and he was quite certain some horrible cad would detain her till four o'clock, and then going would be of no use. Nevertheless he was miserable till Gillian had put on her hat, and then she could do nothing that would content him and keep him out of Aunt Ada's way, but walk him up and down in the little front court with the copper beeches, while she thought they must present to the neighbours a lively tableau of a couple of leopards in a cage.

However, precisely as the clock struck three, Aunt Jane walked up to the iron gate. She had secured an order from Mr. Stebbing, the managing partner, without which they would not have penetrated beyond the gate where 'No admittance except on business' was painted.

Mr. Stebbing himself, a man with what Valetta was wont to call a grisly beard, met them a little within the gate, and did the honours of the place with great politeness. He answered all the boy's questions, and seemed much pleased with his intelligence and interest, letting him see what he wished, and even having the machinery slacked to enable him to perceive how it acted, and most delightful of all, in the eyes of Fergus, letting him behold some dynamite, and explaining its downward explosion. He evidently had a great respect for Miss Mohun, because she entered into it all, put pertinent questions, and helped her nephew if he did not understand.

It was all dull work to Gillian, all that blasting and hewing and polishing, which made the place as busy as a hive. She only wished she could have seen the cove as once it was, with the weather-beaten rocks descending to the sea, overhung with wild thrift and bramble, and with the shore, the peaceful haunts of the white sea-birds; whereas now the fresh-cut rock looked red and wounded, and all below was full of ugly slated or iron-roofed sheds, rough workmen, and gratings and screeches of machinery.

It was the Whites whom she wanted to see, and she never came upon the brother at all, nor on the sister, till Mr. Stebbing, perhaps observing her listless looks, said that they were coming to what would be more interesting to Miss Merrifield, and took them into the workrooms, where a number of young women were busy over the very beautiful work by which flowers and other devices were represented by inlaying different coloured marbles and semi-precious stones in black and white, so as to make tables, slabs, and letter-weights, and brooches for those who could not aspire to the most splendid and costly productions.

Miss Mohun shook hands with 'the young ladies' within the magic circle of the G.F.S., and showed herself on friendly terms of interest with all. From a little inner office Miss White was summoned, came out, and met an eager greeting from Gillian, but blushed a little, and perhaps had rather not have had her unusual Christian name proclaimed by the explanation—

'This is Kalliope White, Aunt Jane.'

Miss Mohun shook hands with her, and said her niece had been much pleased at the meeting, and her sister would be glad to hear of her, explaining to Mr. Stebbing that Captain White had been a brother-officer of Sir Jasper Merrifield.

Kalliope had a very prettily-shaped head, with short hair in little curls and rings all over it. Her whole manner was very quiet and unassuming, as she explained and showed whatever Mr. Stebbing wished. It was her business to make the working drawings for the others, and to select the stones used, and there could be no doubt that she was a capable and valuable worker.

Gillian asked her to show something designed by herself, and she produced an exquisite table-weight, bearing a spray of sweet peas. Gillian longed to secure it for her mother, but it was very expensive, owing to the uncommon stones used in giving the tints, and Mr. Stebbing evidently did not regard it with so much favour as the jessamines and snowdrops, which, being of commoner marbles, could be sold at a rate fitter for the popular purse. Several beautiful drawings in her office had been laid aside as impracticable, 'unless we had a carte blanche wedding order,' he said, with what Gillian thought a sneer.

She would gladly have lingered longer, but this was a very dull room in Fergus's estimation, and perhaps Aunt Jane did not desire a long continuance of the conversation under Mr. Stebbing's eyes, so Gillian found herself hurried on.

Mr. Stebbing begged Miss Mohun to come in to his wife, who would have tea ready, and this could not be avoided without manifest incivility. Fergus hoped to have been introduced to the haunts of his hero, but Master George was gone off in attendance on his brother, who was fishing, and there was nothing to relieve the polite circle of the drawing-room—a place most aesthetically correct, from cornice to the little rugs on the slippery floor. The little teacups and the low Turkish table were a perfect study to those who did not—like Fergus—think more of the dainty doll's muffins on the stand, or the long-backed Dachshund who looked for them beseechingly.

Mrs. Stebbing was quite in accordance with the rest, with a little row of curls over her forehead, a terra-cotta dress, and a chain of watch cocks, altogether rather youthful for the mother of a grown-up son, engaged in his father's business.

She was extremely civil and polite, and everything went well except for a certain stiffness. By and by the subject of the Whites came up, and Mr. Stebbing observed that Miss Merrifield seemed to know Miss White.

'Oh yes,' said Gillian eagerly; 'her father was in my father's regiment, the Royal Wardours.'

'A non-commissioned officer, I suppose,' said Mrs. Stebbing.

'Not for a good many years,' said Gillian. 'He was lieutenant for six years, and retired with the rank of captain.'

'I know they said he was a captain,' said Mrs. Stebbing; 'but it is very easy to be called so.'

'Captain White was a real one,' said Gillian, with a tone of offence. 'Every one in the Royal Wardours thought very highly of him.'

'I am sure no one would have supposed it from his family,' said Mrs. Stebbing. 'You are aware, Miss Mohun, that it was under disgraceful circumstances that he ran away and enlisted.'

'Many a youth who gets into a scrape becomes an excellent soldier, even an officer,' said Miss Mohun.

'Exactly so,' said Mr. Stebbing. 'Those high-spirited lads are the better for discipline, and often turn out well under it. But their promotion is an awkward thing for their families, who have not been educated up to the mark.'

'It is an anomalous position, and I have a great pity for them,' said Miss Mohun. 'Miss White must be a very clever girl.'

'Talented, yes,' said Mr. Stebbing. 'She is useful in her department.

'That may be,' said Mrs. Stebbing; 'but it won't do to encourage her. She is an artful, designing girl, I know very well—'

'Do you know anything against her?' asked Miss Mohun, looking volumes of repression at Gillian, whose brown eyes showed symptoms of glaring like a cat's, under her hat.

'I do not speak without warrant, Miss Mohun. She is one of those demure, proper-behaved sort that are really the worst flirts of all, if you'll excuse me.'

Most thankful was Miss Mohun that the door opened at that moment to admit some more visitors, for she saw that Gillian might at any moment explode.

'Aunt Jane,' she exclaimed, as soon as they had accomplished their departure, 'you don't believe it?'

'I do not think Miss White looks like it,' said Miss Mohun. 'She seemed a quiet, simple girl.'

'And you don't believe all that about poor Captain White?'

'Not the more for Mrs. Stebbing's saying so.'

'But you will find out and refute her. There must be people who know.'

'My dear, you had better not try to rake up such things. You know that the man bore an excellent character for many years in the army, and you had better be satisfied with that,' said Miss Jane for once in her life, as if to provoke Gillian, not on the side of curiosity.

'Then you do believe it!' went on Gillian, feeling much injured for her hero's sake, and wearing what looked like a pertinacious pout.

'Truth compels me to say, Gillian, that the sons of men, even in a small way of business, are not apt to run away and enlist without some reason.'

'And I am quite sure it was all that horrid old White's fault.'

'You had better content yourself with that belief.'

Gillian felt greatly affronted, but Fergus, who thought all this very tiresome, broke in, after a third attempt—

'Aunt Jane, if the pulley of that crane—'

And all the way home they discussed machinery, and Gillian's heart swelled.

'I am afraid Gillian was greatly displeased with me,' said Miss Mohun that evening, talking it over with her sister. 'But her captain might have a fall if she went poking into all the gossip of the place about him.'

'Most likely whatever he did would be greatly exaggerated,' said Adeline.

'No doubt of it! Besides, those young men who are meant by nature for heroes are apt to show some Beserkerwuth in their youth, like Hereward le Wake.'

'But what did you think of the girl?'

'I liked her looks very much. I have seen her singing in the choruses at the choral society concert, and thought how nice her manner was. She does justice to her classical extraction, and is modest and ladylike besides. Mrs. Stebbing is spiteful! I wonder whether it is jealousy. She calls her artful and designing, which sounds to me very much as if Master Frank might admire the damsel. I have a great mind to have the two girls to tea, and see what they are made of.'

'We had much better wait till we hear from Lily. We cannot in the least tell whether she would wish the acquaintance to be kept up. And if there is anything going on with young Stebbing, nothing could be more unadvisable than for Gillian to be mixed up in any nonsense of that sort.'

CHAPTER VI. — SINGLE MISFORTUNES NEVER COME ALONE

On Sunday, Gillian's feet found their way to the top of the garden, where she paced meditatively up and down, hoping to see Kalliope; and just as she was giving up the expectation, the slender black figure appeared on the other side of the railings.

'Oh, Miss Gillian, how kind!'

'Kally, I am glad!'

Wherewith they got into talk at once, for Lady Merrifield's safe arrival and Sir Jasper's improvement had just been telegraphed, and there was much rejoicing over the good news. Gillian had nearly made up her mind to confute the enemy by asking why Captain White had left Rockquay; but somehow when it came to the point, she durst not make the venture, and they skimmed upon more surface subjects.

The one point of union between the parishes of Rockstone and Rockquay was a choral society, whereof Mr. Flight of St. Kenelm's was a distinguished light, and which gave periodical concerts in the Masonic Hall. It being musical, Miss Mohun had nothing to do with it except the feeling it needful to give her presence to the performances. One of these was to take place in the course of the week, and there were programmes in all the shops, 'Mr. Alexis White' being set down for more than one solo, and as a voice in the glees.

'Shall not you sing?' asked Gillian, remembering that her sisters had thought Kalliope had a good ear and a pretty voice.

'I? Oh, no!'

'I thought you used to sing.'

'Yes; but I have no time to keep it up.'

'Not even in the choruses?'

'No, I cannot manage it'—and there was a little glow in the clear brown cheek.

'Does your designing take up so much time?'

'It is not that, but there is a great deal to do at home in after hours. My mother is not strong, and we cannot keep a really efficient servant.'

'Oh! but you must be terribly hard-worked to have no time for relaxation.'

'Not quite that, but—it seems to me,' burst out poor Kalliope, 'that relaxation does nothing but bring a girl into difficulties—an unprotected girl, I mean.'

'What do you mean?' cried Gillian, quite excited; but Kalliope had caught herself up.

'Never mind, Miss Gillian; you have nothing to do with that kind of thing.'

'But do tell me, Kally; I do want to be your friend,' said Gillian, trying to put her hand through.

'There's nothing to tell,' said Kalliope, smiling and evidently touched, but still somewhat red, 'only you know when a girl has nobody to look after her, she has to look after herself.'

'Doesn't Alexis look after you?' said Gillian, not at all satisfied to be put off with this truism.

'Poor Alex! He is younger, you know, and he has quite enough to do. Oh, Miss Gillian, he is such a very dear, good boy.'

'He has a most beautiful voice, Aunt Ada said.'

'Yes, poor fellow, though he almost wishes he had not. Oh dear I there's the little bell! Good-bye, Miss Merrifield, I must run, or Mrs. Smithson will be gone to church, and I shall be locked in.'

So Gillian was left to the enigma why Alexis should regret the beauty of his own voice, and what Kalliope could mean by the scrapes of unprotected girls. It did not occur to her that Miss White was her elder by six or seven years, and possibly might not rely on her judgment and discretion as much as she might have done on those of Alethea.

Meantime the concert was coming on. It was not an amusement that Aunt Ada could attempt, but Miss Mohun took both her nieces, to the extreme pride and delight of Valetta, who had never been, as she said, 'to any evening thing but just stupid childish things, only trees and magic-lanterns'; and would not quite believe Gillian, who assured her in a sage tone that she would find this far less entertaining than either, judging by the manner in which she was wont to vituperate her music lesson.

'Oh! but that's only scales, and everybody hates them! And I do love a German band.'

'Especially in the middle of lesson-time,' said Gillian.

However, Fergus was to spend the evening with Clement Varley; and Kitty was to go with her mother and sister, the latter of whom was to be one of the performers; but it was decreed by the cruel authorities that the two bosom friends would have their tongues in better order if they were some chairs apart; and therefore, though the members of the two families at Beechcroft and the Tamarisks were consecutive, Valetta was quartered between her aunt and Gillian, with Mrs. Varley on the other side of Miss Mohun, and Major Dennis flanking Miss Merrifield. When he had duly inquired after Sir Jasper, and heard of Lady Merrifield's arrival, he had no more conversation for the young lady; and Valetta, having perceived by force of example that in this waiting-time it was not like being in church, poured out her observations and inquiries on her sister.

'What a funny room! And oh! do look at the pictures! Why has that man got on a blue apron? Freemasons! What are Freemasons? Do they work in embroidered blue satin aprons because they are gentlemen? I'll tell Fergus that is what he ought to be; he is so fond of making things—only I am sure he would spoil his apron. What's that curtain for? Will they sing up there? Oh, there's Emma Norton just come in! That must be her father. That's Alice Gidding, she comes to our Sunday class, and do you know, she thought it was Joseph who was put into the den of lions. Has not her mother got a funny head?'

'Hush now, Val. Here they come,' as the whole chorus trooped in and began the 'Men of Harlech.'

Val was reduced to silence, but there was a long instrumental performance afterwards, during which bad examples of chattering emboldened her to whisper—

'Did you see Beatrice Varley? And Miss Berry, our singing-mistress—and Alexis White? Maura says—'

Aunt Jane gave a touch and a frown which reduced Valetta to silence at this critical moment; and she sat still through a good deal, only giving a little jump when Alexis White, with various others, came to sing a glee.

Gillian could study the youth, who certainly was, as Aunt Ada said, remarkable for the cameo-like cutting of his profile, though perhaps no one without an eye for art would have remarked it, as he had the callow unformed air of a lad of seventeen or eighteen, and looked shy and grave; but his voice was a fine one, and was heard to more advantage in the solos to a hunting song which shortly followed.

Valetta had been rather alarmed at the applause at first, but she soon found out what an opportunity it gave for conversation, and after a good deal of popping her head about, she took advantage of the encores to excuse herself by saying, 'I wanted to see if Maura White was there. She was to go if Mrs.

Lee—that's the lodger—would take her. She says Kally won't go, or sing, or anything, because—'

How tantalising! the singers reappeared, and Valetta was reduced to silence. Nor could the subject be renewed in the interval between the parts, for Major Dennis came and stood in front, and talked to Miss Mohun; and after that Valetta grew sleepy, and nothing was to be got out of her till all was over, when she awoke into extra animation, and chattered so vehemently all the way home that her aunt advised Gillian to get her to bed as quietly as possible, or she would not sleep all night, and would be good for nothing the next day.

Gillian, however, being given to think for herself in all cases of counsel from Aunt Jane, thought it could do no harm to beguile the brushing of the child's hair by asking why Kalliope would not come to the concert.

'Oh, it's a great secret, but Maura told me in the cloakroom. It is because Mr. Frank wants to be her—to be her—her admirer,' said Valetta, cocking her head on one side, and adding to the already crimson colour of her cheeks.

'Nonsense, Val, what do you and Maura know of such things?'

'We aren't babies, Gill, and it is very unkind of you, when you told me I was to make friends with Maura White; and Kitty Varley is quite cross with me about it.'

'I told you to be kind to Maura, but not to talk about such foolish things.'

'I don't see why they should be foolish. It is what we all must come to. Grown-up people do, as Lois says. I heard Aunt Ada going on ever so long about Beatrice Varley and that gentleman.'

'It is just the disadvantage of that kind of school that girls talk that sort of undesirable stuff. Gillian said to herself; but curiosity, or interest in the Whites, prompted her to add, 'What did she tell you?'

'If you are so cross, I shan't tell you. You hurt my head, I say.'

'Come, Val, I ought to know.'

'It's a secret.'

'Then you should not have told me so much.'

Val laughed triumphantly, and called her sister Mrs. Curiosity, and at that moment Aunt Jane knocked at the door, and said Val was not to talk.

Val made an impatient face and began to whisper, but Gillian had too much proper feeling to allow this flat disobedience, and would not listen, much as she longed to do so. She heard her little sister rolling and tossing about a good deal, but made herself hard-hearted on principle, and acted sleep. On her own judgment, she would not waken the child in the morning, and Aunt Jane said she was quite right, it would be better to let Val have her sleep out, than send her to school fretful and half alive. 'But you ought not to have let her talk last night.'

As usual, reproof was unpleasing, and silenced Gillian. She hoped to extract the rest of the story in the course of the day. But before breakfast was over Valetta rushed in with her hat on, having scrambled into her clothes in a hurry, and consuming her breakfast in great haste, for she had no notion either of losing her place in the class, or of missing the discussion of the entertainment with Kitty, from whom she had been so cruelly parted.

Tete-a-tetes were not so easy as might have been expected between two sisters occupying the same room, for Valetta went to bed and to sleep long before Gillian, and the morning toilette was a hurry; besides, Gillian had scruples, partly out of pride and partly out of conscientiousness, about encouraging Valetta in gossip or showing her curiosity about it. Could she make anything out from Kalliope herself? However, fortune favoured her, for she came out of her class only a few steps behind little Maura; and as some of Mr. Edgar's boys were about, the child naturally regarded her as a protector.

Maura was quite as pretty as her elders, and had more of a southern look. Perhaps she was proportionably precocious, for she returned Gillian's greeting without embarrassment, and was quite ready to enter into conversation and show her gratification at compliments upon her brother's voice.

'And does not Kalliope sing? I think she used to sing very nicely in the old times.'

'Oh yes,' said Maura; 'but she doesn't now.'

'Why not? Has not she time?'

'That's not all' said Maura, looking significant, and an interrogative sound sufficed to bring out—'It is because of Mr. Frank.'

'Mr. Frank Stebbing?'

'Yes. He was always after her, and would walk home with her after the practices, though Alexis was always there. I know that was the reason for I heard la mamma mia trying to persuade her to go on with the society, and she was determined, and would not. Alex said she was quite right, and it is very tiresome of him, for now she never walks with us on Sunday, and he used to come and give us bonbons and crackers.'

71

'Then she does not like him?'

'She says it is not right or fitting, because Mr. and Mrs. Stebbing would be against it; but mamma said he would get over them, if she would not be so stupid, and he could make her quite a lady, like an officer's daughter, as we are. Is it not a pity she won't, Miss Gillian?'

'I do not know. I think she is very good,' said Gillian.

'Oh! but if she would, we might all be well off again,' said little worldly-minded Maura; 'and I should not have to help her make the beds, and darn, and iron, and all sorts of horrid things, but we could live properly, like ladies.'

'I think it is more ladylike to act uprightly,' said Gillian.

Wherewith, having made the discovery, and escorted Maura beyond the reach of her enemies, she parted with the child, and turned homewards. Gillian was at the stage in which sensible maidens have a certain repugnance and contempt for the idea of love and lovers as an interruption to the higher aims of life and destruction to family joys. Romance in her eyes was the exaltation of woman out of reach, and Maura's communications inclined her to glorify Kalliope as a heroine, molested by a very inconvenient person, 'Spighted by a fool, spighted and angered both,' as she quoted Imogen to herself.

It would be a grand history to tell Alethea of her friend, when she should have learnt a little more about it, as she intended to do on Sunday from Kalliope herself, who surely would be grateful for some sympathy and friendship. Withal she recollected that it was Indian-mail day, and hurried home to see whether the midday post had brought any letters. Her two aunts were talking eagerly, but suddenly broke off as she opened the door.

'Well, Gillian—' began Aunt Ada.

'No, no, let her see for herself,' said Aunt Jane.

'Oh! I hope nothing is the matter?' she exclaimed, seeing a letter to herself on the table.

'No; rather the reverse.'

A horrible suspicion, as she afterwards called it, came over Gillian as she tore open the letter. There were two small notes. The first was—

'DEAR LITTLE GILL—I am going to give you a new brother. Mother will tell you all.—Your loving sister,

'P. E. M.'

She gasped, and looked at the other.

'DEAREST GILLIAN—After all you have heard about Frank, perhaps you will know that I am very happy. You cannot guess how happy, and it is so delightful that mamma is charmed with him. He has got two medals and three clasps. There are so many to write to, I can only give my poor darling this little word. She will find it is only having another to be as fond of her as her old Alley.'

Gillian looked up in a bewildered state, and gasped 'Both!'

Aunt Jane could not help smiling a little, and saying, 'Yes, both at one fell swoop.'

'It's dreadful,' said Gillian.

'My dear, if you want to keep your sisters to yourself, you should not let them go to India, said Aunt Ada.

'They said they wouldn't! They were quite angry at the notion of being so commonplace,' said Gillian.

'Oh, no one knows till her time comes!' said Aunt Jane.

Gillian now applied herself to her mother's letter, which was also short.

'MY DEAREST GILLYFLOWER—I know this will be a great blow to you, as indeed it was to me; but we must not be selfish, and must remember that the sisters' happiness and welfare is the great point. I wish I could write to you more at length; but time will not let me, scattered as are all my poor flock at home. So I must leave you to learn the bare public facts from Aunt Jane, and only say my especial private words to you. You are used to being brevet eldest daughter to me, now you will have to be so to papa, who is mending fast, but, I think, will come home with me. Isn't that news?

'Your loving mother.'

'They have told you all about it, Aunt Jane!' said Gillian.

'Yes; they have been so cruel as not even to tell you the names of these robbers? Well, I dare say you had rather read my letter than hear it.'

'Thank you very much, Aunt Jane! May I take it upstairs with me?'

Consent was readily given, and Gillian had just time for her first cursory reading before luncheon.

'DEAREST JENNY—Fancy what burst upon me only the day after my coming—though really we ought to be very thankful. You might perhaps have divined what was brewing from the letters. Jasper knew of one and suspected the other before the accident, and he says it prevented him from telegraphing to stop me, for he was sure one or both the girls would want their mother.

Phyllis began it. Hers is a young merchant just taken into the great Underwood firm. Bernard Underwood, a very nice fellow, brother to the husband of one of Harry May's sisters—very much liked and respected, and, by the way, an uncommonly handsome man. That was imminent before Jasper's accident, and the letter to prepare me must be reposing in Harry's care. Mr. Underwood came down with Claude to meet me when I landed, and I scented danger in his eye. But it is all right—only his income is entirely professional, and they will have to live out here for some time to come.

'The other only spoke yesterday, having abstained from worrying his General. He is Lord Francis Somerville, son to Lord Liddesdale, and a captain in the Glen Lorn Highlanders, who have not above a couple of years to stay in these parts. He was with the riding party when Jasper fell, and was the first to lift him; indeed, he held him all the time of waiting, for poor Claude trembled too much. He was an immense help through the nursing, and they came to know and depend on him as nothing else would have made them do; and they proved how sincerely right-minded and good he is. There is some connection with the Underwoods, though I have not quite fathomed it. There is no fear about home consent, for it seems that he is given to outpourings to his mother, and had heard that if he thought of Sir Jasper Merrifield's daughter his parents would welcome her, knowing what Sir J. is. There's for you! considering that we have next to nothing to give the child, and Frank has not much fortune, but Alethea is trained to the soldierly life, and they will be better off than Jasper and I were.

'The worst of it is leaving them behind; and as neither of the gentlemen can afford a journey home, we mean to have the double wedding before Lent. As to outfit, the native tailors must be chiefly trusted to, or the stores at Calcutta, and I must send out the rest when I come home. Only please send by post my wedding veil (Gillian knows where it is), together with another as like it as may be. Any slight lace decorations to make us respectable which suggest themselves to you and her might come; I can't recollect or mention them now. I wish Reginald could come and tell you all, but the poor fellow has to go home full pelt about those Irish. Jasper is writing to William, and you must get business particulars from him, and let Gillian and the little ones hear, for there is hardly any time to write. Phyllis, being used to the idea, is very quiet and matter-of-fact about it. She hoped, indeed, that I guessed nothing till I was satisfied about papa, and had had time to rest. Alethea is in a much more April condition, and I am glad Frank waited till I was here on her account and on her father's. He is going on well, but must keep still. He declares that being nursed by two pair of lovers is highly amusing. However, such homes being found for two of the tribe is a great relief to his mind. I suppose it is to one's rational mind, though it is a terrible tug at one's heart-strings. You shall

hear again by the next mail. A brown creature waits to take this to be posted.
—

Your loving sister,

L. M.'

Gillian came down to dinner quite pale, and to Aunt Ada's kind 'Well, Gillian?' she could only repeat, 'It is horrid.'

'It is hard to lose all the pretty double wedding,' said Aunt Ada.

'Gillian does not mean that,' hastily put in Miss Mohun.

'Oh no,' said Gillian; 'that would be worse than anything.'

'So you think,' said Aunt Jane; 'but believe those who have gone through it all, my dear, when the wrench is over, one feels the benefit.'

Gillian shook her head, and drank water. Her aunts went on talking, for they thought it better that she should get accustomed to the prospect; and, moreover, they were so much excited that they could hardly have spoken of anything else. Aunt Jane wondered if Phyllis's betrothed were a brother of Mr. Underwood of St. Matthew's, Whittingtown, with whom she had corresponded about the consumptive home; and Aunt Ada regretted the not having called on Lady Liddesdale when she had spent some weeks at Rockstone, and consoled herself by recollecting that Lord Rotherwood would know all about the family. She had already looked it out in the Peerage, and discovered that Lord Francis Cunningham Somerville was the only younger son, that his age was twenty-nine, and that he had three sisters, all married, as well as his elder brother, who had children enough to make it improbable that Alethea would ever be Lady Liddesdale. She would have shown Gillian the record, but received the ungracious answer, 'I hate swells.'

'Let her alone, Ada,' said Aunt Jane; 'it is a very sore business. She will be better by and by.'

There ensued a little discussion how the veil at Silverfold was to be hunted up, or if Gillian and her aunt must go to do so.

'Can you direct Miss Vincent?' asked Miss Mohun.

'No, I don't think I could; besides, I don't like to set any one to poke and meddle in mamma's drawers.'

'And she could hardly judge what could be available,' added Miss Ada.

'Gillian must go to find it,' said Aunt Jane; 'and let me see, when have I a day? Saturday is never free, and Monday—I could ask Mrs. Hablot to take the cutting out, and then I could look up Lily's Brussels—'

There she caught a sight of Gillian's face. Perhaps one cause of the alienation the girl felt for her aunt was, that there was a certain kindred likeness between them which enabled each to divine the other's inquiring disposition, though it had different effects on the elder and younger character. Jane Mohun suspected that she had on her ferret look, and guessed that Gillian's disgusted air meant that the idea of her turning over Lady Merrifield's drawers was almost as distasteful as that of the governess's doing it.

'Suppose Gillian goes down on Monday with Fanny,' she said. 'She could manage very well, I am sure.'

Gillian cleared up a little. There is much consolation in being of a little importance, and she liked the notion of a day at home, a quiet day, as she hoped in her present mood, of speaking to nobody. Her aunt let her have her own way, and only sent a card to Macrae to provide for meeting and for food, not even letting Miss Vincent know that she was coming. That feeling of not being able to talk about it or be congratulated would wear off, Aunt Jane said, if she was not worried or argued with, in which case it might become perverse affectation.

It certainly was not shared by the children. Sisters unseen for three years could hardly be very prominent in their minds. Fergus hoped that they would ride to the wedding upon elephants, and Valetta thought it very hard to miss the being a bridesmaid, when Kitty Varley had already enjoyed the honour. However, she soon began to glorify herself on the beauty of Alethea's future title.

'What will Kitty Varley and all say?' was her cry.

'Nothing, unless they are snobs, as girls always are,' said Fergus.

'It is not a nice word,' said Miss Adeline.

'But there's nothing else that expresses it, Aunt Ada,' returned Gillian.

'I agree to a certain degree,' said Miss Mohun; 'but still I am not sure what it does express.'

'Just what girls of that sort are,' said Gillian. 'Mere worshippers of any sort of handle to one's name.'

'Gillian, Gillian, you are not going in for levelling,' cried Aunt Adeline.

'No,' said Gillian; 'but I call it snobbish to make more fuss about Alethea's concern than Phyllis's—just because he calls himself Lord—'

'That is to a certain degree true,' said Miss Mohun. 'The worth of the individual man stands first of all, and nothing can be sillier or in worse taste than to parade one's grand relations.'

'To parade, yes,' said Aunt Adeline; 'but there is no doubt that good connections are a great advantage.'

'Assuredly,' said Miss Mohun. 'Good birth and an ancestry above shame are really a blessing, though it has come to be the fashion to sneer at them. I do not mean merely in the eyes of the world, though it is something to have a name that answers for your relations being respectable. But there are such things as hereditary qualities, and thus testimony to the existence of a distinguished forefather is worth having.'

'Lily's dear old Sir Maurice de Mohun to wit,' said Miss Adeline. 'You know she used to tease Florence by saying the Barons of Beechcroft had a better pedigree than the Devereuxes.'

'I'd rather belong to the man who made himself,' said Gillian.

'Well done, Gill! But though your father won his own spurs, you can't get rid of his respectable Merrifield ancestry wherewith he started in life.'

'I don't want to. I had rather have them than horrid robber Borderers, such as no doubt these Liddesdale people were.'

There was a little laughing at this; but Gillian was saying in her own mind that it was a fine thing to be one's own Rodolf of Hapsburg, and in that light she held Captain White, who, in her present state of mind, she held to have been a superior being to all the Somervilles—perhaps to all the Devereuxes who ever existed.

CHAPTER VII. — AN EMPTY NEST

There had been no injunctions of secrecy, and though neither Miss Mohun nor Gillian had publicly mentioned the subject, all Rockquay who cared for the news knew by Sunday morning that Lady Merrifield's two elder daughters were engaged.

Gillian, in the course of writing her letters, had become somewhat familiarised with the idea, and really looked forward to talking it over with Kalliope. Though that young person could hardly be termed Alethea's best friend, it was certain that Alethea stood foremost with her, and that her interest in the matter would be very loving.

Accordingly, Kalliope was at the place of meeting even before Gillian, and anxiously she looked as she said—

'May I venture—may I ask if it is true?'

'True? Oh yes, Kally, I knew you would care.'

'Indeed, I well may. There is no expressing how much I owe to dear Miss Alethea and Lady Merrifield, and it is such a delight to hear of them.'

Accordingly, Gillian communicated the facts as she knew them, and offered to give any message.

'Only my dear love and congratulations,' said Kalliope, with a little sigh. 'I should like to have written, but—'

'But why don't you, then?'

'Oh no; she would be too much engaged to think of us, and it would only worry her to be asked for her advice.'

'I think I know what it is about,' said Gillian.

'How? Oh, how do you know? Did Mr. Flight say anything?'

'Mr. Flight?' exclaimed Gillian. 'What has he to do with it?'

'It was foolish, perhaps; but I did hope he might have helped Alexis, and now he seems only to care for his music.'

'Helped him! How?'

'Perhaps it was unreasonable, but Alexis has always been to good schools. He was getting on beautifully at Leeds, and we thought he would have gained a scholarship and gone on to be a clergyman. That was what his mind has always been fixed upon. You cannot think how good and devoted he is,' said

Kalliope with a low trembling voice; 'and my father wished it very much too. But when the break-up came, Mr. White made our not being too fine, as he said, to work, a sort of condition of doing anything for us. Mr. Moore did tell him what Alexis is, but I believe he thought it all nonsense, and there was nothing to be done. Alexis—dear fellow—took it so nicely, said he was thankful to be able to help mother, and if it was his duty and God's will, it was sure to come right; and he has been plodding away at the marble works ever since, quite patiently and resolutely, but trying to keep up his studies in the evening, only now he has worked through all his old school-books.'

'And does not Mr. Flight know that I will help him?'

'Well, Mr. Flight means to be kind, and sometimes seems to think much of him; but it is all for his music, I am afraid. He is always wanting new things to be learnt and practised, and those take up so much time; and though he does lend us books, they are of no use for study, though they only make the dear boy long and long the more to get on.'

'Does not Mr. Flight know?'

'I am not sure. I think he does; but in his ardour for music he seems to forget all about it. It does seem such a pity that all Alexis's time should be wasted in this drudgery. If I could only be sure of more extra work for my designs, I could set him free; and if Sir Jasper were only at home, I am sure he would put the boy in the way of earning his education. If it were only as a pupil teacher, he would be glad, but then he says he ought not to throw all on me.'

'Oh, he must be very good!' exclaimed Gillian. 'I am sure papa will help him! I wish I could. Oh!'—with a sudden recollection—'I wonder what books he wants most. I am going to Silverfold to-morrow, and there are lots of old school-books there of the boys', doing nothing, that I know he might have.'

'Oh, Miss Gillian, how good of you! How delighted he would be!'

'Do you know what he wants most?'

'A Greek grammar and lexicon most of all,' was the ready answer. 'He has been trying to find them at the second-hand shop ever so long, but I am afraid there is no hope of a lexicon. They are so large and expensive.'

'I think there is an old one of Jasper's, if he would not mind its back being off, and lots of blots.'

'He would mind nothing. Oh, Miss Gillian, you can't think how happy he will be.

'If there is anything else he wants very much, how could he let me know?'

mused Gillian. 'Oh, I see! What time are you at the works?'

'Alex is there at seven; I don't go till nine.'

'I am to be at the station at 8.40. Could you or Maura meet me there and tell me?'

To this Kalliope agreed, for she said she could be sure of getting to her post in time afterwards, and she seemed quite overjoyed. No one could look at her without perceiving that Alexis was the prime thought of her heart, and Gillian delighted her by repeating Aunt Adeline's admiration of his profile, and the general opinion of his singing.

'I am so sorry you have had to give it up,' she added.

'It can't be helped,' Kalliope said; 'and I really have no time.'

'But that's not all,' said Gillian, beginning to blush herself.

'Oh! I hope there's no gossip or nonsense about *that*,' cried Kalliope, her cheeks flaming.

'Only—'

'Not Maura? Naughty little girl, I did not think she knew anything. Not that there is anything to tell,' said Kalliope, much distressed; 'but it is dreadful that there should be such talk.'

'I thought it was *that* you meant when you said you wanted advice.'

'No one could advise me, I am afraid,' said the girl. 'If we could only go away from this place! But that's impossible, and I dare say the fancy will soon go off!'

'Then you don't care for him?'

'My dear Miss Gillian, when I have seen *gentlemen*!' said Kalliope, in a tone that might have cured her admirer.

They had, however, talked longer than usual, and the notes of the warning bell came up, just when Gillian had many more questions to ask, and she had to run down the garden all in a glow with eagerness and excitement, so that Aunt Ada asked if she had been standing in the sea wind. Her affirmative was true enough, and yet she was almost ashamed of it, as not the whole truth, and there was a consciousness about her all the afternoon which made her soon regret that conversation was chiefly absorbed by the younger one's lamentations that they were not to accompany her to Silverfold, and by their commissions. Fergus wanted a formidable amount of precious tools, and inchoate machines, which Mrs. Halfpenny had regarded as 'mess,' and utterly refused to let his aunts be 'fashed' with; while Valetta's orders were chiefly for the visiting all the creatures, so as to bring an exact account of the health and spirits of Rigdum Funnidos, etc., also for some favourite story-books which she wished to lend to Kitty Varley and Maura White.

'For do you know, Gill, Maura has never had a new story-book since mamma gave her Little Alice and her Sister, when she was seven years old! Do bring her Stories They Tell Me, and On Angel's Wings.'

'But is not that Mysie's?'

'Oh yes, but I know Mysie would let her have it. Mysie always let Maura have everything of hers, because the boys teased her.'

'I will bring it; but I think Mysie ought to be written to before it is lent.'

'That is right, Gillian,' said Miss Mohun; 'it is always wiser to be above-board when dealing with other people's things, even in trifles.'

Why did this sound like a reproach, and as if it implied suspicion that Gillian was not acting on that principle? She resented the feeling. She knew she might do as she liked with the boys' old books, for which they certainly had no affection, and which indeed her mother had talked of offering to some of those charities which have a miscellaneous appetite, and wonderful power of adaptation of the disused. Besides, though no one could have the least objection to their being bestowed on the Whites, the very fact of this being her third secret meeting with Kalliope was beginning to occasion an awkwardness in accounting for her knowledge of their needs. It was obvious to ask why she had not mentioned the first meeting, and this her pride would not endure. She had told her parents by letter. What more could be desired?

Again, when she would not promise to see either Miss Vincent or the Miss Hackets, because 'she did not want to have a fuss,' Aunt Jane said she thought it a pity, with regard at least to the governess, who might feel herself hurt at the neglect, 'and needless secrets are always unadvisable.'

Gillian could hardly repress a wriggle, but her Aunt Ada laughed, saying, 'Especially with you about, Jenny, for you always find them out.'

At present, however, Miss Mohun certainly had no suspicion. Gillian was very much afraid she would think proper to come to the station in the morning; but she was far too busy, and Gillian started off in the omnibus alone with Mrs. Mount in handsome black silk trim, to be presented to Mr. Macrae, and much enjoying the trip, having been well instructed by Fergus and Valetta in air that she was to see.

Kalliope was descried as the omnibus stopped, and in a few seconds Gillian had shaken hands with her, received the note, and heard the ardent thanks sent from Alexis, and which the tattered books—even if they proved to be right—would scarcely deserve. He would come with his sister to receive the parcel at the station on Gillian's return—at 5.29, an offer which obviated any further difficulties as to conveyance.

Mrs. Mount was intent upon the right moment to run the gauntlet for the tickets; and had it been otherwise, would have seen nothing remarkable in her charge being accosted by a nice-looking ladylike girl. So on they rushed upon their way, Gillian's spirits rising in a curious sense of liberty and holiday-making.

In due time they arrived, and were received by Macrae with the pony carriage, while the trees of Silverfold looked exquisite in their autumn red, gold, and brown.

But the dreariness of the deserted house, with no one on the steps but Quiz, and all the furniture muffled in sheets, struck Gillian more than she had expected, though the schoolroom had been wakened up for her, a bright fire on the hearth, and the cockatoo highly conversational, the cats so affectionate that it was difficult to take a step without stumbling over one of them.

When the business had all been despatched, the wedding veil disinterred, and the best Brussels and Honiton safely disposed in a box, when an extremely dilapidated and much-inked collection of school-books had been routed out of the backstairs cupboard (commonly called Erebus) and duly packed, when a selection of lighter literature had been made with a view both to Valetta and Lilian; when Gillian had shown all she could to Mrs. Mount, visited all the animals, gone round the garden, and made two beautiful posies of autumn flowers, one for her little sister and the other for Kalliope, discovered that Fergus's precious machine had been ruthlessly made away with, but secured his tools,—she found eating partridge in solitary grandeur rather dreary work, though she had all the bread-sauce to herself, and cream to her apple tart, to say nothing of Macrae, waiting upon her as if she had been a duchess, and conversing in high exultation upon the marriages, only regretting that one gentleman should be a civilian; he had always augured that all his young ladies would be in the Service, and begging that he might be made aware of the wedding-day, so as to have the bells rung.

To express her own feelings to the butler was not possible, and his glee almost infected her. She was quite sorry when, having placed a choice of pears and October peaches before her, he went off to entertain Mrs. Mount; and after packing a substratum of the fruit in the basket for the Whites, she began almost to repent of having insisted on not returning to Rockstone till the four o'clock train, feeling her solitary liberty oppressive; and finally she found herself walking down the drive in search of Miss Vincent.

She had to confess to herself that her aunt was quite right, and that the omission would have been a real unkindness, when she saw how worn and tired the governess looked, and the brightness that flashed over the pale face at sight of her. Mrs. Vincent had been much worse, and though slightly better for the present was evidently in a critical state, very exhausting to her daughter.

Good Miss Hacket at that moment came in to sit with her, and send the daughter out for some air; and it was well that Gillian had had some practice in telling her story not too disconsolately, for it was received with all the delight that the mere notion of a marriage seems to inspire, though Phyllis and Alethea had scarcely been seen at Silverfold before they had gone to India with their father.

Miss Hacket had to be content with the names before she hastened up to the patient; but Miss Vincent walked back through the paddock with Gillian, talking over what was more personally interesting to the governess, the success of her own pupils, scattered as they were, and comparing notes upon Mysie's letters. One of these Miss Vincent had just received by the second post, having been written to announce the great news, and it continued in true Mysie fashion:—

'Cousin Rotherwood knows all about them, and says they will have a famous set of belongings. He will take me to see some of them if we go to London before mamma comes home. Bernard Underwood's sister is married to Mr. Grinstead, the sculptor who did the statue of Mercy at the Gate that Harry gave a photograph of to mamma, and she paints pictures herself. I want to see them; but I do not know whether we shall stay in London, for they do not think it agrees with Fly. I do more lessons than she does now, and I have read through all Autour de mon Jardin. I have a letter from Dolores too, and she thinks that Aunt Phyllis and all are coming home to make a visit in England for Uncle Harry to see his father, and she wishes very much that they would bring her; but it is not to be talked about for fear they should be hindered, and old Dr. May hear of it and be disappointed; but you won't see any one to tell.'

'There, what have I done?' exclaimed Miss Vincent in dismay. 'But I had only just got the letter, and had barely glanced through it.'

'Besides, who would have thought of Mysie having any secrets?' said Gillian.

'After all, I suppose no harm is done; for you can't have any other connection with these Mays.'

'Oh yes, there will be; for I believe a brother of this man of Phyllis's married one of the Miss Mays, and I suppose we shall have to get mixed up with the whole lot. How I do hate strangers! But I'll take care, Miss Vincent, indeed I will. One is not bound to tell one's aunts everything like one's mother.'

'No,' said Miss Vincent decidedly, 'especially when it is another person's secret betrayed through inadvertence.' Perhaps she thought Gillian looked dangerously gratified, for she added: 'However, you know poor Dolores did not find secrecy answer.'

'Oh, there are secrets and secrets, and aunts and aunts!' said Gillian. 'Dolores had no mother.'

'It makes a difference,' said Miss Vincent. 'I should never ask you to conceal anything from Lady Merrifield. Besides, this is not a matter of conduct, only a report.'

Gillian would not pursue the subject. Perhaps she was a little disingenuous with her conscience, for she wanted to carry off the impression that Miss Vincent had pronounced concealment from her aunts to be justifiable; and she knew at the bottom of her heart that her governess would condemn a habit of secret intimacy with any one being carried on without the knowledge of her hostess and guardian for the time being,—above all when it was only a matter, of waiting.

It is a fine thing for self-satisfaction to get an opinion without telling the whole of the facts of the case, and Gillian went home in high spirits, considerably encumbered with parcels, and surprising Mrs. Mount by insisting that two separate packages should be made of the books.

Kalliope and Alexis were both awaiting her at the station, their gratitude unbounded, and finding useful vent by the latter fetching a cab and handing in the goods.

It was worth something to see how happy the brother and sister looked, as they went off in the gaslight, the one with the big brown paper parcel, the other with the basket of fruit and flowers; and Gillian's explanation to Mrs. Mount that they were old friends of her soldiering days was quite satisfactory.

There was a grand unpacking. Aunt Ada was pleased with the late roses, and Aunt Jane that there had been a recollection of Lilian Giles, to whom she had thought her niece far too indifferent. Valetta fondled the flowers, and was gratified to hear of the ardent affection of the Begum and the health of Rigdum, though Gillian was forced to confess that she had not transferred to him the kiss that she had been commissioned to convey. Nobody was disappointed except Fergus, who could not but vituperate the housemaids for the destruction of his new patent guillotine for mice, which was to have been introduced to Clement Varley. To be sure it would hardly ever act, and had never cut off the head of anything save a dandelion, but that was a trifling consideration.

A letter from Mysie was awaiting Gillian, not lengthy, for there was a long interval between Mysie's brains and her pen, and saying nothing about the New Zealand report. The selection of lace was much approved, and the next day there was to be an expedition to endeavour to get the veil matched as nearly as possible. The only dangerous moment was at breakfast the next day, when Miss Mohun said—

'Fanny was delighted with Silverfold. Macrae seems to have been the pink of politeness to her.'

'She must come when the house is alive again,' said Gillian. 'What would she think of it then!'

'Oh, that would be perfectly delicious,' cried Valetta. 'She would see Begum and Rigdum—'

'And I could show her how to work the lawn cutter,' added Fergus.

'By the bye,' said Aunt Jane, 'whom have you been lending books to?'

'Oh, to the Whites,' said Gillian, colouring, as she felt more than she could wish. 'There were some old school-books that I thought would be useful to them, and I was sure mamma would like them to have some flowers and fruit.'

She felt herself very candid, but why would Aunt Jane look at those tell- tale cheeks.

Sunday was wet, or rather 'misty moisty,' with a raw sea-fog overhanging everything—not bad enough, however, to keep any one except Aunt Ada from church or school, though she decidedly remonstrated against Gillian's going out for her wandering in the garden in such weather; and, if she had been like the other aunt, might almost have been convinced that such determination must be for an object. However, Gillian encountered the fog in vain, though she walked up and down the path till her clothes were quite limp and flabby with damp. All the view that rewarded her was the outline of the shrubs looming through the mist like distant forests as mountains. Moreover, she got a scolding from Aunt Ada, who met her coming in, and was horrified at the misty atmosphere which she was said to have brought in, and insisted on her going at once to change her dress, and staying by the fireside all the rest of the afternoon.

'I cannot think what makes her so eager about going out in the afternoon,' said the younger aunt to the elder. 'It is impossible that she can have any reason for it.'

'Only Sunday restlessness,' said Miss Mohun, 'added to the reckless folly of the "Bachfisch" about health.'

'That's true,' said Adeline, 'girls must be either so delicate that they are quite helpless, or so strong as to be absolutely weather-proof.'

Fortune, however, favoured Gillian when next she went to Lily Giles. She had never succeeded in taking real interest in the girl, who seemed to her to be so silly and sentimental that an impulse to answer drily instantly closed up all inclination to effusions of confidence. Gillian had not yet learnt breadth of charity enough to understand that everybody does not feel, or express feeling, after the same pattern; that gush is not always either folly or insincerity; and that girls of Lily's class are about at the same stage of culture as the young ladies of whom her namesake in the Inheritance is the type. When Lily showed her in some little magazine the weakest of poetry, and called it so sweet, just like 'dear Mr. Grant's lovely sermon, the last she had heard. Did he not look so like a saint in his surplice and white stole, with his holy face and beautiful blue eyes; it was enough to make any one feel good to look at him,' Gillian simply replied, 'Oh, *I* never think of the clergyman's looks,' and hurried to her book, feeling infinitely disgusted and contemptuous, never guessing that these poor verses, and the curate's sermons and devotional appearance were, to the young girl's heart, the symbols of all that was sacred, and all that was refined, and that the thought of them was the solace of her lonely and suffering hours. Tolerant sympathy is one of the latest lessons of life, and perhaps it is well that only

'The calm temper of our age should be
  Like the high leaves upon the holly-tree,'

for the character in course of formation needs to be guarded by prickles.

However, on this day Undine was to be finished, for Gillian was in haste to begin Katharine Ashton, which would, she thought, be much more wholesome reality, so she went on later than usual, and came away at last, leaving her auditor dissolved in tears over poor Undine's act of justice.

As Mrs. Giles, full of thanks, opened the little garden-gate just as twilight was falling, Gillian beheld Kalliope and Alexis White coming up together from the works, and eagerly met and shook hands with them. The dark days were making them close earlier, they explained, and as Kalliope happened to have nothing to finish or purchase, she was able to come home with her brother.

Therewith Alexis began to express, with the diffidence of extreme gratitude, his warm thanks for the benefaction of books, which were exactly what he had wanted and longed for. His foreign birth enabled him to do this much more prettily and less clumsily than an English boy, and Gillian was pleased, though she told him that her brother's old ill-used books were far from worthy of such thanks.

'Ah, you cannot guess how precious they are to me!' said Alexis. 'They are the restoration of hope.'

'And can you get on by yourself?' asked Gillian. 'Is it not very difficult without any teacher?'

'People have taught themselves before,' returned the youth, 'so I hope to do so myself; but of course there are many questions I long to ask.'

'Perhaps I could answer some,' said Gillian; 'I have done some classics with a tutor.'

'Oh, thank you, Miss Merrifield,' he said eagerly. 'If you could make me understand the force of the aorist.

It so happened that Gillian had the explanation at her tongue's end, and it was followed by another, and another, till one occurred which could hardly be comprehended without reference to the passage, upon which Alexis pulled a Greek Testament out of his pocket, and his sister could not help exclaiming—

'Oh, Alexis, you can't ask Miss Merrifield to do Greek with you out in the street.'

Certainly it was awkward, the more so as Mrs. Stebbing just then drove by in her carriage.

'What a pity!' exclaimed Gillian. 'But if you would set down any difficulties, you could send them to me by Kalliope on Sunday.'

'Oh, Miss Merrifield, how very good of you!' exclaimed Alexis, his face lighting up with joy.

But Kalliope looked doubtful, and began a hesitating 'But—'

'I'll tell you of a better way!' exclaimed Gillian. 'I always go once a week to read to this Lilian Giles, and if I come down afterwards to Kalliope's office after you have struck work, I could see to anything you wanted to ask.'

Alexis broke out into the most eager thanks. Kalliope said hardly anything, and as they had reached the place where the roads diverged, they bade one another good-evening.

Gillian looked after the brother and sister just as the gas was being lighted, and could almost guess what Alexis was saying, by his gestures of delight. She did not hear, and did not guess how Kalliope answered, 'Don't set your heart on it too much, dear fellow, for I should greatly doubt whether Miss Gillian's aunts will consent. Oh yes, of course, if they permit her, it will be all right.

So Gillian went her way feeling that she had found her 'great thing.' Training a minister for the Church! Was not that a 'great thing'?

CHAPTER VIII. — GILLIAN'S PUPIL

Gillian was not yet seventeen, and had lived a home life totally removed from gossip, so that she had no notion that she was doing a more awkward or remarkable thing than if she had been teaching a drummer-boy. She even deliberated whether she should mention her undertaking to her mother, or produce the grand achievement of Alexis White, prepared for college, on the return from India; but a sense that she had promised to tell everything, and that, while she did so, she could defy any other interference, led her to write the design in a letter to Ceylon, and then she felt ready to defy any censure or obstructions from other Quarters.

Mystery has a certain charm. Infinite knowledge of human nature was shown in the text, 'Stolen waters are sweet, and bread eaten in secret is pleasant'; and it would be hard to define how much Gillian's satisfaction was owing to the sense of benevolence, or to the pleasure of eluding Aunt Jane, when, after going through her chapter of Katharine Ashton, in a somewhat perfunctory manner, she hastened away to Miss White's office. This, being connected with the showroom, could be entered without passing through the gate with the inscription—'No admittance except on business.' Indeed, the office had a private door, which, at Gillian's signal, was always opened to her. There, on the drawing-desk, lay a Greek exercise and a translation, with queries upon the difficulties for Gillian to correct, or answer in writing. Kalliope had managed to make that little room a pleasant place, bare as it was, by pinning a few of her designs on the walls, and always keeping a terracotta vase of flowers or coloured leaves upon the table. The lower part of the window she had blocked with transparencies delicately cut and tinted in cardboard—done, as she told Gillian, by her little brother Theodore, who learnt to draw at the National School, and had the same turn for art as herself. Altogether, the perfect neatness and simplicity of the little room gave it an air of refinement, which rendered it by no means an unfit setting for the grave beauty of Kalliope's countenance and figure.

The enjoyment of the meeting was great on both sides, partly from the savour of old times, and partly because there was really much that was uncommon and remarkable about Kalliope herself. Her father's promotion had come exactly when she and her next brother were at the time of life when the changes it brought would tell most on their minds and manners. They had both been sent to schools where they had associated with young people of gentle breeding, which perhaps their partly foreign extraction, and southern birth and childhood, made it easier for them to assimilate. Their beauty and brightness had led to a good deal of kindly notice from the officers and ladies of the regiment, and they had thus acquired the habits and ways of the class to which they had been raised. Their father, likewise, had been a man of a chivalrous nature, whose youthful mistakes had been the outcome of high spirit and romance, and who, under discipline, danger, suffering, and responsibility, had become earnestly religious. There had besides been his Colonel's influence on him, and on his children that of Lady Merrifield and Alethea.

It had then been a piteous change and darkening of life when, after the crushing grief of his death, the young people found themselves in such an entirely different stratum of society. They were ready to work, but they could not help feeling the mortification of being relegated below the mysterious line of gentry, as they found themselves at Rockquay, and viewed as on a level with the clerks and shop-girls of the place. Still more, as time went on, did they miss the companionship and intercourse to which they had been used. Mr. Flight, the only person in a higher rank who took notice of them, and perceived that there was more in them than was usual, was after all only a patron—not a friend, and perhaps was not essentially enough of a gentleman to be free from all airs of condescension even with Alexis, while he might be wise in not making too much of an approach to so beautiful a girl as Kalliope. Besides, after a fit of eagerness, and something very like promises, he had apparently let Alexis drop, only using him for his musical services, and not doing anything to promote the studies for which the young man thirsted, nor proposing anything for the younger boys, who would soon outgrow the National School.

Alexis had made a few semi-friends among the musical youth of the place; but there was no one to sympathise with him in his studious tastes, and there was much in his appearance and manners to cause the accusation of being 'stuck-up'—music being really the only point of contact with most of his fellows of the lower professional class.

Kalliope had less time, but she had, on principle, cultivated kindly terms with the young women employed under her. Her severe style of beauty removed her from any jealousy of her as a rival, and she was admired— almost worshipped—by them as the glory of the workshop. They felt her superiority, and owned her ability; but nobody there was capable of being a companion to her. Thus the sister and brother had almost wholly depended upon one another; and it was like a breath from what now seemed the golden age of their lives when Gillian Merrifield walked into the office, treating Kalliope with all the freedom of an equal and the affection of an old friend. There was not very much time to spare after Gillian had looked at the exercises, noted and corrected the errors, and explained the difficulties or mistakes in the translation from Testament and Delectus, feeling all the time how much more mastery of the subject her pupil had than Mr. Pollock's at home had ever attained to.

However, Kalliope always walked home with her as far as the opening of Church Cliff Road, and they talked of the cleverness and goodness of the brothers, except Richard at Leeds, who never seemed to be mentioned; how Theodore kept at the head of the school, and had hopes of the drawing prize, and how little Petros devoured tales of battles, and would hear of nothing but being a soldier. Now and then, too, there was a castle in the air of a home for little Maura at Alexis's future curacy. Kalliope seemed to look to working for life for poor mother, while Theodore should cultivate his art. Oftener the two recalled old adventures and scenes of their regimental days, and discussed the weddings of the two Indian sisters.

Once, however, Kalliope was obliged to suggest, with a blushing apology, that she feared Gillian must go home alone, she was not ready.

'Can't I help you? what have you to do?'

Kalliope attempted some excuse of putting away designs, but presently peeped from the window, and Gillian, with excited curiosity, imitated her, and beheld, lingering about, a young man in the pink of fashion, with a tea-rose in his buttonhole and a cane in his hand.

'Oh, Kally,' she cried, 'does he often hang about like this waiting for you?'

'Not often, happily. There! old Mr. Stebbing has come out, and they are walking away together. We can go now.'

'So he besets you, and you have to keep out of his way,' exclaimed Gillian, much excited. 'Is that the reason you come to the garden all alone on Sunday?'

'Yes, though I little guessed what awaited me there,' returned Kalliope; 'but we had better make haste, for it is late for you to be returning.'

It was disappointing that Kalliope would not discuss such an interesting affair; but Gillian was sensible of the danger of being so late as to cause questions, and she allowed herself to be hurried on too fast for conversation, and passing the two Stebbings, who, no doubt, took her for a 'hand.'

'Does this often happen?' asked Gillian.

'No; Alec walks home with me, and the boys often come and meet me. Oh, did I tell you that the master wants Theodore to be a pupil-teacher? I wish I knew what was best for him.'

'Could not he be an artist?'

'I should like some one to tell me whether he really has talent worth cultivating, dear boy, or if he would be safer and better in an honourable occupation like a school-master.'

'Do you call it honourable?'

'Oh yes, to be sure. I put it next to a clergyman's or a doctor's life.'

'Not a soldier's?'

'That depends,' said Kalliope.

'On the service he is sent upon, you mean? But that is his sovereign's look-out. He "only has to obey, to do or die."'

'Yes, it is the putting away of self, and possible peril of life, that makes all those grandest,' said Kalliope, 'and I think the schoolmaster is next in opportunities of doing good.'

Gillian could not help thinking that none of all these could put away self more entirely than the girl beside her, toiling away her beauty and her youth in this dull round of toil, not able to exercise the instincts of her art to the utmost, and with no change from the monotonous round of mosaics, which were forced to be second rate, to the commonest household works, and the company of the Queen of the White Ants.

Gillian perceived enough of the nobleness of such a life to fill her with a certain enthusiasm, and make her feel a day blank and uninteresting if she could not make her way to the little office.

One evening, towards the end of the first fortnight, Alexis himself came in with a passage that he wanted to have explained. His sister looked uneasy all the time, and hurried to put on her hat, and stand demonstratively waiting, telling Gillian that they must go, the moment the lesson began to tend to discursive talk, and making a most decided sign of prohibition to her brother when he showed a disposition to accompany them.

'I think you are frightfully particular, Kally,' said Gillian, when they were on their way up the hill. 'Such an old friend, and you there, too.'

'It would never do here! It would be wrong,' answered Kalliope, with the authority of an older woman. 'He must not come to the office.'

'Oh, but how could I ever explain to him? One can't do everything in writing. I might as well give up the lessons as never speak to him about them.'

There was truth in this, and perhaps Alexis used some such arguments on his side, for at about every third visit of Gillian's he dropped in with some important inquiry necessary to his progress, which was rapid enough to compel Gillian to devote some time to preparation, in order to keep ahead of him.

Kalliope kept diligent guard, and watched against lengthening the lessons into gossip, and they were always after hours when the hands had gone away. The fear of being detected kept Gillian ready to shorten the time.

'How late you are!' were the first words she heard one October evening on entering Beechcroft Cottage; but they were followed by 'Here's a pleasure for you!'

'It's from papa himself! Open it! Open it quick,' cried Valetta, dancing round her in full appreciation of the honour and delight.

Sir Jasper said that his daughter must put up with him for a correspondent, since two brides at once were as much as any mother could be supposed to undertake. Indeed, as mamma would not leave him, Phyllis was actually going to Calcutta, chaperoned by one of the matrons of the station, to make purchases for both outfits, since Alethea would not stir from under the maternal wing sooner than she could help.

At the end came, 'We are much shocked at poor White's death. He was an excellent officer, and a good and sensible man, though much hampered with his family. I am afraid his wife must be a very helpless being. He used to talk about the good promise of one of his sons—the second, I think. We will see whether anything can be done for the children when we come home. I say we, for I find I shall have to be invalided before I can be entirely patched up, so that mamma and I shall have a sort of postponed silver wedding tour, a new variety for the old folks "from home."'

'Oh, is papa coming home?' cried Valetta.

'For good! Oh, I hope it will be for good,' added Gillian.

'Then we shall live at dear Silverfold all the days of our life,' added Fergus.

'And I shall get back to Rigdum.'

'And I shall make a telephone down to the stables,' were the cries of the children.

The transcendent news quite swallowed up everything else for some time; but at last Gillian recurred to her father's testimony as to the White family.

'Is the second son the musical one?' she was asked, and on her affirmative, Aunt Jane remarked, 'Well, though the Rev. Augustine Flight is not on a pinnacle of human wisdom, his choir practices, etc., will keep the lad well out of harm's way till your father can see about him.'

This would have been an opportunity of explaining the youth's aims and hopes, and her own share in forwarding them; but it had become difficult to avow the extent of her intercourse with the brother and sister, so entirely without the knowledge of her aunts. Even Miss Mohun, acute as she was, had no suspicions, and only thought with much satisfaction that her niece was growing more attentive to poor Lilian Giles, even to the point of lingering.

'I really think, she said, in consultation with Miss Adeline, 'that we might gratify that damsel by having the White girls to drink tea.'

'Well, we can add them to your winter party of young ladies in business.'

'Hardly. These stand on different ground, and I don't want to hurt their feelings or Gillian's by mixing them up with the shopocracy.'

'Have you seen the Queen of the White Ants?'

'Not yet; but I mean to reconnoitre, and if I see no cause to the contrary, I shall invite them for next Tuesday.'

'The mother? You might as well ask her namesake.'

'Probably; but I shall be better able to judge when I have seen her.'

So Miss Mohun trotted off, made her visit, and thus reported, 'Poor woman! she certainly is not lovely now, whatever she may have been; but I should think there was no harm in her, and she is effusive in her gratitude to all the Merrifield family. It is plain that the absent eldest son is the favourite, far more so than the two useful children at the marble works; and Mr. White is spoken of as a sort of tyrant, whereas I should think they owed a good deal to his kindness in giving them employment.'

'I always thought he was an old hunks.'

'The town thinks so because he does not come and spend freely here; but I have my doubts whether they are right. He is always ready to do his part in subscriptions; and the employing these young people as he does is true kindness.'

'Unappreciated.'

'Yes, by the mother who would expect to be kept like a lady in idleness, but perhaps not so by her daughter. From all I can pick up, I think she must be a very worthy person, so I have asked her and the little schoolgirl for Tuesday evening, and I hope it will not be a great nuisance to you, Ada.'

'Oh no,' said Miss Adeline, good humouredly, 'it will please Gillian, and I shall be interested in seeing the species, or rather the variety.'

'Var Musa Groeca Hibernica Militaris,' laughed Aunt Jane.

'By the bye, I further found out what made the Captain enlist.'

'Trust you for doing that!' laughed her sister.

'Really it was not on purpose, but old Zack Skilly was indulging me with some of his ancient smuggling experiences, in what he evidently views as the heroic age of Rockquay. "Men was men, then," he says. "Now they be good for nought, but to row out the gentlefolks when the water is as smooth as glass." You should hear the contempt in his voice. Well, a promising young hero of his was Dick White, what used to work for his uncle, but liked a bit of a lark, and at last hit one of the coastguard men in a fight, and ran away, and folks said he had gone for a soldier. Skilly had heard he was dead, and his wife had come to live in these parts, but there was no knowing what was true and what wasn't. Folks would talk! Dick was a likely chap, with more life about him than his cousin Jem, as was a great man now, and owned all the marble works, and a goodish bit of the town. There was a talk as how the two lads had both been a courting of the same maid, that was Betsy Polwhele, and had fallen out about her, but how that might be he could not tell. Anyhow, she was not wed to one nor t'other of them, but went into a waste and died.'

'I wonder if it was for Dick's sake. So Jem was not constant either.'

'Except to his second love. That was a piteous little story too.'

'You mean his young wife's health failing as soon as he brought her to that house which he was building for her, and then his taking her to Italy, and never enduring to come back here again after she and her child died. But he made a good thing of it with his quarries in the mountains.'

'You sordid person, do you think that was all he cared for!'

'Well, I always thought of him as a great, stout, monied man, quite incapable of romance and sensitiveness.'

'If so, don't you think he would have let that house instead of keeping it up in empty state! There is a good deal of character in those Whites.'

'The Captain is certainly the most marked man, except Jasper, in that group of officers in Gillian's photograph-book.'

'Partly from the fact that a herd of young officers always look so exactly alike—at least in the eyes of elderly spinsters.'

'Jane!'

'Let us hope so, now that it is all over. This same Dick must have had something remarkable about him, to judge by the impression he seems to have left on all who came in his way, and I shall like to see his children.'

'You always do like queer people.'

'It is plain that we ought to take notice of them,' said Miss Mohun, 'and it is not wholesome for Gillian to think us backward in kindness to friends about whom she plainly has a little romance.'

She refrained from uttering a suspicion inspired by her visit that there had been more 'kindnesses' on her niece's part than she could quite account for. Yet she believed that she knew how all the girl's days were spent; was certain that the Sunday wanderings never went beyond the garden, and, moreover, she implicitly trusted Lily's daughter.

Gillian did not manifest as much delight and gratitude at the invitation as her aunts expected. In point of fact, she resented Aunt Jane's making a visit of investigation without telling her, and she was uneasy lest there should have been or yet should be a disclosure that should make her proceedings appear clandestine. 'And they are not!' said she to herself with vehemence. 'Do I not write them all to my own mother? And did not Miss Vincent allow that one is not bound to treat aunts like parents?'

Even the discovery of Captain White's antecedents was almost an offence, for if her aunt would not let her inquire, why should she do so herself, save to preserve the choice morceau for her own superior intelligence? Thus all the reply that Gillian deigned was, 'Of course I knew that Captain White could never have done anything to be ashamed of.'

The weather was too wet for any previous meetings, and it was on a wild stormy evening that the two sisters appeared at seven o'clock at Beechcroft Cottage. While hats and waterproofs were being taken off upstairs, Gillian found opportunity to give a warning against mentioning the Greek lessons. It was received with consternation.

'Oh, Miss Merrifield, do not your aunts know?'

'No. Why should they? Mamma does.'

'Not yet. And she is so far off! I wish Miss Mohun knew! I made sure that she did,' said Kalliope, much distressed.

'But why? It would only make a fuss.'

'I should be much happier about it.'

'And perhaps have it all upset.'

'That is the point. I felt that it must be all right as long as Miss Mohun sanctioned it; but I could not bear that we should be the means of bringing you into a scrape, by doing what she might disapprove while you are under her care.'

'Don't you think you can trust me to know my own relations?' said Gillian somewhat haughtily.

'Indeed, I did not mean that we are not infinitely obliged to you,' said Kalliope. 'It has made Alexis another creature to have some hope, and feel himself making progress.'

'Then why do you want to have a fuss, and a bother, and a chatter? If my father and mother don't approve, they can telegraph.'

With which argument she appeased or rather silenced Kalliope, who could not but feel the task of objecting alike ungracious and ungrateful towards the instructor, and absolutely cruel and unkind towards her brother, and who spoke only from a sense of the treachery of allowing a younger girl to transgress in ignorance. Still she was conscious of not understanding on what terms the niece and aunts might be, and the St. Kenelm's estimate of the Beechcroft ladies was naturally somewhat different from that of the St. Andrew's congregation. Miss Mohun was popularly regarded in those quarters as an intolerable busybody, and Miss Adeline as a hypochondriacal fine lady, so that Gillian might perhaps reasonably object to put herself into absolute subjection; so, though Kalliope might have a presentiment of breakers ahead, she could say no more, and Gillian, feeling that she had been cross, changed the subject by admiring the pretty short curly hair that was being tied back at the glass.

'I wish it would grow long,' said Kalliope. 'But it always was rather short and troublesome, and ever since it was cut short in the fever, I have been obliged to keep it like this.'

'But it suits you,' said Gillian. 'And it is exactly the thing now.'

'That is the worst of it. It looks as if I wore it so on purpose. However, all our hands know that I cannot help it, and so does Lady Flight.'

The girl looked exceedingly well, though little Alice, the maid, would not have gone out to tea in such an ancient black dress, with no relief save a rim of white at neck and hands, and a tiny silver Maltese cross at the throat. Maura had a comparatively new gray dress, picked out with black. She was a pretty creature, the Irish beauty predominating over the Greek, in her great long-lashed brown eyes, which looked radiant with shy happiness. Miss Adeline was perfectly taken by surprise at the entrance of two such uncommon forms and faces, and the quiet dignity of the elder made her for a moment suppose that her sister must have invited some additional guest of undoubted station.

Valetta, who had grown fond of Maura in their school life, and who dearly loved patronising, pounced upon her guest to show her all manner of treasures and curiosities, at which she looked in great delight; and Fergus was so well satisfied with her comprehension of the principles of the letter balance, that he would have taken her upstairs to be introduced to all his mechanical inventions, if the total darkness and cold of his den had not been prohibitory.

Kalliope looked to perfection, but was more silent than her sister, though, as Miss Mohun's keen eye noted, it was not the shyness of a conscious inferior in an unaccustomed world, but rather that of a grave, reserved nature, not chattering for the sake of mere talk.

Gillian's photograph-book was well looked over, with all the brothers and sisters at different stages, and the group of officers. Miss Mohun noted the talk that passed over these, as they were identified one by one, sometimes with little reminiscences, childishly full on Gillian's part, betraying on Kalliope's side friendly acquaintance, but all in as entirely ladylike terms as would have befitted Phyllis or Alethea. She could well believe in the words with which Miss White rather hastened the turning of the page, 'Those were happy days—I dare not dwell on them too much!'

'Oh, I like to do so!' cried Gillian. 'I don't want the little ones ever to forget them.'

'Yes—you! But with you it would not be repining.'

This was for Gillian's ear alone, as at that moment both the aunts were, at the children's solicitation, engaged on the exhibition of a wonderful musical-box—Aunt Adeline's share of her mother's wedding presents—containing a bird that hovered and sung, the mechanical contrivance of which was the chief merit in Fergus's eyes, and which had fascinated generations of young people for the last sixty years. Aunt Jane, however, could hear through anything—even through the winding-up of what the family called 'Aunt Ada's Jackdaw,' and she drew her conclusions, with increasing respect and pity for the young girl over whose life such a change had come.

But it was not this, but what she called common humanity, which prompted her, on hearing a heavy gust of rain against the windows, to go into the lower regions in quest of a messenger boy to order a brougham to take the guests home at the end of the evening.

The meal went off pleasantly on the whole, though there loomed a storm as to the ritual of St. Kenelm's; but this chiefly was owing to the younger division of the company, when Valetta broke into an unnecessary inquiry why they did not have as many lights on the altar at St. Andrew's as at St. Kenelm's, and Fergus put her down with unceremoniously declaring that Stebbing said Flight was a donkey.

Gillian came down with what she meant for a crushing rebuke, and the indignant colour rose in the cheeks of the guests; but Fergus persisted, 'But he makes a guy of himself and a mountebank.'

Aunt Jane thought it time to interfere. 'Fergus,' she said, 'you had better not repeat improper sayings, especially about a clergyman.'

Fergus wriggled.

'And,' added Aunt Ada, with equal severity, 'you know Mr. Flight is a very kind friend to little Maura and her sister.'

'Indeed he is,' said Kalliope earnestly; and Maura, feeling herself addressed, added, 'Nobody but he ever called on poor mamma, till Miss Mohun did; no, not Lady Flight.'

'We are very grateful for his kindness,' put in Kalliope, in a repressive tone.

'But,' said Gillian, 'I thought you said he had seemed to care less of late.'

'I do not know,' said Miss White, blushing; 'music seems to be his chief interest, and there has not been anything fresh to get up since the concert.'

'I suppose there will be for the winter,' said Miss Mohun, and therewith the conversation was safely conducted away to musical subjects, in which some of the sisters' pride and affection for their brothers peeped out; but Gillian was conscious all the time that Kalliope was speaking with some constraint when she mentioned Alexis, and that she was glad rather to dwell on little Theodore, who had good hopes of the drawing prize, and she seriously consulted Miss Mohun on the pupil-teachership for him, as after he had passed the seventh standard he could not otherwise go on with his education, though she did not think he had much time for teaching.

'Would not Mr. White help him further?' asked Miss Mohun.

'I do not know. I had much rather not ask,' said Kalliope. 'We are too many to throw ourselves on a person who is no near relation, and he has not seemed greatly disposed to help.'

'Your elder brother?'

'Oh, poor Richard, he is not earning anything yet. I can't ask him. If I only knew of some school I could be sure was safe and good and not too costly, Alexis and I would try to manage for Theodore after the examination in the spring.'

The Woodward schools were a new light to her, and she was eagerly interested in Miss Mohun's explanations and in the scale of terms.

Meantime Miss Adeline got on excellently with the younger ones, and when the others were free, proposed for their benefit a spelling game. All sat round the table, made words, and abstracted one another's with increasing animation, scarcely heeding the roaring of the wind outside, till there was a ring at the bell.

'My brother has come for us,' said Kalliope.

'Oh, but it is not fit for you to walk home,' said Miss Mohun. 'The brougham is coming by and by; ask Mr. White to come in,' she added, as the maid appeared with the message that he was come for his sisters.

There was a confusion of acknowledgments and disclaimers, and word was brought back that Mr. White was too wet to come in. Miss Mohun, who was not playing, but prompting Fergus, jumped up and went out to investigate, when she found a form in an ancient military cloak, trying to keep himself from dripping where wet could do mischief. She had to explain her regret at his having had such a walk in vain; but she had taken alarm on finding that rain was setting in for the night, and had sent word by the muffin-boy that the brougham would be wanted, contriving to convey that it was not to be paid for.

Nothing remained to be said except thanks, and Alexis emerged from the cloak, which looked as if it had gone through all his father's campaigns, took off his gaiters, did his best for his boots, and, though not in evening costume, looked very gentleman-like and remarkably handsome in the drawing-room, with no token of awkward embarrassment save a becoming blush.

Gillian began to tremble inwardly again, but the game had just ended in her favour, owing to Fergus having lost all his advantages in Aunt Jane's absence, besides signalising himself by capturing Maura's 'bury,' under the impression that an additional R would combine that and straw into a fruit.

So the coast being cleared, Miss Adeline greatly relieved her niece's mind by begging, as a personal favour, to hear the song whose renown at the concert had reached her; and thus the time was safely spent in singing till the carriage was announced, and good-nights exchanged.

Maura's eyes grew round with delight, and she jumped for joy at the preferment.

'Oh!' she said, as she fervently kissed Valetta, 'it is the most delightful evening I ever spent in the whole course of my life, except at Lady Merrifield's Christmas-tree! And now to go home in a carriage! I never went in one since I can remember!'

And Kalliope's 'Thank you, we have enjoyed ourselves very much,' was very fervent.

'Those young people are very superior to what I expected,' said Aunt Adeline. 'What fine creatures, all so handsome; and that little Maura is a perfect darling.'

'The Muse herself is very superior,' said Miss Mohun. 'One of those home heroines who do the work of Atlas without knowing it. I do not wonder that the marble girls speak of her so enthusiastically.'

How Gillian might have enjoyed all this, and yet she could not, except so far that she told herself that thus there could be no reasonable objection made by her aunts to intercourse with those whom they so much admired.

Yet perhaps even then she would have told all, but that, after having bound over Kalliope to secrecy, it would be awkward to confess that she had told all. It would be like owning herself in the wrong, and for that she was not prepared. Besides, where would be the secrecy of her 'great thing'?

CHAPTER IX. — GAUGING AJEE

Without exactly practising to deceive, Gillian began to find that concealment involved her in a tangled web; all the more since Aunt Jane had become thoroughly interested in the Whites, and was inquiring right and left about schools and scholarships for the little boys.

She asked their master about them, and heard that they were among his best scholars, and that their home lessons had always been carefully attended to by their elder brother and sister. In fact, he was most anxious to retain Theodore, to be trained for a pupil-teacher, the best testimony to his value! Aunt Jane came home full of the subject, relating what the master said of Alexis White, and that he had begun by working with him at Latin and mathematics; but that they had not had time to go on with what needed so much study and preparation.

'In fact, said Miss Mohun, 'I have a suspicion that if a certificated schoolmaster could own any such thing, the pupil knew more than the teacher. When your father comes home, I hope he will find some way of helping that lad.'

Gillian began to crimson, but bethought herself of the grandeur of its being found that she was the youth's helper. 'I am glad you have been lending him books,' added Aunt Jane.

What business had she to know what had not been told her? The sense of offence drove back any disposition to consult her. Yet to teach Alexis was no slight task, for, though he had not gone far in Greek, his inquiries were searching, and explaining to him was a different thing from satisfying even Mr. Pollock. Besides, Gillian had her own studies on hand. The Cambridge examinations were beginning to assume larger proportions in the Rockquay mind, and 'the General Screw Company,' as Mr. Grant observed, was prevailing.

Gillian's knowledge was rather discursive, and the concentration required by an examination was hard work to her, and the time for it was shortened by the necessity of doing all Alexis's Greek exercises and translations beforehand, and of being able to satisfy him why an error was not right, for, in all politeness, he always would know why it did not look right. And there was Valetta, twisting and groaning. The screw was on her form, who, unless especially exempted, were to compete for a prize for language examination.

Valetta had begun by despising Kitty Varley for being excepted by her mother's desire and for not learning Latin; but now she envied any one who had not to work double tides at the book of Caesar that was to be taken up, and Vercingetorix and his Arverni got vituperated in a way that would have made the hair of her hero-worshipping mother fairly stand on end.

But then Lilias Mohun had studied him for love of himself, not for dread of failure.

Gillian had been displeased when Fergus deserted her for Aunt Jane as an assistant, but she would not have been sorry if Valetta had been off her hands, when she was interrupted in researches after an idiom in St. John's Gospel by the sigh that this abominable dictionary had no verb oblo, or in the intricacies of a double equation by despair at this horrid Caesar always hiding away his nominatives out of spite.

Valetta, like the American child, evidently regarded the Great Julius in no other light than as writer of a book for beginners in Latin, and, moreover, a very unkind one; and she fully reciprocated the sentiment that it was no wonder that the Romans conquered the world, since they knew the Latin grammar by nature.

Nor was Gillian's hasty and sometimes petulant assistance very satisfactory to the poor child, since it often involved hearing 'Wait a minute,' and a very long one, 'How can you be so stupid?' 'I told you so long ago'; and sometimes consisted of a gabbling translation, with rapidly pointed finger, very hard to follow, and not quite so painstaking as when Alexis deferentially and politely pointed out the difficulties, with a strong sense of the favour that she was doing him.

Not that these personal lessons often took place. Kalliope never permitted them without dire necessity, and besides, there was always an uncertainty when Gillian might come down, or when Alexis might be able to come in.

One day when Aunt Jane had come home with a story of how one of her 'business girls' had confessed to Miss White's counsel having only just saved her from an act of folly, it occurred to Aunt Adeline to say—

'It is a great pity you have not her help in the G.F.S.'

'I did not understand enough about her before, and mixed her up with the ordinary class of business girls. I had rather have her a member for the sake of example; but if not, she would be a valuable associate. Could not you explain this to her without hurting her feelings, as I am afraid I did, Gill? I did not understand enough about her when I spoke to her before.'

Gillian started. The conversation that should have been so pleasant to her was making her strangely uncomfortable.

'I do not see how Gill is to get at her,' objected the other aunt. 'It would be of no great use to call on her in the nest of the Queen of the White Ants. I can't help recollecting the name, it was so descriptive.'

'Yes; it was on her mother's account that she refused, and of course her office must not be invaded in business hours.'

'I might call on her there before she goes home,' suggested Gillian, seeing daylight.

'You cannot be walking down there at dusk, just as the workmen come away' exclaimed Aunt Ada, making the colour so rush into Gillian's cheeks that she was glad to catch up a screen.

'No,' said Miss Mohun emphatically; 'but I could leave her there at five o'clock, and go to Tideshole to take old Jemmy Burnet his jersey, and call for her on the way back.'

'Or she could walk home with me,' murmured the voice behind the screen.

Gillian felt with dismay that all these precautions as to her escort would render her friend more scrupulous than ever as to her visits. To have said, 'I have several times been at the office,' would have been a happy clearance of the ground, but her pride would not bend to possible blame, nor would she run the risk of a prohibition. 'It would be the ruin of hope to Alexis, and mamma knows all,' said she to herself.

It was decided that she should trust to Kalliope to go back with her, for when once Aunt Jane get into the very fishy hamlet of Tideshole, which lay beyond the quarries, there was no knowing when she might get away, since

'Alike to her were time and tide,
    November's snow or July's pride.'

So after a few days, too wet and tempestuous for any expedition, they set forth accompanied by Fergus, who rushed in from school in time to treat his aunt as a peripatetic 'Joyce's scientific dialogues.' Valetta had not arrived, and Gillian was in haste to elude her, knowing that her aunt would certainly not take her on to Tideshole, and that there would be no comfort in talking before her; but it was a new thing to have to regard her little sister in the light of a spy, and again she had to reason down a sense of guiltiness. However, her aunt wanted Valetta as little as she did; and she had never so rejoiced in Fergus's monologue, 'Then this small fly-wheel catches into the Targe one, and so— Don't you see?'—only pausing for a sound of assent.

Unacquainted with the private door, Miss Mohun entered the office through the showroom, exchanging greetings with the young saleswomen, and finding Miss White putting away her materials.

Shaking hands, Miss Mohun said—

'I have brought your friend to make a visit to you while I go on to Tideshole. She tells me that you will be kind enough to see her on her way home, if you are going back at the same time.'

'I shall be delighted,' said Kalliope, with eyes as well as tongue, and no sooner were she and Gillian alone together than she joyfully exclaimed—

'Then Miss Mohun knows! You have told her.

'No—'

'Oh!' and there were volumes in the intonation. 'I was alarmed when she came in, and then so glad if it was all over. Dear Miss Merrifield—'

'Call me Gillian; I have told you to do so before! Phyllis is Miss Merrifield, and I won't be so before my time,' said Gillian, interrupting in a tone more cross than affectionate.

'I was going to say,' pursued Kalliope, 'that the shock her entrance gave to me proved all the more that we cannot be treating her properly.

'Never mind that! I did not come about that. She is quite taken with you, Kally, and wants you more than ever to be a Friendly Girl, because she thinks it would be so good for the others who are under you.'

'They have told me something about it,' said Kalliope thoughtfully.

'She fancied' added Gillian, 'that perhaps she did not make you understand the rights of it, not knowing that you were different from the others.'

'Oh no, it was not that,' said Kalliope. 'Indeed, I hope there is no such nonsense in me. It was what my dear father always warned us against; only poor mamma always gets vexed if she does not think we are keeping ourselves up, and she had just been annoyed at—something, and we did not know then that it was Lady Merrifield's sister.'

This was contradictory, but it was evident that, while Kalliope disowned conceit of station for herself, she could not always cross her mother's wishes. It was further elicited that if Lady Flight had taken up the matter there would have been no difficulty. Half a year ago the Flights had seemed to the young Whites angelic and infallible, and perhaps expectations had been founded on their patronage; but there had since been a shadow of disappointment, and altogether Kalliope was less disposed to believe that my Lady was correct in pronouncing Miss Mohun's cherished society as 'dissentish,' and only calculated for low servant girls and ladies who wished to meddle in families.

Clanship made Gillian's indignation almost bring down the office, and her eloquence was scarcely needed, since Kalliope had seen the value to some of her 'hands' from the class, the library, the recreation-room, and the influence of the ladies, above all, the showing them that it was possible to have variety and amusement free from vulgar and perilous dissipation; but still she hesitated. She had no time, she said; she could not attend classes, and she was absolutely necessary at home in the evenings; but Gillian assured her that nothing was expected from her but a certain influence in the right direction, and the showing the younger and giddier that she did not think the Society beneath her.

'I see all that,' said Kalliope; 'I wish I had not been mistaken at first; but, Miss Mer—Gillian, I do not see how I can join it now.'

'Why not? What do you mean?'

Kalliope was very unwilling to speak, but at last it came.

'How can I do this to please your aunt, who thinks better of me than I deserve, when—Oh! excuse me—I know it is all your kindness—but when I am allowing you to deceive her—almost, I mean—'

'Deceive! I never spoke an untrue word to my aunt in my life,' said Gillian, in proud anger; 'but if you think so, Miss White, I had better have no more to do with it.'

'I feel,' said Kalliope, with tears in her eyes, 'as if it might be better so, unless Miss Mohun knew all about it.'

'Well, if you think so, and like to upset all your brother's hopes—'

'It would be a terrible grief to him, I know, and I don't undervalue your kindness, indeed I don't; but I cannot be happy about it while Miss Mohun does not know. I don't understand why you do not tell her.'

'Because I know there would be a worry and a fuss. Either she would say we must wait for letters from mamma, or else that Alexis must come to Beechcroft, and all the comfort would be over, and it would be gossiped about all over the place. Can't you trust me, when I tell you I have written it all to my own father and mother, and surely I know my own family best?'

Kalliope looked half convinced, but she persisted—

'I suppose you do; only please, till there is a letter from Lady Merrifield, I had rather not go into this Society.'

'But, Kally, you don't consider. What am I to say to my aunt? What will she think of you?'

'I can't help that! I cannot do this while she could feel I was conniving at what she might not like. Indeed, I cannot. I beg your pardon, but it goes against me. When shall you be able to hear from Lady Merrifield?'

'I wrote three weeks ago. I suppose I shall hear about half-way through December, and you know they could telegraph if they wanted to stop it, so I think you might be satisfied.'

Still Kalliope could not be persuaded, and finally, as a sort of compromise, Gillian decided on saying that she would think about it and give her answer at Christmas; to which she gave a reluctant assent, with one more protest that if there were no objection to the lessons, she could not see why Miss Mohun should not know of them.

Peace was barely restored before voices were heard, and in came Fergus, bringing Alexis with him. They had met on the beach road in front of the works, and Fergus, being as usual full of questions about a crane that was swinging blocks of stone into a vessel close to the little pier, his aunt had allowed him to stay to see the work finished, after which Alexis would take him to join his sister.

So it came about that they all walked home together very cheerfully, though Gillian was still much vexed under the surface at Kalliope's old-maidish particularity.

However, the aunts were not as annoyed at the delay as she expected. Miss Mohun said she would look out some papers that would be convincing and persuasive, and that it might be as well not to enrol Miss White too immediately before the Christmas festivities, but to wait till the books were begun next year. Plans began to prevail for the Christmas diversions and entertainments, but the young Merrifields expected to have nothing to do with these, as they were to meet the rest of the family at their eldest uncle's house at Beechcroft; all except Harry, who was to be ordained in the Advent Ember week, and at once begin work with his cousin David Merrifield in the Black Country. Their aunts would not go with them, as Beechcroft breezes, though her native air, were too cold for Adeline in the winter, and Jane could leave neither her, nor her various occupations, and the festivities of all Rockstone.

It is not easy to say which Gillian most looked forward to: Mysie's presence, or the absence of the supervision which she imagined herself to suffer from, because she had set herself to shirk it. She knew she should feel more free. But behold! a sudden change, produced by one morning's letters.

'It is a beastly shame!'

'Oh, Fergus! That's not a thing to say,' cried Valetta.

'I don't care! It is a beastly shame not to go to Beechcroft, and be poked up here all the holidays.'

'But you can't when Primrose has got the whooping-cough.'

'Bother the whooping-cough.'

'And welcome; but you would find it bother you, I believe.'

'I shouldn't catch it. I want Wilfred, and to ride the pony, and see the sluice that Uncle Maurice made.'

'You couldn't if you had the cough.'

'Then I should stay there instead of coming back to school! I say it is horrid, and beastly, and abominable, and—'

'Come, come, Fergus,' here put in Gillian, 'that is very wrong.'

'You don't hear Gill and me fly out in that way,' added Valetta, 'though we are so sorry about Mysie and Fly.'

'Oh, you are girls, and don't know what is worth doing. I *will* say it is beast —'

'Now don't, Fergus; it is very rude and ungrateful to the aunts. None of us like having to stay here and lose our holiday; but it is very improper to say so in their own house, and I thought you were so fond of Aunt Jane.'

'Aunt Jane knows a thing or two, but she isn't Wilfred.'

'And Wilfred is always teasing you.'

'Fergus is quite right,' said Miss Mohun, who had been taking off her galoshes in the vestibule while this colloquy was ending in the dining-room; 'it is much better to be bullied by a brother than made much of by an aunt, and you know I am very sorry for you all under the infliction.'

'Oh, Aunt Jane, we know you are very kind, and—' began Gillian.

'Never mind, my dear; I know you are making the best of us, and I am very much obliged to you for standing up for us. It is a great disappointment, but I was going to give Fergus a note that I think will console him.'

And out of an envelope which she had just taken from the letter-box she handed him a note, which he pulled open and then burst out, 'Cousin David! Hurrah! Scrumptious!' commencing a war-dance at the same moment.

'What is it? Has David asked you?' demanded both his sisters at the same moment.

'Hurrah! Yes, it is from him. "My dear Fergus, I hope"—hurrah—"Harry, mm—mm—mm—brothers, 20th mm—mm. Your affectionate cousin, David

Merrifield."'

'Let me read it to you,' volunteered Gillian.

'Wouldn't you like it?'

'How can you be so silly, Ferg? You can't read it yourself. You don't know whether he really asks you.'

Fergus made a face, and bolted upstairs to gloat, and perhaps peruse the letter, while Valetta rushed after him, whether to be teased or permitted to assist might be doubtful.

'He really does ask him,' said Aunt Jane. 'Your cousin David, I mean. He says that he and Harry can put up all the three boys between them, and that they will be very useful in the Christmas festivities of Coalham.'

'It is very kind of him,' said Gillian in a depressed tone.

'Fergus will be very happy.'

'I only hope he will not be bent on finding a coal mine in the garden when he comes back,' said Aunt Jane, smiling; 'but it is rather dreary for you, my dear. I had been hoping to have Jasper here for at least a few days. Could he not come and fetch Fergus?'

Gillian's eyes sparkled at the notion; but they fell at once, for Jasper would be detained by examinations until so late that he would only just be able to reach Coalham before Christmas Day. Harry was to be ordained in a fortnight's time to work under his cousin, Mr. David Merrifield, and his young brothers were to meet him immediately after.

'I wish I could go too,' sighed Gillian, as a hungry yearning for Jasper or for Mysie took possession of her.

'I wish you could,' said Miss Mohun sympathetically; 'but I am afraid you must resign yourself to helping us instead.'

'Oh, Aunt Jane, I did not mean to grumble. It can't be helped, and you are very kind.'

'Oh, dear!' said poor Miss Jane afterwards in private to her sister, 'how I hate being told I am very kind! It just means, "You are a not quite intolerable jailor and despot," with fairly good intentions.'

'I am sure you are kindness itself, dear Jenny,' responded Miss Adeline. 'I am glad they own it! But it is very inconvenient and unlucky that that unjustifiable mother should have sent her child to the party to carry the whooping-cough to poor little Primrose, and Mysie, and Phyllis.'

'All at one fell swoop! As for Primrose, the worthy Halfpenny is quite enough for her, and Lily is well out of it; but Fly is a little shrimp, overdone all round, and I don't like the notion of it for her.'

'And Rotherwood is so wrapped up in her. Poor dear fellow, I hope all will go well with her.'

'There is no reason it should not. Delicate children often have it the most lightly. But I am sorry for Gillian, though, if she would let us, I think we could make her happy.'

Gillian meantime, after her first fit of sick longing for her brother and sister, and sense of disappointment, was finding some consolation in the reflection that had Jasper discovered her instructions to Alexis White, he would certainly have 'made no end of a row about it,' and have laughed to scorn the bare notion of her teaching Greek to a counting-house clerk! But then Jasper was wont to grumble and chafe at all employments—especially beneficent ones—that interfered with devotion to his lordly self, and on the whole, perhaps he was safer out of the way, as he might have set on the aunts to put a stop to her proceedings. Of Mysie's sympathy she was sure, yet she would have her scruples about the aunts, and she was a sturdy person, hard to answer—poor Mysie, whooping away helplessly in the schoolroom at Rotherwood! Gillian felt herself heroically good-humoured and resigned. Moreover, here was the Indian letter so long looked for, likely by its date to be an answer to the information as to Alexis White's studies. Behold, it did not appear to touch on the subject at all! It was all about preparations for the double wedding, written in scraps by different hands, at different times, evidently snatched from many avocations and much interruption. Of mamma there was really least of all; but squeezed into a corner, scarcely legible, Gillian read, 'As to lessons, if At. J. approves.' It was evidently an afterthought; and Gillian *could*, and chose to refer it to a certain inquiry about learning the violin, which had never been answered—for the confusion that reigned at Columbo was plainly unfavourable to attending to minute details in home letters.

The longest portions of the despatch were papa's, since he was still unable to move about. He wrote:—'Our two "young men" think it probable you will have invitations from their kith and kin. If this comes to pass, you had better accept them, though you will not like to break up the Christmas party at Beechcroft Court.'

There being no Christmas party at Beechcroft Court, Gillian, in spite of her distaste to new people, was not altogether sorry to receive a couple of notes by the same post, the first enclosed in the second, both forwarded from thence.

'VALE LESTON PRIORY,

'9th December.

'MY DEAR MISS MERRIFIELD—We are very anxious to make acquaintance with my brother Bernard's new belongings, since we cannot greet our new sister Phyllis ourselves. We always have a family gathering at Christmas between this house and the Vicarage, and we much hope that you and your brother will join it. Could you not meet my sister, Mrs. Grinstead, in London, and travel down with her on the 23rd? I am sending this note to her, as I think she has some such proposal to make.—Yours very sincerely,

'WILMET U. HAREWOOD.'

The other letter was thus—

'BROMPTON, 10th December.

'MY DEAR GILLIAN—It is more natural to call you thus, as you are becoming a sort of relation—very unwillingly, I dare say—for "in this storm I too have lost a brother." However, we will make the best of it, and please don't hate us more than you can help. Since your own home is dispersed for the present, it seems less outrageous to ask you to spend a Christmas Day among new people, and I hope we may make you feel at home with us, and that you will enjoy our beautiful church at Vale Leston. We are so many that we may be less alarming if you take us by driblets, so perhaps it will be the best way if you will come up to us on the 18th or 19th, and go down with us on the 23rd. You will find no one with us but my nephew—almost son— Gerald Underwood, and my niece, Anna Vanderkist, who will be delighted to make friends with your brother Jasper, who might perhaps meet you here. You must tell me all about Phyllis, and what she would like best for her Cingalese home.—Yours affectionately,

GERALDINE GRINSTEAD.

Thus then affairs shaped themselves. Gillian was to take Fergus to London, where Jasper would meet them at the station, and put the little boy into the train for Coalham, whither his brother Wilfred had preceded him by a day or two.

Jasper and Gillian would then repair to Brompton for two or three days before going down with Mr. and Mrs. Grinstead to Vale Leston, and they were to take care to pay their respects to old Mrs. Merrifield, who had become too infirm to spend Christmas at Stokesley.

What was to happen later was uncertain, whether they were to go to Stokesley, or whether Jasper would join his brothers at Coalham, or come down to Rockstone with his sister for the rest of the holidays. Valetta must remain there, and it did not seem greatly to distress her; and whereas nothing had been said about children, she was better satisfied to stay within reach of Kitty and mamma, and the Christmas-trees that began to dawn on the horizon, than to be carried into an unknown region of 'grown-ups.'

While Gillian was not only delighted at the prospect of meeting Jasper, her own especial brother, but was heartily glad to make a change, and defer the entire question of lessons, confessions, and G.F.S. for six whole weeks. She might get a more definite answer from her parents, or something might happen to make explanation to her aunt either unnecessary or much more easy —and she was safe from discovery. But examinations had yet to be passed.

116

CHAPTER X. — AUT CAESAR AUT NIHIL

Examinations were the great autumn excitement. Gillian was going up for the higher Cambridge, and Valetta's form was under preparation for competition for a prize in languages. The great Mr. White, on being asked to patronise the High School at its first start, four years ago, had endowed it with prizes for each of the four forms for the most proficient in two tongues.

As the preparation became more absorbing, brows were puckered and looks were anxious, and the aunts were doubtful as to the effect upon the girls' minds or bodies. It was too late, however, to withdraw them, and Miss Mohun could only insist on air and exercise, and permit no work after the seven- o'clock tea.

She was endeavouring to chase cobwebs from the brains of the students by the humours of Mrs. Nickleby, when a message was brought that Miss Leverett, the head-mistress of the High School, wished to speak to her in the dining-room. This was no unusual occurrence, as Miss Mohun was secretary to the managing committee of the High School. But on the announcement Valetta began to fidget, and presently said that she was tired and would go to bed. The most ordinary effect of fatigue upon this young lady was to make her resemble the hero of the nursery poem—

```
'I do not want to go to bed,
    Sleepy little Harry said.'
```

Nevertheless, this willingness excited no suspicion, till Miss Mohun came to the door to summon Valetta.

'Is there anything wrong!' exclaimed sister and niece together.

'Gone to bed! Oh! I'll tell you presently. Don't you come, Gillian.'

She vanished again, leaving Gillian in no small alarm and vexation.

'I wonder what it can be,' mused Aunt Ada.

'I shall go and find out!' said Gillian, jumping up, as she heard a door shut upstairs.

'No, don't,' said Aunt Ada, 'you had much better not interfere.'

'It is my business to see after my own sister,' returned Gillian haughtily.

'I see what you mean, my dear,' said her aunt, stretching out her hand, kindly; 'but I do not think you can do any good. If she is in a scrape, you have nothing to do with the High School management, and for you to burst in would only annoy Miss Leverett and confuse the affair. Oh, I know your impulse of defence, dear Gillian; but the time has not come yet, and you can't have any reasonable doubt that Jane will be just, nor that your mother would wish that you should be quiet about it.'

'But suppose there is some horrid accusation against her!' said Gillian hotly.

'But, dear child, if you don't know anything about it, how can you defend her?'

'I ought to know!'

'So you will in time; but the more people there are present, the more confusion there is, and the greater difficulty in getting at the rights of anything.''

More by her caressing tone of sympathy than by actual arguments, Adeline did succeed in keeping Gillian in the drawing-room, though not in pacifying her, till doors were heard again, and something so like Valetta crying as she went upstairs, that Gillian was neither to have nor to hold, and made a dash out of the room, only to find her aunt and the head-mistress exchanging last words in the hall, and as she was going to brush past them, Aunt Jane caught her hand, and said—

'Wait a moment, Gillian; I want to speak to you.'

There was no getting away, but she was very indignant. She tugged at her aunt's hand more than perhaps she knew, and there was something of a flouncing as she flung into the drawing-room and demanded—

'Well, what have you been doing to poor little Val?'

'We have done nothing,' said Miss Mohun quietly. 'Miss Leverett wanted to ask her some questions. Sit down, Gillian. You had better hear what I have to say before going to her. Well, it appears that there has been some amount of cribbing in the third form.'

'I'm sure Val never would,' broke out Gillian. And her aunt answered—

'So was I; but—'

'Oh—'

'My dear, do hush,' pleaded Adeline. 'You must let yourself listen.'

Gillian gave a desperate twist, but let her aunt smooth her hand.

'All the class—almost—seem to have done it in some telegraphic way, hard to understand,' proceeded Aunt Jane. 'There must have been some stupidity on the part of the class-mistress, Miss Mellon, or it could not have gone on; but there has of late been a strong suspicion of cribbing in Caesar in Valetta's class. They had got rather behindhand, and have been working up somewhat too hard and fast to get through the portion for examination. Some of them translated too well—used terms for the idioms that were neither literal, nor could have been forged by their small brains; so there was an examination, and Georgie Purvis was detected reading off from the marks on the margin of her notebook.'

'But what has that to do with Val?'

'Georgie, being had up to Miss Leverett, made the sort of confession that implicates everybody.'

'Then why believe her?' muttered Gillian. But her aunt went on—

'She said that four or five of them did it, from the notes that Valetta Merrifield brought to school.'

'Never!' interjected Gillian.

'She said,' continued Miss Mohun, 'it was first that they saw her helping Maura White, and they thought that was not fair, and insisted on her doing the same for them.'

'It can't be true! Oh, don't believe it!' cried the sister.

'I grieve to remind you that I showed you in the drawer in the dining-room chiffonier a translation of that very book of Caesar that your mother and I made years ago, when she was crazy upon Vercingetorix.'

'But was that reason enough for laying it upon poor Val?'

'She owned it.'

There was a silence, and then Gillian said—

'She must have been frightened, and not known what she was saying.'

'She was frightened, but she was very straightforward, and told without any shuffling. She saw the old copy-books when I was showing you those other remnants of our old times, and one day it seems she was in a great puzzle over her lessons, and could get no help or advice, because none of us had come in. I suppose you were with Lilian, and she thought she might just look at the passage. She found Maura in the same difficulty, and helped her; and then Georgie Purvis and Nelly Black found them out, and threatened to tell unless she showed them her notes; but the copying whole phrases was only done quite of late in the general over-hurry.'

'She must have been bullied into it,' cried Gillian. 'I shall go and see about her.'

Aunt Ada made a gesture as of deprecation; but Aunt Jane let her go without remonstrance, merely saying as the door closed—

'Poor child! Esprit de famille!'

'Will it not be very bad for Valetta to be petted and pitied?'

'I don't know. At any rate, we cannot separate them at night, so it is only beginning it a little sooner; and whatever I say only exasperates Gillian the more. Poor little Val, she had not a formed character enough to be turned loose into a High School without Mysie to keep her in order.'

'Or Gillian.'

'I am not so sure of Gillian. There's something amiss, though I can't make out whether it is merely that I rub her down the wrong way. I wonder whether this holiday time will do us good or harm! At any rate, I know how Lily felt about Dolores.'

'It must have been that class-mistress's fault.'

'To a great degree; but Miss Leverett has just discovered that her cleverness does not compensate for a general lack of sense and discipline. Poor little Val—perhaps it is her turning-point!'

Gillian, rushing up in a boiling state of indignation against everybody, felt the family shame most acutely of all; and though, as a Merrifield, she defended her sister below stairs, on the other hand she was much more personally shocked and angered at the disgrace than were her aunts, and far less willing to perceive any excuse for the culprit.

There was certainly no petting or pitying in her tone as she stood over the little iron bed, where the victim was hiding her head on her pillow.

'Oh, Valetta, how could you do such a thing? The Merrifields have never been so disgraced before!'

'Oh, don't, Gill! Aunt Jane and Miss Leverett were—not so angry—when I said—I was sorry.'

'But what will papa and mamma say?'

'Must they—must they hear?'

'You would not think of deceiving them, I hope.'

'Not deceiving, only not telling.'

'That comes to much the same.'

'You can't say anything, Gill, for you are always down at Kal's office, and nobody knows.'

This gave Gillian a great shock, but she rallied, and said with dignity, 'Do you think I do not write to mamma everything I do?'

It sufficed for the immediate purpose of annihilating Valetta, who had just been begging off from letting mamma hear of her proceedings; but it left Gillian very uneasy as to how much the child might know or tell, and this made her proceed less violently, and more persuasively, 'Whatever I do, I write to mamma; and besides, it is different with a little thing like you, and your school work. Come, tell me how you got into this scrape.'

'Oh, Gill, it was so hard! All about those tiresome Gauls, and there were bits when the nominative case would go and hide itself, and those nasty tenses one doesn't know how to look out, and I knew I was making nonsense, and you were out of the way, and there was nobody to help; and I knew mamma's own book was there—the very part too—because Aunt Jane had shown it to us, so I did not think there was any harm in letting her help me out of the muddle.'

'Ah! that was the beginning.'

'If you had been in, I would not have done it. You know Aunt Jane said there was no harm in giving a clue, and this was mamma.'

'But that was not all.'

'Well, then, there was Maura first, as much puzzled, and her brother is so busy he hasn't as much time for her as he used to have, and it does signify to her, for perhaps if she does not pass, Mr. White may not let her go on at the High School, and that would be too dreadful, for you know you said I was to do all I could for Maura. So I marked down things for her and she copied them off, and then Georgie and Nelly found it out, and, oh! they were dreadful! I never knew it was wrong till they went at me. And they were horrid to Maura, and said she was a Greek and I a Maltese, and so we were both false, and cheaty, and sly, and they should tell Miss Leverett unless I would help them.'

'Oh! Valetta, why didn't you tell me?'

'I never get to speak to you, said Val. 'I did think I would that first time, and ask you what to do, but then you came in late, and when I began something, you said you had your Greek to do, and told me to hold my tongue.'

'I am very sorry,' said Gillian, feeling convicted of having neglected her little sister in the stress of her own work and of the preparation for that of her pupil, who was treading on her heels; 'but indeed, Val, if you had told me it was important, I should have listened.'

'Ah I but when one is half-frightened, and you are always in a hurry,' sighed the child. And, indeed, I did do my best over my own work before ever I looked; only those two are so lazy and stupid, they would have ever so much more help than Maura or I ever wanted; and at last I was so worried and hurried with my French and all the rest, that I did scramble a whole lot down, and that was the way it was found out. And I am glad now it is over, whatever happens.'

'Yes, that is right,' said Gillian, 'and I am glad you told no stories; but I wonder Emma Norton did not see what was going on.'

'Oh, she is frightfully busy about her own.'

'And Kitty Varley?'

'Kitty is only going up for French and German. Miss Leverett is so angry. What do you think she will do to me, Gill? Expel me?'

'I don't know—I can't guess. I don't know High School ways.'

It would be so dreadful for papa and mamma and the boys to know,' sobbed Valetta. 'And Mysie! oh, if Mysie was but here!'

'Mysie would have been a better sister to her,' said Gillian's conscience, and her voice said, 'You would never have done it if Mysie had been here.'

'And Mysie would be nice,' said the poor child, who longed after her companion sister as much for comfort as for conscience. 'Is Aunt Jane very very angry?' she went on; 'do you think I shall be punished?'

'I can't tell. If it were I, I should think you were punished enough by having disgraced the name of Merrifield by such a dishonourable action.'

'I—I didn't know it was dishonourable.'

'Well,' said Gillian, perhaps a little tired of the scene, or mayhap dreading another push into her own quarters, 'I have been saying what I could for you, and I should think they would feel that no one but our father and mother had a real right to punish you, but I can't tell what the School may do. Now, hush, it is of no use to talk any more. Good-night; I hope I shall find you asleep when I come to bed.'

Valetta would have detained her, but off she went, with a consciousness that she had been poor comfort to her little sister, and had not helped her to the right kind of repentance. But then that highest ground—the strict rule of perfect conscientious uprightness—was just what she shrank from bringing home to herself, in spite of those privileges of seniority by which she had impressed poor Valetta.

The worst thing further that was said that night, when she had reported as much of Valetta's confidence as she thought might soften displeasure, was Aunt Ada's observation: 'Maura! That's the White child, is it not? No doubt it was the Greek blood.'

'The English girls were much worse,' hastily said Gillian, with a flush of alarm, as she thought of her own friends being suspected.

'Yes; but it began with the little Greek,' said Aunt Ada. 'What a pity, for she is such an engaging child! I would take the child away from the High School, except that it would have the appearance of her being dismissed.

'We must consider of that,' said Aunt Jane. 'There will hardly be time to hear from Lilias before the next term begins. Indeed, it will not be so very long to wait before the happy return, I hope.'

'Only two months,' said Gillian; 'but it would be happier but for this.'

'No,' said Aunt Jane. 'If we made poor little Val write her confession, and I do the same for not having looked after her better, it will be off our minds, and need not cloud the meeting.'

'The disgrace!' sighed Gillian; 'the public disgrace!'

'My dear, I don't want to make you think lightly of such a thing. It was very wrong in a child brought up as you have all been, with a sense of honour and uprightness; but where there has been no such training, the attempt to copy is common enough, for it is not to be looked on as an extraordinary and indelible disgrace. Do you remember Primrose saying she had broken mamma's heart when she had knocked down a china vase? You need not be in that state of mind over what was a childish fault, made worse by those bullying girls. It is of no use to exaggerate. The sin is the thing—not the outward shame.'

'And Valetta told at once when asked,' added Aunt Ada.

'That makes a great difference.'

'In fact, she was relieved to have it out,' said Miss Mohun. 'It is not at all as if she were in the habit of doing things underhand.'

Everything struck on Gillian like a covert reproach. It was pain and shame to her that a Merrifield should have lowered herself to the common herd so as to need these excuses of her aunts, and then in the midst of that indignation came that throb of self-conviction which she was always confuting with the recollection of her letter to her mother.

She was glad to bid good-night and rest her head.

The aunts ended by agreeing that it was needful to withdraw Valetta from the competition. It would seem like punishment to her, but it would remove her from the strain that certainly was not good for her. Indeed, they had serious thoughts of taking her from the school altogether, but the holidays would not long be ended before her parents' return.

'I am sorry we ever let her try for the prize,' said Ada.

'Yes,' said Aunt Jane, 'I suppose it was weakness; but having opposed the acceptance of the system of prizes by competition at first, I thought it would look sullen if I refused to let Valetta try. Stimulus is all very well, but competition leads to emulation, wrath, strife, and a good deal besides.'

'Valetta wished it too, and she knew so much Latin to begin with that I thought she would easily get it, and certainly she ought not to get into difficulties.'

'After the silken rein and easy amble of Silverfold, the spur and the race have come severely.'

'It is, I suppose, the same with Gillian, though there it is not competition. Do you expect her to succeed?'

'No. She has plenty of intelligence, and a certain sort of diligence, but does not work to a point. She wants a real hand over her! She will fail, and it will be very good for her.'

'I should say the work was overmuch for her, and had led her to neglect Valetta.'

'Work becomes overmuch when people don't know how to set about it, and resent being told—No, not in words, but by looks and shoulders. Besides, I am not sure that it is her proper work that oppresses her. I think she has some other undertaking in hand, probably for Christmas, or for her mother's return; but as secrecy is the very soul of such things, I shut my eyes.'

'Somehow, Jane, I think you have become so much afraid of giving way to curiosity that you sometimes shut your eyes rather too much.'

'Well, perhaps in one's old age one suffers from the reaction of one's bad qualities. I will think about it, Ada. I certainly never before realised how very different school supervision of young folks is from looking after them all round. Moreover, Gillian has been much more attentive to poor Lily Giles of late, in spite of her avocations.'

Valetta was not at first heartbroken on hearing that she was not to go in for the language examination. It was such a relief from the oppression of the task, and she had so long given up hopes of having the prize to show to her mother, that she was scarcely grieved, though Aunt Jane was very grave while walking down to school with her in the morning to see Miss Leverett, and explain the withdrawal.

That lady came to her private room as soon as she had opened the school. From one point of view, she said, she agreed with Miss Mohun that it would be better that her niece should not go up for the examination.

'But,' she said, 'it may be considered as a stigma upon her, since none of the others are to give up.'

'Indeed! I had almost thought it a matter of course.'

'On the contrary, two of the mothers seem to think nothing at all of the matter. Mrs. Black—'

'The Surveyor's wife, isn't she?'

'Yes, she writes a note saying that all children copy, if they can, and she wonders that I should be so severe upon such a frequent occurrence, which reflects more discredit on the governesses than the scholars.'

'Polite that! And Mrs. Purvis? At least, she is a lady!'

'She is more polite, but evidently has no desire to be troubled. She hopes that if her daughter has committed a breach of school discipline, I will act as I think best.'

'No feeling of the real evil in either! How about Maura White?'

'That is very different. It is her sister who writes, and so nicely that I must show it to you.'

'MY DEAR MADAM—I am exceedingly grieved that Maura should have acted in a dishonourable manner, though she was not fully aware how wrongly she was behaving. We have been talking to her, and we think she is so truly sorry as not to be likely to fall into the same temptation again. As far as we can make out, she has generally taken pains with her tasks, and only obtained assistance in unusually difficult passages, so that we think that she is really not ill-prepared. If it is thought right that all the pupils concerned should abstain from the competition, we would of course readily acquiesce in the justice of the sentence; but to miss it this year might make so serious a difference to her prospects, that I hope it will not be thought a necessary act of discipline, though we know that we have no right to plead for any exemption for her. With many thanks for the consideration you have shown for her, I remain, faithfully yours,

'A very different tone indeed, and it quite agrees with Valetta's account,' said Miss Mohun.

'Yes, the other two girls were by far the most guilty.'

'And morally, perhaps, Maura the least; but I retain my view that, irrespective of the others, Valetta's parents had rather she missed this examination, considering all things.'

Valetta came home much more grieved when she had found she was the only one left out, and declared it was unjust.

No,' said Gillian, 'for you began it all. None of the others would have got into the scrape but for you.'

'It was all your fault for not minding me!'

'As if I made you do sly things.'

'You made me. You were so cross if I only asked a question,' and Val prepared to cry.

'I thought people had to do their own work and not other folks'! Don't be so foolish.'

'Oh dear! oh dear! how unkind you are! I wish—I wish Mysie was here; every one is grown cross! Oh, if mamma would but come home!'

'Now, Val, don't be such a baby! Stop that!'

And Valetta went into one of her old agonies of crying and sobbing, which brought Aunt Jane in to see what was the matter. She instantly stopped the scolding with which Gillian was trying to check the outburst, and which only added to its violence.

'It is the only thing to stop those fits,' said Gillian. 'She can if she will! It is all temper.'

'Leave her to me!' commanded Aunt Jane. 'Go!'

Gillian went away, muttering that it was not the way mamma or Nurse Halfpenny treated Val, and quite amazed that Aunt Jane, of all people, should have the naughty child on her lap and in her arms, soothing her tenderly.

The cries died away, and the long heaving sobs began to subside, and at last a broken voice said, on Aunt Jane's shoulder, 'It's—a—little bit—like mamma.'

For Aunt Jane's voice had a ring in it like mamma's, and this little bit of tenderness was inexpressibly comforting.

'My poor dear child,' she said, 'mamma will soon come home, and then you will be all right.'

'I shouldn't have done it if mamma had been there!'

'No, and now you are sorry.'

'Will mamma be very angry?'

'She will be grieved that you could not hold out when you were tempted; but I am sure she will forgive you if you write it all to her. And, Val, you know you can have God's forgiveness at once if you tell Him.'

'Yes,' said Valetta gravely; then, 'I did not before, because I thought every one made so much of it, and were so cross. And Georgie and Nellie don't care at all.'

'Nor Maura?'

'Oh, Maura does, because of Kalliope.'

'How do you mean?'

Valetta sat up on her aunt's lap, and told.

'Maura told me! She said Kally and Alec both were at her, but her mamma was vexed with them, and said she would not have her scolded at home as well as at school about nothing; and she told Theodore to go and buy her a tart to make up to her, but Theodore wouldn't, for he said he was ashamed of her. So she sent the maid. But when Maura had gone to bed and to sleep, she woke up, and there was Kally crying over her prayers, and whispering half aloud, "Is she going too? My poor child! Oh, save her! Give her the Spirit of truth—"'

'Poor Kalliope! She is a good sister.'

'Yes; Maura says Kally is awfully afraid of their telling stories because of Richard—the eldest, you know. He does it dreadfully. I remember nurse used to tell us not to fib like Dick White. Maura said he used to tell his father stories about being late and getting money, and their mother never let him be punished. He was her pet. And Maura remembers being carried in to see poor Captain White just before he died, when she was getting better, but could not stand, and he said, "Truth before all, children. Be true to God and man." Captain White did care so much, but Mrs. White doesn't. Isn't that very odd, for she isn't a Roman Catholic?' ended Valetta, obviously believing that falsehood was inherent in Romanists, and pouring out all this as soon as her tears were assuaged, as if, having heard it, she must tell.

'Mrs. White is half a Greek, you know,' said Aunt Jane, 'and the Greeks are said not to think enough about truth.'

'Epaminondas did,' said Valetta, who had picked up a good deal from the home atmosphere, 'but Ulysses didn't.'

'No; and the Greeks have been enslaved and oppressed for a great many years, and that is apt to make people get cowardly and false. But that is not our concern, Val, and I think with such a recollection of her good father, and such a sister to help her, Maura will not fall into the fault again. And, my dear, I quite see that neither you nor she entirely realised that what you did was deception, though you never spoke a word of untruth.'

'No, we did not,' said Valetta.

'And so, my dear child, I do forgive you, quite and entirely, as we used to say, though I have settled with Miss Leverett that you had better not go up for the examination, since you cannot be properly up to it. And you must write the whole history to your mother. Yes; I know it will be very sad work, but it will be much better to have it out and done with, instead of having it on your mind when she comes home.'

'Shall you tell her!'

'Yes, certainly,' said the aunt, well knowing that this would clench the matter. 'But I shall tell her how sorry you are, and that I really think you did not quite understand what you were about at first. And I shall write to Miss White, and try to comfort her about her sister.'

'You won't say I told!'

'Oh no; but I shall have quite reason enough for writing in telling her that I am sorry my little niece led her sister into crooked paths.'

Gillian knew that this letter was written and sent, and it did not make her more eager for a meeting with Kalliope. So that she was not sorry that the weather was a valid hindrance, though a few weeks ago she would have disregarded such considerations. Besides, there was her own examination, which for two days was like a fever, and kept her at her little table, thinking of nothing but those questions, and dreaming and waking over them at night.

It was over; and she was counselled on all sides to think no more about it till she should hear of success or failure. But this was easier said than done, and she was left in her tired state with a general sense of being on a wrong tack, and of going on amiss, whether due to her aunt's want of assimilation to herself, or to her mother's absence, she did not know, and with the further sense that she had not been the motherly sister she had figured to herself, but that both the children should show a greater trust and reliance on Aunt Jane than on herself grieved her, not exactly with jealousy, but with sense of failure and dissatisfaction with herself. She had a universal distaste to her surroundings, and something very like dread of the Whites, and she rejoiced in the prospect of quitting Rockstone for the present.

She felt bound to run down to the office to wish Kalliope good-bye. There she found an accumulation of exercises and translations waiting for her.

'Oh, what a quantity! It shows how long it is since I have been here.'

'And indeed,' began Kalliope, 'since your aunt has been so very kind about poor little Maura—'

'Oh, please don't talk to me! There's such a lot to do, and I have no time. Wait till I have done.'

And she nervously began reading out the Greek exercise, so as effectually to stop Kalliope's mouth. Moreover, either her own uneasy mind, or the difficulty of the Greek, brought her into a dilemma. She saw that Alexis's phrase was wrong, but she did not clearly perceive what the sentence ought to be, and she perplexed herself over it till he came in, whether to her satisfaction or not she could not have told, for she had not wanted to see him on the one hand, though, on the other, it silenced Kalliope.

She tried to clear her perceptions by explanations to him, but he did not seem to give his mind to the grammar half as much as to the cessation of the lessons and her absence.

'You must do the best you can,' she said, 'and I shall find you gone quite beyond me.'

'I shall never do that, Miss Merrifield.'

'Nonsense!' she said, laughing uncomfortably 'a pretty clergyman you would be if you could not pass a girl. There! good-bye. Make a list of your puzzles and I will do my best with them when I come back.'

'Thank you,' and he wrung her hand with an earnestness that gave her a sense of uneasiness.

CHAPTER XI. — LADY MERRIFIELD'S CHRISTMAS LETTER-BAG

(PRIMROSE.)

'MY DEAR MAMMA—I wish you a merry Christmas, and papa and sisters and Claude too. I only hooped once to-day, and Nurse says I may go out when it gets fine. Fly is better. She sent me her dolls' house in a big box in a cart, and Mysie sent a new frock of her own making for Liliana, and Uncle William gave me a lovely doll, with waxen arms and legs, that shuts her eyes and squeals, and says Mamma; but I do not want anything but my own dear mamma, and all the rest. I am mamma's own little PRIMROSE.'

(FERGUS.)

'COALHAM.

'MY DEAR MAMMA—I wish you and papa, and all, a happy Crismas, and I send a plan of the great coal mine for a card. It is much jollier here than at Rockquay, for it is all black with cinders, and there are little fires all night, and there are lots of oars and oxhide and fossils and ferns and real curiozitys, and nobody minds noises nor muddy boots, and they aren't at one to wash your hands, for they can't be clean ever; and there was a real row in the street last night just outside. We are to go down a mine some day when Cousin David has time. I mean to be a great jeologist and get lots of specimens, and please bring me home all the minerals in Ceylon. Harry gave me a hammer.— I am, your affectionate son, FERGUS MERRIFIELD.'

(VALETTA.)

'MY DEAREST MAMMA—I hope you will like my card. Aunt Ada did none of it, only showed me how, and Aunt Jane says I may tell you I am really trying to be good. I am helping her gild fir-cones for a Christmas-tree for the quire, and they will sing carols. Macrae brought some for us the day before yesterday, and a famous lot of holly and ivy and mistletoe and flowers, and three turkeys and some hams and pheasants and partridges. Aunt Jane sent the biggest turkey and ham in a basket covered up with holly to Mrs. White, and another to Mrs. Hablot, and they are doing the church with the holly and ivy. We are to eat the other the day after to-morrow, and Mr. Grant and Miss Burne, who teaches the youngest form, are coming. It was only cold beef to-day, to let Mrs. Mount go to church; but we had mince pies, and I am going to Kitty's Christmas party to-morrow, and we shall dance—so Aunt Ada has given me a new white frock and a lovely Roman sash of her own. Poor old Mrs. Vincent is dead, and Fergus's great black rabbit, and poor little

Mary Brown with dip—(blot). I can't spell it, and nobody is here to tell me how, but the thing in people's throats, and poor Anne has got it, and Dr. Ellis says it was a mercy we were all away from home, for we should have had it too, and that would have been ever so much worse than the whooping-cough.

'I have lots of cards, but my presents are waiting for my birthday, when Maura is to come to tea. It is much nicer than I thought the holidays would be. Maura White has got the prize for French and Latin. It is a lovely Shakespeare. I wish I had been good, for I think I should have got it. Only she does want more help than I do—so perhaps it is lucky I did not. No, I don't mean lucky either.—

Your affectionate little daughter,

VAL.'

(WILFRED.)

'DEAR MOTHER—Fergus is such a little ape that he will send you that disgusting coal mine on his card, as if you would care for it. I know you will like mine much better—that old buffer skating into a hole in the ice. I don't mind being here, for though Harry and Davy get up frightfully early to go to church, they don't want us down till they come back, and we can have fun all day, except when Harry screws me down to my holiday task, which is a disgusting one, about the Wars of the Roses. Harry does look so rum now that he is got up for a parson that we did not know him when he met us at the station. There was an awful row outside here last night between two sets of Waits. David went out and parted them, and I thought he would have got a black eye. All the choir had supper here, for there was a service in the middle of the night; but they did not want us at it, and on Tuesday we are to have a Christmas ship, and a magic-lantern, and Rollo and Mr. Bowater are coming to help—he is the clergyman at the next place—and no end of fun, and the biggest dog you ever saw. Fergus has got one of his crazes worse than ever about old stones, and is always in the coal hole, poking after ferns and things. Wishing you a merry Christmas.—Your affectionate son,

'WILFRED MERRIFIELD.'

(MYSIE.)

'ROTHERWOOD, Christmas Day.

'MY OWN DEAREST MAMMA—A very happy Christmas to you, and papa and Claude and my sisters, and here are the cards, which Miss Elbury helped me about so kindly that I think they are better than usual: I mean that she advised me, for no one touched them but myself. You will like your text, I hope, I chose it because it is so nice to think we are all one, though we are in so many different places. I did one with the same for poor Dolores in New

Zealand. Uncle William was here yesterday, and he said dear little Primrose is almost quite well. Fly is much better to-day; her eyes look quite bright, and she is to sit up a little while in the afternoon, but I may not talk to her for fear of making her cough; but she slept all night without one whoop, and will soon be well now. Cousin Rotherwood was so glad that he was quite funny this morning, and he gave me the loveliest writing-case you ever saw, with a good lock and gold key, and gold tops to everything, and my three M's engraved on them all. I have so many presents and cards that I will write out a list when I have finished my letter. I shall have plenty of time, for everybody is gone to church except Cousin Florence, who went early.

'I am to dine at the late dinner, which will be early, because of the church singers, and Cousin Rotherwood says he and I will do snapdragon, if I will promise not to whoop.

'4.30.—I had to stop again because of the doctor. He says he does not want to have any more to do with me, and that I may go out the first fine day, and that Fly is much better. And only think! He says Rockquay is the very place for Fly, and as soon as we are not catching, we are all to go there. Cousin Rotherwood told me so for a great secret, but he said I might tell you, and that he would ask Aunt Alethea to let Primrose come too. It does warm one up to think of it, and it is much easier to feel thankful and glad about all the rest of the right sort of Christmas happiness, now I am so near having Gill and Val again.—Your very loving child,

M. M. MERRIFIELD.'

(JASPER.)

'VALE LESTON PRIORY,

'25th December.

'DEAREST MOTHER—Here are my Christmas wishes that we may all be right again at home this year, and that you could see the brace of pheasants I killed. However, Gill and I are in uncommonly nice quarters. I shall let her tell the long story about who is who, for there is such a swarm of cousins, and uncles, and aunts, and when you think you have hold of the right one, it turns out to be the other lot. There are three houses choke full of them, and more floating about, and all running in and out, till it gets like the little pig that could not be counted, it ran about so fast. They are all Underwood or Harewood, more or less, except the Vanderkists, who are all girls except a little fellow in knickerbockers. Poor little chap, his father was a great man on the turf, and ruined him horse and foot before he was born, and then died of D. T., and his mother is a great invalid, and very badly off, with no end of daughters—the most stunning girls you ever saw—real beauties, and no mistake, especially Emily, who is great fun besides. She is to be Helena when we act Midsummer Night's Dream on Twelfth Night for all the natives, and I am Demetrius, dirty cad that he is! She lives with the Grinsteads, and Anna with the Travis Underwoods, Phyllis's young man's bosses. If he makes as good a thing of it as they have done, she will be no end of a swell. Mr. Travis Underwood has brought down his hunters and gives me a mount. Claude would go stark staring mad to see his Campeador.

'They are awfully musical here, and are always at carols or something, and that's the only thing against them. As to Gill, she is in clover, in raptures with every one, especially Mrs. Grinstead, and I think it is doing her good.—Your affectionate son, J. R. M.'

(GILLIAN.)

'DEAREST MAMMA—All Christmas love, and a message to Phyllis that I almost forgive her desertion for the sake of the set of connections she has brought us, like the nearest and dearest relations or more, but Geraldine—for so she told me to call her—is still the choicest of all. It is so pretty to see her husband—the great sculptor—wait on her, as if she was a queen and he her knight! Anna told me that he had been in love with her ever so long, and she refused him once; but after the eldest brother died, and she was living at St. Wulstan's, he tried again, and she could not hold out. I told you of her charming house, so full of lovely things, and about Gerald, all cleverness and spirit, but too delicate for a public school. He is such a contrast to Edward Harewood, a great sturdy, red-haired fellow, who is always about with Jasper, except when he—Japs, I mean—is with Emily Vanderkist. She is the prettiest of the Vanderkists. There are eight of them besides little Sir Adrian. Mary always stays to look after her mother, who is in very bad health, and has weak eyes. They call Mary invaluable and so very good, but she is like a homely little Dutchwoman, and nobody would think she was only twenty. Sophy, the next to her, calls herself pupil-teacher to Mrs. William Harewood, and together they manage the schoolroom for all the younger sisters the two little girls at the Vicarage, and Wilmet, the only girl here at the Priory; but, of course, no lessons are going on now, only learning and rehearsing the parts, and making the dresses, painting the scenes, and learning songs. They all do care so much about music here that I find I really know hardly anything about it, and Jasper says it is their only failing.

'They say Mr. Lancelot Underwood sings and plays better than any of them; but he is at Stoneborough. However, he is coming over with all the Mays for our play, old Dr. May and all. I was very much surprised to find he was an organist and a bookseller, but Geraldine told me about it, and how it was for the sake of the eldest brother—"my brother," they all say; and somehow it seems as if the house was still his, though it is so many years since he died. And yet they are all such happy, merry people. I wish I could let you know how delightful it all is. Sometimes I feel as if I did not deserve to have such a pleasant time. I can't quite explain, but to be with Geraldine Grinstead makes one feel one's self to be of a ruder, more selfish mould, and I know I have not been all I ought to be at Rockstone; but I don't mind telling you, now you are so soon to be at home, Aunt Jane seems to worry me—I can't tell how, exactly—while there is something about Geraldine that soothes and brightens, and all the time makes one long to be better.

'I never heard such sermons as Mr. Harewood's either; it seems as if I had never listened before, but these go right down into one. I cannot leave off thinking about the one last Sunday, about "making manifest the counsels of all hearts." I see now that I was not as much justified in not consulting Aunt Jane about Kalliope and Alexis as I thought I was, and that the concealment was wrong. It came over me before the beautiful early Celebration this morning, and I could not feel as if I ought to be there till I had made a resolution to tell her all about it, though I should like it not to be till you are come home, and can tell her that I am not really like Dolores, as she will be sure to think me, for I really did it, not out of silliness and opposition, but because I knew how good they were, and I did tell you. Honestly, perhaps there was some opposition in the spirit of it; but I mean to make a fresh start when I come back, and you will be near at hand then, and that will help me.

'26th.—The afternoon service of song began and I was called off. I never heard anything so lovely, and we had a delightful evening. I can't tell you about it now, for I am snatching a moment when I am not rehearsing, as this must go to-day. Dr. and Miss May, and the Lances, as they call them, are just come. The Doctor is a beautiful old man. All the children were round him directly, and he kissed me, and said that he was proud to meet the daughter of such a distinguished man.

'This must go.—Your loving daughter,

'JULIANA MERRIFIELD.'

(HARRY.)

'COALHAM, Christmas Day.

'It is nearly St. Stephen's Day, for, dear mother, I have not had a minute before to send you or my father my Christmas greeting. We have had most joyous services, unusually well attended, David tells me, and that makes up for the demonstration we had outside the door last night. David is the right fellow for this place, though we are disapproved of as south country folk. The boys are well and amused, Wilfred much more comfortable for being treated more as a man, and Fergus greatly come on, and never any trouble, being always dead-set on some pursuit. It is geology, or rather mineralogy, at present, and if he carries home all the stones he has accumulated in the back yard, he will have a tolerable charge for extra luggage. David says there is the making of a great man in him, I think it is of an Uncle Maurice. Macrae writes to me in a state of despair about the drains at Silverfold; scarlet fever and diphtheria abound at the town, so that he says you cannot come back there till something has been done, and he wants me to come and look at them; but I do not see how I can leave David at present, as we are in the thick of classes for Baptism and Confirmation in Lent, and I suspect Aunt Jane knows more about the matter than I do.

'Gillian and Jasper seem to be in a state of great felicity at Vale Leston— and Mysie getting better, but poor little Phyllis Devereux has been seriously ill.—Your affectionate son, H. MERRIFIELD.'

(AUNT JANE AND AUNT ADELINE.)

'11.30, Christmas Eve. 'MY DEAREST LILY—This will be a joint letter, for Ada will finish it to-morrow, and I must make the most of my time while waiting for the Waits to dwell on unsavoury business. Macrae came over here with a convoy of all sorts of "delicacies of the season," for which thank you heartily in the name of Whites, Hablots, and others who partook thereof, according, no doubt, to your kind intention. He was greatly perturbed, poor man, for your cook has been very ill with diphtheria, and the scarlet fever is severe all round; there have been some deaths, and the gardener's child was in great danger. The doctor has analysed the water, and finds it in a very bad state, so that your absence this autumn is providential. If you are in haste, telegraph to me, and I will meet your landlord there, and the sanitary inspector, and see what can be done, without waiting for Jasper. At any rate, you cannot go back there at once. Shall I secure a furnished house for you here? The Rotherwoods are coming to the hotel next door to us, as soon as Phyllis is fit to move and infection over. Victoria will stay there with the children, and he go back and forwards. If Harry and Phyllis May should come home, I suppose their headquarters will be at Stoneborough; but still this would be the best place for a family gathering. Moreover, Fergus gets on very nicely at Mrs. Edgar's, and it would be a pity to disturb him. On the other hand, I am not sure of the influences of the place upon the—

'Christmas Day, 3 P.M.—There came the Waits I suppose, and Jane had to stop and leave me to take up the thread. Poor dear Jenny, the festival days are no days of rest to her, but I am not sure that she would enjoy repose, or that it would not be the worse possible penance to her. She is gone down now to the workhouse with Valetta to take cards and tea and tobacco to the old people, not sending them, because she says a few personal wishes and the sight of a bright child will be worth something to the old bodies. Then comes tea for the choir-boys, before Evensong and carols, and after that my turn may come for what remains of the evening. I must say the church is lovely, thanks to your arums and camellias, which Macrae brought us just in time. It is very unfortunate that Silverfold should be in such a state, but delightful for us if it sends you here; and this brings me to Jenny's broken thread, which I must spin on, though I tell her to take warning by you, when you so repented having brought Maurice home by premature wails about Dolores. Perhaps impatience is a danger to all of us, and I believe there is such a thing as over- candour.

'What Jane was going to say was that she did not think the place had been good for either of the girls; but all that would be obviated by your presence. If poor Miss Vincent joins you, now that she is free, you would have your own schoolroom again, and the locality would not make much difference. Indeed, if the Rotherwood party come by the end of the holidays, I have very little doubt that Victoria will allow Valetta to join Phyllis and Mysie in the schoolroom, and that would prevent any talk about her removal from the High School. The poor little thing has behaved as well as possible ever since, and is an excellent companion; Jane is sure that it has been a lesson that will last her for life, and I am convinced that she was under an influence that you can put an end to—I mean that White family. Jane thinks well of the eldest daughter, in spite of her fringe and of her refusal to enter the G.F.S.; but I have good reason for knowing that she holds assignations in Mr. White's garden on Sunday afternoons with young Stebbing, whose mother knows her to be a most artful and dangerous girl, though she is so clever at the mosaic work that there is no getting her discharged. Mrs. Stebbing called to warn us against her, and, as I was the only person at home, told me how she had learnt from Mr. White's housekeeper that this girl comes every Sunday alone to walk in the gardens— she was sure it must be to meet somebody, and they are quite accessible to an active young man on the side towards the sea. He is going in a few days to join the other partner at the Italian quarries, greatly in order that the connection may be broken off. It is very odd that Jane, generally so acute, should be so blind here. All she said was, "That's just the time Gillian is so bent on mooning in the garden." It is a mere absurdity; Gillian always goes to the children's service, and besides, she was absent last Sunday, when Miss White was certainly there. But Gillian lends the girl books, and altogether patronises her in a manner which is somewhat perplexing to us; though, as it cannot last long, Jane thinks it better not to interfere before your return to judge for yourself. These young people are members of the Kennel Church congregation, and I had an opportunity of talking to Mr. Flight about them.

He says he had a high opinion of the brother, and hoped to help him to some higher education, with a view perhaps to Holy Orders; but that it was so clearly the youth's duty to support his mother, and it was so impossible for her to get on without his earnings, that he (Mr. Flight, I mean) had decided to let him alone that his stability might be proved, or till some opening offered; and of late there had been reason for disappointment, tokens of being unsettled, and reports of meetings with some young woman at his sister's office. It is always the way when one tries to be interested in those half-and- half people,—the essential vulgarity is sure to break out, generally in the spirit of flirtation conducted in an underhand manner. And oh! that mother! I write all this because you had better be aware of the state of things before your return. I am afraid, however, that between us we have not written you a very cheering Christmas letter.

'There is a great question about a supply of water to the town. Much excitement is caused by the expectation of Rotherwood's visit, and it is even said that he is to be met here by the great White himself, whom I have always regarded as a sort of mythical personage, not to say a harpy, always snatching away every promising family of Jane's to the Italian quarries.

'You will have parted with the dear girls by this time, and be feeling very sad and solitary; but it is altogether a good connection, and a great advantage. I have just addressed to Gillian, at Vale Leston, a coroneted envelope, which must be an invitation from Lady Liddesdale. I am very glad of it. Nothing is so likely as such society to raise her above the tone of these Whites.—Your loving A. M.'

'10.30 P.M.—These Whites! Really I don't think it as bad as Ada supposes, so don't be uneasy, though it is a pity she has told you so much of the gossip respecting them. I do not believe any harm of that girl Kalliope; she has such an honest, modest pair of eyes. I dare say she is persecuted by that young Stebbing, for she is very handsome, and he is an odious puppy. But as to her assignations in the garden, if they are with any one, it is with Gillian, and I see no harm in them, except that we might have been told—only that would have robbed the entire story of its flavour, I suppose. Besides, I greatly disbelieve the entire story, so don't be worried about it! There—as if we had not been doing our best to worry you! But come home, dearest old Lily. Gather your chicks under your wing, and when you cluck them together again, all will be well. I don't think you will find Valetta disimproved by her crisis. It is curious to hear how she and Gillian both declare that Mysie would have prevented it, as if naughtiness or deceit shrank from that child's very face.

'It has been a very happy, successful Christmas Day, full of rejoicing. May you be feeling the same; that joy has made us one in many a time of separation.—Your faithful old Brownie,

J. MOHUN.'

(GILLIAN AGAIN.)

'ROWTHORPE, 20th January.

'DEAREST MAMMA—This is a Sunday letter. I am writing it in a beautiful place, more like a drawing-room than a bed-room, and it is all very grand; such long galleries, such quantities of servants, so many people staying in the house, that I should feel quite lost but for Geraldine. We came so late last night that there was only just time to dress for dinner at eight o'clock. I never dined with so many people before, and they are all staying in the house. I have not learnt half of them yet, though Lady Liddesdale, who is a nice, merry old lady, with gray hair, called her eldest granddaughter, Kitty Somerville, and told her to take care of me, and tell me who they all were. One of them is that Lord Ormersfield, whom Mysie ran against at Rotherwood, and, do you know, I very nearly did the same; for there is early Celebration at the little church just across the garden. Kitty talked of calling for me, but I did not make sure, because I heard some one say she was not to go if she had a cold; and, when I heard the bell, I grew anxious and started off, and I lost my way, and thought I should never get to the stairs; but just as I was turning back, out came Lord and Lady Ormersfield. He looks quite young, though he is rather lame—I shall like all lame people, for the sake of Geraldine—and Lady Ormersfield has such a motherly face. He laughed, and said I was not the first person who had lost my way in the labyrinths of passages, so I went on with them, and after all Kitty was hunting for me! I sat next him at breakfast, and, do you know, he asked me whether I was the sister of a little downright damsel he met at Rotherwood two years ago, and said he had used her truthfulness about the umbrella for a favourite example to his small youngest!

'When I hear of truthfulness I feel a sort of shock. "Oh, if you knew!" I am ready to say, and I grow quite hot. That is what I am really writing about to-day. I never had time after that Christmas Day at Vale Leston to do more than keep you up to all the doings; but I did think: and there were Mr. Harewood's sermons, which had a real sting in them, and a great sweetness besides. I have tried to set some down for you, and that is one reason I did not say more. But to-day, after luncheon, it is very quiet, for Kitty and Constance are gone to their Sunday classes, and the gentlemen and boys are out walking, except Lord Somerville, who has a men's class of his own, and all the old ladies are either in their rooms, or talking in pairs. So I can tell you that I see now that I did not go on in a right spirit with Aunt Jane, and that I did poor Val harm by my example, and went very near deception, for I did not choose to believe that when you said "If Aunt J. approves," you meant about Alexis White's lessons; so I never told her or Kalliope, and I perceive now that it was not right towards either; for Kally was very unhappy about her not knowing. I am very sorry; I see that I was wrong all round, and that I should have understood it before, if I had examined myself in the way Mr. Harewood dwelt upon in his last Sunday in Advent sermon, and never gone on in such a way.

'I am not going to wait for you now, but shall confess it all to Aunt Jane as soon as I go home, and try to take it as my punishment if she asks a terrible number of questions. Perhaps I shall write it, but it would take such a quantity of explanation, and I don't want Aunt Ada to open the letter, as she does any that come while Aunt Jane is out.

'Please kiss my words and forgive me, as you read this, dear mamma; I never guessed I was going to be so like Dolores.

'Kitty has come to my door to ask if I should like to come and read something nice and Sundayish with them in her grandmamma's dressing-room.—So no more from your loving GILL.'

CHAPTER XII. — TRANSFORMATION

'Well, now for the second stage of our guardianship!' said Aunt Ada, as the two sisters sat over the fire after Valetta had gone to bed. 'Fergus comes back to-morrow, and Gillian—when?'

'She does not seem quite certain, for there is to be a day or two at Brompton with this delightful Geraldine, so that she may see her grandmother —also Mr. Clement Underwood's church, and the Merchant of Venice—an odd mixture of ecclesiastics and dissipations.'

'I wonder whether she will be set up by it.'

'So do I! They are all remarkably good people; but then good people do sometimes spoil the most of all, for they are too unselfish to snub. And on the other hand, seeing the world sometimes has the wholesome effect of making one feel small—'

'My dear Jenny!'

'Oh! I did not mean you, who are never easily effaced; but I was thinking of youthful bumptiousness, fostered by country life and elder sistership.'

'Certainly, though Valetta is really much improved, Gillian has not been as pleasant as I expected, especially during the latter part of the time.'

'Query, was it her fault or mine, or the worry of the examination, or all three?'

'Perhaps you did superintend a little too much at first. More than modern independence was prepared for, though I should not have expected recalcitration in a young Lily; but I think there was more ruffling of temper and more reserve than I can quite understand.'

'It has not been a success. As dear old Lily would have said, "My dream has vanished," of a friend in the younger generation, and now it remains to do the best I can for her in the few weeks that are left, before we have her dear mother again.'

'At any rate, you have no cause to be troubled about the other two. Valetta is really the better for her experience, and you have always got on well with the boy.'

Fergus was the first of the travellers to appear at Rockstone. Miss Mohun, who went to meet him at the station, beheld a small figure lustily pulling at a great canvas bag, which came bumping down the step, assisted by a shove from the other passengers, and threatening for a moment to drag him down between platform and carriages.

'Fergus, Fergus, what have you got there? Give it to me. How heavy!'

'It's a few of my mineralogical specimens,' replied Fergus. 'Harry wouldn't let me put any more into my portmanteau—but the peacock and the dendrum are there.'

Already, without special regard to peacock or dendrum, whatever that article might be, Miss Mohun was claiming the little old military portmanteau, with a great M and 110th painted on it, that held Fergus's garments.

He would scarcely endure to deposit the precious bag in the omnibus, and as he walked home his talk was all of tertiary formations, and coal measures, and limestones, as he extracted a hammer from his pocket, and looked perilously disposed to use it on the vein of crystals in a great pink stone in a garden wall. His aunt was obliged to begin by insisting that the walls should be safe from geological investigations.

'But it is such waste, Aunt Jane. Only think of building up such beautiful specimens in a stupid old wall.'

Aunt Jane did not debate the question of waste, but assured him that equally precious specimens could be honestly come by; while she felt renewed amusement and pleasure at anything so like the brother Maurice of thirty odd years ago being beside her.

It made her endure the contents of the bag being turned out like a miniature rockery for her inspection on the floor of the glazed verandah outside the drawing-room, and also try to pacify Mrs. Mount's indignation at finding the more valuable specimens, or, as she called them, 'nasty stones' and bits of dirty coal, within his socks.

Much more information as to mines, coal, or copper, was to be gained from him than as to Cousin David, or Harry, or Jasper, who had spent the last ten days of his holidays at Coalham, which had procured for Fergus the felicity of a second underground expedition. It was left to his maturer judgment and the next move to decide how many of his specimens were absolutely worthless; it was only stipulated that he and Valetta should carry them, all and sundry, up to the lumber-room, and there arrange them as he chose;—Aunt Jane routing out for him a very dull little manual of mineralogy, and likewise a book of Maria Hack's, long since out of print, but wherein 'Harry Beaufoy' is instructed in the chief outlines of geology in a manner only perhaps inferior to that of "Madame How and Lady Why," which she reserved for a birthday present. Meantime Rockstone and its quarries were almost as excellent a field of research as the mines of Coalham, and in a different line.

'How much nicer it is to be a boy than a girl!' sighed Valetta, as she beheld her junior marching off with all the dignity of hammer and knapsack to look up Alexis White and obtain access to the heaps of rubbish, which in his eyes held as infinite possibilities as the diamond fields of Kimberley. And Alexis was only delighted to bestow on him any space of daylight when both were free from school or from work, and kept a look-out for the treasures he desired. Of course, out of gratitude to his parents—or was it out of gratitude to his sister? Perhaps Fergus could have told, if he had paid the slightest attention to such a trifle, how anxiously Alexis inquired when Miss Gillian was expected to return. Moreover, he might have told that his other model, Stebbing, pronounced old Dick White a beast and a screw, with whom his brother Frank was not going to stop.

Gillian came back a fortnight later, having been kept at Rowthorpe, together with Mrs. Grinstead, for a family festival over the double marriage in Ceylon, after which she spent a few days in London, so as to see her grandmother, Mrs. Merrifield, who was too infirm for an actual visit to be welcome, since her attendant grandchild, Bessie Merrifield, was so entirely occupied with her as to have no time to bestow upon a guest of more than an hour or two. Gillian was met at the station by her aunt, and when all her belongings had been duly extracted, proving a good deal larger in bulk than when she had left Rockstone, and both were seated in the fly to drive home through a dismal February Fill-dyke day, the first words that were spoken were,

'Aunt Jane, I ought to tell you something.'

Hastily revolving conjectures as to the subject of the coming confession, Miss Mohun put herself at her niece's service.

'Aunt Jane, I know I ought to have told you how much I was seeing of the Whites last autumn.'

'Indeed, I know you wished to do what you could for them.'

'Yes,' said Gillian, finding it easier than she expected. 'You know Alexis wants very much to be prepared for Holy Orders, and he could not get on by himself, so I have been running down to Kalliope's office after reading to Lily Giles, to look over his Greek exercises.'

'Meeting him?'

'Only sometimes. But Kally did not like it. She said you ought to know, and that was the reason she would not come into the G.F.S. She is so good and honourable, Aunt Jane.'

'I am sure she is a very excellent girl,' said Aunt Jane warmly. 'But certainly it would have been better to have these lessons in our house. Does your mother know?'

'Yes,' said Gillian, 'I wrote to her all I was doing, and how I have been talking to Kally on Sunday afternoons through the rails of Mr. White's garden. I thought she could telegraph if she did not approve, but she does not seem to have noticed it in my letters, only saying something I could not make out— about "if you approved."'

'And is that the reason you have told me?'

'Partly, but I got the letter before the holidays. I think it has worked itself up, Aunt Jane, into a sense that it was not the thing. There was Kally, and there was poor Valetta's mess, and her justifying herself by saying I did more for the Whites than you knew, and altogether, I grew sorry I had begun it, for I was sure it was not acting honestly towards you, Aunt Jane, and I hope you will forgive me.'

Miss Mohun put her arm round the girl and kissed her heartily.

'My dear Gill, I am glad you have told me! I dare say I seemed to worry you, and that you felt as if you were watched; I will do my very best to help you, if you have got into a scrape. I only want to ask you not to do anything more till I can see Kally, and settle with her the most suitable way of helping the youth.'

But do you think there is a scrape, aunt? I never thought of that, if you forgave me.'

'My dear, I see you did not; and that you told me because you are my Lily's daughter, and have her honest heart. I do not know that there is anything amiss, but I am afraid young ladies can't do—well, impulsive things without a few vexations in consequence. Don't be so dismayed, I don't know of anything, and I cannot tell you how glad I am of your having spoken out in this way.'

'I feel as if a load were off my back!' said Gillian.

And a bar between her and her aunt seemed to have vanished, as they drove up the now familiar slope, and under the leafless copper beeches. Blood is thinker than water, and what five months ago had seemed to be exile, had become the first step towards home, if not home itself, for now, like Valetta, she welcomed the sound of her mother's voice in her aunt's. And there were Valetta and Fergus rushing out, almost under the wheels to fly at her, and

Aunt Ada's soft embraces in the hall.

The first voice that came out of the melee was Valetta's. 'Gill is grown quite a lady!'

'How much improved!' exclaimed Aunt Ada.

'The Bachfisch has swum into the river,' was Aunt Jane's comment.

'She'll never be good for anything jolly—no scrambling!' grumbled Fergus.

'Now Fergus! didn't Kitty Somerville and I scramble when we found the gate locked, and thought we saw the spiteful stag, and that he was going to run at us?'

'I'm afraid that was rather on compulsion, Gill.'

'It wasn't the spiteful stag after all, but we had such a long way to come home, and got over the park wall at last by the help of the limb of a tree. We had been taking a bit of wedding-cake to Frank Somerville's old nurse, and Kitty told her I was her maiden aunt, and we had such fun—her uncle's wife's sister, you know.'

'We sent a great piece of our wedding-cake to the Whites,' put in Valetta. 'Fergus and I took it on Saturday afternoon, but nobody was at home but Mrs. White, and she is fatter than ever.'

'I say, Gill, which is the best formation, Vale Leston or Rowthorpe?'

'Oh, nobody is equal to Geraldine; but Kitty is a dear thing.'

'I didn't mean that stuff, but which had the best strata and specimens?'

'Geological, he means—not of society,' interposed Aunt Jane.

'Oh yes! Harry said he had gone geology mad, and I really did get you a bit of something at Vale Leston, Fergus, that Mr. Harewood said was worth having. Was it an encrinite? I know it was a stone-lily.'

'An encrinite! Oh, scrumptious!'

Then ensued such an unpacking as only falls to the lot of home-comers from London, within the later precincts of Christmas, gifts of marvellous contrivance and novelty, as well as cheapness, for all and sundry, those reserved for others almost as charming to the beholders as those which fell to their own lot. The box, divided into compartments, transported Fergus as much as the encrinite; Valetta had a photograph-book, and, more diffidently, Gillian presented Aunt Ada with a graceful little statuette in Parian, and Aunt Jane with the last novelty in baskets. There were appropriate keepsakes for the maids, and likewise for Kalliope and Maura. Aunt Jane was glad to see that discretion had prevailed so as to confine these gifts to the female part of the White family. There were other precious articles in reserve for the absent; and the display of Gillian's own garments was not without interest, as she had been to her first ball, under the chaperonage of Lady Somerville, and Mrs. Grinstead had made her white tarletan available by painting it and its ribbons with exquisite blue nemophilas, too lovely for anything so fleeting.

Mrs. Grinstead and her maid had taken charge of the damsel's toilette at Rowthorpe, had perhaps touched up her dresses, and had certainly taught her how to put them on, and how to manage her hair, so that though it had not broken out into fringes or tousles, as if it were desirable to imitate savages 'with foreheads marvellous low,' the effect was greatly improved. The young brown-skinned, dark-eyed face, and rather tall figure were the same, even the clothes the very same chosen under her aunt Ada's superintendence, but there was an indescribable change, not so much that of fashion as of distinction, and something of the same inward growth might be gathered from her conversation.

All the evening there was a delightful outpouring. Gillian had been extremely happy, and considerably reconciled to her sisters' marriages; but she had been away from home and kin long enough to make her feel her nearness to her aunts, and to appreciate the pleasure of describing her enjoyment without restraint, and of being with those whose personal family interests were her own, not only sympathetic, like her dear Geraldine's. They were ready for any amount of description, though, on the whole, Miss Mohun preferred to hear of the Vale Leston charities and church details, and Miss Adeline of the Rowthorpe grandees and gaieties, after the children had supped full of the diversions of their own kind at both places, and the deeply interesting political scraps and descriptions of great men had been given.

It had been, said Aunt Jane, a bit of education. Gillian had indeed spent her life with thoughtful, cultivated, and superior people; but the circumstances of her family had confined her to a schoolroom sort of existence ever since she had reached appreciative years, retarding, though not perhaps injuring, her development; nor did Rockquay society afford much that was elevating, beyond the Bureau de Charite that Beechcroft Cottage had become. Details were so much in hand that breadth of principle might be obscured.

At Vale Leston, however, there was a strong ecclesiastical atmosphere; but while practical parish detail was thoroughly kept up, there was a wider outlook, and constant conversation and discussion among superior men, such as the Harewood brothers, Lancelot Underwood, Mr. Grinstead, and Dr. May, on the great principles and issues of Church and State matters, religion, and morals, together with matters of art, music, and literature, opening new vistas to her, and which she could afterwards go over with Mrs. Grinstead and Emily and Anna Vanderkist with enthusiasm and comprehension. It was something different from grumbling over the number of candles at St. Kenelm's, or the defective washing of the St. Andrew's surplices.

At Rowthorpe she had seen and heard people with great historic names, champions in the actual battle. There had been a constant coming and going of guests during her three weeks' visit, political meetings, entertainments to high and low, the opening of a public institute in the next town, the exhibition of tableaux in which she had an important share, parties in the evenings, and her first ball. The length of her visit and her connection with the family had made her share the part of hostess with Lady Constance and Lady Katharine Somerville, and she had been closely associated with their intimates, the daughters of these men of great names. Of course there had been plenty of girlish chatter and merry trifling, perhaps some sharp satirical criticism, and the revelations she had heard had been a good deal of the domestic comedy of political and aristocratic life; but throughout there had been a view of conscientious goodness, for the young girls who gave a tone to the rest had been carefully brought up, and were earnest and right-minded, accepting representation, gaiety, and hospitality as part of the duty of their position, often involving self-denial, though there was likewise plenty of enjoyment.

Such glimpses of life had taught Gillian more than she yet realised. As has been seen, the atmosphere of Vale Leston had deepened her spiritual life, and the sermons had touched her heart to the quick, and caused self-examination, which had revealed to her the secret of her dissatisfaction with herself, and her perception was the clearer through her intercourse on entirely equal terms with persons of a high tone of refinement.

The immediate fret of sense of supervision and opposition being removed, she had seen things more justly, and a distaste had grown on her for stolen expeditions to the office, and for the corrections of her pupil's exercises. She recoiled from the idea that this was the consequence either of having swell friends, or of getting out of her depth in her instructions; but reluctance recurred, while advance in knowledge of the world made her aware that Alexis White, after hours, in his sister's office, might justly be regarded by her mother and aunts as an undesirable scholar for her, and that his sister's remonstrances ought not to have been scouted. She had done the thing in her simplicity, but it was through her own wilful secretiveness that her ignorance had not been guarded.

Thus she had, as a matter of truth, conscience, and repentance, made the confession which had been so kindly received as to warm her heart with gratitude to her aunt, and she awoke the next morning to feel freer, happier, and more at home than she had ever yet done at Rockstone.

When the morning letters were opened, they contained the startling news that Mysie might be expected that very evening, with Fly, the governess, and Lady Rotherwood,—at least that was the order of precedence in which the party represented itself to the minds of the young Merrifields. Primrose had caught a fresh cold, and her uncle and aunt would not part with her till her mother's return, but the infection was over with the other two, and sea air was recommended as soon as possible for Lady Phyllis; so, as the wing of the hotel, which was almost a mansion in itself, had been already engaged, the journey was to be made at once, and the arrival would take place in the afternoon. The tidings were most rapturously received; Valetta jumped on and off all the chairs in the room unchidden, while Fergus shouted, 'Hurrah for Mysie and Fly!' and Gillian's heart felt free to leap.

This made it a very busy day, since Lady Rotherwood had begged to have some commissions executed for her beforehand, small in themselves, but, with a scrupulously thorough person, occupying all the time left from other needful engagements; so that there was no chance of the promised conversation with Kalliope, nor did Gillian trouble herself much about it in her eagerness, and hardly heard Fergus announce that Frank Stebbing had come home, and the old boss was coming, 'bad luck to him.'

All the three young people were greatly disappointed that their aunts would not consent to their being on the platform nor in front of the hotel, nor even in what its mistress termed the reception-room, to meet the travellers.

'There was nothing Lady Rotherwood would dislike more than a rush of you all,' said Aunt Adeline, and they had to submit, though Valetta nearly cried when she was dragged in from demonstratively watching at the gate in a Scotch mist.

However, in about a quarter of an hour there was a ring at the door, and in another moment Mysie and Gillian were hugging one smother, Valetta hanging round Mysie's neck, Fergus pulling down her arm. The four creatures seemed all wreathed into one like fabulous snakes for some seconds, and when they unfolded enough for Mysie to recollect and kiss her aunts, there certainly was a taller, better-equipped figure, but just the same round, good- humoured countenance, and the first thing, beyond happy ejaculations, that she was heard in a dutiful voice to say was, 'Miss Elbury brought me to the door. I may stay as long as my aunts like to have me this evening, if you will be so kind as to send some one to see me back.'

Great was the jubilation, and many the inquiries after Primrose, who had once been nearly well, but had fallen back again, and Fly, who, Mysie said, was quite well and as comical as ever when she was well, but quickly tired. She had set out in high spirits, but had been dreadfully weary all the latter part of the journey, and was to go to bed at once. She still coughed, but Mysie was bent on disproving Nurse Halfpenny's assurance that the recovery would not be complete till May, nor was there any doubt of her own air of perfect health.

It was an evening of felicitous chatter, of showing off Christmas cards, of exchanging of news, of building of schemes, the most prominent being that Valetta should be in the constant companionship of Mysie and Fly until her own schoolroom should be re-established. This had been proposed by Lord Rotherwood, and was what the aunts would have found convenient; but apparently this had been settled by Lord Rotherwood and the two little girls, but Lady Rotherwood had not said anything about it, and quoth Mysie, 'Somehow things don't happen till Lady Rotherwood settles them, and then they always do.'

'And shall I like Miss Elbury?' asked Valetta.

'Yes, if—if you take pains,' said Mysie; 'but you mustn't bother her with questions in the middle of a lesson, or she tells you not to chatter. She likes to have them all kept for the end; and then, if they aren't foolish, she will take lots of trouble.'

'Oh, I hate that!' said Valetta. 'I shouldn't remember them, and I like to have done with it. Then she is not like Miss Vincent?'

'Oh no! She couldn't be dear Miss Vincent; but, indeed, she is very kind and nice.'

'How did you get on altogether, Mysie! Wasn't it horrid?' asked Gillian.

'I was afraid it was going to be horrid,' said Mysie. 'You see, it wasn't like going in holiday time as it was before. We had to be almost always in the schoolroom; and there were lots of lessons—more for me than Fly.'

'Just like a horrid old governess to slake her thirst on you,' put in Fergus; and though his aunts shook their heads at him, they did not correct him.

'And one had to sit bolt upright all the time, and never twist one's ankles,' continued Mysie; 'and not speak except French and German—good, mind! It wouldn't do to say, "La jambe du table est sur mon exercise?"'

'Oh, oh! No wonder Fly got ill!'

'Fly didn't mind one bit. French and German come as naturally to her as the days of the week, and they really begin to come to me in the morningnow when I see Miss Elbury.'

'But have you to go on all day?' asked Valetta disconsolately.

'Oh no! Not after one o'clock.'

'And you didn't say that mamma thinks it only leads to slovenly bad grammar!' said Gillian.

'That would have been impertinent,' said Mysie; 'and no one would have minded either.'

'Did you never play?'

'We might play after our walk—and after tea; but it had to be quiet play, not real good games, even before Fly was ill—at least we did have some real games when Primrose came over, or when Cousin Rotherwood had us down in his study or in the hall; but Fly got tired, and knocked up very soon even then. Miss Elbury wanted us always to play battledore and shuttlecock, or Les Graces, if we couldn't go out.'

'Horrid woman!' said Valetta.

'No, she isn't horrid,' said Mysie stoutly; 'I only fancied her so when she used to say, "Vos coudes, mademoiselle," or "Redresses-vous," and when she would not let us whisper; but really and truly she was very, very kind, and I came to like her very much and see she was not cross—only thought it right.'

'And redressez-vous has been useful, Mysie,' said Aunt Ada; 'you are as much improved as Gillian.'

'I thought it would be dreadful,' continued Mysie, 'when the grown-ups went out on a round of visits, and we had no drawing-room, and no Cousin Rotherwood; but Cousin Florence came every day, and once she had us to dinner, and that was nice; and once she took us to Beechcroft to see Primrose, and if it was not fine enough for Fly to go out, she came for me, and I went to her cottages with her. Oh, I did like that! And when the whooping-cough came, you can't think how very kind she was, and Miss Elbury too. They both seemed only to think how to make me happy, though I didn't feel ill a bit, except when I whooped, but they seemed so sorry for me, and so pleased that I didn't make more fuss. I couldn't, you know, when poor Fly was so ill. And when she grew better, we were all so glad that somehow it made us all like a sort of a kind of a home together, though it could not be that.'

Mysie's English had scarcely improved, whatever her French had done; but Gillian gathered that she had had far more grievances to overcome, and had met them in a very different spirit from herself.

As to the schoolroom arrangements, which would have been so convenient to the aunts, it was evident that the matter had not yet been decisively settled, though the children took it for granted. It was pretty to see how Mysie was almost devoured by Fergus and Valetta, hanging on either side of her as she sat, and Gillian, as near as they would allow, while the four tongues went on unceasingly.

It was only horrid, Valetta said, that Mysie should sleep in a different house; but almost as much of her company was vouchsafed on the ensuing day, Sunday, for Miss Elbury had relations at Rockquay, and was released for the entire day; and Fly was still so tired in the morning that she was not allowed to get up early in the day.

Her mother, however, came in to go to church with Adeline Mohun, and Gillian, who had heard so much of the great Marchioness, was surprised to see a small slight woman, not handsome, and worn-looking about the eyes. At the first glance, she was plainly dressed; but the eye of a connoisseur like Aunt Ada could detect the exquisiteness of the material and the taste, and the slow soft tone of her voice; and every gesture and phrase showed that she had all her life been in the habit of condescending—in fact, thought Gillian, revolving her recent experience, though Lady Liddesdale and all her set are taller, finer-looking people, they are not one bit so grand—no, not that—but so unapproachable, as I am sure she is. She is gracious, while they are just good-natured!

Aunt Ada was evidently pleased with the graciousness, and highly delighted to have to take this distinguished personage to church. Mysie was with her sisters, Valetta was extremely anxious to take her to the Sunday drawing-room class—whether for the sake of showing her to Mrs. Hablot, or Mrs. Hablot to her, did not appear.

Gillian was glad to be asked to sit with Fly in the meantime. It was a sufficient reason for not repairing to the garden, and she hoped that Kalliope was unaware of her return, little knowing of the replies by which Fergus repaid Alexis for his assistance in mineral hunting. She had no desire to transgress Miss Mohun's desire that no further intercourse should take place till she herself had spoken with Kalliope.

She found little Phyllis Devereux a great deal taller and thinner than the droll childish being who had been so amusing two years before at Silverfold, but eagerly throwing herself into her arms with the same affectionate delight. All the table was spread with pretty books and outlined illuminations waiting to be painted, and some really beautiful illustrated Sunday books; but as Gillian touched the first, Fly cried out, 'Oh, don't! I am so tired of all those things! And this is such a stupid window. I thought at least I should see the people going to church, and this looks at nothing but the old sea and a tiresome garden.'

'That is thought a special advantage,' said Gillian, smiling.

'Then I wish some one had it who liked it!'

'You would not be so near us.'

'No, and that is nice, and very nice for Mysie. How are all the dear beasts at Silverfold—Begum, and all?'

'I am afraid I do not know more about them than Mysie does. Aunt Jane heard this morning that she must go down there to-morrow to meet the health-man and see what he says; but she won't take any of us because of the diphtheria and the scarlet fever being about.'

'Oh dear, how horrid those catching things are! I've not seen Ivinghoe all this winter! Ah! but they are good sometimes! If it had not been for the measles, I should never have had that most delicious time at Silverfold, nor known Mysie. Now, please tell me all about where you have been, and what you have been doing.'

Fly knew some of the younger party that Gillian had met at Rowthorpe; but she was more interested in the revels at Vale Leston, and required a precise description of the theatricals, or still better, of the rehearsals. Never was there a more appreciative audience, of how it all began from Kit Harewood, the young sailor, having sent home a lion's skin from Africa, which had already served for tableaux of Androcles and of Una—how the boy element had insisted on fun, and the child element on fairies, and how Mrs. William Harewood had suggested Midsummer Night's Dream as the only combination of the three essentials, lion, fun, and fairy, and pronounced that education had progressed far enough for the representation to be 'understanded of the people,' at least by the 6th and 7th standards. On the whole, however, comprehension seemed to have been bounded by intense admiration of the little girl fairies, whom the old women appeared to have taken for angels, for one had declared that to hear little Miss Cherry and Miss Katie singing their hymns like the angels they was, was just like Heaven. She must have had an odd notion of 'Spotted snakes with double tongues.' Moreover, effect was added to the said hymns by Uncle Lance behind the scenes.

Then there was the account of how it had been at first intended that Oberon should be represented by little Sir Adrian, with his Bexley cousin, Pearl Underwood, for his Titania; but though she was fairy enough for anything, he turned out so stolid, and uttered 'Well met by moonlight, proud Titania,' the only lines he ever learnt, exactly like a lesson, besides crying whenever asked to study his part, that the attempt had to be given up, and the fairy sovereigns had to be of large size, Mr. Grinstead pronouncing that probably this was intended by Shakespeare, as Titania was a name of Diana, and he combined

Grecian nymphs with English fairies. So Gerald Underwood had to combine the part of Peter Quince (including Thisbe) with that of Oberon, and the queen was offered to Gillian.

'But I had learnt Hermia,' she said, 'and I saw it was politeness, so I wouldn't, and Anna Vanderkist is ever so much prettier, besides being used to acting with Gerald. She did look perfectly lovely, asleep on the moss in the scene Mrs. Grinstead painted and devised for her! There was—'

'Oh! not only the prettiness, I don't care for that. One gets enough of the artistic, but the fun—the dear fun.'

'There was fun enough, I am sure,' said Gillian. 'Puck was Felix—Pearl's brother, you know—eleven years old, so clever, and an awful imp—and he was Moon besides; but the worst of it was that his dog—it was a funny rough terrier at the Vicarage—was so furious at the lion, when Adrian was roaring under the skin, that nobody could hear, and Adrian got frightened, as well he might, and crept out from under it, screaming, and there fell the lion, collapsing flat in the middle of the place. Even Theseus—Major Harewood, you know, who had tried to be as grave as a judge, and so polite to the actors —could not stand that interpolation, as he called it, of "the man in the moon —not to say the dog," came down too soon—Why, Fly—'

For Fly was in such a paroxysm of laughter as to end in a violent fit of coughing, and to bring Lady Rotherwood in, vexed and anxious.

'Oh, mother! it was only—it was only the lion's skin—' and off went Fly, laughing and coughing again.

'I was telling her about the acting or Midsummer Night's Dream at Vale Leston,' explained Gillian.

'I should not have thought that a suitable subject for the day,' said the Marchioness gravely, and Fly's endeavour to say it was her fault for asking about it was silenced by choking; and Gillian found herself courteously dismissed in polite disgrace, and, as she felt, not entirely without justice.

It was a great disappointment that Aunt Jane did not think it well to take any of the young people to their home with her. As she said, she did not believe that they would catch anything; but it was better to be on the safe side, and she fully expected that they would spend most of the day with Mysie and Fly.

'I wish I could go and talk to Kalliope, my dear,' she said to Gillian; 'but I am afraid it must wait another day.'

'Oh, never mind,' said Gillian, as they bade each other good-night at their doors; 'they don't know that I am come home, so they will not expect me.'

CHAPTER XIII. — ST. VALENTINE'S DAY

Miss Mohun came back in the dark after a long day, for once in her life quite jaded, and explaining that the health-officer and the landlord had been by no means agreed, and that nothing could be done till Sir Jasper came home and decided whether to retain the house or not.

All that she was clear about, and which she had telegraphed to Aden, was, that there must be no going back to Silverfold for the present, and she was prepared to begin lodging-hunting as soon as she received an answer.

'And how have you got on?' she asked, thinking all looked rather blank.

'We haven't been to see Fly,' broke out Valetta, 'though she went out on the beach, and Mysie must not stay out after dark, for fear she should cough.'

'Mysie says they are afraid of excitement,' said Gillian gloomily.

'Then you have seen nothing of the others?'

'Yes, I have seen Victoria, said Aunt Adeline, with a meaning smile.

Miss Mohun went up to take off her things, and Gillian followed her, shutting the door with ominous carefulness, and colouring all over.

'Aunt Jane, I ought to tell you. A dreadful thing has happened!'

'Indeed, my dear! What?'

'I have had a valentine.'

'Oh!' repressing a certain inclination to laugh at the bathos from the look of horror and shame in the girl's eyes.

'It is from that miserable Alexis! Oh, I know I brought it on myself, and I have been so wretched and so ashamed all day.'

'Was it so very shocking! Let me see—'

'Oh! I sent it back at once by the post, in an envelope, saying, "Sent by mistake."'

'But what was it like? Surely it was not one of the common shop things?'

'Oh no; there was rather a pretty outline of a nymph or muse, or something of that sort, at the top—drawn, I mean—and verses written below, something about my showing a lodestar of hope, but I barely glanced at it. I hated it too much.'

'I am sorry you were in such a hurry,' said Aunt Jane. 'No doubt it was a shock; but I am afraid you have given more pain than it quite deserved.'

'It was so impertinent!' cried Gillian, in astonished, shame-stricken indignation.

'So it seems to you,' said her aunt, 'and it was very bad taste; but you should remember that this poor lad has grown up in a stratum of society where he may have come to regard this as a suitable opportunity of evincing his gratitude, and perhaps it may be very hard upon him to have this work of his treated as an insult.'

'But you would not have had me keep it and tolerate it?' exclaimed Gillian.

'I can hardly tell without having seen it; but you might have done the thing more civilly, through his sister, or have let me give it back to him. However, it is too late now; I will make a point of seeing Kalliope to-morrow, but in the meantime you really need not be so horribly disgusted and ashamed.'

'I thought he was quite a different sort!'

'Perhaps, after all, your thoughts were not wrong; and he only fancied, poor boy, that he had found a pretty way of thanking you.'

This did not greatly comfort Gillian, who might prefer feeling that she was insulted rather than that she had been cruelly unkind, and might like to blame Alexis rather than herself. And, indeed, in any case, she had sense enough to perceive that this very unacceptable compliment was the consequence of her own act of independence of more experienced heads.

The next person Miss Mohun met was Fergus, lugging upstairs, step by step, a monstrous lump of stone, into which he required her to look and behold a fascinating crevice full of glittering spar.

'Where did you get that, Fergus?'

'Up off the cliff over the quarry.'

'Are you sure that you may have it?'

'Oh yes; White said I might. It's so jolly, auntie! Frank Stebbing is gone away to the other shop in the Apennines, where the old boss lives. What splendiferous specimens he must have the run of! Our Stebbing says 'tis because Kally White makes eyes at him; but any way, White has got to do his work while he's away, and go all the rounds to see that things are right, so I go after him, and he lets me have just what I like—such jolly crystals.'

'I am sure I hope it is all right.'

'Oh yes, I always ask him, as you told me; but he is awfully slow and mopy and down in the mouth to-day. Stebbing says he is sweet upon Gill; but I told him that couldn't be, White knew better. A general's daughter, indeed! and Will remembers his father a sergeant.'

'It is very foolish, Fergus. Say no more about it, for it is not nice talk about your sister.'

'I'll lick any one who does,' said Fergus, bumping his stone up another step.

Poor Aunt Jane! There was more to fall on her as soon as the door was finally shut on the two rooms communicating with one another, which the sisters called their own. Mrs. Mount's manipulations of Miss Adeline's rich brown hair were endured with some impatience, while Miss Mohun leant back in her chair in her shawl-patterned dressing-gown, watching, with a sort of curious wonder and foreboding, the restlessness that proved that something was in store, and meantime somewhat lazily brushing out her own thinner darker locks.

'You are tired, Miss Jane,' said the old servant, using the pet name in private moments. 'You had better let me do your hair.'

'No, thank you, Fanny; I have very nearly done,' she said, marking the signs of eagerness on her sister's part. 'Oh, by the bye, did that hot bottle go down to Lilian Giles?'

'Yes, ma'am; Mrs. Giles came up for it.'

'Did she say whether Lily was well enough to see Miss Gillian?'

Mrs. Mount coughed a peculiar cough that her mistresses well knew to signify that she could tell them something they would not like to hear, if they chose to ask her, and it was the younger who put the question—

'Fanny, did she say anything?'

'Well, Miss Ada, I told her she must be mistaken, but she stuck to it, though she said she never would have breathed a word if Miss Gillian had not come back again, but she thought you should know it.'

'Know what?' demanded Jane.

'Well, Miss Jane, she should say 'tis the talk that Miss Gillian, when you have thought her reading to the poor girl, has been running down to the works —and 'tis only the ignorance of them that will talk, but they say it is to meet a young man. She says, Mrs. Giles do, that she never would have noticed such talk, but that the young lady did always seem in a hurry, only just reading a chapter, and never stopping to talk to poor Lily after it; and she has seen her herself going down towards the works, instead of towards home, ma'am. And she said she could not bear that reading to her girl should be made a colour for such doings.'

'Certainly not, if it were as she supposes,' said Miss Mohun, sitting very upright, and beating her own head vigorously with a very prickly brush; 'but you may tell her, Fanny, that I know all about it, and that her friend is Miss White, who you remember spent an evening here.'

Fanny's good-humoured face cleared up. 'Yes, ma'am, I told her that I was quite sure that Miss Gillian would not go for to do anything wrong, and that it could be easy explained; but people has tongues, you see.'

'You were quite right to tell us, Fanny. Good-night.'

'People has tongues!' repeated Adeline, when that excellent person had disappeared. 'Yes, indeed, they have. But, Jenny, do you really mean to say that you know all about this?'

'Yes, I believe so.'

'Oh, I wish you had been at home to-day when Victoria came in. It really is a serious business.'

'Victoria! What has she to do with it? I should have thought her Marchioness-ship quite out of the region of gossip, though, for that matter, grandees like it quite as much as other people.'

'Don't, Jane, you know it does concern her through companionship for Phyllis, and she was very kind.'

'Oh yes, I can see her sailing in, magnificently kind from her elevation. But how in the world did she manage to pick up all this in the time?' said poor Jane, tired and pestered into the sharpness of her early youth.

'Dear Jenny, I wish I had said nothing to-night. Do wait till you are rested.'

'I am not in the least tired, and if I were, do you think I could sleep with this half told?'

'You said you knew.'

'Then it is only about Gillian being so silly as to go down to Miss White's office at the works to look over the boy's Greek exercises.'

'You don't mean that you allowed it!'

'No, Gillian's impulsiveness, just like her mother's, began it, as a little assertion of modern independence; but while she was away that little step from brook to river brought her to the sense that she had been a goose, and had used me rather unfairly, and so she came and confessed it all to me on the way home from the station the first morning after her return. She says she had written it all to her mother from the first.'

'I wonder Lily did not telegraph to put a stop to it.'

'Do you suppose any mother, our poor old Lily especially, can marry a couple of daughters without being slightly frantic! Ten to one she never realised that this precious pupil was bigger than Fergus. But do tell me what my Lady had heard, and how she heard it.'

'You remember that her governess, Miss Elbury, has connections in the place.'

'"The most excellent creature in the world." Oh yes, and she spent Sunday with them. So that was the conductor.'

'I can hardly say that Miss Elbury was to be blamed, considering that she had heard the proposal about Valetta! It seems that that High School class-mistress, Miss Mellon, who had the poor child under her, is her cousin.'

'Oh dear!'

'It is exactly what I was afraid of when we decided on keeping Valetta at home. Miss Mellon told all the Caesar story in plainly the worst light for poor Val, and naturally deduced from her removal that she was the most to blame.'

'Whereas it was Miss Mellon herself! But nobody could expect Victoria to see that, and no doubt she is quite justified in not wishing for the child in her schoolroom! But, after all, Valetta is only a child; it won't hurt her to have this natural recoil of consequences, and her mother will be at home in three weeks' time. It signifies much more about Gillian. Did I understand you that the gossip about her had reached those august ears?'

'Oh yes, Jane, and it is ever so much worse. That horrid Miss Mellon seems to have told Miss Elbury that Gillian has a passion for low company, that she is always running after the Whites at the works, and has secret meetings with the young man in the garden on Sunday, while his sister carries on her underhand flirtation with another youth, Frank Stebbing, I suppose. It really was too preposterous, and Victoria said she had no doubt from the first that there was exaggeration, and had told Miss Elbury so; but still she thought Gillian must have been to blame. She was very nice about it, and listened to all my explanation most kindly, as to Gillian's interest in the Whites, and its having been only the sister that she met, but plainly she is not half convinced. I heard something about a letter being left for Gillian, and really, I don't know whether there may not be more discoveries to come. I never felt before the force of our dear father's saying, apropos of Rotherwood himself, that no one knows what it is to lose a father except those who have the care of his children.'

'Whatever Gillian did was innocent and ladylike, and nothing to be ashamed of,' said Aunt Jane stoutly; 'of that I am sure. But I should like to be equally sure that she has not turned the head of that poor foolish young man, without in the least knowing what she was about. You should have seen her state of mind at his sending her a valentine, which she returned to him, perfectly ferociously, at once, and that was all the correspondence somebody seems to have smelt out.'

'A valentine! Gillian must have behaved very ill to have brought that upon herself! Oh dear! I wish she had never come here; I wish Lily could have stayed at home, instead of scattering her children about the world. The Rotherwoods will never get over it.'

'That's the least part of the grievance, in my eyes,' said her sister. 'It won't make a fraction of difference to the dear old cousin Rotherwood; and as to my Lady, it is always a liking from the teeth outwards.'

'How can you say so! I am sure she has always been most cordial.'

'Most correct, if you please. Oh, did she say anything about Mysie?'

'She said nothing but good of Mysie; called her delightful, and perfectly good and trustworthy, said they could never have got so well through Phyllis's illness without her, and that they only wished to keep her altogether.'

'I dare say, to be humble companion to my little lady, out of the way of her wicked sisters.'

'Jane!'

'My dear, I don't think I can stand any more defence of her just now! No, she is an admirable woman, I know. That's enough. I really must go to bed, and consider which is to be faced first, she or Kalliope.'

It was lucky that Miss Mohun could exist without much sleep, for she was far too much worried for any length of slumber to visit her that night, though she was afoot as early as usual. She thought it best to tell Gillian that Lady Rotherwood had heard some foolish reports, and that she was going to try to clear them up, and she extracted an explicit account as to what the extent of her intercourse with the Whites had been, which was given willingly, Gillian being in a very humble frame, and convinced that she had acted foolishly. It surprised her likewise that Aunt Adeline, whom she had liked the best, and thought the most good-natured, was so much more angry with her than Aunt Jane, who, as she felt, forgave her thoroughly, and was only anxious to help her out of the scrape she had made for herself.

Miss Mohun thought her best time for seeing Kalliope would be in the dinner-hour, and started accordingly in the direction of the marble works. Not far from them she met that young person walking quickly with one of her little brothers.

'I was coming to see you,' Miss Mohun said. 'I did not know that you went home in the middle of the day.'

'My mother has been so unwell of late that I do not like to be entirely out of reach all day,' returned Kalliope, who certainly looked worn and sorrowful; 'so I manage to run home, though it is but for a quarter of an hour.'

'I will not delay you, I will walk with you,' and when Petros had been dismissed, 'I am afraid my niece has not been quite the friend to you that she intended.'

'Oh, Miss Mohun, do you know all about it? It is such a relief! I have felt so guilty towards you, and yet I did not know what to do.'

'I have never thought that the concealment was your fault,' said Jane.

'I did think at first that you knew,' said Kalliope, 'and when I found that was not the case, I suppose I should have insisted on your being told; but I could not bear to seem ungrateful, and my brother took such extreme delight in his lessons and Miss Merrifield's kindness, that—that I could not bear to do what might prevent them. And now, poor fellow, it shows how wrong it was, since he has ventured on that unfortunate act of presumption, which has so offended her. Oh, Miss Mohun, he is quite broken-hearted.'

'I am afraid Gillian was very discourteous. I was out, or it should not have been done so unkindly. Indeed, in the shock, Gillian did not recollect that she might be giving pain.'

'Yes, yes! Poor Alexis! He has not had any opportunity of understanding how different things are in your class of life, and he thought it would show his gratitude and—and—Oh, he is so miserable!' and she was forced to stop to wipe away her tears.

'Poor fellow! But it was one of those young men's mistakes that are got over and outgrown, so you need not grieve over it so much, my dear. My brother-in-law is on his way home, and I know he means to see what can be done for Alexis, for your father's sake.'

'Oh, Miss Mohun, how good you are! I thought you could never forgive us. And people do say such shocking things.'

'I know they do, and therefore I am going to ask you to tell me exactly what intercourse there has been with Gillian.'

Kalliope did so, and Miss Mohun was struck with the complete accordance of the two accounts, and likewise by the total absence of all attempt at self-justification on Miss White's part. If she had in any way been weak, it had been against her will, and her position had been an exceedingly difficult one. She spoke in as guarded a manner as possible; but to such acute and experienced ears as those of her auditor, it was impossible not to perceive that, while Gillian had been absolutely simple, and unconscious of all but a kind act of patronage, the youth's imagination had taken fire, and he had become her ardent worshipper; with calf-love, no doubt, but with a distant, humble adoration, which had, whether fortunately or unfortunately, for once found expression in the valentine so summarily rejected. The drawing and the composition had been the work of many days, and so much against his sister's protest that it had been sent without her knowledge, after she had thought it given up. She had only extracted the confession through his uncontrollable despair, which made him almost unfit to attend to his increased work, perhaps by his southern nature exaggerated.

'The stronger at first, the sooner over,' thought Miss Mohun; but she knew that consolation betraying her comprehension would not be safe.

One further discovery she made, namely, that on Sunday, Alexis, foolish lad, had been so wildly impatient at their having had no notice from Gillian since her return, that he had gone to the garden to explain, as he said, his sister's non-appearance there, since she was detained by her mother's illness. It was the only time he had ever been there, and he had met no one; but Miss Mohun felt a sinking of heart at the foreboding that the mauvaises langues would get hold of it.

The only thing to be decided on was that there must be a suspension of intercourse, at any rate, till Lady Merrifield's arrival; not in unkindness, but as best for all. And, indeed, Kalliope had no time to spare from her mother, whose bloated appearance, poor woman, was the effect of long-standing disease.

The daughter's heart was very full of her, and evidently it would have been a comfort to discuss her condition with this kind friend; but no more delay was possible; and Miss Mohun had to speed home, in a quandary how much or how little about Alexis's hopeless passion should be communicated to its object, and finally deciding that Gillian had better only be informed that he had been greatly mortified by the rude manner of rejection, but that the act itself proved that she must abstain from all renewal of the intercourse till her parents should return.

But that was not all the worry of the day. Miss Mohun had still to confront Lady Rotherwood, and, going as soon as the early dinner was over, found the Marchioness resting after an inspection of houses in Rockquay. She did not like hotels, she said, and she thought the top of the cliff too bleak for Phyllis, so that they must move nearer the sea if the place agreed with her at all, which was doubtful. Miss Mohun was pretty well convinced that the true objection was the neighbourhood of Beechcroft Cottage. She said she had come to give some explanation of what had been said to her sister yesterday.

'Oh, my dear Jane, Adeline told me all about it yesterday. I am very sorry for you to have had such a charge, but what could you expect of girls cast about as they have been, always with a marching regiment?'

'I do not think Mysie has given you any reason to think her ill brought up.'

'A little uncouth at first, but that was all. Oh, no! Mysie is a dear little girl. I should be very glad to have her with Phyllis altogether, and so would Rotherwood. But she was very young when Sir Jasper retired.'

'And Valetta was younger. Poor little girl! She was naughty, but I do not think she understood the harm of what she was doing.'

Lady Rotherwood smiled.

'Perhaps not; but she must have been deeply involved, since she was the one amongst all the guilty to be expelled.'

'Oh, Victoria! Was that what you heard?'

'Miss Elbury heard it from the governess she was under. Surely she was the only one not permitted to go up for the examination and removed.'

'True, but that was our doing—no decree of the High School. Her own governess is free now, and her mother on her way, and we thought she had better not begin another term. Yes, Victoria, I quite see that you might doubt her fitness to be much with Phyllis. I am not asking for that—I shall try to get her own governess to come at once; but for the child's sake and her mother's I should like to get this cleared up. May I see Miss Elbury?'

'Certainly; but I do not think you will find that she has exaggerated, though of course her informant may have done so.

Miss Elbury was of the older generation of governesses, motherly, kind, but rather prim and precise, the accomplished element being supplied with diplomaed foreigners, who, since Lady Phyllis's failure in health, had been dispensed with. She was a good and sensible woman, as Jane could see, in spite of the annoyance her report had occasioned, and it was impossible not to assent when she said she had felt obliged, under the circumstances, to mention to Lady Rotherwood what her cousin had told her.

'About both my nieces,' said Jane. 'Yes, I quite understand. But, though of course the little one's affair is the least important, we had better get to the bottom of that first, and I should like to tell you what really happened.'

She told her story, and how Valetta had been tempted and then bullied into going beyond the first peeps, and finding she did not produce the impression she wished, she begged Miss Elbury to talk it over with the head-mistress. It was all in the telling. Miss Elbury's young cousin, Miss Mellon, had been brought under rebuke, and into great danger of dismissal, through Valetta Merrifield's lapse; and it was no wonder that she had warned her kinswoman against 'the horrid little deceitful thing,' who had done so much harm to the whole class. 'Miss Mohun was running about over the whole place, but not knowing what went on in her own house!' And as to Miss White, Miss Elbury mentioned at last, though with some reluctance, that it was believed that she had been on the point of a private marriage, and of going to Italy with young Stebbing, when her machinations were detected, and he was forced to set off without her.

With this in her mind, the governess could not be expected to accept as satisfactory what was not entire confutation or contradiction, and Miss Mohun saw that, politely as she was listened to, it was all only treated as excuse; since there could be no denial of Gillian's folly, and it was only a question of degree.

And, provoking as it was, the disappointment might work well for Valetta. The allegations against Gillian were a far more serious affair, but much more of these could be absolutely disproved and contradicted; in fact, all that Miss Mohun herself thought very serious, i.e. the flirtation element, was shown to be absolutely false, both as regarded Gillian and Kalliope; but it was quite another thing to convince people who knew none of the parties, when there was the residuum of truth undeniable, that there had been secret meetings not only with the girl, but the youth. To acquit Gillian of all but modern independence and imprudent philanthropy was not easy to any one who did not understand her character, and though Lady Rotherwood said nothing more in the form of censure, it was evident that she was unconvinced that Gillian was not a fast and flighty girl, and that she did not desire more contact than was necessary.

No doubt she wished herself farther off! Lord Rotherwood, she said, was coming down in a day or two, when he could get away, and then they should decide whether to take a house or to go abroad, which, after all, might be the best thing for Phyllis.

'He will make all the difference,' said Miss Adeline, when the unsatisfactory conversation was reported to her.

'I don't know! But even if he did, and I don't think he will, I won't have

Valetta waiting for his decision and admitted on sufferance.'

'Shall you send her back to school?'

'No. Poor Miss Vincent is free, and quite ready to come here. Fergus shall go and sleep among his fossils in the lumber-room, and I will write to her at once. She will be much better here than waiting at Silverton, though the Hacketts are very kind to her.'

'Yes, it will be better to be independent. But all this is very unfortunate. However, Victoria will see for herself what the children are. She has asked me to take a drive with her to-morrow if it is not too cold.'

'Oh yes, she is not going to make an estrangement. You need not fear that, Ada. She does not think it your fault.'

Aunt Jane pondered a little as to what to say to the two girls, and finally resolved that Valetta had better be told that she was not to do lessons with Fly, as her behaviour had made Lady Rotherwood doubt whether she was a good companion. Valetta stamped and cried, and said it was very hard and cross when she had been so sorry and every one had forgiven her; but Gillian joined heartily with Aunt Jane in trying to make the child understand that consequences often come in spite of pardon and repentance. To Gillian herself, Aunt Jane said as little as possible, not liking even to give the veriest hint of the foolish gossip, or of the extent of poor Alexis White's admiration; for it was enough for the girl to know that concealment had brought her under a cloud, and she was chiefly concerned as to how her mother would look on it. She had something of Aunt Jane's impatience of patronage, and perhaps thought it snobbish to seem concerned at the great lady's displeasure.

Mysie was free to run in and out to her sisters, but was still to do her lessons with Miss Elbury, and Fly took up more of her time than the sisters liked. Neither she nor Fly were formally told why their castles vanished into empty air, but there certainly was a continual disappointment and fret on both sides, which Fly could not bear as well as when she was in high health, and poor Mysie's loving heart often found it hard to decide between her urgent claims and those of Valetta!

But was not mamma coming? and papa? Would not all be well then? Yes, hearts might bound at the thought. But where was Gillian's great thing?'

Miss Vincent's coming was really like a beginning of home, in spite of her mourning and depressed look. It was a great consolation to the lonely woman to find how all her pupils flew at her, with infinite delight. She had taken pains to bring a report of all the animals for Valetta, and she duly admired all Fergus's geological specimens, and even undertook to print labels for them.

Mysie would have liked to begin lessons again with her; but this would have been hard on Fly, and besides, her mother had committed her to the Rotherwoods, and it was better still to leave her with them.

The aunts were ready with any amount of kindness and sympathy for the governess's bereavement, and her presence was a considerable relief in the various perplexities.

Even Lady Rotherwood and Miss Elbury had been convinced, and by no means unwillingly, that Gillian had been less indiscreet than had been their first impression; but she had been a young lady of the period in her independence, and was therefore to be dreaded. No more garden trysts would have been possible under any circumstances, for the house and garden were in full preparation for the master, who was to meet Lord Rotherwood to consult about the proposed water-works and other designs for the benefit of the town where they were the chief landowners.

CHAPTER XIV. — THE PARTNER

The expected telegram arrived two days later, requesting Miss Mohun to find a lodging at Rockstone sufficient to contain Sir Jasper and Lady Merrifield, and a certain amount of sons and daughters, while they considered what was to be done about Silverfold.

'So you and I will go out house-hunting, Gillian?' said Aunt Jane, when she had opened it, and the exclamations were over.

'I am afraid there is no house large enough up here,' said her sister.

'No, it is an unlucky time, in the thick of the season.'

'Victoria said she had been looking at some houses in Bellevue.'

'I am afraid she will have raised the prices of them.'

'But, oh, Aunt Jane, we couldn't go to Bellevue Church!' cried Gillian.

'Your mother would like to be so near the daily services at the Kennel,' said Miss Mohun. 'Yes, we must begin with those houses. There's nothing up here but Sorrento, and I have heard enough of its deficiencies!'

At that moment in came a basket of game, grapes, and flowers, with Lady Rotherwood's compliments.

'Solid pudding,' muttered Miss Mohun. 'In this case, I should almost prefer empty praise. Look here, Ada, what a hamper they must have had from home! I think I shall, as I am going that way, take a pheasant and some grapes to the poor Queen of the White Ants; I believe she is really ill, and it will show that we do not want to neglect them.'

'Oh, thank you, Aunt Jane!' cried Gillian, the colour rising in her face, and she was the willing bearer of the basket as she walked down the steps with her aunt, and along the esplanade, only pausing to review the notices of palatial, rural, and desirable villas in the house-agent's window, and to consider in what proportion their claims to perfection might be reduced.

As they turned down Ivinghoe Terrace, and were approaching the rusty garden-gate, they overtook Mrs. Lee, the wife of the organist of St. Kenelm's, who lodged at Mrs. White's. In former times, before her marriage, Mrs. Lee had been a Sunday-school teacher at St. Andrew's, and though party spirit considered her to have gone over to the enemy, there were old habits of friendly confidence between her and Miss Mohun, and there was an exchange of friendly greetings and inquiries. When she understood their errand she rejoiced in it, saying that poor Mrs. White was very poorly, and rather fractious, and that this supply would be most welcome both to her and her daughter.

'Ah, I am afraid that poor girl goes through a great deal!'

'Indeed she does, Miss Mohun; and a better girl never lived. I cannot think how she can bear up as she does; there she is at the office all day with her work, except when she runs home in the middle of the day—all that distance to dish up something her mother can taste, for there's no dependence on the girl, nor on little Maura neither. Then she is slaving early and late to keep the house in order as well as she can, when her mother is fretting for her attention; and I believe she loses more than half her night's rest over the old lady. How she bears up, I cannot guess; and never a cross word to her mother, who is such a trial, nor to the boys, but looking after their clothes and their lessons, and keeping them as good and nice as can be. I often say to my husband, I am sure it is a lesson to live in the house with her.'

'I am sure she is an excellent girl,' said Miss Mohun. 'I wish we could do anything to help her.'

'I know you are a real friend, Miss Mohun, and never was there any young person who was in greater need of kindness; though it is none of her fault. She can't help her face, poor dear; and she has never given any occasion, I am sure, but has been as guarded and correct as possible.'

'Oh, I was in hopes that annoyance was suspended at least for a time!'

'You are aware of it then, Miss Mohun? Yes, the young gentleman is come back, not a bit daunted. Yesterday evening what does he do but drive up in a cab with a great bouquet, and a basketful of grapes, and what not! Poor Kally, she ran in to me, and begged me as a favour to come downstairs with her, and I could do no less. And I assure you, Miss Mohun, no queen could be more dignified, nor more modest than she was in rejecting his gifts, and keeping him in check. Poor dear, when he was gone she burst out crying—a thing I never knew of her before; not that she cared for him, but she felt it a cruel wrong to her poor mother to send away the grapes she longed after; and so she will feel these just a providence.'

'Then is Mrs. White confined to her room?'

'For more than a fortnight. For that matter the thing was easier, for she had encouraged the young man as far as in her lay, poor thing, though my husband and young Alexis both told her what they knew of him, and that it would not be for Kally's happiness, let alone the offence to his father.'

'Then it really went as far as that?'

'Miss Mohun, I would be silent as the grave if I did not know that the old lady went talking here and there, never thinking of the harm she was doing. She was so carried away by the idea of making a lady of Kally. She says she was a beauty herself, though you would not think it now, and she is perfectly puffed up about Kally. So she actually lent an ear when the young man came persuading Kally to get married and go off to Italy with him, where he made sure he could come over Mr. White with her beauty and relationship and all— among the myrtle groves—that was his expression—where she would have an association worthy of her. I don't quite know how he meant it to be brought about, but he is one who would stick at nothing, and of course Kally would not hear of it, and answered him so as one would think he would never have had the face to address her again, but poor Mrs. White has done nothing but fret over it, and blame her daughter for undutifulness, and missing the chance of making all their fortunes—breaking her heart and her health, and I don't know what besides. She is half a foreigner, you see, and does not understand, and she is worse than no one to that poor girl.'

'And you say he is come back as bad as ever.'

'Or worse, you may say, Miss Mohun; absence seems only to have set him the more upon her, and I am afraid that Mrs. White's talk, though it may not have been to many, has been enough to set it about the place; and in cases like that, it is always the poor young woman as gets the blame—especially with the gentleman's own people.'

'I am afraid so.'

'And you see she is in a manner at his mercy, being son to one of the heads of the firm, and in a situation of authority.'

'What can she do all day at the office?'

'She keeps one or two of the other young ladies working with her,' said Mrs. Lee; 'but if any change could be made, it would be very happy for her; though, after all, I do not see how she could leave this place, the house being family property, and Mr. White their relation, besides that Mrs. White is in no state to move; but, on the other hand, Mr. and Mrs. Stebbing know their son is after her, and the lady would not stick at believing or saying anything against her, though I will always bear witness, and so will Mr. Lee, that never was there a more good, right-minded young woman, or more prudent and guarded.'

'So would Mr. Flight and his mother, I have no doubt.'

'Mr. Flight would, Miss Mohun, but'—with an odd look—'I fancy my lady thinks poor Kally too handsome for it to be good for a young clergyman to have much to say to her. They have not been so cordial to them of late, but that is partly owing to poor Mrs. White's foolish talk, and in part to young Alexis having been desultory and mopy of late—not taking the interest in his music he did. Mr. Lee says he is sure some young woman is at the bottom of it.'

Miss Mohun saw her niece's ears crimson under her hat, and was afraid Mrs. Lee would likewise see them. They had reached the front of the house, and she made haste to take out a visiting-card and to beg Mrs. Lee kindly to give it with the basket, saying that she would not give trouble by coming to the door.

And then she turned back with Gillian, who was in a strange tumult of shame and consternation, yet withal, feeling that first strange thrill of young womanhood at finding itself capable of stirring emotion, and too much overcome by these strange sensations—above all by the shock of shame—to be able to utter a word.

I must make light of it, but not too light, thought Miss Mohun, and she broke the ice by saying, 'Poor foolish boy—'

'Oh, Aunt Jane, what shall I do?'

'Let it alone, my dear.'

'But that I should have done so much harm and upset him so'—in a voice betraying a certain sense of being flattered. 'Can't I do anything to undo it?'

'Certainly not. To be perfectly quiet and do nothing is all you can do. My dear, boys and young men have such foolish fits—more in that station than in ours, because they have none of the public school and college life which keeps people out of it. You were the first lady this poor fellow was brought into contact with, and—well, you were rather a goose, and he has been a greater one; but if he is let alone, he will recover and come to his senses. I could tell you of men who have had dozens of such fits. I am much more interested about his sister. What a noble girl she is!'

'Oh, isn't she, Aunt Jane. Quite a real heroine! And now mamma is coming, she will know what to do for her!'

'I hope she will, but it is a most perplexing case altogether.'

'And that horrid young Stebbing is come back too. I am glad she has that nice Mrs. Lee to help her.'

'And to defend her,' added Miss Mohun. 'Her testimony is worth a great deal, and I am glad to know where to lay my hand upon it. And here is our first house, "Les Rochers." For Madame de Sevigne's sake, I hope it will do!'

But it didn't! Miss Mohun got no farther than the hall before she detected a scent of gas; and they had to betake themselves to the next vacant abode. The investigating nature had full scope in the various researches that she made into parlour, kitchen, and hall, desperately wearisome to Gillian, whose powers were limited to considering how the family could sit at ease in the downstairs rooms, how they could be stowed away in the bedrooms, and where there were the prettiest views of the bay. Aunt Jane, becoming afraid that while she was literally 'ferreting' in the offices Gillian might be meditating on her conquest, picked up the first cheap book that looked innocently sensational, and left her to study it on various sofas. And when daylight failed for inspections, Gillian still had reason to rejoice in the pastime devised for her, since there was an endless discussion at the agent's, over the only two abodes that could be made available, as to prices, repairs, time, and terms. They did not get away till it was quite dark and the gas lighted, and Miss Mohun did not think the ascent of the steps desirable, so that they went round by the street.

'I declare,' exclaimed Miss Mohun, 'there's Mr. White's house lighted up. He must be come!'

'I wonder whether he will do anything for Kalliope,' sighed Gillian.

'Oh, Jenny,' exclaimed Miss Adeline, as the two entered the drawing-room. 'You have had such a loss; Rotherwood has been here waiting to see you for an hour, and such an agreeable man he brought with him!'

'Who could it have been?'

'I didn't catch his name—Rotherwood was mumbling in his quick way— indeed, I am not sure he did not think I knew him. A distinguished-looking man, like a picture, with a fine white beard, and he was fresh from Italy; told me all about the Carnival and the curious ceremonies in the country villages.'

'From Italy? It can't have been Mr. White.'

'Mr. White! My dear Jane! this was a gentleman—quite a grand-looking man. He might have been an Italian nobleman, only he spoke English too well for that, though I believe those diplomates can speak all languages. However, you will see, for we are to go and dine with them at eight o'clock—you, and I, and Gillian.'

'You, Ada!'

'Oh! I have ordered the chair round; it won't hurt me with the glasses up. Gillian, my dear, you must put on the white dress that Mrs. Grinstead's maid did up for you—it is quite simple, and I should like you to look nice! Well— oh, how tired you both look! Ring for some fresh tea, Gillian. Have you found a house?'

So excited and occupied was Adeline that the house-hunting seemed to have assumed quite a subordinate place in her mind. It really was an extraordinary thing for her to dine out, though this was only a family party next door; and she soon sailed away to hold counsel with Mrs. Mount on dresses and wraps, and to get her very beautiful hair dressed. She made by far the most imposing appearance of the three when they shook themselves out in the ante-room at the hotel, in her softly-tinted sheeny pale-gray dress, with pearls in her hair, and two beautiful blush roses in her bosom; while her sister, in black satin and coral, somehow seemed smaller than ever, probably from being tired, and from the same cause Gillian had dark marks under her brown eyes, and a much more limp and languid look than was her wont.

Fly was seated on her father's knee, looking many degrees better and brighter, as if his presence were an elixir of life, and when he put her down to greet the arrivals, both she and Mysie sprang to Gillian to ask the result of the quest of houses. The distinguished friend was there, and was talking to Lady Rotherwood about Italian progress, and there was only time for an inquiry and reply as to the success of the search for a house before dinner was announced —the little girls disappeared, and the Marquess gave his arm to his eldest cousin.

'Grand specimen of marble, isn't he!' he muttered.

'Ada hasn't the least idea who he is. She thinks him a great diplomate,' communicated Jane in return, and her arm received an ecstatic squeeze.

It was amusing to Jane Mohun to see how much like a dinner at Rotherwood this contrived to be, with my lady's own footman, and my lord's valet waiting in state. She agreed mentally with her sister that the other guest was a very fine-looking man, with a picturesque head, and he did not seem at all out of place or ill-at-ease in the company in which he found himself. Lord Rotherwood, with a view, perhaps, to prolonging Adeline's mystification, turned the conversation to Italian politics, and the present condition and the industries of the people, on all of which subjects much ready information was given in fluent, good English, with perhaps rather unnecessarily fine words. It was only towards the end of the dinner that a personal experience was mentioned about the impossibility of getting work done on great feast days, or of knowing which were the greater—and the great dislike of the peasant mind to new methods.

When it came to 'At first, I had to superintend every blasting with gelatine,' the initiated were amused at the expression of Adeline's countenance, and the suppressed start of frightful conviction that quivered on her eyelids and the corners of her mouth, though kept in check by good breeding, and then smoothed out into a resolute complacency, which convinced her sister that having inadvertently exalted the individual into the category of the distinguished, she meant to abide staunchly by her first impression.

Lady Rotherwood, like most great ladies in public life, was perfectly well accustomed to have all sorts of people brought home to dinner, and would have been far less astonished than her cousins at sitting down with her grocer; but she gave the signal rather early, and on reaching the sitting-room, where Miss Elworthy was awaiting them, said—

'We will leave them to discuss their water-works at their ease. Certainly residence abroad is an excellent education.'

'A very superior man,' said Adeline.

'Those self-made men always are.'

'In the nature of things, added Miss Mohun, 'or they would not have mounted.'

'It is the appendages that are distressing,' said Lady Rotherwood, 'and they seldom come in one's way. Has this man left any in Italy?'

'Oh no, none alive. He took his wife there for her health, and that was the way he came to set up his Italian quarries; but she and his child both died there long ago, and he has never come back to this place since,' explained Ada.

'But he has relations here,' said Jane. 'His cousin was an officer in Jasper Merrifield's regiment.'

She hoped to have been saying a word in the cause of the young people, but she regretted her attempt, for Lady Rotherwood replied—

'I have heard of them. A very undeserving family, are they not?'

Gillian, whom Miss Elworthy was trying to entertain, heard, and could not help colouring all over, face, neck, and ears, all the more for so much hating the flush and feeling it observed.

Miss Mohun's was a very decided, 'I should have said quite the reverse.'

'Indeed! Well, I heard the connection lamented, for his sake, by—what was her name? Mrs. Stirling—or—'

'Mrs. Stebbing,' said Adeline. 'You don't mean that she has actually called on you?'

'Is there any objection to her?' asked Lady Rotherwood, with a glance to see whether the girl was listening.

'Oh no, no! only he is a mere mason—or quarryman, who has grown rich,' said Adeline.

The hostess gave a little dry laugh.

'Is that all? I thought you had some reason for disapproving of her. I thought her rather sensible and pleasing.'

Cringing and flattering, thought Jane; and that is just what these magnificent ladies like in the wide field of inferiors. But aloud she could not help saying, 'My principal objection to Mrs. Stebbing is that I have always thought her rather a gossip—on the scandalous side.' Then, bethinking herself that it would not be well to pursue the subject in Gillian's presence, she explained where the Stebbings lived, and asked how long Lord Rotherwood could stay.

'Only over Sunday. He is going to look over the place to-morrow, and next day there is to be a public meeting about it. I am not sure that we shall not go with him. I do not think the place agrees with Phyllis.'

The last words were spoken just as the two gentlemen had come in from the dining-room, rather sooner than was expected, and they were taken up.

'Agrees with Phyllis! She looks pounds—nay, hundred-weights better than when we left home. I mean to have her down to-morrow on the beach for a lark—castle-building, paddling—with Mysie and Val, and Fergus and all. That's what would set her up best, wouldn't it, Jane?'

Jane gave a laughing assent, wondering how much of this would indeed prove castle-building, though adding that Fergus was at school, and that it was not exactly the time of year for paddling.

'Oh, ah, eh! Well, perhaps not—forestalling sweet St. Valentine—stepping into their nests they paddled. Though St. Valentine is past, and I thought our fortunes had been made, Mr. White, by calling this the English Naples, and what not.'

'Those are the puffs, my lord. There is a good deal of difference even between this and Rocca Marina, which is some way up the mountain.'

'It must be very beautiful,' said Miss Ada.

'Well, Miss Mohun, people do say it is striking.' And he was drawn into describing the old Italian mansion, purchased on the extinction of an ancient family of nobles, perched up on the side of a mountain, whose feet the sea laved, with a terrace whence there was a splendid view of the Gulf of Genoa, and fine slopes above and below of chestnut-trees and vineyards; and therewith he gave a hearty invitation to the company present to visit him there if ever they went to Italy, when he would have great pleasure in showing them many bits of scenery, and curious remains that did not fall in the way of ordinary tourists.

Lady Rotherwood gratefully said she should remember the invitation if they went to the south, as perhaps they should do that very spring.

'And,' said Ada, 'you are not to be expected to remain long in this climate when you have a home like that awaiting you.'

'Don't call it home, Miss Mohun,' he said. 'I have not had that these many years; but I declare, the first sound of our county dialect, when I got out at the station, made my heart leap into my mouth. I could have shaken hands with the fellow.'

'Then I hope you will remain here for some time. There is much wanting to be set going,' said Jane.

'So I thought of doing, and I had out a young fellow, who I thought might take my place—my partner's son, young Stebbing. They wrote that he had been learning Italian, with a view to being useful to me, and so on; but when he came out, what was he but a fine gentleman—never had put his hand to a pick, nor a blasting-iron; and as to his Italian, he told me it was the Italian of Alfieri and Leopardi. Leopardi's Italian it might be, for it was a very mottled or motley tongue, but he might as well have talked English or Double-Dutch to our hands, or better, for they had picked up the meaning of some orders from me before I got used to their lingo. And then he says 'tis office work and superintendence he understands. How can you superintend, I told him, what you don't know yourself? No, no; go home and bring a pair of hands fit for a quarryman, before I make you overlooker.'

This was rather delightful, and it further appeared that he could answer all Jane's inquiries after her beloved promising lads whom he had deported to the Rocca Marina quarries.

They were evidently kindly looked after, and she began to perceive that it was not such a bad place after all for them, more especially as he was in the act of building them a chapel, and one of his objects in coming to England was to find a chaplain; and as Lord Rotherwood said, he had come to the right shop, since Rockquay in the spring was likely to afford a choice of clergy with weak chests, or better still, with weak-chested wives, to whom light work in a genial climate would be the greatest possible boon.

Altogether the evening was very pleasant, only too short. It was a curious study for Jane Mohun how far Lady Rotherwood would give way to her husband. She always seemed to give way, but generally accomplished her own will in the end, and it was little likely that she would allow the establishment to await the influx of Merrifields, though certainly Gillian had done nothing displeasing all that evening except that terrible blushing, for which piece of ingenuousness her aunt loved her all the better.

At half-past ten next morning, however, Lord Rotherwood burst in to borrow Valetta for a donkey-ride, for which his lady had compounded instead of the paddling and castle-building, and certainly poor Val could not do much to corrupt Fly on donkey back, and in his presence. He further routed out Gillian, nothing loth, from her algebra, bidding her put on her seven-leagued boots, and not get bent double—and he would fain have seized on his cousin Jane, but she was already gone off for an interview with the landlord of the most eligible of the two houses.

Gillian and Valetta came back very rosy, and in fits of merriment. Lord Rotherwood had paid the donkey-boys to stay at home, and let him and Gillian take their place. They had gone out on the common above the town, with most amusing rivalries as to which drove the beast worst, making Mysie umpire. Then having attained a delightfully lonely place, Fly had begged for a race with Valetta, which failed, partly because Val's donkey would not stir, and partly because Fly could not bear the shaking; and then Lord Rotherwood himself insisted on riding the donkey that wouldn't go, and racing Gillian on the donkey that would—and he made his go so effectually that it ran away with him, and he pulled it up at last only just in time to save himself from being ignominiously stopped by an old fishwoman!

He had, as Aunt Jane said, regularly dipped Gill back into childhood, and she looked, spoke, and moved all the better for it.

CHAPTER XV. — THE ROCKS OF ROCKSTONE

Lord Rotherwood came in to try to wile his cousin to share in the survey of the country; but she declared it to be impossible, as all her avocations had fallen into arrear, and she had to find a couple of servants as well as a house for the Merrifields. This took her in the direction of the works, and Gillian proposed to go with her as far as the Giles's, there to sit a little while with Lilian, for whom she had a new book.

'My dear, surely you must be tired out!' exclaimed the stay-at-home aunt.

'Oh no, Aunt Ada! Quite freshened by that blow on the common.'

And Miss Mohun was not sorry, thinking that to leave Gillian free to come home by herself would be the best refutation of Mrs. Mount's doubts of her.

They had not, however, gone far on their way—on the walk rather unfrequented at this time of day—before Gillian exclaimed, 'Is that Kally? Oh! and who is that with her?' For there certainly was a figure in somewhat close proximity, the ulster and pork-pie hat being such as to make the gender doubtful.

'How late she is! I am afraid her mother is worse,' said Miss Mohun, quickening her steps a little, and, at the angle of the road, the pair in front perceived them. Kalliope turned towards them; the companion—about whom there was no doubt by that time—gave a petulant motion and hastened out of sight.

In another moment they were beside Kalliope, who looked shaken and trembling, with tears in her eyes, which sprang forth at the warm pressure of her hand.

'I am afraid Mrs. White is not so well,' said Miss Mohun kindly.

'She is no worse, I think, thank you, but I was delayed. Are you going this way? May I walk with you?'

'I will come with you to the office,' said Miss Mohun, perceiving that she was in great need of an escort and protector.

'Oh, thank you, thank you, if it is not too much out of your way.'

A few more words passed about Mrs. White's illness and what advice she was having. Miss Mohun could not help thinking that the daughter did not quite realise the extent of the illness, for she added—

'It was a good deal on the nerves and mind. She was so anxious about Mr.

James White's arrival.'

'Have you not seen him?'

'Oh no! Not yet.'

'I think you will be agreeably surprised,' said Gillian. And here they left her at Mrs. Giles's door.

'Yes,' added Miss Mohun, 'he gave me the idea of a kind, just man.'

'Miss Mohun,' said the poor girl, as soon as they were tete-a-tete, 'I know you are very good. Will you tell me what I ought to do? You saw just now—'

'I did; and I have heard.'

Her face was all in a flame and her voice choked. 'He says—Mr. Frank does—that his mother has found out, and that she will tell her own story to Mr. White; and—and we shall all get the sack, as he calls it; and it will be utter misery, and he will not stir a finger to vindicate me; but if I will listen to him, he will speak to Mr. White, and bear me through; but I can't—I can't. I know he is a bad man; I know how he treated poor Edith Vane. I never can; and how shall I keep out of his way?'

'My poor child,' said Miss Mohun, 'it is a terrible position for you; but you are doing quite right. I do not believe Mr. White would go much by what that young man says, for I know he does not think highly of him.'

'But he does go altogether by Mr. Stebbing—altogether, and I know he— Mr. Stebbing, I mean—can't bear us, and would not keep us on if he could help it. He has been writing for another designer—an artist—instead of me.'

'Still, you would be glad to have the connection severed?'

'Oh yes, I should be glad enough to be away; but what would become of my mother and the children?'

'Remember your oldest friends are on their way home; and I will try to speak to Mr. White myself.'

They had reached the little door of Kalliope's office, which she could open with a latch-key, and Miss Mohun was just about to say some parting words, when there was a sudden frightful rumbling sound, something between a clap of thunder and the carting of stones, and the ground shook under their feet, while a cry went up—loud, horror-struck men and women's voices raised in dismay.

Jane had heard that sound once before. It was the fall of part of the precipitous cliff, much of which had been quarried away. But in spite of all precautions, frost and rain were in danger of loosening the remainder, and wire fences were continually needing to be placed to prevent the walking above on edges that might be perilous.

Where was it? What had it done? was the instant thought. Kalliope turned as pale as death; the girls came screaming and thronging out of their workshop, the men from their sheds, the women from the cottages, as all thronged to the more open space beyond the buildings where they could see, while Miss Mohun found herself clasped by her trembling niece.

Others were rushing up from the wharf. One moment's glance showed all familiar with the place that a projecting point, forming a sort of cusp in the curve of the bay, had gone, and it lay, a great shattered mass, fragments spreading far and wide, having crashed through the roof of a stable that stood below.

There was a general crowding forward to the spot, and crying and exclamation, and a shouting of 'All right' from above and below. Had any one come down with it? A double horror seized Miss Mohun as she remembered that her cousin was to inspect those parts that very afternoon.

She caught at the arm of a man and demanded, 'Was any one up there?'

'Master's there, and some gentlemen; but they hain't brought down with it,' said the man. 'Don't be afraid, miss. Thank the Lord, no one was under the rock—horses even out at work.'

'Thank God, indeed!' exclaimed Miss Mohun, daring now to look up, and seeing, not very distinctly, some figures of men, who, however, were too high up and keeping too far from the dangerous broken edge for recognition.

Room was made for the two ladies, by the men who knew Miss Mohun, to push forward, so as to have a clearer view of the broken wall and roof of the stable, and the great ruddy blue and white veined mass of limestone rock, turf, and bush adhering to what had been the top.

There was a moment's silence through the crowd, a kind of awe at the spectacle and the possibilities that had been mercifully averted.

Then one of the men said—

'That was how it was. I saw one of them above—not Stebbing—No— coming out to the brow; and after this last frost, not a doubt but that must have been enough to bring it down.'

'Not railed off, eh?' said the voice of young Stebbing from among the crowd.

'Well, it were marked with big stones where the rail should go,' said another. 'I know, for I laid 'em myself; but there weren't no orders given.'

'There weren't no stones either. Some one been and took 'em away,' added the first speaker.

'I see how it is,' Frank Stebbing's metallic voice could plainly be heard, flavoured with an oath. 'This is your neglect, White, droning, stuck-up sneak as you always were and will be! I shall report this. Damage to property, and maybe life, all along of your confounded idleness.'

And there were worse imprecations, which made Miss Mohun break out in a tone of shocked reproof—

'Mr. Stebbing!'

'I beg your pardon, Miss Mohun; I was not aware of your presence—'

'Nor of a Higher One,' she could not help interposing, while he went on justifying himself.

'It is the only way to speak to these fellows; and it is enough to drive one mad to see what comes of the neglect of a conceited young ass above his business. Life and property—'

'But life is safe, is it not?' she interrupted with a shudder.

'Ay, ay, ma'am,' said the voice of the workman, 'or we should know it by this time.'

But at that moment a faint, gasping cry caught Jane's ear.

Others heard it too. It was a child's voice, and grew stronger after a moment. It came from the corner of the shed outside the stable.

'Oh, oh!' cried the women, pressing forward, 'the poor little Fields!'

Then it was recollected that Mrs. Field—one of those impracticable women on whom the shafts of school officers were lost, and who was always wandering in the town—had been seen going out, leaving two small children playing about, the younger under the charge of the elder. The father was a carter, and had been sent on some errand with the horses.

This passed while anxious hands were struggling with stones and earth, foremost among them Alexis White. The utmost care was needful to prevent the superincumbent weight from falling in and crushing the life there certainly was beneath, happily not the rock from above, but some of the debris of the stable. Frank Stebbing and the foreman had to drive back anxious crowds, and keep a clear space.

Then came running, shrieking, pushing her way through the men, the poor mother, who had to be forcibly withheld by Miss Mohun and one of the men from precipitating herself on the pile of rubbish where her children were buried, and so shaking it as to make their destruction certain.

Those were terrible moments; but when the mother's voice penetrated to the children, a voice answered—

'Mammy, mammy get us out, there's a stone on Tommy,'—at least so the poor woman understood the lispings, almost stifled; and she shrieked again, 'Mammy's coming, darlings!'

The time seemed endless, though it was probably only a few minutes before it was found that the children were against the angle of the shed, where the wall and a beam had protected the younger, a little girl of five, who seemed to be unhurt. But, alas! though the boy's limbs were not crushed, a heavy stone had fallen on his temple.

The poor woman would not believe that life was gone. She disregarded the little one, who screamed for mammy and clutched her skirts, in spite of the attempts of the women to lift her up and comfort her; and gathering the poor lifeless boy in her arms, she alternately screamed for the doctor and uttered coaxing, caressing calls to the child.

She neither heard nor heeded Miss Mohun, with whom, indeed, her relations had not been agreeable; and as a young surgeon, sniffing the accident from afar, had appeared on the scene, and had, at the first glance, made an all too significant gesture, Jane thought it safe to leave the field to him and a kind, motherly, good neighbour, who promised her to send up to Beechcroft Cottage in case there was anything to be done for the unhappy woman or the poor father. Mr. Hablot, who now found his way to the spot, promised to walk on and prepare him: he was gone with a marble cross to a churchyard some five miles off.

Gillian had not spoken a word all this time. She felt perfectly stunned and bewildered, as if it was a dream, and she could not understand it. Only for a moment did she see the bleeding face and prone limbs of the poor boy, and that sent a shuddering horror over her, so that she felt like fainting; but she had so much recollection and self-consciousness, that horror of causing a sensation and giving trouble sent the blood back to her heart, and she kept her feet by holding hard to her aunt's arm and presently Miss Mohun felt how tight and trembling was the grasp, and then saw how white she was.

'My dear, we must get home directly,' she said kindly. 'Lean on me—there.'

There was leisure now, as they turned away, for others to see the young lady's deadly paleness, and there were invitations to houses and offers of all succours at hand, but the dread of 'a fuss' further revived Gillian, and all that was accepted was a seat for a few moments and a glass of water, which Aunt Jane needed almost as much as she did.

Though the girl's colour was coming back, and she said she could walk quite well, both had such aching knees and such shaken limbs that they were glad to hold by each other as they mounted the sloping road, and half-way up Gillian came to a sudden stop.

'Aunt Jane,' she said, panting and turning pale again, 'you heard that dreadful man. Oh! do you think it was true? Fergus's bit of spar—Alexis not minding. Oh! then it is all our doing!'

'I can't tell. Don't you think about it now,' said Aunt Jane, feeling as if the girl were going to swoon on the spot in the shock. 'Consequences are not in our hands. Whatever it came from, and very sad it was, there was great mercy, and we have only to thank God it was no worse.'

When at last aunt and niece reached home, they had no sooner opened the front door than Adeline came almost rushing out of the drawing-room.

'Oh! my dearest Jane,' she cried, clasping and kissing her sister, 'wasn't it dreadful? Where were you? Mr. White knows no one was hurt below, but I could not be easy till you came in.'

'Mr. White!'

'Yes; Mr. White was so kind as to come and tell me—and about Rotherwood.'

'What about Rotherwood?' exclaimed Miss Mohun, advancing into the drawing-room, where Mr. White had risen from his seat.

'Nothing to be alarmed about. Indeed, I assure you, his extraordinary presence of mind and agility—'

'What was it?' as she and Gillian each sank into a chair, the one breathless, the other with the faintness renewed by the fresh shock, but able to listen as Mr. White told first briefly, then with more detail, how—as the surveying party proceeded along the path at the top of the cliffs, he and Lord Rotherwood comparing recollections of the former outline, now much changed by quarrying—the Marquis had stepped out to a slightly projecting point; Mr. Stebbing had uttered a note of warning, knowing how liable these promontories were to break away in the end of winter, and happily Lord Rotherwood had turned and made a step or two back, when the rock began to give way under his feet, so that, being a slight and active man, a spring and bound forward had actually carried him safely to the firm ground, and the others, who had started back in self-preservation, then in horror, fully believing him borne down to destruction, saw him the next instant lying on his face on the path before them. When on his feet, he had declared himself unhurt, and solely anxious as to what the fall of rock might have done beneath; but he was reassured by those cries of 'All right' which were uttered before the poor little Fields were discovered; and then, when the party were going to make their way down to inspect the effects of the catastrophe, he had found that he had not escaped entirely unhurt. Of course he had been forced to leap with utter want of heed, only as far and wide as he could, and thus, though he had lighted on his feet, he had fallen against a stone, and pain and stiffness of shoulder made themselves apparent; though he would accept no help in walking back to the hotel, and was only anxious not to frighten his wife and daughter, and desired Mr. White, who had volunteered to go, to tell the ladies next door that he was convinced it was nothing, or, if anything, only a trifle of a collar-bone. Mr. White had, since the arrival of the surgeon, made an expedition of inquiry, and heard this verdict confirmed, with the further assurance that there was no cause for anxiety. The account of the damage and disaster below was new to him, as his partner had declared the stables to be certain to be empty, and moreover in need of being rebuilt; and he departed to find Mr. Stebbing and make inquiries.

Miss Mohun, going to the hotel, saw the governess, and heard that all was going on well, and that Lord Rotherwood insisted that nothing was the matter, and would not hear of going to bed, but was lying on the sofa in the sitting-room. Her ladyship presently came out, and confirmed the account; but Jane agreed with her that, if possible, the knowledge of the poor child's death should be kept from him that night, lest the shock should make him feverish. However, in that very moment when she was off guard, the communication had been made by his valet, only too proud to have something to tell, and with the pleasing addition that Miss Mohun had had a narrow escape. Whereupon ensued an urgent message to Miss Mohun to come and tell him all about it.

Wife and cousin exchanged glances of consternation, and perhaps each knew she might be thankful that he did not come himself instead of sending, and yet feared that the abstinence was a proof more of incapacity than of submission.

Lying there in a dressing-gown over a strapped shoulder, he showed his agitation by being more than usually unable to finish a sentence.

'Jenny, Jenny—you are—are you all safe? not frightened?'

'Oh no, no, I was a great way off; I only heard the noise, and I did not know you were there.'

'Ah! there must be—something must be meant for me to do. Heaven must mean—thank Him! But is it true—a poor child? Can't one ever be foolish without hurting more than one's self?'

Jane told him the truth calmly and quietly, explaining that the survivor was entirely unhurt, and the poor little victim could not have suffered; adding with all her heart, 'The whole thing was full of mercy, and I do not think you need blame yourself for heedlessness, for it was an accident that the place was not marked.'

'Shameful neglect' said Lady Rotherwood.

'The partner—what's-his-name—Stebbing—said something about his son being away. An untrustworthy substitute, wasn't there?' said Lord Rotherwood.

'The son was the proficient in Leopardine Italian we heard of last night,' said Jane. 'I don't know what he may be as an overlooker here. He certainly fell furiously on the substitute, a poor cousin of Mr. White's own, but I am much afraid the origin of the mischief was nearer home—Master Fergus's geological researches.'

'Fergus! Why, he is a mite.'

'Yes, but Maurice encore. However, I must find out from him whether this is only a foreboding of my prophetic soul!'

'Curious cattle,' observed Lord Rotherwood.

'Well,' put in his wife, 'I do not think Ivinghoe has ever given us cause for anxiety.'

'Exactly the reason that I am always expecting him to break out in some unexpected place! No, Victoria,' he added, seeing that she did not like this, 'I am quite ready to allow that we have a model son, and I only pity him for not having a model father.'

'Well, I am not going to stay and incite you to talk nonsense,' said Jane, rising to depart; 'I will let you know my discoveries.'

She found Fergus watching for her at the gate, with the appeal, 'Aunt Jane, there's been a great downfall of cliff, and I want to see what formations it has brought to light, but they won't let me through to look at it, though I told them White always did.'

'I do not suppose that they will allow any one to meddle with it at present,' said Aunt Jane; then, as Fergus made an impatient exclamation, she added, 'Do you know that a poor little boy was killed, and Cousin Rotherwood a good deal hurt?'

'Yes,' said Fergus, 'Big Blake said so.'

'And now, Fergus, I want to know where you took that large stone from that you showed me with the crack of spar.'

'With the micaceous crystals,' corrected Fergus. 'It was off the top of that very cliff that fell down, so I am sure there must be more in it; and some one else will get them if they won't let me go and see for them.'

'And Alexis White gave you leave to take it?'

'Oh yes, I always ask him.'

'Were you at the place when you asked him, Fergus?'

'At the place on the cliff? No. For I couldn't find him for a long time, and I carried it all the way down the steps.'

'And you did not tell him where it came from?'

'He didn't ask. Indeed, Aunt Jane, I always did show him what I took, and he would have let me in now, only he was not at the office; and the man at the gate, Big Blake, was as savage as a bear, and slammed the door on me, and said they wouldn't have no idle boys loafing about there. And when I said I wasn't an idle boy but a scientific mineralogist, and that Mr. Alexis White always let me in, he laughed in my face, and said Mr. Alexis had better look out for himself. I shall tell Stebbing how cheeky he was.'

'My dear Fergus, there was good reason for keeping you out. You did not know it, nor Alexis; but those stones were put to show that the cliff was getting dangerous, and to mark where to put an iron fence; and it was the greatest of mercies that Rotherwood's life was saved.'

The boy looked a little sobered, but his aunt had rather that his next question had not been: 'Do you think they will let me go there again!'

However, she knew very well that conviction must slowly soak in, and that nothing would be gained by frightening him, so that all she did that night was to send a note by Mysie to her cousin, explaining her discovery; and she made up her mind to take Fergus to the inquest the next day, since his evidence would exonerate Alexis from the most culpable form of carelessness.

Only, however, in the morning, when she had ascertained the hour of the inquest, did she write a note to Mrs. Edgar to explain Fergus's absence from school, or inform the boy of what she intended. On the whole he was rather elated at being so important as to be able to defend Alexis White, and he was quite above believing that scientific research could be reckoned by any one as mischief.

Just as Miss Mohun had gone up to get ready, Mysie ran in to say that Cousin Rotherwood would be at the door in a moment to take Fergus down.

'Lady Rotherwood can't bear his going,' said Mysie, 'and Mr. White and Mr. Stebbing say that he need not; but he is quite determined, though he has got his arm in a sling, for he says it was all his fault for going where he ought not. And he won't have the carriage, for he says it would shake his bones ever so much more than Shank's mare.'

'Just like him,' said Aunt Jane. 'Has Dr. Dagger given him leave?'

'Yes; he said it wouldn't hurt him; but Lady Rotherwood told Miss Elbury she was sure he persuaded him.'

Mysie's confused pronouns were cut short by Lord Rotherwood's own appearance.

'You need not go, Jane,' he said. 'I can take care of this little chap. They'll not chop off his head in the presence of one of the Legislature.'

'Nice care to begin by chaffing him out of his wits,' she retorted. 'The question is, whether you ought to go.'

'Yes, Jenny, I must go. It can't damage me; and besides, to tell the truth, it strikes me that things will go hard with that unlucky young fellow if some one is not there to stand up for him and elicit Fergus's evidence.'

'Alexis White!'

'White—ay, a cousin or something of the exemplary boss. He's been dining with his partners—the old White, I mean—and they've been cramming him—I imagine with a view to scapegoat treatment—jealousy, and all the rest of it. If there is not a dismissal, there's a hovering on the verge.'

'Exactly what I was afraid of,' said Jane. 'Oh, Rotherwood, I could tell you volumes. But may I not come down with you? Could not I do something?'

'Well, on the whole, you are better away, Jenny. Consider William's feelings. Womankind, even Brownies, are better out of it. Prejudice against proteges, whether of petticoats or cassocks—begging your pardon. I can fight battles better as an unsophisticated stranger coming down fresh, though I don't expect any one from the barony of Beechcroft to believe it, and maybe the less I know of your volumes the better till after—'

'Oh, Rotherwood, as if I wasn't too thankful to have you to send for me!'

'There! I've kept the firm out there waiting an unconscionable time. They'll think you are poisoning my mind. Come along, you imp of science. Trust me, I'll not bully him, though it's highly tempting to make the chien chasser de race.'

'Oh, Aunt Jane, won't you go?' exclaimed Gillian in despair, as her cousin waved a farewell at the gate.

'No, my dear; it is not for want of wishing, but he is quite right. He can do much better than I could.'

'But is he in earnest, aunt?'

'Oh yes, most entirely, and I quite see that he is right—indeed I do, Gillian. People pretend to defer to a lady, but they really don't like her poking her nose in, and, after all, I could have no right to say anything. My only excuse for going was to take care of Fergus.'

A further token of Lord Rotherwood's earnestness in the cause was the arrival of his servant, who was to bring down the large stone which Master Merrifield had moved, and who conveyed it in a cab, being much too grand to carry it through the streets.

Gillian was very unhappy and restless, unable to settle to anything, and linking cause and effect together disconsolately in a manner Mysie, whom she admitted to her confidence, failed to understand.

'It was a great pity Fergus did not show Alexis where the stone came from, but I don't see what your not giving him his lessons had to do with it. Made him unhappy? Oh! Gilly dear, you don't mean any one would be too unhappy to mind his business for such nonsense as that! I am sure none of us would be so stupid if Mr. Pollock forgot our Greek lessons.'

'Certainly not,' said Gillian, almost laughing; 'but you don't understand, Mysie. It was the taking him up and letting him down, and I could not explain it, and it looked so nasty and capricious.'

'Well, I suppose you ought to have asked Aunt Jane's leave; but I do think he must be a ridiculous young man if he could not attend to his proper work because you did not go after him when you were only just come home.'

'Ah, Mysie, you don't understand!'

Mysie opened a round pair of brown eyes, and said, 'Oh! I did think people were never so silly out of poetry. There was Wilfrid in Hokeby, to be sure. He was stupid enough about Matilda; but do you mean that he is like that!'

'Don't, don't, you dreadful child; I wish I had never spoken to you,' cried Gillian, overwhelmed with confusion. 'You must never say a word to any living creature.'

'I am sure I shan't,' said Mysie composedly; 'for, as far as I can see, it is all stuff. This Alexis never found out what Fergus was about with the stone, and so the mark was gone, and Cousin Rotherwood trod on it, and the poor little boy was killed; but as to the rest, Nurse Halfpenny would say it was all conceited maggots; and how you can make so much more fuss about that than about the poor child being crushed, I can't make out.'

'But if I think it all my fault?'

'That's maggots,' returned Mysie with uncompromising common-sense. 'You aren't old enough, nor pretty enough, for any of that kind of stuff, Gill!'

And Gillian found that either she must go without comprehension, or have a great deal more implied, if she turned for sympathy to any one save Aunt Jane, who seemed to know exactly how the land lay.

CHAPTER XVI. — VANISHED

It seemed to be a very long time before the inquest was over, and Aunt Jane had almost yielded to her niece's impatience and her own, and consented to walk down to meet the intelligence, when Fergus came tearing in, 'I've seen the rock, and there is a flaw of crystallisation in it! And the coroner-man called me an incipient geologist.'

'But the verdict?'

'They said it was accidental death, and something about more care being taken and valuable lives endangered.'

'And Alexis White—'

'Oh! there was a great bother about his not being there. They said it looked very bad; but they could not find him.'

'Not find him! Oh! Where is Cousin Rotherwood?'

'He is coming home, and he said I might run on, and tell you that if you had time to come in to the hotel he would tell you about it.'

With which invitation Miss Mohun hastened to comply; Gillian was ardent to come too, and it seemed cruel to prevent her; but, besides that Jane thought that her cousin might be tired enough to make his wife wish him to see as few people as possible, she was not sure that Gillian might not show suspicious agitation, and speech and action would not be free in her presence. So the poor girl was left to extract what she could from her little brother, which did not amount to much.

It was a propitious moment, for Jane met Lord Rotherwood at the door of the hotel, parting with Mr. White; she entered with him, and his wife, after satisfying herself that he was not the worse for his exertions, was not sorry that he should have his cousin to keep him quiet in his easy-chair while she went off to answer a pile of letters which had just been forwarded from home.

'Well, Jenny,' he said, 'I am afraid your protege does not come out of it very well; that is, if he is your protege. He must be an uncommonly foolish young man.'

'I reserve myself on that point. But is it true that he never appeared?'

'Quite true.'

'Didn't they send for him?'

'Yes; but he could not be found, either at the works or at home. However, the first might be so far accounted for, since he met at his desk a notice of dismissal from White and Stebbing.'

'No! Really. Concocted at that unlucky dinner yesterday! But, of course, it was not immediate.'

'Of course not, and perhaps something might have been done for him; but a man who disappears condemns himself.'

'But what for? I hope Fergus explained that the stone was not near the spot when he showed it.'

'Yes; Fergus spoke up like a little man, and got more credit than he deserved. If they had known that of all varieties of boys the scientific is the worst imp of mischief! It all went in order due—surgeon explained injuries to poor little being—men how the stone came down and they dug him out—poor little baby-sister made out her sad little story. That was the worst part of all. Something must be done for that child—orphanage or something—only unluckily there's the father and mother. Poor father! he is the one to be pitied. I mean to get at him without the woman. Well, then came my turn, and how I am afflicted with the habit of going where I ought not, and, only by a wonderful mercy, was saved from being part of the general average below. Then we got to the inquiry, Were not dangerous places railed off? Yes, Stebbing explained that it was the rule of the firm to have the rocks regularly inspected once a month, and once a fortnight in winter and spring, when the danger is greater. If they were ticklish, the place was marked at the moment with big stones, reported, and railed off. An old foreman-sort of fellow swore to having detected the danger, and put stones. He had reported it. To whom? To Mr. Frank. Yes, he thought it was Mr. Frank, just before he went away. It was this fellow's business to report it and send the order, it seems, and in his absence Alexander White, or whatever they call him, took his work. Well, the old man doesn't seem to know whether he mentioned the thing to young White or not, which made his absence more unlucky; but, anyway, the presence of the stones was supposed to be a sufficient indication of the need of the rail, or to any passenger to avoid the place. In fact, if Master White had been energetic, he would have seen to the thing. I fancy that is the long and short of it. But when the question came how the stones came to be removed, I put Fergus forward. The foreman luckily could identify his stone by the precious crack of spar; and the boy explained how he had lugged it down, and showed it to his friend far away from its place—had, in fact, turned over and displaced all the lot.'

'Depend upon it, Alexis has gone out of the way to avoid accusing Fergus!'

'Don't make me start, it hurts; but do you really believe that, Jane—you, the common-sense female of the family?'

'Indeed I do, he is a romantic, sensitive sort of fellow, who would not defend himself at the boy's expense.'

'Whew! He might have stood still and let Fergus defend him, then, instead of giving up his own cause.'

'And how did it end?'

'Accidental death, of course; couldn't be otherwise; but censure on the delay and neglect of precaution, which the common opinion of the Court naturally concentrated on the absent; though, no doubt, the first omission was young Stebbing's; but owing to the hurry of his start for Italy, that was easily excused. And even granting that Fergus did the last bit of mischief, your friend may be romantically generous, if you please; but he must have been very slack in his work.'

'Poor fellow—yes. Now before I tell you what I know about him, I should like to hear how Mr. Stebbing represents him. You know his father was a lieutenant in the Royal Wardours.'

'Risen from the ranks, a runaway cousin of White's. Yes, and there's a son in a lawyer's office always writing to White for money.'

'Oh! I never had much notion of that eldest—'

'They have no particular claim on White; but when the father died he wrote to Stebbing to give those that were old enough occupation at the works, and see that the young ones got educated.'

'So he lets the little boys go to the National School, though there's no great harm in that as yet.'

'He meant to come and see after them himself, and find out what they are made of. But meantime this youth, who did well at first, is always running after music and nonsense of all kinds, thinking himself above his business, neglecting right and left; while as to the sister, she is said to be very clever at designing—both ways in fact—so determined to draw young Stebbing in, that, having got proof of it at last, they have dismissed her too. And, Jane, I hardly like to tell you, but somehow they mix Gillian up in the business. They ate it up again when I cut them short by saying she was my cousin, her mother and you like my sisters. I am certain it is all nonsense, but had you any notion of any such thing? It is insulting you, though, to suppose you had not,' he added, as he saw her air of acquiescence; 'so, of course, it is all right.'

'It is not all right, but not so wrong as all that. Oh no! and I know all about it from poor Gill herself and the girl. Happily they are both too good girls to need prying. Well, the case is this. There was a quarrel about a love story between the two original Whites, who must both have had a good deal of stuff in them. Dick ran away, enlisted, rose, and was respected by Jasper, etc., but was married to a Greco-Hibernian wife, traditionally very beautiful, poor woman, though rather the reverse at present. Lily and her girls did their best for the young people with good effect on the eldest girl, who really in looks and ways is worthy of her Muse's name, Kalliope. Father had to retire with rank of captain, and died shortly after. Letters failed to reach the Merrifields, who were on the move. This Quarry cousin was written to, and gave the help he described to you. Perhaps it was just, but it disappointed them, and while the father lived, Alexis had been encouraged to look to getting to the University and Holy Orders. He has a good voice, and the young curate at the Kennel patronised him, perhaps a little capriciously, but I am not quite sure. All this was unknown to me till the Merrifield children came, and Gillian, discovering these Whites, flew upon them in the true enthusiastic Lily- fashion, added to the independence of the modern maiden mistrustful of old cats of aunts. Like a little goose, she held trystes with Kalliope, through the rails at the top of the garden on Sunday afternoons.'

'Only Kalliope!'

'Cela va sans dire. The brother was walking the young ones on the cliffs whence she had been driven by the attentions of Master Frank Stebbing. Poor thing, she is really beautiful enough to be a misfortune to her, and so is the youth—Maid of Athens, Irish eyes, plus intellect. Gill lent books, and by and by volunteered to help the lad with his Greek.'

'Whew—'

'Just as she would teach a night-school class. She used to give him lessons at his sister's office. I find that as soon as Kalliope found it was unknown to me she protested, and did all in her power to prevent it, but Gillian had written all to her mother, and thought that sufficient.'

'And Lily—? Victoria would have gone crazy—supposing such a thing possible,' he added, sotto voce.

'Lily was probably crazy already between her sick husband and her bridal daughters, for she answered nothing intelligible. However, absence gave time for reflection, and Gillian came home after her visits convinced by her own good sense and principle that she had not acted fairly towards us, so that, of her own accord, the first thing she did was to tell me the whole, and how much the sister had always objected. She was quite willing that I should talk it over with Kalliope before she went near them again, but I have never been able really to do so.'

'Then it was all Greek and—"Lilyism!" Lily's grammar over again, eh!'

'On her side, purely so—but I am afraid she did upset the boy's mind. He seems to have been bitterly disappointed at what must have appeared like neglect and offence—and oh! you know how silly youths can be—and he had Southern blood too, poor fellow, and he went mooning and moping about, I am afraid really not attending to his business; and instead of taking advantage of the opening young Stebbing's absence gave him of showing his abilities, absolutely gave them the advantage against him, by letting them show him up as an idle fellow.'

'Or worse. Stebbing talked of examining the accounts, to see if there were any deficiency.'

'That can be only for the sake of prejudicing Mr. White—they cannot really suspect him.'

'If not, it was very good acting, and Stebbing appears to me just the man to suspect a parson's pet, and a lady's—as he called this unlucky fellow.'

'Ask any of the workmen—ask Mr. Flight.'

'Well, I wish he had come to the front. It looks bad for him, and your plea, Jenny, is more like Lily than yourself.'

'Thank you; I had rather be like Lily than myself.'

'And you are equally sure that the sister is maligned?'

'Quite sure—on good evidence—the thing is how to lay it all before Mr. White, for you see these Stebbings evidently want to prevent him from taking to his own kindred—you must help me, Rotherwood.'

'When I am convinced,' he said. 'My dear Jenny, I beg your pardon—I have an infinite respect for your sagacity, but allow me to observe, though your theory holds together, still it has rather an ancient and fish-like smell.'

'I only ask you to investigate, and make him do so. Listen to any one who knows, to any one but the Stebbings, and you will find what an admirable girl the sister is, and that the poor boy is perfectly blameless of anything but being forced into a position for which he was never intended, and of all his instincts rebelling.'

They were interrupted by the arrival of the doctor, whom Lady Rotherwood had bound over to come and see whether her husband was the worse for his exertions. He came in apologising most unnecessarily for his tardiness. And in the midst of Miss Mohun's mingled greeting and farewell, she stood still to hear him say that he had been delayed by being called in to that poor woman, Mrs. White, who had had a fit on hearing the policeman inquiring for that young scamp, her son.

'The policeman!' ejaculated Jane in consternation.

'It was only to summon him to attend the inquest,' explained Dr. Dagger, 'but there was no one in the house with her but a little maid, and the shock was dreadful. If he has really absconded, it looks exceedingly ill for him.'

'I believe he has only been inattentive,' said Jane firmly, knowing that she ought to go, and yet feeling constrained to wait long enough to ask what was the state of the poor mother, and if her daughter were with her.

'The daughter was sent for, and seems to be an effective person— uncommonly handsome, by the bye. The attack was hysteria, but there is evidently serious disease about her, which may be accelerated.'

'I thought so. I am afraid she has had no advice.'

'No; I promised the daughter to come and examine her to-morrow when she is calmer, and if that son is good for anything, he may have returned.'

And therewith Jane was forced to go away, to carry this wretched news to poor Gillian.

Aunt and niece went as soon as the mid-day meal was over to inquire for poor Mrs. White, and see what could be done. She was sleeping under an opiate, and Kalliope came down, pale as marble, but tearless. She knew nothing of her brother since she had given him his breakfast that morning. He had looked white and haggard, and had not slept, neither did he eat. She caught at the theory that had occurred to Miss Mohun, that he did not like to accuse Fergus, for even to her he had not mentioned who had removed the stone. In that case he might return at night. Yet it was possible that he did not know even now whence the stone had come, and it was certain that he had been at his office that morning, and opened the letter announcing his dismissal. Kalliope, going later, had found the like notice, but had had little time to dwell on it before she had been summoned home to her mother. Poor Mrs. White had been much shaken by the first reports of yesterday's accident, which had been so told to her as to alarm her for both her children; and when her little maid rushed in to say that 'the pelis was come after Mr. Alec,' it was no wonder that her terror threw her into a most alarming state, which made good Mrs. Lee despatch her husband to bring home Kalliope; and as the attack would not yield to the soothing of the women or to their domestic remedies, but became more and more delirious and convulsive, the nearest doctor was sent for, and Dr. Dagger, otherwise a higher flight than would have been attempted, was caught on his way and brought in to discover how serious her condition already was.

This Kalliope told them with the desperate quietness of one who could not afford to give way. Her own affairs were entirely swallowed up in this far greater trouble, and for the present there were no means of helping her. Mr. and Mrs. Lee were thoroughly kind, and ready to give her efficient aid in her home cares and her nursing; and it could only be hoped that Alexis might come back in the evening, and set the poor patient's mind at rest.

'We will try to make Mr. White come to a better understanding,' said Miss Mohun kindly.

'Thank you' said Kalliope, pushing back her hair with a half-bewildered look. 'I remember my poor mother was very anxious about that. But it seems a little thing now.'

'May God bless and help you, my dear,' said Miss Mohun, with a parting kiss.

Gillian had not spoken all the time; but outside she said—'Oh, aunt! is this my doing?'

'Not quite,' said Aunt Jane kindly. 'There were other causes.'

'Oh, if I could do anything!'

'Alas! it is easier to do than to undo.'

Aunt Jane was really kind, and Gillian was grateful, but oh, how she longed for her mother!

There was no better news the next morning. Nothing had been heard of Alexis, and nothing would persuade his mother in her half-delirious and wholly unreasonable state that he had not been sent to prison, and that they were not keeping it from her. She was exceedingly ill, and Kalliope had been up all night with her.

Such was the report in a note sent up by Mrs. Lee by one of the little boys early in the morning, and, as soon as she could reasonably do so, Miss Mohun carried the report to Lord Rotherwood, whom she found much better, and anxious to renew the tour of inspection which had been interrupted.

Before long, Mr. White was shown in, intending to resume the business discussion, and Miss Mohun was about to retreat with Lady Rotherwood, when her cousin, taking pity on her anxiety, said—

'If you will excuse me for speaking about your family matters, Mr. White, my cousin knows these young people well, and I should like you to hear what she has been telling me.'

'A gentleman has just been calling on me about them,' said Mr. White, not over-graciously.

'Mr. Flight?' asked Jane anxiously.

'Yes; a young clergyman, just what we used to call Puseyite when I left England; but that name seems to be gone out now.'

'Anyway,' said Jane, 'I am sure he had nothing but good to say of Miss White, or indeed of her brother; and I am afraid the poor mother is very ill.'

'That's true, Miss Mohun; but you see there may be one side to a lady or a parson, and another to a practical man like my partner. Not but that I should be willing enough to do anything in reason for poor Dick's widow and children, but not to keep them in idleness, or letting them think themselves too good to work.'

'That I am sure these two do not. Their earnings quite keep the family. I know no one who works harder than Miss White, between her business, her lodgers, the children, and her helpless mother.'

'I saw her mosaics—very fair, very clever, some of them; but I'm afraid she is a sad little flirt, Miss Mohun.'

'Mr. White,' said Lord Rotherwood, 'did ever you hear of a poor girl beset by an importunate youth, but his family thought it was all her fault?'

'If Mr. White would see her,' said Jane, 'he would understand at a glance that the attraction is perfectly involuntary; and I know from other sources how persistently she has avoided young Stebbing; giving up Sunday walks to prevent meeting him, accepting nothing from him, always avoiding tete-a-tetes.'

'Hum! But tell me this, madam,' said Mr. White eagerly, 'how is it that, if these young folks are so steady and diligent as you would make out, that eldest brother writes to me every few months for help to support them?'

'Oh!' Jane breathed out, then, rallying, 'I know nothing about that eldest. Yes, I do though! His sister told my niece that all the rents of the three houses went to enable Richard to appear as he ought at the solicitor's office at Leeds.'

'There's a screw loose somewhere plainly,' said Lord Rotherwood.

'The question is, where it is,' said Mr. White.

'And all I hope, said Jane, 'is that Mr. White will judge for himself when he has seen Kalliope and made inquiries all round. I do not say anything for the mother, poor thing, except that she is exceedingly ill just now, but I do thoroughly believe in the daughter.'

'And this runaway scamp, Miss Mohun?'

'I am afraid he is a runaway; but I am quite sure he is no scamp,' said Jane.

'Only so clever as to be foolish, eh?' said the Marquis, rather provokingly.

'Exactly so,' she answered; 'and I am certain that if Mr. White will trust to his own eyes and his own inquiries, he will find that I am right.'

She knew she ought to go, and Lord Rotherwood told her afterwards, 'That was not an ill-aimed shaft, Jane. Stebbing got more than one snub over the survey. I see that White is getting the notion that there's a system of hoodwinking going on, and of not letting him alone, and he is not the man to stand that.'

'If he only would call on Kalliope!'

'I suspect he is afraid of being beguiled by such a fascinating young woman.'

It was a grievous feature in the case to Gillian that she could really do nothing. Mrs. White was so ill that going to see Kalliope was of no use, and Maura was of an age to be made useful at home; and there were features in the affair that rendered it inexpedient for Gillian to speak of it except in the strictest confidence to Aunt Jane or Mysie. It was as if she had touched a great engine, and it was grinding and clashing away above her while she could do nothing to stay its course.

CHAPTER XVII. — 'THEY COME, THEY COME'

Dr. Dagger examined Mrs. White and pronounced that there had been mortal disease of long standing, and that she had nearly, if not quite, reached the last stage. While people had thought her selfish, weak, and exacting, she must really have concealed severe suffering, foolishly perhaps, but with great fortitude.

And from hearing this sentence, Kalliope had turned to find at last tidings of her brother in a letter written from Avoncester, the nearest garrison town. He told his sister that, heart-broken already at the result of what he knew to be his own presumption, and horrified at the fatal consequences of his unhappy neglect, he felt incapable of facing any of those whom he had once called his friends, and the letter of dismissal had removed all scruples. Had it not been for his faith and fear, he would have put an end to his life, but she need have no alarms on that score. He had rushed away, scarce knowing what he was doing, till he had found himself on the road to Avoncester and then had walked on thither and enlisted in the regiment quartered there, where he hoped to do his duty, having no other hope left in life!

Part of this letter Kalliope read to Miss Mohun, who had come down to hear the doctor's verdict. It was no time to smile at the heart being broken by the return of a valentine, or all hope in life being over before twenty. Kalliope, who knew what the life of a private was, felt wretched over it, and her poor mother was in despair; but Miss Mohun tried to persuade her that it was by no means an unfortunate thing, since Alexis would be thus detained safely and within reach till Sir Jasper arrived to take up the matter, and Mr. White had been able to understand it.

'Yes; but he cannot come to my poor mother. And Richard will be so angry —think it such a degradation.'

'He ought not. Your father—'

'Oh! but he will. And I must write to him. Mother has been asking for him.'

'Tell me, my dear, has Richard ever helped you?'

'Oh no, poor fellow, he could not. He wants all we can send him, or we would have put the little boys to a better school.'

'I would not write before it is absolutely necessary,' said Miss Mohun. 'A young man hanging about with nothing to do, even under these circumstances, might make things harder.'

'Yes, I know,' said Kalliope, with a trembling lip. 'And if it was urgent, even Alexis might come. Indeed, I ought to be thankful that he is safe, after all my dreadful fears, and not far off.'

Miss Mohun refrained from grieving the poor girl by blaming Alexis for the impetuous selfish folly that had so greatly added to the general distress of his family, and rendered it so much more difficult to plead his cause. In fact, she felt bound to stand up as his champion against all his enemies, though he was less easy of defence than his sister; and Mr. Flight, the first person she met afterwards, was excessively angry and disappointed, speaking of such a step as utter ruin.

'The lad was capable of so much better things,' said he. 'I had hoped so much of him, and had so many plans for him, that it is a grievous pity; but he had no patience, and now he has thrown himself away. I told him it was his first duty to maintain his mother, and if he had stuck to that, I would have done more for him as soon as he was old enough, and I could see what was to be done for the rest of them; but he grew unsettled and impatient, and this is the end of it!'

'Not the end, I hope,' said Miss Mohun. 'It is not exactly slavery without redemption.'

'He does not deserve it.'

'Who does? Besides, remember what his father was.'

'His father must have been of the high-spirited, dare-devil sort. This lad was made for a scholar—for the priesthood, in fact, and the army will be more uncongenial than these marble works! Foolish fellow, he will soon have had enough of it, with his refinement, among such associates.'

Jane wondered that the young clergyman did not regret that he had sufficiently tried the youth's patience to give the sense of neglect and oblivion. There had been many factors in the catastrophe, and this had certainly been one, since the loan of a few books, and an hour a week of direction of study, would have kept Alexis contented, and have obviated all the perilous intercourse with Gillian; but she scarcely did the Rev. Augustine Flight injustice in thinking that in the aesthetic and the emotional side of religion he somewhat lost sight of the daily drudgery that works on character chiefly as a preventive. 'He was at the bottom of it, little as he knows it,' she said to herself as she walked up the hill. 'How much harm is done by good beginnings of a skein left to tangle.'

Lady Flight provided a trained nurse to help Kalliope, and sent hosts of delicacies; and plenty of abuse was bestowed on Mr. James White for his neglect. Meanwhile Mrs. White, though manifestly in a hopeless state, seemed likely to linger on for some weeks longer.

In the meantime, Miss Mohun at last found an available house, and was gratified by the young people's murmur that 'Il Lido' was too far off from Beechcroft. But then their mother would be glad to be so near St. Andrew's, for she belonged to the generation that loved and valued daily services.

Lord Rotherwood, perhaps owing to his exertions, felt the accident more than he had done at first, and had to be kept very quiet, which he averred to be best accomplished by having the children in to play with him; and as he always insisted on sending for Valetta to make up the party, the edict of separation fell to the ground, when Lady Rotherwood, having written his letters for him, went out for a drive, taking sometimes Miss Elbury, but more often Adeline Mohun, who flattered herself that her representations had done much to subdue prejudice and smooth matters.

'Which always were smooth,' said Jane; 'smooth and polished as a mahogany table, and as easy to get into.'

However, she was quite content that Ada should be the preferred one, and perhaps no one less acute than herself would have felt that the treatment as intimates and as part of the family was part of the duty of a model wife. Both sisters were in request to enliven the captive, and Jane forebore to worry him with her own anxieties about the present disgrace of the Whites. Nothing could be done for Kalliope in her mother's present state, Alexis must drink of his own brewst, and Sir Jasper and Lady Merrifield were past Brindisi! As to Mr. White, he seemed to be immersed in business, and made no sign of relenting; Jane had made one or two attempts to see him, but had not succeeded. Only one of her G.F.S. maidens, who was an enthusiastic admirer of Kalliope, and in perfect despair at her absence, mentioned that Mr. White had looked over all their work and had been immensely struck with Miss White's designs, and especially with the table inlaid with autumn leaves, which had been set aside as expensive, unprofitable, and not according to the public taste, and not shown to him on his first visit to the works with Mr. Stebbing. There were rumours in the air that he was not contented with the state of things, and might remain for some time to set them on a different footing.

Miss Adeline had been driving with Lady Rotherwood, and on coming in with her for the afternoon cup of tea, found Mr. White conversing with Lord Rotherwood, evidently just finishing the subject—a reading-room or institute of some sort for the men at the works.

'All these things are since my time,' said Mr. White. 'We were left pretty much to ourselves in those days.'

'And what do you think? Should you have been much the better for them?' asked the Marquis.

'Some of us would,' was the answer.

'You would not have thought them a bore!'

'There were some who would, as plenty will now; but we were a rough set —we had not so much to start with as the lads, willy nilly, have now. But I should have been glad of books, and diversion free from lawlessness might have prevented poor Dick's scrapes. By the bye, that daughter of his can do good work.'

'Poor thing,' said Miss Adeline, 'she is a very good girl, and in great trouble. I was much pleased with her, and I think, she has behaved remarkably well under very trying circumstances.'

'I observed that the young women in the mosaic department seemed to be much attached to her,' said Mr. White.

'My sister thinks she has been an excellent influence there.'

'She was not there,' said Mr. White.

'No; her mother is too ill to be left—dying, I should think, from what I hear.'

'From the shock of that foolish lad's evasion?' asked Lord Rotherwood.

'She was very ill before, I believe, though that brought it to a crisis. No one would believe how much that poor girl has had depending on her. I wish she had been at the works—I am sure you would have been struck with her.'

'Have you any reason to think they are in any distress, Miss Mohun?'

'Not actually at present; but I do not know what they are to do in future, with the loss of the salaries those two have had,' said Adeline, exceedingly anxious to say neither too much nor too little.

'There is the elder brother.'

'Oh! he is no help, only an expense.'

'Miss Mohun, may I ask, are you sure of that?'

'As sure as I can be of anything. I have always heard that the rents of their two or three small houses went to support Richard, and that they entirely live on the earnings of the brother and sister, except that you are so good as to educate the younger girl. It has come out casually—they never ask for anything.'

Mr. White looked very thoughtful. Adeline considered whether importunity would do most harm or good; but thought her words might work. When she rose to take leave, Mr. White did the same, 'evidently,' thought she, 'for the sake of escorting her home,' and she might perhaps say another word in confidence for the poor young people. She had much reliance, and not unjustly, on her powers of persuasion, and she would make the most of those few steps to her own door.

'Indeed, Mr. White,' she began, 'excuse me, but I cannot help being very much interested in those young people we were speaking of.'

'That is your goodness, Miss Mohun. I have no doubt they are attractive—there's no end to the attractiveness of those Southern folk they belong to—on one side of the house at least, but unfortunately you never know where to have them—there's no truth in them; and though I don't want to speak of anything I may have done for them, I can't get over their professing never to have had anything from me.'

'May I ask whether you sent it through that eldest brother?'

'Certainly; he always wrote to me.'

'Then, Mr. White, I cannot help believing that the family here never heard of it. Do you know anything of that young man?'

'No; I will write to his firm and inquire. Thank you for the hint, Miss Mohun.'

They were at Beechcroft Cottage gate, and he seemed about to see her even to the door. At that instant a little girlish figure advanced and was about to draw back on perceiving that Miss Adeline was not alone, when she exclaimed, 'Maura, is it you, out so late! How is your mother?'

'Much the same, thank you, Miss Adeline!'

'Here is one of the very young folks we were mentioning,' said Ada, seeing her opportunity and glad that there was light enough to show the lady-like little figure. 'This is Maura, Mr. White, whom you are kindly educating.'

Mr. White took the hand, which was given with a pretty respectful gesture, and said something kind about her mother's illness, while Adeline took the girl into the house and asked if she had come on any message.

'Yes, if you please,' said Maura, blushing; 'Miss Mohun was so kind as to offer to lend us an air-cushion, and poor mamma is so restless and uncomfortable that Kally thought it might ease her a little.'

'By all means, my dear. Come in, and I will have it brought,' said Adeline, whose property the cushion was, and who was well pleased that Mr. White came in likewise, and thus had a full view of Maura's great wistful, long-lashed eyes, and delicate refined features, under a little old brown velvet cap, and the slight figure in a gray ulster. He did not speak while Maura answered Miss Adeline's inquiries, but when the cushion had been brought down, and she had taken it under her arm, he exclaimed—

'Is she going back alone?'

'Oh yes,' said Maura cheerfully; 'it is not really dark out of doors yet.'

'I suppose it could not be helped,' said Miss Adeline.

'No; Theodore is at the school. They keep him late to get things ready for the inspection, and Petros had to go to the doctor's to fetch something; but he will meet me if he is not kept waiting.'

'It is not fit for a child like that to go alone so late,' said Mr. White, who perhaps had imbibed Italian notions of the respectability of an escort. 'I will walk down with her.'

Maura looked as if darkness were highly preferable to such a cavalier; but Miss Adeline was charmed to see them walk off together, and when her sister presently came in with Gillian and Fergus, she could not but plume herself a little on her achievement.

'Then it was those two!' exclaimed Jane. 'I thought so from the other side of the street, but it was too dark to be certain; and besides, there was no believing it.'

'Did not they acknowledge you?'

'Oh no; they were much too busy.'

'Talking. Oh, what fun!' Adeline could not help observing in such glee that she looked more like 'our youngest girl' than the handsome middle-aged aunt.

'But,' suggested Fergus, somewhat astonished, 'Stebbing says he is no end of a horrid brute of a screw.'

'Indeed. What has he been doing?'

'He only tipped him a coach wheel.'

'Well, to tip over as a coach wheel is the last thing I should have expected of Mr. White,' said Aunt Jane, misunderstanding on purpose.

'A crown piece then,' growled Fergus; 'and of course he thought it would be a sovereign, and so he can't pay me my two ten—shillings, I mean, that I lent him, and so I can't get the lovely ammonite I saw at Nott's.'

'How could you be so silly as to lend him any money?'

'I didn't want to; but he said he would treat us all round if I wouldn't be mean, and after all I only got half a goody, with all the liqueur out of it.'

'It served you right,' said Gillian. 'I doubt whether you would see the two shillings again, even if he had the sovereign.'

'He faithfully promised I should,' said Fergus, whose allegiance was only half broken. 'And old White is a beast, and no mistake. He was perfectly savage to Stebbing's major, and he said he wouldn't be under him, at no price.'

'Perhaps Mr. White might say the same,' put in Aunt Ada.

'He is a downright old screw and a bear, I tell you,' persisted Fergus. 'He jawed Frank Stebbing like a pickpocket for just having a cigar in the quarry.'

'Close to the blasting powder, eh?' said Miss Mohun.

'And he is boring and worrying them all out of their lives over the books,' added Fergus. 'Poking his nose into everything, so that Stebbing says his governor vows he can't stand it, and shall cut the concern it the old brute does not take himself off to Italy before long.'

'What a good thing!' thought both sisters, looking into each other's eyes and auguring well for the future.

All were anxious to hear the result of Maura's walk, and Gillian set out in the morning on a voyage of discovery with a glass of jelly for Mrs. White; but all she could learn was that the great man had been very kind to Maura, though he had not come in, at which Gillian was indignant.

'Men are often shy of going near sickness and sorrow,' said her aunt Ada. 'You did not hear what they talked about?'

'No; Maura was at school, and Kally is a bad person to pump.'

'I should like to pump Mr. White,' was Aunt Jane's comment.

'If I could meet him again,' said Aunt Ada, 'I feel sure he would tell me.'

Her sister laughed a little, so well did she know that little half-conscious, half-gratified tone of assumption of power over the other sex; but Miss Adeline proved to be right. Nay, Mr. White actually called in the raw cold afternoon, which kept her in when every one else was out. He came for the sake of telling her that he was much pleased with the little girl—a pretty creature, and simple and true, he really believed. Quite artlessly, in answer to his inquiries, she had betrayed that her eldest brother never helped them. 'Oh no! Mamma was always getting all the money she could to send to him, because he must keep up appearances at his office at Leeds, and live like a gentleman, and it did not signify about Kalliope and Alexis doing common work.'

'That's one matter cleared up,' rejoiced Jane. 'It won't be brought up against them now.'

'And then it seems he asked the child about her sister's lovers.'

'Oh!'

'It was for a purpose. Don't be old maidish, Jenny!'

'Well, he isn't a gentleman.'

'Now, Jane, I'm sure—'

'Never mind. I want to hear; only I should have thought you would have been the first to cry out.'

'Little Maura seems to have risen to the occasion, and made a full explanation as far as she knew—and that was more than the child ought to have known, by the bye—of how Mr. Frank was always after Kally, and how she could not bear him, and gave up the Sunday walk to avoid him, and how he had tried to get her to marry him, and go to Italy with him; but she would not hear of it.'

'Just the thing the little chatterbox would be proud of, but it is no harm that "Mon oncle des iles Philippines" should know.'

'"I see his little game" was what Mr. White said,' repeated Adeline. '"The young dog expected to come over me with this pretty young wife—my relation, too; but he would have found himself out in his reckoning."'

'So far so good; but it is not fair.'

'However, the ice is broken. What's that? Is the house coming down?'

No; but Gillian and Valetta came rushing in, almost tumbling over one another, and each waving a sheet of a letter. Papa and mamma would land in three days' time if all went well; but the pity was that they must go to London before coming to Rockquay, since Sir Jasper must present himself to the military and medical authorities, and likewise see his mother, who was in a very failing state.

The children looked and felt as if the meeting were deferred for years; but Miss Mohun, remembering the condition of 'Il Lido,' alike as to the presence of workmen and absence of servants, felt relieved at the respite, proceeded to send a telegram to Macrae, and became busier than ever before in her life.

The Rotherwoods were just going to London. The Marquis was wanted for a division, and though both he and Dr. Dagger declared his collar-bone quite repaired, his wife could not be satisfied without hearing for herself a verdict to the same effect from the higher authorities, being pretty sure that whatever their report might be, his abstract would be 'All right. Never mind.'

Fly had gained so much in flesh and strength, and was so much more like her real self, that she was to remain at the hotel with Miss Elbury, the rooms being kept for her parents till Easter. Mysie was, however, to go with them to satisfy her mother, 'with a first mouthful of children,' said Lord Rotherwood. 'Gillian had better come too; and we will write to the Merrifields to come to us, unless they are bound to the old lady.'

This, however, was unlikely, as she was very infirm, and her small house was pretty well filled by her attendants. Lady Rotherwood seconded the invitation like a good wife, and Gillian was grateful. Such a forestalling was well worth even the being the Marchioness's guest, and being treated with careful politeness and supervision as a girl of the period, always ready to break out. However, she would have Mysie, and she tried to believe Aunt Jane, who told her that she had conjured up a spectre of the awful dame. There was a melancholy parting on the side of poor little Lady Phyllis. 'What shall I do without you, Mysie dear?'

'It is only for a few days.'

'Yes; but then you will be in a different house, all down in the town—it will be only visiting—not like sisters.'

'Sisters are quite a different thing,' said Mysie stoutly; 'but we can be the next thing to it in our hearts.'

'It is not equal,' said Fly. 'You don't make a sister of me, and I do of you.'

'Because you know no better! Poor Fly, I do wish I could give you a sister of your own.'

'Do you know, Mysie, I think—I'm quite sure, that daddy is going to ask your father and mother to give you to us, out and out.'

'Oh! I'm sure they won't do that,' cried Mysie in consternation. 'Mamma never would!'

'And wouldn't you? Don't you like me as well as Gill and Val?'

'I *like* you better. Stop, don't, Fly; you are what people call more of a companion to me—my friend; but friends aren't the same as sisters, are they? They may be more, or they may be less, but it is not the same kind. And then it is not only you, there are papa and mamma and all my brothers.'

'But you *do* love daddy, and you have not seen yours for four years, and Aunt Florence and all the cousins at Beechcroft say they were quite afraid of him.'

'Because he is so—Oh! I don't know how to say it, but he is just like Epaminondas, or King Arthur, or Robert Bruce, or—'

'Well, that's enough' said Fly; 'I am sure my daddy would laugh if you said he was like all those.'

'To be sure he would!' said Mysie. 'And do you think I would give mine for him, though yours is so kind and good and such fun?'

'And I'm sure I'd rather have him than yours,' said Fly.

'Well, that's right. It would be wicked not to like one's own father and mother best.'

'But if they thought it would be good for you to have all my governesses and advantages, and they took pity on my loneliness. What then?'

'Then? Oh! I'd try to bear it,' said unworldly and uncomplimentary Mysie. 'And you need not be lonely now. There's Val!'

The two governesses had made friends, and the embargo on intercourse with Valetta had been allowed to drop; but Fly only shook her head, and allowed that Val was better than nothing.'

Mysie had a certain confidence that mamma would not give her away if all the lords and ladies in the world wanted her; and Gillian confirmed her in that belief, so that no misgiving interfered with her joy at finding herself in the train, where Lord Rotherwood declared that the two pair of eyes shone enough to light a candle by.

'I feel,' said Mysie, jumping up and down in her seat, 'like the man who said he had a bird in his bosom.'

'Or a bee in his bonnet, eh?' said Lord Rotherwood, while Mysie obeyed a sign from my lady to moderate the restlessness of her ecstasies.

'It really was a bird in his bosom,' said Gillian gravely, 'only he said so when he was dying in battle, and he meant his faith to his king.'

'And little Mysie has kept her faith to her mother,' said their cousin, putting out his hand to turn the happy face towards him. 'So the bird may well sing to her.'

'In spite of parting with Phyllis?' asked Lady Rotherwood.

'I can't help it, *indeed*,' said Mysie, divided between her politeness and her dread of being given away; 'it has been very nice, but one's own, own papa and mamma must be more than any one.'

'So they ought,' said Lord Rotherwood, and there it ended, chatter in the train not being considered desirable.

Gillian longed to show Mysie and Geraldine Grinstead to each other, and the first rub with her hostess occurred when the next morning she proposed to take a cab and go to Brompton.

'Is not your first visit due to your grandmother?' said Lady Rotherwood. 'You might walk there, and I will send some one to show you the way.'

'We must not go there till after luncheon,' said Gillian. 'She is not ready to see any one, and Bessie Merrifield cannot be spared; but I know Mrs. Grinstead will like to see us, and I do so want Mysie to see the studio.'

'My dear' (it was not a favourable my dear), 'I had rather you did not visit any one I do not know while you are under my charge.'

'She is Phyllis's husband's sister,' pleaded Gillian.

Lady Rotherwood made a little bend of acquiescence, but said no more, and departed, while Gillian inly raged. A few months ago she would have acted on her own responsibility (if Mysie would not have been too much shocked), but she had learnt the wisdom of submission in fact, if not in word, for she growled about great ladies and exclusiveness, so that Mysie looked mystified.

It was certainly rather dull in the only half-revivified London house, and Belgrave Square in Lent did not present a lively scene from the windows. The Liddesdales had a house there, but they were not to come up till the season began; and Gillian was turning with a sigh to ask if there might not be some books in Fly's schoolroom, when Mysie caught the sound of a bell, and ventured on an expedition to find her ladyship and ask leave to go to church.

There, to their unexpected delight, they beheld not only Bessie, but a clerical-looking back, which, after some watching, they so identified that they looked at one another with responsive eyes, and Gillian doubted whether this were recompense for submission, or reproof for discontent.

Very joyful was the meeting on the steps of St. Paul's, Knightsbridge, and an exchange of 'Oh! how did you come here? Where are you?'

Harry had come up the day before, and was to go and meet the travellers at Southampton with his uncle, Admiral Merrifield, who had brought his eldest daughter Susan to relieve her sister or assist her. Great was the joy and eager the talk, as first Bessie was escorted by the whole party back to grandmamma's house, and then Harry accompanied his sisters to Belgrave Square, where he was kept to luncheon, and Lady Rotherwood was as glad to resign his sisters to his charge as he could be to receive them.

He had numerous commissions to execute for his vicar, and Gillian had to assist the masculine brains in the department of Church needlework, actually venturing to undertake some herself, trusting to the tuition of Aunt Ada, a proficient in the same; while Mysie reverently begged at least to hem the borders.

Then they revelled in the little paradises of books and pictures in Northumberland Avenue and Westminster Sanctuary, and went to Evensong at the Abbey, Mysie's first sight thereof, and nearly the like to Gillian, since she only remembered before a longing not to waste time in a dull place instead of being in the delightful streets.

'It is a thing never to forget,' she said under her breath, as they lingered in the nave.

'I never guessed anything could make one feel so,' added Mysie, with a little sigh of rapture.

'That strange unexpected sense of delight always seems to me to explain, "Eye hath not seen, nor ear heard, neither hath it entered into the heart of man to conceive,"' said Harry.

Mysie whispered—

```
'Beneath thy contemplation
      Sink heart and voice opprest!'
```

'Oh, Harry, can't we stay and see Henry VII.'s Chapel, and Poets' Corner, and Edward I.'s monument?' pleaded the sister.

'I am afraid we must not, Gill. I have to see after some vases, and to get a lot of things at the Stores, and it will soon be dark. If I don't go to Southampton to-morrow, I will take you then. Now then, feet or cab?'

'Oh, let us walk! It is ten times the fun.'

'Then mind you don't jerk me back at the crossings.'

There are few pleasures greater of their kind than that of the youthful country cousin under the safe escort of a brother or father in London streets. The sisters looked in at windows, wondered and enjoyed, till they had to own their feet worn out, and submit to a four-wheeler.

'An hour of London is more than a month of Rockquay, or a year of Silverfold,' cried Gillian.

'Dear old Silverfold,' said Mysie; 'when shall we go back?'

'By the bye,' said Harry, 'how about the great things that were to be done for mother?'

'Primrose is all right,' said Mysie. 'The dear little thing has written a nice copybook, and hemmed a whole set of handkerchiefs for papa. She is so happy with them.'

'And you, little Mouse?'

'I have done my translation—not quite well, I am afraid, and made the little girl's clothes. I wonder if I may go and take them to her.'

'And Val has finished her crewel cushion, thanks to the aunts,' said Gillian.

'Fergus's machine, how about that? Perpetual motion, wasn't it?'

'That has turned into mineralogy, worse luck,' said Gillian.

'Gill has done a beautiful sketch of Rockquay,' added Mysie.

'Oh! don't talk of me,' said Gillian. 'I have only made a most unmitigated mess of everything.'

But here attention was diverted by Harry's exclaiming—

'Hullo! was that Henderson?'

'Nonsense; the Wardours are at Cork.'

'He may be on leave.'

'Or retired. He is capable of it.'

'I believe it was old Fangs.'

The discussion lasted to Belgrave Square.

And then Sunday was spent upon memorable churches and services under the charge of Harry, who was making the most of his holiday. The trio went to Evensong at St. Wulstan's, and a grand idea occurred to Gillian—could not Theodore White become one of those young choristers, who had their home in the Clergy House.

CHAPTER XVIII. — FATHER AND MOTHER

The telegram came early on Monday morning. Admiral Merrifield and Harry started by the earliest train, deciding not to take the girls; whereupon their kind host, to mitigate the suspense, placed himself at the young ladies' disposal for anything in the world that they might wish to see. It was too good an opportunity of seeing the Houses of Parliament to be lost, and the spell of Westminster Abbey was upon Mysie.

Cousin Rotherwood was a perfect escort, and declared that he had not gone through such a course of English history since he had taken his cousin Lilias and his sister Florence the same round more years ago than it was civil to recollect. He gave a sigh to the great men he had then let them see and hear, and regretted the less that there was no possibility of regaling the present pair with a debate. It was all like a dream to the two girls. They saw, but suspense was throbbing in their hearts all the time, and qualms were crossing Gillian as she recollected that in some aspects her father could be rather a terrible personage when one was wilfully careless, saucy to authorities, or unable to see or confess wrong-doing; and the element of dread began to predominate in her state of expectation. The bird in the bosom fluttered very hard as the possible periods after the arrivals of trains came round; and it was not till nearly eight o'clock that the decisive halt of wheels was heard, and in a few moments Mysie was in the dearest arms in the world, and Gillian feeling the moustached kiss she had not known for nearly four long years, and which was half-strange, half-familiar.

In drawing-room light, there was the mother looking none the worse for her journey, her clear brown skin neither sallow nor lined, and the soft brown eyes as bright and sweet as ever; but the father must be learnt over again, and there was awe enough as well as enthusiastic love to make her quail at the thought of her record of self-will.

There was, however, no disappointment in the sight of the fine, tall soldierly figure, broad shouldered, but without an ounce of superfluous flesh, and only altered by his hair having become thinner and whiter, thus adding to the height of his forehead, and making his very dark eyebrows and eyes have a different effect, especially as he was still pallid beneath the browning of many years, though he declared himself so well as to be ashamed of being invalided.

Time was short. Harry and the Admiral, who were coming to dinner, had rushed home to dress and to fetch Susan; and Lady Merrifield was conducted in haste to her bedroom, and left to the almost too excited ministrations of her daughters.

It was well that attentive servants had unfastened the straps, for when Gillian had claimed the keys of the dear old familiar box, her hand shook so much that they jingled; the key would not go into the hole, and she had to resign them to sober Mysie, who had been untying the bonnet, with a kiss, and answering for the health of Primrose, whom Uncle William was to bring to London in two days' time.

'My dear silly child,' said her mother, surprised at Gillian's emotion.

And the reply was a burst of tears. 'Oh, so silly! so wrong! I have so wanted you.'

'I know all about it. You told us all, like an honest child.'

'Oh, such dreadful things—the rock—the poor child killed—Cousin Rotherwood hurt.'

'Yes, yes, I heard! We can't have it out now. Here's papa! she is upset about these misadventures,' added Lady Merrifield, looking up to her husband, who stood amazed at the sobs that greeted him.

'You must control yourself, Gillian,' he said gravely. 'Stop that! Your mother is tired, and has to dress! Don't worry her. Go, if you cannot leave off.'

The bracing tone made Gillian swallow her tears, the more easily because of the familiarity of home atmosphere, confidence, and protection; and a mute caress from her mother was a promise of sympathy.

The sense of that presence was the chief pleasure of the short evening, for there were too many claimants for the travellers' attention to enable them to do more than feast their eyes on their son and daughters, while they had to talk of other things, the weddings, the two families, the home news, all deeply interesting in their degree, though not touching Gillian quite so deeply as the tangle she had left at Rockstone, and mamma's view of her behaviour; even though it was pleasant to hear of Phyllis's beautiful home in Ceylon, and Alethea's bungalow, and how poor Claude had to go off alone to Rawul Pindee. She felt sure that her mother was far more acceptable to her hostess than either of the aunts, and that, indeed, she might well be so!

Gillian's first feeling was like Mysie's in the morning, that nothing could go wrong with her again, but she must perforce have patience before she could be heard. Harry could not be spared for another day from his curacy, and to him was due the first tete-a-tete with his mother, after that most important change his life had yet known, and in which she rejoiced so deeply. 'The dream of her heart,' she said, 'had always been that one of her sons should be dedicated;' and now that the fulfilment had come in her absence, it was precious to her to hear all those feelings and hopes and trials that the young man could have uttered to no other ears.

Sir Jasper, meantime, had gone out on business, and was to meet the rest at luncheon at his mother's house, go with them to call on the Grinsteads, and then do some further commissions, Lady Rotherwood placing the carriage at their disposal. As to 'real talk,' that seemed impossible for the girls, they could only, as Mysie expressed it, 'bask in the light of mamma's eyes' and after Harry was gone on an errand for his vicar, there were no private interviews for her.

Indeed, the mother did not know how much Gillian had on her mind, and thought all she wanted was discussion, and forgiveness for the follies explained in the letter, the last received. Of any connection between that folly and the accident to Lord Rotherwood of course she was not aware, and in fact she had more on her hands than she could well do in the time allotted, and more people to see. Gillian had to find that things could not be quite the same as when she had been chief companion in the seclusion of Silverfold.

And just as she was going out the following letter was put into her hands, come by one of the many posts from Rockstone:—

'MY DEAR GILLIAN—I write to you because you can explain matters, and I want your father's advice, or Cousin Rotherwood's. As I was on the way to Il Lido just now I met Mr. Flight, looking much troubled and distressed. He caught at me, and begged me to go with him to tell poor Kalliope that her brother Alexis is in Avoncester Jail. He knew it from having come down in the train with Mr. Stebbing. The charge is for having carried away with him L15 in notes, the payment for a marble cross for a grave at Barnscombe. You remember that on the day of the accident poor Field was taking it in the waggon, when he came home to hear of his child's death.

'The receipt for the price was inquired for yesterday, and it appeared that the notes had been given to Field in an envelope. In his trouble, the poor man forgot to deliver this till the morning; when on his way to the office he met young White and gave it to him. Finding it had not been paid in, nor entered in the books, and knowing the poor boy to have absconded, off went Mr. Stebbing, got a summons, and demanded to have him committed for trial.

'Alexis owned to having forgotten the letter in the shock of the dismissal, and to having carried it away with him, but said that as soon as he had discovered it he had forwarded it to his sister, and had desired her to send it to the office. He did not send it direct, because he could only, at the moment, get one postage-stamp. On this he was remanded till Saturday, when his sisters' evidence can be taken at the magistrates meeting. This was the news that Mr. Flight and I had to take to that poor girl, who could hardly be spared from her mother to speak to us, and how she is to go to Avoncester it is hard to say; but she has no fear of not being able to clear her brother, for she says she put the dirty and ragged envelope that no doubt contained the notes into another, with a brief explanation, addressed it to Mr. Stebbing, and sent it by Petros, who told her that he had delivered it.

'I thought nothing could be clearer, and so did Mr. Flight, but unluckily Kalliope had destroyed her brother's letter, and had not read me this part of it, so that she can bring no actual tangible proof, and it is a much more serious matter than it appeared when we were talking to her. Mr. White has just been here, whether to condole or to triumph I don't exactly know. He has written to Leeds, and heard a very unsatisfactory account of that eldest brother, who certainly has deceived him shamefully, and this naturally adds to the prejudice against the rest of the family. We argued about Kalliope's high character, and he waved his hand and said, "My dear ladies, you don't understand those Southern women—the more pious, devoted doves they are, the blacker they will swear themselves to get off their scamps of men." To represent that Kalliope is only one quarter Greek was useless, especially as he has been diligently imbued by Mrs. Stebbing with all last autumn's gossip, and, as he confided to Aunt Ada, thinks "that they take advantage of his kindness!"

'Of course Mr. Flight, and all who really know Alexis and Kalliope, feel the accusation absurd; but it is only too possible that the Avoncester magistrates may not see the evidence in the same light, as its weight depends upon character, and the money is really missing, so that I much fear their committing him for trial at the Quarter Sessions. It will probably be the best way to employ a solicitor to watch the case at once, and I shall speak to Mr. Norton tomorrow, unless your father can send me any better advice by post. I hope it is not wicked to believe that the very fact of Mr. Norton's being concerned might lead to the notes finding themselves.

'Meantime, I am of course doing what I can. Kally is very brave in her innocence and her brother's, but, shut up in her mother's sickroom, she little guesses how bad things are made to look, or how Greek and false are treated as synonymous.

'Much love to your mother. I am afraid this is a damper on your happiness, but I am sure that your father would wish to know. Aunt Ada tackles Mr. White better than I do, and means if possible to make him go to Avoncester himself when the case comes on, so that he should at least see and hear for himself.—Your affectionate aunt,

J. M.'

What a letter for poor Gillian! She had to pocket it at first, and only opened it while taking off her hat at grandmamma's house, and there was only time for a blank feeling of uncomprehending consternation before she had to go down to luncheon, and hear her father and uncle go on with talk about India and Stokesley, to which she could not attend.

Afterwards, Lady Merrifield was taken to visit grandmamma, and Bessie gratified the girls with a sight of her special den, where she wrote her stories, showing them the queer and flattering gifts that had come to her in consequence of her authorship, which was becoming less anonymous, since her family were growing hardened to it, and grandmamma was past hearing of it or being distressed. It was in Bessie's room that Gillian gathered the meaning of her aunt's letter, and was filled with horror and dismay. She broke out with a little scream, which brought both Mysie and Bessie to her side; but what could they do? Mysie was shocked and sympathising enough, and Bessie was trying to understand the complicated story, when the summons came for the sisters. There were hopes of communicating the catastrophe in the carriage; but no, the first exclamation of 'Oh, mamma!' was lost.

Sir Jasper had something so important to tell his wife about his interviews at the Horse Guards, that the attempt to interrupt was silenced by a look and sign. It was a happy thing to have a father at home, but it was different from being mamma's chief companion and confidante, and poor Gillian sat boiling over with something very like indignation at not being allowed even to allow that she had something to tell at least as important as anything papa could be relating.

She hardly knew whether to be glad or sorry that the Grinsteads proved to be out of town; but at any rate she might be grateful to Lady Rotherwood for preventing a vain expedition—a call on another old friend, Mrs. Crayon, the Marianne Weston of early youth, and now a widow, as she too was out. Then followed some shopping that the parents wanted to do together, but at the door of the stores Lady Merrifield said—

'I have a host of things to get here for the two brides. Suppose, papa, that you walk home with Gillian across the Park. It will suit you better than this fearful list.'

Lady Merrifield only thought of letting father and daughter renew their acquaintance, and though she saw that Gillian was in an agony to speak about something, did not guess what an ordeal the girl felt it to have to begin with the father, unseen for four years, and whose searching eyes and grave politeness gave a sense of austerity, so that trepidation was spoiling all the elation at having a father, and such a father, to walk with.

'Well, Gillian,' he said, 'we have a great deal of lee way to make up. I want to hear of poor White's children. I am glad you have had the opportunity of showing them some kindness.'

'Oh, papa! it is so dreadful! If you would read this letter.'

'I cannot do so here,' said Sir Jasper, who could not well make trial of his new spectacles in Great George Street. What is dreadful?'

'This accusation. Poor Alexis! Oh! you don't know. The accident and all—our fault—mine really,' gasped Gillian.

'I am not likely to know at this rate,' said Sir Jasper. 'I hope you have not caught the infection of incoherency from Lord Rotherwood. Do you mean his accident?'

'Yes; they have turned them both off, and now they have gone and put Alexis in prison.'

'For the accident? I thought it was a fall of rock.'

'Oh no—I mean yes—it wasn't for that; but it came of that, and Fergus and I were at the bottom of it,' said Gillian, in such confusion that her words seemed to tumble out without her own control.

'How did you escape with your lives?'

Was he misunderstanding her on purpose, or giving a lesson on slipslop at such a provoking moment? Perhaps he was really only patient with the daughter who must have seemed to him half-foolish, but she was forced to collect her senses and say—

'I only meant that we were the real cause. Fergus is wild about geology, and took away a stone that was put to show where the cliff was unsafe. He showed the stone to Alexis White, who did not know where it came from and let him have it, and that was the way Cousin Rotherwood came to tread on the edge of the precipice.'

'What had you to do with it?'

'I—oh! I had disappointed Alexis about the lessons,' said Gillian, blushing a little;' and he was out of spirits, and did not mind what he was about.'

'H'm! But you cannot mean that this youth can have been imprisoned for such a cause.'

'No; that was about the money, but of course he sent it back. He ran away when he was dismissed, because he was quite in despair, and did not know what he was about.'

'I think not, indeed!'

'Papa,' said Gillian, steadying her voice, 'you must not, please, blame him so much, for it was really very much my fault, and that is what makes me doubly unhappy. Did you read my last letter to mamma?'

'Yes. I understood that you thought you had not treated your aunts rightly by not consulting them about your intercourse with the Whites, and that you had very properly resolved to tell them all. I hope you did so.'

'Indeed I did, and Aunt Jane was very kind, or else I should have had no comfort at all. Was mamma very much shocked at my teaching Alexis?'

'I do not remember. We concluded that whatever you did had your aunts' sanction.'

'Ah! that was the point.'

'Did these young people persuade you to secrecy?'

'Oh no, no; Kalliope protested, and I overpowered her, because—because I was foolish, and I thought Aunt Jane interfering.'

'I see,' said Sir Jasper, with perhaps more comprehension of the antagonism than sisterly habit and affection would have allowed to his wife. 'I am glad you saw your error, and tried to repair it; but what could you have done to affect this boy so much. How old is he? We thought of him as twelve or fourteen, but one forgets how time goes on, and you speak of him as in a kind of superintendent's position.'

'He is nineteen.'

Sir Jasper twirled his moustache.

'I begin to perceive,' he said, 'you rushed into an undertaking that became awkward, and when you had to draw off, the young fellow was upset and did not mind his business. So far I understand, but you said something about prison.'

The worst part of the personal confession was over now, and Gillian could go on to tell the rest of the Stebbing enmity, of Mr. White's arrival, and of the desire to keep his relations aloof from him.

'This is guess work,' said Sir Jasper.

'I think Cousin Rotherwood would say the same' rejoined Gillian, and then she explained the dismissal, the flight, and the unfortunate consequences, and that Aunt Jane hoped for advice by the morning's post.

'I am afraid it is too late for that,' said Sir Jasper, looking at his watch. 'I must read her letter and consider.'

Gillian gave a desperate sigh, and felt more desperate when at that moment the very man they had had a glimpse of on Saturday met them, exclaiming in a highly delighted tone—

'Sir Jasper Merrifield!'

Any Royal Wardour ought to have been welcome to the Merrifields, but this individual had not been a particular favourite with the young people. They knew he was the son of a popular dentist, who had made his fortune, and had put his son into the army to make a gentleman of him, and prevent him from becoming an artist. In the first object there had been very fair success; but the taste for art was unquenchable, and it had been the fashion of the elder half of the Merrifield family to make a joke, and profess to be extremely bored, when 'Fangs,' as they naughtily called him among themselves, used to arrive from leave, armed with catalogues, or come in with his drawings to find sympathy in his colonel's wife. Gillian had caught enough from her four elders to share in an unreasoning way their prejudice, and she felt doubly savage and contemptuous when she heard—

'Yes, I retired.'

'And what are you doing now?'

'My mother required me as long as she lived' (then Gillian noticed that he was in mourning). 'I think I shall go abroad, and take lessons at Florence or Rome, though it is too late to do anything seriously—and there are affairs to be settled first.'

Then came a whole shoal of other inquiries, and even though they actually included 'poor White' and his family, Gillian was angered and dismayed at the wretch being actually asked by her father to come in with them and see Lady Merrifield, who would be delighted to see him.

'What would Lady Rotherwood think of the liberty?' the displeased mood whispered to Gillian.

But Lady Rotherwood, presiding over her pretty Worcester tea-set, was quite ready to welcome any of the Merrifield friends. There were various people in the room besides Lady Merrifield and Mysie, who had just come in. There was the Admiral talking politics with Lord Rotherwood, and there was Clement Underwood, who had come with Harry from the city, and Bessie discussing with them boys' guilds and their amusements.

Gillian felt frantic. Would no one cast a thought on Alexis in prison? If he had been to be hanged the next day, her secret annoyance at their indifference to his fate could not have been worse.

And yet at the first opportunity Harry brought Mr. Underwood to talk to her about his choir-boys, and to listen to her account of the 7th Standard boy, a member of the most musical choir in Rockquay, and the highest of the high.

'I hope not cockiest of the cocky,' said Mr. Underwood, smiling. 'Our experience is that superlatives may often be so translated.'

'I don't think poor Theodore is cocky,' said Gillian; 'the Whites have always been so bullied and sat upon.'

'Is his name Theodore?' asked Mr. Underwood, as if he liked the name, which Gillian remembered to have seen on a cross at Vale Leston.

'Being sat upon is hardly the best lesson in humility,' said Harry.

'There's apt to be a reaction,' said Mr. Underwood; 'but the crack voice of a country choir is not often in that condition, as I know too well. I was the veriest young prig myself under those circumstances!'

'Don't be too hard on cockiness,' said Lord Rotherwood, who had come up to them, 'there must be consciousness of powers. How are you to fly, if you mustn't flap your wings and crow a little?'

'On a les defauts de ses qualites,' put in Lady Merrifield.

'Yes,' added Mr. Underwood. 'It is quite true that needful self-assertion and originality, and sense of the evils around—'

'Which the old folk have outgrown and got used to,' said Lord Rotherwood.

'May be condemned as conceit,' concluded Mr. Underwood.

'Ay, exactly as Eliab knew David's pride and the naughtiness of his heart,' said Lord Rotherwood. 'If you won't fight your giant yourself, you've no business to condemn those who feel it in them to go at him.'

'Ah! we have got to the condemnation of others, instead of the exaltation of self,' said Lady Merrifield.

'It is better to cultivate humility in one's self than other people, eh?' said the Marquis, and his cousin thought, though she did not say, that he was really the most humble and unself-conscious man she had ever known. What she did say was, 'It is a plant that grows best uncultivated.'

'And if you have it not by happy nature, what then?' said Clement

Underwood.

'Then I suppose you must plant it, and there will be plenty of tears of repentance to water it,' returned she.

'Thank you,' said Clement. 'That is an idea to work upon.'

'All very fine!' sighed Gillian to Mysie, 'but oh, how about Alexis in prison! There's papa, now he has got rid of Fangs, actually going to walk off with Uncle Sam, and mamma has let Lady Rotherwood get hold of her. Will nobody care for anybody?'

'I think I would trust papa,' said Mysie.

He was not long gone, and when he came back he said, 'You may give me that letter, Gillian. I posted a card to tell your aunt she should hear to- morrow.'

All that Gillian could say to her mother in private that evening consisted of, 'Oh, mamma, mamma,' but the answer was, 'I have heard about it from papa, my dear; I am glad you told him. He is thinking what to do. Be patient.'

Externally, awe and good manners forced Gillian to behave herself; but internally she was so far from patient, and had so many bitter feelings of indignation, that she felt deeply rebuked when she came down next morning to find her father hurrying through his breakfast, with a cab ordered to convey him to the station, on his way to see what could be done for Alexis White.

That day Gillian had her confidential talk with her mother—a talk that she never forgot, trying to dig to the roots of her failures in a manner that only the true mother-confessor of her own child can perhaps have patience and skill for, and that only when she has studied the creature from babyhood. The concatenation, ending (if it was so to end) in the committal to Avoncester Jail, and beginning with the interview over the rails, had to be traced link by link, and was almost as long as 'the house that Jack built.'

'And now I see,' said Gillian, 'that it all came of a nasty sort of antagonism to Aunt Jane. I never guessed how like I was to Dolores, and I thought her so bad. But if I had only trusted Aunt Jane, and had no secrets, she would have helped me in it all, I know now, and never have brought the Whites into trouble.'

'Yes,' said Lady Merrifield; 'perhaps I should have warned you a little more, but I went off in such a hurry that I had no time to think. You children are all very loyal to us ourselves; but I suppose you are all rather infected by the modern spirit, that criticises when it ought to submit to authorities.'

'But how can one help seeing what is amiss? As some review says, how respect what does not make itself respectable? You know I don't mean that for my aunts. I have learnt now what Aunt Jane really is—how very kind and wise and clever and forgiving—but I was naughty enough to think her at first —'

'Well, what? Don't be afraid.'

'Then I did think she was fidgety and worrying—always at one, and wanting to poke her nose into everything.'

'Poor Aunt Jane! Those are the faults of her girlhood, which she has been struggling against all her life!'

'But in your time, mamma, would such difficulties really not have been seen—I mean, if she had been actually what I thought her?'

'I think the difference was that no faults of the elders were dwelt upon by a loyal temper. To find fault was thought so wrong that the defects were scarcely seen, and were concealed from ourselves as well as others. It would scarcely, I suppose, be possible to go back to that unquestioning state, now the temper of the times is changed; but I belong enough to the older days to believe that the true safety is in submission in the spirit as well as the letter.'

'I am sure I should have found it so,' said Gillian. 'And oh! I hope, now that papa is come, the Whites may be spared any more of the troubles I have brought on them.'

'We will pray that it may be so.' said her mother.

CHAPTER XIX. — THE KNIGHT AND THE DRAGON

A telegram had been received in the morning, which kept Valetta and Fergus on the qui vive all day. Valetta was an unspeakable worry to the patient Miss Vincent, and Fergus arranged his fossils and minerals.

Both children flew out to meet their father at the gate, but words failed them as he came into the house, greeted the aunts, and sat down with Fergus on his knee, and Valetta encircled by his arm.

'Yes, Lilias is quite well, very busy and happy—with her first instalment of children.'

'I am so thankful that you are come,' said Adeline. 'Jane ventured to augur that you would, but I thought it too much to hope for.'

'There was no alternative,' said Sir Jasper.

'I infer that you halted at Avoncester.'

'I did so; I saw the poor boy.'

'What a comfort for his sister!'

'Poor fellow! Mine was the first friendly face he had seen, and he was almost overcome by it'—and the strong face quivered with emotion at the recollection of the boy's gratitude.

'He is a nice fellow,' said Jane. 'I am glad you have seen him, for neither Mr. White nor Rotherwood can believe that he is not utterly foolish, if not worse.'

'A boy may do foolish things without being a fool,' said Sir Jasper. 'Not that this one is such another as his father. I wish he were.'

'I suppose he has more of the student scholarly nature.'

'Yes. The enlistment, which was the making of his father, was a sort of moral suicide in him. I got him to tell me all about it, and I find that the idea of the inquest, and of having to mention you, you monkey, drove him frantic, and the dismissal completed the business.'

'I told them about it,' said Fergus.

'Quite right, my boy; the pity was that he did not trust to your honour, but he seems to have worked himself into the state of mind when young men run amuck. I saw his colonel, Lydiard, and the captain and sergeant of his company, who had from the first seen that he was a man of a higher class under a cloud, and had expected further inquiry, though, even from the little that had been seen of him, there was a readiness to take his word. As the sergeant said, he was not the common sort of runaway clerk, and it was a thousand pities that he must go to the civil power—in which I am disposed to agree. What sort of man is the cousin at the marble works?'

'A regular beast,' murmured Fergus.

'I think,' said Jane, 'that he means to be good and upright.'

'More than means,' said Ada, 'but he is cautious, and says he has been so often deceived.'

'As far as I can understand,' said Jane, 'there was originally desperate enmity between him and his cousin.'

'He forgave entirely,' said Ada; 'and he really has done a great deal for the family, who own that they have no claim upon him.'

'Yes,' said Jane, 'but from a distance, with no personal knowledge, and a contempt for the foreign mother, and the pretensions to gentility. He would have been far kinder if his cousin had remained a sergeant.'

'He only wished to try them,' said Adeline, 'and he always meant to come and see about them; besides, that eldest son has been begging of him on false pretences all along.'

'That I can believe,' said Sir Jasper. 'I remember his father's distress at his untruth in the regimental school, and his foolish mother shielding him. No doubt he might do enough to cause distrust of his family; but has Mr. White actually never gone near them, as Gillian told me?'

'Excepting once walking Maura home,' said Jane, 'no; but I ascribe all that to the partner, Mr. Stebbing, who has had it all his own way here, and seems to me to have systematically kept Alexis down to unnecessarily distasteful drudgery. Kalliope's talent gave her a place; but young Stebbing's pursuit of her, though entirely unrequited, has roused his mother's bitter enmity, and there are all manner of stories afloat. I believe I could disprove every one of them; but together they have set Mr. White against her, and he cannot see her in her office, as her mother is too ill to be left. I do believe that if the case against Alexis is discharged, they will think she has the money.'

'Stebbing said Maura changed a five-pound note,' put in Fergus; 'and when I told him to shut up, for it was all bosh, he punched me.'

I hope Richard sent it' said Ada, 'but you see the sort of report that is continually before Mr. White—not that I think he believes half, or is satisfied

—with the Stebbings.'

'I am sure he is not with Frank Stebbing,' said Jane. 'I do think and hope that he is only holding off in order to judge; and I think your coming may have a great effect upon him, Jasper.'

The Rotherwoods had requested Sir Jasper to use their apartments at the hotel, and he went thither to dress, being received, as he said, by little Lady Phyllis with much grace and simplicity.

The evening passed brightly, and when the children were gone to bed, their father said rather anxiously that he feared the aunts had had a troublesome charge hastily thrust on them.

'We enjoyed it very much,' said Adeline politely.

'We were thankful to have a chance of knowing the young people,' added Jane. 'I am only glad you did not come home at Christmas, when I was not happy about the two girls.'

'Yes, Valetta got into trouble and wrote a piteous little letter of confession about copying.'

'Yes, but you need not be uneasy about that; it was one of those lapses that teach women without any serious loss. She did not know what she was about, and she told no falsehoods; indeed, each one of your children has been perfectly truthful throughout.'

'That is the great point, after all. Lilias could hardly fail to make her children true.'

'Fergus is really an excellent little boy, and Gillian—poor Gillian—I think she really did want more experience, and was only too innocent.'

'That is what you really think,' said the father anxiously.

'Yes, I do,' said Jane. 'If she had been a fast girl, she would have been on her guard against the awkward situation, and have kept out of this mess; but very likely would have run into a worse one.'

'I do not think that her elder sisters would have done like her.'

'Perhaps not; but they were living in your regimental world at the age when her schoolroom life was going on. I think you have every reason to be satisfied with her tone of mind. As you said of the boy, a person may commit an imprudence without being imprudent.'

'I quite agree to that,' he said, 'and, indeed, I see that you have managed her most wisely, and obtained her affection and gratitude, as indeed you have mine!' he added, with a tone in his voice that touched Jane to the core of her heart.

'I never heard anything like it before,' she said to her sister over their fire at night, with a dew of pleasure in her eyes.

'I never liked Jasper so well before. He is infinitely pleasanter and more amiable. Do you remember our first visit? No, it was not you who went with me, it was Emily. I am sure he felt bound to be on guard all the time against any young officer's attentions to his poor little sister-in-law,' said Ada, with her Maid-of-Athens look. 'The smallest approach brought those hawk's eyes of his like a dart right through one's backbone. It all came back to me to- night, and the way he used to set poor Lily to scold me.'

'So that you rejoiced to be grown old. I beg your pardon, but I did. My experience was when I went to help Lily pack for foreign service, when I suppose my ferret look irritated him, for he snubbed me extensively, and I am sure he rejoiced to carry his wife out of reach of all the tribe. I dare say I richly deserved it, but I hope we are all "mellered down," as Wat Greenwood used to say of his brewery for the pigs.'

'My dear, what a comparison!'

'Redolent of the Old Court, and of Lily, waiting for her swan's nest among the reeds, till her stately warrior came, and made her day dreams earnest in a way that falls to the lot of few. I don't think his severity ever dismayed her for a moment, there was always such sweetness in it.

'True knight and lady! Yes. He is grown handsomer than ever, too!'

'I hope he will get those poor children out of their hobble! It is chivalrous enough of him to come down about it, in the midst of all his business in London.'

Sir Jasper started the next morning with Fergus on his way to school, getting on the road a good deal of information, mingled together about forms and strata, cricket and geology. Leaving his little son at Mrs. Edgar's door, he proceeded to Ivinghoe Terrace, where he waited long at the blistered door of the dilapidated house before the little maid informed him that Mr. Richard was gone out, and missus was so ill that she didn't know as Miss White could see nobody; but she took his card and invited him to walk into the parlour, where the breakfast things were just left.

Down came Kalliope, with a wan face and eyes worn with sleeplessness, but a light of hope and gratitude flashing over her features as she met the kind eyes, and felt the firm hand of her father's colonel, a sort of king in the eyes of all Royal Wardours.

'My poor child,' he said gently, 'I am come to see if I can help you.'

'Oh! so good of you,' and she squeezed his hand tightly, in the effort perhaps not to give way.

'I fear your mother is very ill.'

'Very ill,' said Kalliope. 'Richard came last night, and he let her know what we had kept from her; but she is calmer now.'

'Then your brother Richard is here.'

'Yes; he is gone up to Mr. White's.'

'He is in a solicitor's office, I think. Will he be able to undertake the case?'

'Oh no, no'—the white cheek flushed, and the hand trembled. 'There is a Leeds family here, and he is afraid of their finding out that he has any connection with this matter. He says it would be ruin to his prospects.'

'Then we must do our best without him,' Sir Jasper said in a fatherly voice, inexpressively comforting to the desolate wounded spirit. 'I will not keep you long from your mother, but will you answer me a few questions? Your brother tells me—'

She looked up almost radiantly, 'You have seen him?'

'Yes. I saw him yesterday,' and as she gazed as if the news were water to a thirsty soul—'he sent his love, and begged his mother and you to forgive the distress his precipitancy has caused. I did not think him looking ill; indeed, I think the quiet of his cell is almost a rest to him, as he makes sure that he can clear himself.'

'Oh, Sir Jasper! how can we ever be grateful enough!'

'Never mind that now, only tell me what is needful, for time is short. Your brother sent these notes in their own envelope, he says.'

'Yes, a very dirty one. I did not open it or see them, but enclosed it in one of my own, and sent it by my youngest brother, Petros.'

'How was yours addressed?'

'Francis Stebbing, Esq., Marble Works; and I put in a note in explanation.'

'Is the son's name likewise Francis?'

'Francis James.'

'Petros delivered it?'

'Yes, certainly.'

Here they were interrupted by Maura's stealing timidly in with the message that poor mamma had heard that Sir Jasper was here, and would he be so very good as to come up for one minute and speak to her.

'It is asking a great deal,' said Kalliope, 'but it would be very kind, and it might ease her mind.'

He was taken to the poor little bedroom full of oppressive atmosphere, though the window was open to relieve the labouring breath. It seemed absolutely filled with the enormous figure of the poor dropsical woman with white ghastly face, sitting pillowed up, incapable of lying down.

'Oh, so good! so angelic!' she gasped.

'I am sorry to see you so ill, Mrs. White.'

'Ah! 'tis dying I am, Colonel Merrifield—begging your pardon, but the sight of you brings back the times when my poor captain was living, and I was the happy woman. 'Tis the thought of my poor orphans that is vexing me, leaving them as I am in a strange land where their own flesh and blood is unnatural to them,' she cried, trying to clasp her swollen hands, in the excitement that brought out the Irish substructure of her nature. 'Ah, Colonel dear, you'll bear in mind their father that would have died for you, and be good to them.'

'Indeed, I hope to do what I can for them.'

'They are good children, Sir Jasper, all of them, even the poor boy that is in trouble out of the very warmth of his heart; but 'tis Richard who would be the credit to you, if you would lend him the helping hand. Where is the boy, Kally?'

'He is gone to call on Mr. White.'

'Ah! and you'll say a good word for him with his cousin,' she pleaded, 'and say how 'tis no discredit to him if things are laid on his poor brother that he never did.'

The poor woman was evidently more anxious to bespeak patronage for her first-born, the pride and darling of her heart, than for those who might be thought to need it more, but she became confused and agitated when she thought of Alexis, declaring that the poor boy might have been hasty, and have disgraced himself, but it was hard, very hard, if they swore away his liberty, and she never saw him more, and she broke into distressing sobs. Sir Jasper, in a decided voice, assured her that he expected with confidence that her son would be freed the next day, and able to come to see her.

'It's the blessing of a dying mother will be on you, Colonel dear! Oh! bring him back, that his mother's eyes may rest on the boy that has always been dutiful. No—no, Dick, I tell you 'tis no disgrace to wear the coat his father wore.' Wandering was beginning, and she was in no condition for Kalliope to leave her. The communicative Maura, who went downstairs with him, said that Richard was so angry about Alexis that it had upset poor mamma sadly. And could Alexis come?' she asked, 'even when he is cleared?'

'I will ask for furlough for him.'

'Oh! thank you—that would do mamma more good than anything. She is so fond of Richard, he is her favourite, but Alexis is the real help and comfort.'

'I can quite believe so. And now will you tell me where I shall find your brother who took the letter, Peter or Petros?'

'Petros is his name, but the boys call him Peter. He is at school—the Bellevue National School—up that street.'

Repairing to that imposing building, Sir Jasper knocked at the door, and sent in his card by an astonished pupil-teacher with a request to the master that he might speak to Petros White, waiting in the porch till a handsome little fellow appeared, stouter, rosier, and more English looking than the others of his family, but very dusty, and rather scared.

'You don't remember me,' said Sir Jasper, 'but I was your father's colonel, and I want to find some way of helping your brother. Your sister tells me she gave you a letter to carry to Mr. Stebbing.'

'Yes, sir.'

'Where did you take it?'

'To his house, Carrara.'

'Was it not directed to the Marble Works?'

'Yes, but—'

'But what? Speak out, my man.'

'At the gate Blake, the porter, was very savage, and would not let us in. He said he would have no boys loafing about, we had done harm enough for one while, and he would set his dog at us.'

'Then you did not give him the letter?'

'No. I wouldn't after the way he pitched into me. I didn't know if he would give it. And he wouldn't hear a word, so we went up to Rockstone to the house.'

'Whom did you give it to there?'

'I dropped it into the slit in the door.'

'You only told your sister that you delivered it.'

'Yes, sir. Theodore said I must not tell sister; it would only vex her more to hear how every one pitches into us, right and left,' he said, with trembling lip.

'Is Theodore your next brother?'

'Yes sir.'

'Was he with you?'

'No; it was Sydney Grove.'

'Is he here? Or—Did any one else see you leave the letter?'

'Mr. Stebbing's son—the young one, George, was in the drive and slanged us for not going to the back door.'

'That is important. Thank you, my boy. Give my—my compliments to your master, and ask him to be kind enough to spare this Sydney Grove to me for a few moments.'

This proved to be an amphibious-looking boy, older and rougher than Petros, and evidently his friend and champion. He was much less shy, and spoke out boldly, saying how he had gone with little Peter, and the porter had rowed them downright shameful, but it was nothing to that there young Stebbing ordering them out of the grounds for a couple of beastly cads, after no good. He (Grove) had a good mind to ha' give 'un a good warming, only 'twas school time, and they was late as it was. Everybody was down upon the Whites, and it was a shame when they hadn't done nothing, and he didn't see as they was stuck up, not he.

Sir Jasper made a note of Master Grove's residence, and requested an interview with the master, from whom he obtained an excellent character of both the Whites, especially Theodore. The master lamented that this affair of their brother should have given a handle against them, for he wanted the services of the elder one as a monitor, eventually as a pupil-teacher, but did not know whether the choice would be advisable under the present circumstances. The boys' superiority made them unpopular, and excited jealousy among a certain set, though they were perfectly inoffensive, and they had much to go through in consequence of the suspicion that had fallen on their brother. Petros and Sydney should have leave from school whenever their testimony was wanted.

As Sir Jasper walked down the street, his elder sister-in-law emerged from a tamarisk-flanked gateway. 'This is our new abode, Jasper,' she said. 'Come in and see what you think of it! Well, have you had any success?'

He explained how the letter could be traced to Mr. Stebbing's house, and then consulted her whether to let all come out at the examination before the magistrates, or to induce the Stebbings to drop the prosecution.

'It would serve them right if it all came out in public,' she said.

'But would it be well?'

'One must not be vindictive! And to drag poor Kalliope to Avoncester would be a dreadful business in her mother's state. Besides, Frank Stebbing is young, and it may be fair to give them a chance of hushing it up. I ought to be satisfied with clearing Alexis.'

'Then I will go to the house. When shall I be likely to find Mr. Stebbing!'

'Just after luncheon, I should say.'

'And shall I take the lawyer?'

'I should say not. If they hope to keep the thing secret, they will be the more amenable, but you should have the two boys within reach. Let us ask for them to come up after their dinner to Beechcroft. No, it must not be to dinner. Petros must not be sent to the kitchen, and Ada would expire if the other came to us! Now, do you like to see your house? Here is Macrae dying to see you.'

The old soldier had changed his quarters too often to be keenly interested in any temporary abode, provided it would hold the requisite amount of children, and had a pleasant sitting-room for his Lily, but he inspected politely and gratefully, and had a warmly affectionate interview with Macrae, who had just arrived with a great convoy of needfuls from Silverfold, and who undertook to bring up and guard the two boys from any further impertinences that might excite Master Grove's pugnacity.

It was a beautiful day, of the lamb-like entrance weather of March, and on the way home Miss Adeline was met taking advantage of the noontide sunshine to exchange her book at the library, 'where,' she said, 'I found Mr. White reading the papers, so I asked him to meet Jasper at luncheon, thinking that may be useful.'

If Sir Jasper would rather have managed matters by himself, he forebore to say so, and he got on very well with Mr. White on subjects of interest, but, to the ladies' vexation, he waited to be alone before he began, 'I have come down to see what can be done for this poor young man, Mr. White, a connection of yours, I believe.

'A bad business, Sir Jasper, a bad business.'

'I am sorry to hear you say so. I have seen a great deal of service with his father, and esteemed him very highly—'

'Ay, ay, very likely. I had a young man's differences with my cousin, as lads will fall out, but there was the making of a fine fellow in him. But it was the wife, bringing in that Greek taint, worse even than the Italian, so that there's no believing a word out of any of their mouths.'

'Well, the schoolmaster has just given me a high character of the younger one, for truthfulness especially.'

'All art, Sir Jasper, all art. They are deeper than your common English sort, and act it out better. I'll just give you an instance or two. That eldest son has been with me just now, a smart young chap, who swears he has been keeping his mother all this time—he has written to me often enough for help to do so. On the other hand, the little sister tells me, "Mamma always wants money to send to poor Richard." Then again, Miss Mohun assures me that the elder one vows that she never encouraged Frank Stebbing for a moment, and to his mother's certain knowledge she is keeping up the correspondence.'

'Indeed,' said Sir Jasper. 'And may I ask what is your opinion as to this charge? I never knew a young man enlist with fifteen pounds in his pocket.'

'Spent it by the way, sir. Ran through it at billiards. Nothing more probable; it is the way with those sober-looking lads when something upsets them. Then when luck went against him, enlisted out of despair. Sister, like all women, ready to lie through thick and thin to save him, most likely even on oath.'

'However,' said Sir Jasper, 'I can produce independent witness that the youngest boy set off with the letter for the office, and the porter not admitting him, carried it to the house.'

'What became of it then?'

'Mr. Stebbing will have to answer that. I propose to lay the evidence before him in his own house, so that he may make inquiry, and perhaps find it, and drop the prosecution. Will you come with me?'

'Certainly, Sir Jasper. I should be very glad to think as you do. I came prepared to act kindly by these children, the only relations I have in the world; but I confess that what I have seen and heard has made me fear that they, at least the elder ones, are intriguing and undeserving. I should be glad of any proof to the contrary.'

Carrara was not far off, and they were just in time to catch Mr. Stebbing in his arm-chair, looking over his newspaper, before repairing to his office. Mrs. Stebbing stood up, half-flattered, half-fluttered, at the call of this stately gentleman, and was scarcely prepared to hear him say—

'I have come down about this affair of young White's. His father was my friend and brother-officer, and I am very anxious about him.'

'I have been greatly disappointed in those young people, Sir Jasper,' said Mr. Stebbing uneasily.

'I understand that you are intending to prosecute Alexis White for the disappearance of the fifteen pounds he received on behalf of the firm.'

'Exactly so, Sir Jasper. There's no doubt that the carter, Field, handed it to him; he acknowledges as much, but he would have us believe that after running away with it, he returned it to his sister to send to me. Where is it? I ask.'

'Yes,' put in Mrs. Stebbing, 'and the girl, the little one, changed a five-pound note at Glover's.'

'I can account for that,' said Mr. White, with somewhat of an effort. 'I gave her one for her sister, and charged them not to mention it.'

He certainly seemed ashamed to mention it before those who accounted it a weakness; and Sir Jasper broke the silence by proposing to produce his witnesses.

'Really, Sir Jasper, this should be left for the court,' said Mr. Stebbing.

'It might be well to settle the matter in private, without dragging Miss White into Avoncester away from her dying mother.'

'Those things are so exaggerated,' said the lady.

'I have seen her,' said Sir Jasper gravely.

'May I ask who these witnesses are?' demanded Mr. Stebbing.

'Two are waiting here—the messenger and his companion. Another is your porter at the marble works, and the fourth is your youngest son.'

This caused a sensation, and Mrs. Stebbing began—

'I am sure I can't tell what you mean, Sir Jasper.'

'Is he in the house?'

'Yes; he has a bad cold.'

Mrs. Stebbing opened the door and called 'George,' and on the boy's appearance, Sir Jasper asked him—

'Do you remember the morning of the 17th of last month—three days after the accident? I want to know whether you saw any one in the approach to the house.'

'I don't know what day it was,' said the boy, somewhat sulkily.

'You did see some one, and warned them off!'

'I saw two little ca—two boys out of the town on the front door steps.'

'Did you know them?'

'No—that is to say, one was a fisherman's boy.'

'And the other?'

'I thought he belonged to the lot of Whites.'

'Should you know them again?'

'I suppose so.'

'Will you excuse me, and I will call them into the hall?' said Sir Jasper.

This was effected, and Master George had to identify the boys, after which Sir Jasper elicited that Petros had seen the dirty envelope come out of his brother's letter, and that his sister had put it into another, which she addressed as he described, and gave into his charge to deliver. Then came the account of the way he had been refused admittance by the porter.

'Why didn't you give him the letter?' demanded Mr. Stebbing.

'Catch us,' responded Sydney Grove, rejoiced at the opportunity, 'when what we got was, "Get out, you young rascals!"'

Petros more discreetly added—

'My sister wanted it to be given to Mr. Stebbing, so we went up to the house to wait for him, but it got late for school, and I saw the postman drop the letters into the slit in the door, so I thought that would be all right.'

'Did you see him do so?' asked Sir Jasper of the independent witness.

'Yes, sir, and he there'—pointing to George—'saw it too, and—'

'Did you?'

'Ay, and thought it like their impudence.'

'That will do, my boys,' said Sir Jasper. 'Now run away.'

Mr. White put something into each paw as the door was opened and the pair made their exit.

If Sir Jasper acted as advocate, Mr. White seemed to take the position of judge.

'There can be no doubt,' he said, 'that the letter containing the notes reached this house.'

'No,' said Mr. Stebbing hotly. 'Why was I not told? Who cleared the letter-box?'

It was the page's business, but to remember any particular letter on any particular day was quite beyond him, and he only stared wildly and said, 'Dun no,' on which he was dismissed to the lower regions.

'The address was "Francis Stebbing, Esq.,"' said Sir Jasper meditatively, perhaps like a spider pulling his cord. 'Francis—your son's name. Can he—'

'Mr. White, I'll thank you to take care what you say of my son!' exclaimed Mrs. Stebbing; but there was a blank look of alarm on the father's face.

'Where is he?' asked Mr. White.

'He may be able to explain'—courtesy and pity made the General add.

'No, no,' burst out the mother. 'He knows nothing of it. Mr. Stebbing, can't you stand up for your own son?'

'Perhaps,' began the poor man, his tone faltering with a terrible anxiety, but his wife exclaimed hastily—

'He never saw nor heard of it. I put it in the fire.'

There was a general hush, broken by Mr. Stebbing saying slowly—

'You—put—it—in—the—fire.'

'Yes; I saw those disreputable-looking boys put it into the box. I wasn't going to have that bold girl sending billy-doos on the sly to my son.'

'Under these circumstances,' drily said Sir Jasper, 'I presume that you will think it expedient to withdraw the prosecution.'

'Certainly, certainly,' said Mr. Stebbing, in the tone of one delivered from great alarm. 'I will write at once to my solicitor at Avoncester.' Then turning on his wife, 'How was it that I never heard this before, and you let me go and make a fool of myself?'

'How was I to know, Mr. Stebbing? You started off without a word to me, and all you told me when you came back was that the young man said he had posted the letter to his sister. I should like to know why he could not send it himself to the proper place!'

'Well, Mrs. Stebbing,' said her husband, 'I hope it will be a lesson to you against making free with other people's letters.'

She tossed her head, and was about to retire, when Sir Jasper said—

'Before leaving us, madam, in justice to my old friend's daughter, I should be much obliged if you would let me know your grounds for believing the letter to be what you say.'

'Why—why, Sir Jasper, it has been going on this year or more! She has perfectly infatuated the poor boy.'

'I am not asking about your son's sentiments but can you adduce any proof of their being encouraged!'

'Sir Jasper! a young man doesn't go on in that way without encouragement.'

'What encouragement can you prove?'

'Didn't I surprise a letter from her—?'

'Well'—checked the tone of triumphant conviction.

'A refusal, yes, but we all know what that means, and that there must have been something to lead to it'—and as there was an unconvinced silence —'Besides—oh, why, every one knew of her arts. You did, Mr. Stebbing, and of poor Frank's infatuation. It was the reason of her dismissal.'

'I knew what you told me, Mrs. Stebbing,' he answered grimly, not at all inclined to support her at this moment of anger. 'I am sure I wish I had never listened to you. I never saw anything amiss in the girl's behaviour, and they are all at sixes and sevens without her at the mosaic work—though she is only absent from her mother's illness at present.'

'You! of course she would not show her goings on before you, said the lady.

'Is Master Frank in the house?' put in Mr. White; 'I should like to put the question before him.'

'You can't expect a young man to make mortifying admissions,' exclaimed the mother, and as she saw smiles in answer she added, 'Of course, the girl has played the modest and proper throughout! That was her art, to draw him on, till he did not know what he was about.'

'Setting aside the supposed purpose,' said Sir Jasper, 'you admit, Mrs. Stebbing, that of your own knowledge, Miss White has never encouraged your son's attentions.'

'N—no; but we all know what those girls are.'

'Fatherless and unprotected,' said Sir Jasper, 'dependent on their own character and exertion, and therefore in especial need of kind construction. Good morning, Mrs. Stebbing; I have learnt all that I wish to know.'

Overpowered, but not convinced, Mrs. Stebbing saw her visitors depart.

'And I hope her husband will give it to her well,' said Mr. White, as they left the house.

They looked in at Beechcroft Cottage with the tidings.

'All safe, I see!' cried Miss Jane. 'Is the money found?'

'No; Mrs. Stebbing burnt it, under the impression that it was a love-letter,' drily said Sir Jasper.

Miss Mohun led the way in the hearty fit of laughter, to which the gentlemen gave way the more heartily for recent suppression; and Mr. White added—

'I assure you, it was as good as a play to hear Sir Jasper worm it out. One would think he had been bred a lawyer.'

'And now,' said the General, 'I must go and relieve that poor girl's suspense.'

'I will come with you,' volunteered Mr. White. 'I fully believe that she is a good girl, though this business and Master Richard's applications staggered me; and this soldier fellow must be an ass if he is not a scamp.'

'Scarcely that, I think,' said Miss Adelaide, with her pleading smile.

'Well, discipline will be as good for him as for his father,' said Mr. White. 'He has done for himself, but that was a nice little lad that you had up—too good for a common national school.'

Wherewith they departed, and found that Kalliope must have been on the watch, for she ran down to open the door to them, and the gladness which irradiated her face as Sir Jasper's first 'All right,' lighted up her features, which were so unlike the shop-girl prettiness that Mr. White expected as quite to startle him.

Richard was in the parlour in a cloud of smoke, and began to do the honours.

'Our acknowledgments are truly due to Sir Jasper. Mr. White, we are much honoured. Pray be seated, please to excuse—'

They paid little attention to him, while Sir Jasper told as much to his sister as could well be explained as to the fate of her envelope, and added—

'You will not be wanted at Avoncester, as the case will not come on. I shall go and see all safe, then on to town, but I mean to see your brother's commanding officer, and you may tell your mother that I have no doubt that he will be allowed a furlough.'

'But, Sir Jasper' broke in Richard, 'I beg your pardon; but there is a family from Leeds at Bellevue, the Nortons, and imagine what it would be if they reported me as connected with a common private soldier, just out of prison too!'

'Let him come to me then,' exclaimed Mr. White.

In spite of appearances of disgust, Richard took the invitation to himself, and looked amiable and gratified.

'Thank you, Mr. White, that will obviate the difficulty. When shall I move up?'

'You, sir? Did you think I meant you?' said Mr. White contemptuously. 'No; I prefer a fool to a knave!'

'Mr. White,' interposed Sir Jasper, 'whatever you may have to say to Richard White, consider his sister. Or had you not better report our success to your mother, my dear?'

'One moment,' said Mr. White. 'Tell me, young lady, if you do not object, what assistance have you ever received from me.'

'You have most kindly employed us, and paid for Maura's education,' said Kalliope.

'Is that all? Has nothing been transmitted through this brother?'

'I do not understand,' said Kalliope, trembling, as Richard scowled at her.

'Sir,' said he, 'I always intended, but unforeseen circumstances—'

'That's enough for the present, sir,' said Mr. White. 'I have heard all I wish, and more too.'

'Sir,' said Kalliope, still trembling, 'indeed, Richard is a kind son and brother. My mother is much attached to him. I am generally out all day, and it is quite possible that she did not tell me all that passed between them, as she knew that I did not like you to be applied to.'

'That will do, my dear,' said Mr. White. 'I don't want to say any more about it. You shall have your brother to-morrow, if Sir Jasper can manage it. I will bring him back to Rockstone as my guest, so that his brother need not be molested with his company.'

CHAPTER XX. — IVINGHOE TERRACE

On an east-windy Friday afternoon Valetta and Fergus were in a crowning state of ecstasy. Rigdum Funnidos was in a hutch in the small garden under the cliff, Begum and two small gray kittens were in a basket under the kitchen stairs, Aga was purring under everybody's feet, Cocky was turning out the guard upon his perch—in short, Il Lido was made as like Silverfold as circumstances would permit. Aunt Ada with Miss Vincent was sitting on the sofa in the drawing-room, with a newly-worked cosy, like a giant's fez, over the teapot, and Valetta's crewel cushion fully displayed. She was patiently enduring a rush in and out of the room of both children and Quiz once every minute, and had only requested that it should not be more than once, and that the door should neither be slammed nor left open.

Macrae and the Silverfold carriage were actually gone to the station, and, oh! oh! oh! here it really was with papa on the box, and heaps of luggage, and here were Primrose and Gillian and mamma and Mrs. Halfpenny, all emerging one after another, and Primrose, looking—oh dear! more like a schoolroom than a nursery girl—such a great piece of black leg below the little crimson skirt; but the dear little face as plump as ever.

That was the first apparent fact after the disengaging from the general embrace, when all had subsided into different seats, and Aunt Jane, who had appeared from somewhere in her little round sealskin hat, had begun to pour out the tea. The first sentence that emerged from the melee of greetings and intelligence was—

'Fly met her mother at the station; how well she looks!'

'Then Victoria came down with you?'

'Yes; I am glad we went to her. I really do like her very much.'

Then Primrose and Valetta varied the scene by each laying a kitten in their mother's lap; and Begum, jumping after her progeny, brushed Lady Merrifield's face with her bushy tail, interrupting the information about names.

'Come, children,' said Sir Jasper, 'that's enough; take away the cats.' It was kindly said, but it was plain that liberties with mamma would not continue before him.

'The Whites?' was Gillian's question, as she pressed up to Aunt Jane.

'Poor Mrs. White died the night before last,' was the return. 'I have just come from Kally. She is in a stunned state now—actually too busy to think and feel, for the funeral must be to-morrow.'

Sir Jasper heard, and came to ask further questions.

'She saw Alexis,' went on Miss Mohun. 'They dressed him in his own clothes, and she seemed greatly satisfied when he came to sit by her, and had forgotten all that went before. However, the end came very suddenly at last, and all those poor children show their southern nature in tremendous outbursts of grief—all except Kalliope, who seems not to venture on giving way, will not talk, or be comforted, and is, as it were, dried up for the present. The big brothers give way quite as much as the children, in gusts, that is to say. Poor Alexis reproaches himself with having hastened it, and I am afraid his brother does not spare him. But Mr. White has bought his discharge.'

'You don't mean it.'

'Yes; whether it was the contrast between Alexis's air of refinement and his private soldier's turn-out, or the poor fellow's patience and submission, or the brother's horrid behaviour to him, Mr. White has taken him up, and bought him out.'

'All because of Richard's brutal speech. That is good! Though I confess I should have let the lad have at least a year's discipline for his own good, since he had put himself into it; but I can't be sorry. There is something engaging about the boy.'

'And Mr. White is the right man to dispose of them.'

No more passed, for here were the children eager and important, doing the honours of the new house, and intensely happy at the sense of home, which with them depended more on persons than on place.

One schoolroom again,' said Mysie. 'One again with Val and Prim and Miss Vincent. Oh, it is happiness!'

Even Mrs. Halfpenny was a delightful sight, perhaps the more so that her rightful dominion was over; the nursery was no more, and she was only to preside in the workroom, be generally useful, wait on my lady, and look after Primrose as far as was needful.

The bustle and excitement of settling in prevented much thought of the Whites, even from Gillian, during that evening and the next morning; and she was ashamed of her own oblivion of her friend in the new current of ideas, when she found that her father meant to attend the funeral out of respect to his old fellow-soldier.

Rockquay had outgrown its churchyard, and had a cemetery half a mile off, so that people had to go in carriages. Mr. White had made himself responsible for expenses, and thus things were not so utterly dreary as poverty might have made them. It was a dreary, gusty March day, with driving rushes of rain, which had played wildly with Gillian's waterproof while she was getting such blossoms and evergreen leaves as her aunt's garden afforded, not out of love for the poor Queen of the White Ants herself, but thinking the attention might gratify the daughters; and her elders moralised a little on the use and abuse of wreaths, and how the manifestation of tender affection and respect had in many cases been imitated in empty and expensive compliment.

'The world spoils everything with its coarse finger,' said Lady Merrifield.

'I hope the custom will not be exaggerated altogether out of fashion,' said Jane. 'It is a real comfort to poor little children at funerals to have one to carry, and it is as Mrs. Gaskell's Margaret said of mourning, something to prevent settling to doing nothing but crying; besides that afterwards there is a wholesome sweetness in thus keeping up the memory.'

Sir Jasper shared a carriage with Mr. White, and returned somewhat wet and very cold, and saying that it had been sadly bleak and wretched for the poor young people, who stood trembling, so far as he could see; and he was anxious to know how the poor girls were after it. It had seemed to him as if Kalliope could scarcely stand. He proved to be right. Kalliope had said nothing, not wept demonstratively, perhaps not at all; but when the carriage stopped at the door, she proved to be sunk back in her corner in a dead faint. She was very long in reviving, and no sooner tried to move than she swooned again, and this time it lasted so long that the doctor was sent for. Miss Mohun arrived just as he had partially restored her, and they had a conversation.

'They must get that poor girl to bed as soon as it is possible to undress her,' he said. 'I have seen that she must break down sooner or later, and I'm afraid she is in for a serious illness; but as yet there is no knowing.'

Nursing was not among Jane's accomplishments, except of her sister Ada's chronic, though not severe ailments; but she fetched Mrs. Halfpenny as the most effective person within reach, trusting to that good woman's Scotch height, strong arms, great decision, and the tenderness which real illness always elicited.

Nor was she wrong. Not only did Mrs. Halfpenny get the half-unconscious girl into bed, but she stayed till evening, and then came back to snatch a meal and say—

'My leddy, if you have no objection, I will sit up with that puir lassie the night. They are all men-folk or bairns there, except the lodger-lady, who is worn out with helping the mother, and they want some one with a head on her shoulders.'

Lady Merrifield consented with all her heart; but the Sunday morning's report was no better, when Mrs. Halfpenny came home to dress Primrose, and see her lady.

'That eldest brother, set him up, the idle loon, was off by the mail train that night, and naething wad serve him but to come in and bid good-bye to his sister just as I had gotten her off into something more like a sleep. It startled her up, and she went off her head again, poor dearie, and began to talk about prison and disgrace, and what not, till she fainted again; and when she came to, I was fain to call the other lad to pacify her, for I could see the trouble in her puir een, though she could scarce win breath to speak.'

'Is Alexis there?'

'Surely he is, my leddy; he's no the lad to leave his sister in sic a strait. It was all I could do to gar him lie down when she dozed off again, but there's sair stress setting in for all of them, puir things. I have sent the little laddie off to beg the doctor to look in as soon as he can, for I am much mistaken if there be not fever coming on.'

'Indeed! And what can those poor children do?'

'That's what I'm thinking, my leddy. And since 'tis your pleasure that the nursery be done awa' wi', and I have not ta'en any fresh work, I should like weel to see the puir lassie through wi' it. Ye'll no mind that Captain White and my puir Halfpenny listed the same time, and always forgathered as became douce lads. The twa of them got their stripes thegither, and when Halfpenny got his sunstroke in that weary march, 'twas White who gave him his last sup of water, and brought me his bit Bible. So I'd be fain to tend his daughter in her sickness, if you could spare me, my leddy, and I'd aye rin home to dress Missie Primrose and pit her to bed, and see to matters here.'

'There's no better nurse in the world, dear old Halfpenny,' said Lady Merrifield, with tears in her eyes. 'I do feel most thankful to you for proposing it. Never mind about Primrose, only you must have your meals and a good rest here, and not knock yourself up.'

Mrs. Halfpenny smiled grimly at the notion of her being sooner knocked up than a steam-engine. Dr. Dagger entirely confirmed her opinion that poor Kalliope was likely to have a serious illness, low nervous fever, and failing action of the heart, no doubt from the severe strain that she had undergone, more or less, for many months, and latterly fearfully enhanced by her mother's illness, and the shock and suspense about Alexis, all borne under the necessity of external composure and calmness, so that even Mrs. Lee had never entirely understood how much it cost her. The doctor did not apprehend extreme danger to one young and healthy, but he thought much would depend on good nursing, and on absolute protection from any sort of excitement, so that such care as Mrs. Halfpenny's was invaluable, since she was well known to be a dove to a patient, but a dragon to all outsiders.

Every one around grieved at having done so little to lighten these burthens, and having even increased them, her brother Alexis above all; but on the other hand, he was the only person who was of any use to her, or was suffered to approach her, since his touch and voice calmed the recurring distress, lest he were still in prison and danger.

Alexis went back dutifully on the Monday morning to his post at the works. The young man was much changed by his fortnight's experiences, or rather he had been cured of a temporary fit of distraction, and returned to his better self. How many discussions his friends held about him cannot be recorded, but after a conversation with Mr. Flight, with whom he was really more unreserved than any other being except Kalliope, this was the understanding at which Miss Mohun and Lady Merrifield arrived as to his nature and character.

Refined, studious, and sensitive, thoroughly religious-minded, and of a high tone of thought, his aspirations had been blighted by his father's death, his brother's selfishness, and his mother's favouritism. In a brave spirit of self-abnegation, he had turned to the uncongenial employment set before him for the sake of his family, and which was rendered specially trying by the dislike of his fellows to 'the gentleman cove,' and the jealousy of the Stebbings. Alike for his religious and his refined habits he had suffered patiently, as Mr. Flight had always known more or less, and now bore testimony. The curate, who had opened to him the first door of hope and comfort, had in these weeks begun to see that the apparent fitfulness of his kindness had been unsettling.

Then came the brief dream of felicity excited by Gillian and the darkness of its extinction, just as Frank Stebbing's failure and the near approach of Mr. White had made the malice of his immediate superiors render his situation more intolerable than ever. There was the added sting of self-reproach for his presumption towards Gillian, and the neglect caused by his fit of low spirits. Such a sensitive being, in early youth, wearied and goaded on all sides, might probably have persevered through the darkness till daylight came; but the catastrophe, the dismissal, and the perception that he could only defend himself at the expense of his idol's little brother, all exaggerated by youthful imagination, were too much for his balance of judgment, and he fled without giving himself time to realise how much worse he made it for those he left behind him.

Of course he perceived it all now, and the more bitterly from his sister's wanderings, but the morbid exaggeration was gone. The actual taste of a recruit's life had shown him that there were worse things than employment at the quarries with his home awaiting him, and his cell had been a place of thought and recovery of his senses. He had never seriously expected conviction, and Sir Jasper's visit had given him a spring of hopeful resignation, in which thoughts stirred of doing his duty, and winning his way after his father's example, and taking the trials of his military life as the just cross of his wrong-doing in entering it.

His liberation and Mr. White's kindness had not altered this frame. He was too unhappy to feel his residence in the great house anything but a restraint; he could not help believing that he had hastened his mother's death, and could only bow his head meekly under his brother's reproaches, alike for that and for his folly and imprudence and the disgrace he had brought on the family.

'And now you'll, be currying favour and cutting out every one else,' had been a sting which added fresh force to Alexis's desire to escape from his kinsman's house to sleep at home as soon as his brother had gone; and Richard had seen enough of Sir Jasper and of Mr. White to be anxious to return to his office at Leeds as soon as possible, and to regulate his affairs beyond their reach.

Alexis knew that he had avoided a duty in not working out his three months' term, and likewise that his earnings were necessary to the family all the more for his sister being laid aside. He knew that he hardly deserved to resume his post, and he merely asked permission so to do, and it was granted at once, but curtly and coldly.

Mr. Flight had asked if he had not found the going among the other clerks very trying.

'I had other things to think of,' said Alexis sadly, then recalling himself. 'Yes; Jones did sneer a little, but the others stopped that. They knew I was down, you see.'

'And you mean to go on?'

'If I may. That, and for my sister to get better, is all I can dare to hope. My madness and selfishness have shown me unworthy of all that I once dreamt of.'

In that resolution it was assuredly best to leave him, only giving him such encouragement and sympathy as might prevent that more dangerous reaction of giving up all better things; and Sir Jasper impressed on Mr. Flight, the only friend who could have aided him in fulfilling his former aspirations, that Mr. White had in a manner purchased the youth by buying his discharge, and that interference would not only be inexpedient, but unjust. The young clergyman chafed a little over not being allowed to atone for his neglect; but Sir Jasper was not a person to be easily gainsayed. Nor could there be any doubt that Mr. White was a good man, though in general so much inclined to reserve his hand that his actions were apt to take people by surprise at last, as they had never guessed his intentions, and he had a way of sucking people's brains without in the least letting them know what use he meant to make of their information. The measures he was taking for the temporal, intellectual, and spiritual welfare of the people at the works would hardly have been known except for the murmurs of Mrs. Stebbing, although, without their knowing what he was about with them, Mr. Stebbing himself, Mr. Hablot, Miss Mohun, to say nothing of Alexis, the foremen and the men and their wives, had given him the groundwork of his reforms. Meantime, he came daily to inquire for Kalliope, and lavished on her all that could be an alleviation, greatly offending Mrs. Halfpenny by continually proffering the services of a hospital nurse.

'A silly tawpie that would be mair trouble than half a dozen sick,' as she chose to declare.

She was a born autocrat, and ruled as absolutely in No. 1 as in her nursery, ordering off the three young ones to their schools, in spite of Maura's remonstrances and appeals to Lady Merrifield, who agreed with nurse that the girl was much better away and occupied than where she could be of very little use.

Indeed, Mrs. Halfpenny banished every one from the room except Mrs. Lee and Alexis, whom she would allow to take her place, while she stalked to Il Lido for her meals, and the duties she would not drop. As to rest, she always, in times of sickness, seemed to be made of cast iron, and if she ever slept at all, it was in a chair, while Alexis sat by his sister in the evening.

The fever never ran very high, but constant vigilance was wanted from the extreme exhaustion and faintness. There was no violent delirium, but more of delusion and distress; nor was it easy to tell when she was conscious or otherwise, for she hardly spoke, and as yet the doctor forbade any attempt to rouse her more than was absolutely needful. They were only to give nourishment, watch her, and be patient.

A few months ago Gillian would have fussed herself into a frantic state of anxiety and self-reproach, but her parents, when her mother had once heard as much outpouring as she thought expedient, would not permit what Sir Jasper called 'perpetual harping.'

'You have to do your duties all the same, and not worry your mother and all the family with your feelings,' he said. She thought it very unkind, and went away crying.

'Nobody could hinder her from thinking about Kalliope,' she said to herself, and think she did at her prayers, and when the bulletins came in, but the embargo on discussion prevented her from being so absolutely engrossed, as in weaker hands she might have been, and there was a great deal going on to claim her attention. For one thing, the results of the Cambridge Examination showed that while Emma Norton and a few others had passed triumphantly, she had failed, and conscience carried her back to last autumn's disinclination to do just what Aunt Jane especially recommended.

She cried bitterly over the failure, for she had a feeling that success there would redeem her somewhat in her parents' eyes; but here again she experienced the healing kindness of her father. He would not say that he should not have been much pleased by her success, but he said failure that taught her to do her best without perverseness was really a benefit; and as arithmetic and mathematics had been her weakest points, he would work at them with her and Mysie for an hour every morning.

It was somewhat formidable, but the girls soon found that what their father demanded was application, and that inattention displeased him much more than stupidity. His smile, though rare, was one of the sweetest things in the world, and his approbation was delightful, and gave a stimulus to the entire day's doings. Mysie was more than ever in dread of being handed over to the Rotherwoods, though her love for poor Fly and pity for her solitude were so strong. She would have been much relieved if she had known what had passed; when the offer was seriously made, Lord Rotherwood insisted that his wife should do it.

'Then they will believe in it,' he said.

'I do not know why you should say that,' she returned, always dutifully blinding herself to that which all their intimates knew perfectly well. However, perhaps from having a station and dignity of her own, together with great simplicity, Lady Merrifield had from her first arrival got on so well with her hostess as not quite to enter into Jane's sarcastic descriptions of her efforts at cordiality; and it was with real warmth that Lady Rotherwood begged for Mysie as a permanent companion and adopted sister to Phyllis, who was to be taken back to London after Easter, and in the meantime spent every possible moment with her cousins.

Tears at the unkindness to lonely Fly came into Lady Merrifield's eyes as she said—

'I cannot do it, Victoria; I do not think I ought to give away my child, even if I could.'

'It is not only our feelings,' added Sir Jasper, 'but it is our duty to bring up our own child in her natural station; and though we know she would learn nothing but good in your family, I cannot think it well that a girl should acquire habits, and be used to society ways and of life beyond those which she can expect to continue.'

They both cried out at this, Lord Rotherwood with a halting declaration of perfect equality, which his lady seconded, with a dexterous reference to connections.

'We will not put it on rank then,' said Sir Jasper, 'but on wealth. With you, Maria must become accustomed to much that she could not continue, and had better not become natural to her. I know there are great advantages to manners and general cultivation in being with you, and we shall be most thankful to let her pay long visits, and be as much with Phyllis as is consistent with feeling her home with us, but I cannot think it right to do more.'

'But with introductions,' pleaded Lady Rotherwood, 'she might marry well. With her family and connections, she would be a match for any one.'

'I hope so,' said Sir Jasper; 'but at the same time it would not be well for her to look on such a marriage as the means of continuing the habits that would have become second nature.'

'Poor Mysie,' exclaimed Lord Rotherwood, bursting out laughing at the idea, and at Lady Merrifield's look as she murmured, 'My Mysie!'

'You misunderstand me,' said the Marchioness composedly. 'I was as far as possible from proposing marriage as a speculation for her.'

'I know you were,' said Sir Jasper. 'I know you would deal by Maria as by your own daughter, and I am very grateful to you, Lady Rotherwood, but I can only come back to my old decision, that as Providence did not place her in your rank of life, she had better not become so accustomed to it as to render her own distasteful to her.'

'Exactly what I expected,' said Lord Rotherwood.

'Yes,' returned his wife, with an effort of generosity; 'and I believe you are right, Jasper, though I am sorry for my little solitary girl, and I never saw a friend so perfectly suitable for her as your Mysie.'

'They may be friends still,' said Lord Rotherwood, 'and we will be grateful to you whenever you can spare her to us.'

'Perhaps,' added Sir Jasper, 'all the more helpful friends for seeing different phases of life.'

'And, said his wife, with one of her warm impulses, 'I do thank you, Victoria, for so loving my Mysie.'

'As if any one could help it, after last winter,' said that lady, and an impromptu kiss passed between the two mothers, much to the astonishment of the Marquis, who had never seen his lady so moved towards any one.

The Merrifields were somewhat on the world, for Sir Jasper, on going to Silverfold and corresponding with the trustees of the landlord, had found that the place could not be put in a state either of repair or sanitation, such as he approved, without more expense than either he or the trustees thought advisable, and he decided on giving it up, and remaining at Il Lido till he could find something more suitable.

The children, who had been there during the special homemaking age, bewailed the decision, and were likely always to look back on Silverfold as a sort of Paradise; but the elder ones had been used to changes from infancy, and had never settled down, and their mother said that place was little to her as long as she had her Jasper by her side, and as to the abstract idea of home as a locality, that would always be to her under the tulip-tree and by the pond at the Old Court at Beechcroft, just as her abstract idea of church was in the old family pew, with the carved oak panels, before the restoration, in which she had been the most eager of all.

Thus a fortnight passed, and then the fever was decidedly wearing off, but returning at night. Kalliope still lay weak, languid, silent, fainting at any attempt to move her, not apparently able to think enough to ask how time passed, or to be uneasy about anything, simply accepting the cares given to her, and lying still. One morning, however, Alexis arrived in great distress to speak to Sir Jasper, not that his sister was worse, as he explained, but Richard had been selling the house. The younger ones at home had never troubled themselves as to whose property the three houses in Ivinghoe Terrace were. Perhaps Kalliope knew, but she could not be asked; but the fact was that Captain White had been so lost sight of, that he had not known that this inheritance had fallen to him under the will of his grandfather, who was imbecile at the time of his flight. On his deathbed, the Captain had left the little he owned to his wife, and she had died intestate, as Richard had ascertained before leaving home, so that he, as eldest son, was heir to the ground. He had written to Kalliope, a letter which Alexis had opened, informing her that he had arranged to sell the houses to a Mr. Gudgeon, letting to him their own till the completion of the legal business necessary, and therefore desiring his brothers and sisters to move out with their lodgers, if not by Lady Day itself, thus giving only a week's spare notice, at latest by

Old Lady Day.

'Is he not aware of your sister's state?'

'I do not imagine that he has read the letter that I wrote to him. He was very much displeased with me, and somewhat disposed to be angry at my sister's fainting, and to think that we were all trying to work on his feelings. He used to be rather fond of Maura, so I told her to write to him, but he has taken no notice, and he can have no conception of Kalliope's condition, or he would not have addressed his letter to her. I came to ask if you would kindly write to him how impossible it is to move her.'

'You had better get a certificate from Dr. Dagger. Either I or Lady Merrifield will meet him, and see to that. That will serve both to stay him and the purchaser.'

'That is another misfortune. This Gudgeon is the chief officer, or whatever they call it, of the Salvation Army. I knew they had been looking out for a place for a barracks, and could not get one because almost everythingbelongs to Lord Rotherwood or to Mr. White.'

Sir Jasper could only reply that he would see what could be done in the matter, and that, at any rate, Kalliope should not be disturbed.

Accordingly Lady Merrifield repaired to Ivinghoe Terrace for the doctor's visit, and obtained from him the requisite certificate that the patient could not be removed at present. He gave it, saying, however, to Lady Merrifield's surprise, that though he did not think it would be possible to remove her in a week's time, yet after that he fully believed that she would have more chance of recovering favourably if she could be taken out of the small room and the warm atmosphere beneath the cliffs—though of course all must depend on her state at the time.

Meantime there was a council of the gentlemen about outbidding the Salvation Army. Lord Rotherwood was spending already as much as he could afford, in the days of agricultural depression, on the improvements planned with Mr. White. That individual was too good a man of business to fall, as he said, into the trap, and make a present to that scamp Richard of more than the worth of the houses, and only Mr. Flight was ready to go to any cost to keep off the Salvation Army; but the answer was curt. Richard knew he had no chance with Mr. White, and did not care to keep terms with him.

'Mr. Richard White begs to acknowledge the obliging offer of the Rev. Augustine Flight, and regrets that arrangements have so far progressed with Mr. Gudgeon that he cannot avail himself of it.'

Was this really regret or was the measure out of spite? Only the widest charity could accept the former suggestion, and even Sir Jasper Merrifield's brief and severe letter and Dr. Dagger's certificate did not prevent a letter to Alexis, warning him not to make their sister's illness a pretext for unreasonable delay.

What was to be done? Kalliope was still unfit to be consulted or even informed, and she had been hitherto so entirely the real head and manager of the family that Alexis did not like to make any decision without her; and even the acceptance of the St. Wulstan's choristership for Theodore had been put off for her to make it, look to his outfit, and all that only the woman of the family could do for them.

And here they were at a loss for a roof over their heads, and nowhere to bestow the battered old furniture, of which Richard magnanimously renounced his sixth share; while she who had hitherto toiled, thought, managed, and contrived for all the other four, without care of their own, still lay on her bed, sensible indeed and no longer feverish, but with the perilous failure of heart, renewed by any kind of exertion or excitement, a sudden movement, or a startling sound in the street; and Mrs. Halfpenny, guarding her as ferociously as ever, and looking capable of murdering any one of her substitutes if they durst hint a word of their perplexities. Happily she asked no questions; she was content when allowed to be kissed by the others, and to see they were well. Nature was enforcing repose, and so far "her senses was all as in a dream bound up." Alexis remembered that it had been somewhat thus at Leeds, when, after nursing all the rest, she had succumbed to the epidemic; but then the mother had been able to watch over her, and had been a more effective parent to the rest than she had since become.

The first practical proposal was Mrs. Lee's. They thought of reversing the present position, and taking a small house where their present hosts might become their lodgers. Moreover, Miss Mohun clenched the affair about

Theodore, and overcame Alexis's scruples, while Lady Merrifield, having once or twice looked in, and been smiled at and thanked by Kalliope, undertook to prepare her for his farewell.

Alexis and Maura both declared that she would instantly jump up, and want to begin looking over his socks; but she got no further than—

'Dear boy! It is the sort of thing I always wished for him. People are very good! But his things—'

'Oh yes, dearie, ye need not fash yourself. I've mended them as I sat by you, and packed them all. Lie still. They are all right.'

There was an atmosphere of the Royal Wardours about Mrs. Halfpenny, which was at once congenial and commanding; and Kalliope's mind at once relinquished the burthen of socks, shirts, and even the elbows of the outgrown jacket, nor did any of the family ever know how the deficiencies had been supplied.

And when Theodore, well admonished, came softly and timidly for the parting kiss, his face quivering all over with the effort at self-control, she lay and smiled; but with a great crystal tear on each dark eyelash, and her thin transparent fingers softly stroked his cheeks, as the low weak voice said—

'Be a good boy, dear—speak truth. Praise God well. Write; I'll write when I am better.'

It was the first time she had spoken of being better, and they told Theodore to take comfort from it when all the other three walked him up to the station.

CHAPTER XXI. — BEAUTY AND THE BEAST

In the search for a new abode Mrs. Lee was in much difficulty, for it was needful to be near St. Kenelm's, and the only vacant houses within her means were not desirable for the reception of a feeble convalescent; moreover, Mr. Gudgeon grumbled and inquired, and was only withheld by warnings enhanced by the police from carrying the whole charivari of the Salvation Army along Ivinghoe Terrace on Sunday afternoon.

Perhaps it was this, perhaps it was the fact of having discussed the situation with the two Miss Mohuns, that made Mr. White say to Alexis, 'There are two rooms ready for your sister, as soon as Dagger says she can be moved safely. The person who nurses her had better come with her, and you may as well come back to your old quarters.'

Alexis could hardly believe his ears, but Mr. White waved off all thanks. The Mohun sisters were delighted and triumphant, and Jane came down to talk it over with her elder sister, auguring great things from that man who loved to deal in surprises.

'That is true,' said Sir Jasper.

'What does that mean, Jasper?' said his wife. 'It sounds significant.'

'I certainly should not be amazed if he did further surprise us all. Has it never struck you how that noontide turn of Adeline's corresponds with his walk home from the reading-room?'

Lady Merrifield looked rather startled, but Jane only laughed, and said, 'My dear Jasper, if you only knew Ada as well as I do! Yes, I have seen far too many of those little affairs to be taken in by them. Poor Ada! I know exactly how she looks, but she is only flattered, like a pussy-cat waggling the end of its tail—it means nothing, and never comes to anything. The thing that is likely and hopeful is, that he may adopt those young people as nephews and nieces.'

'Might it not spoil them?' said Lady Merrifield.

'Oh! I did not mean that. They might work with him still. However, there is no use in settling about that. The only thing to be expected of him is the unexpected!'

'And the thing to be done,' added her sister, 'is to see how and when that poor girl can be got up to Cliff House.'

To the general surprise, Dr. Dagger wished the transit to take place without loss of time. A certain look of resigned consternation crossed Kalliope's face on being informed of her destiny, but she justified Mrs. Halfpenny's commendation of her as the maist douce and conformable patient in the world, for she had not energy enough even to plead against anything so formidable, and she had not yet been told that Ivinghoe Terrace was her home no longer.

The next day she was wrapped in cloaks and carried downstairs between her brother and Mrs. Halfpenny, laid on a mattress in the Merrifield waggonette, which went up the hill at a foot's pace, and by the same hands, with her old friend the caretaker's wife going before, was taken upstairs to a beautiful large room, with a window looking out on vernal sky and sea. She was too much exhausted on her arrival to know anything but the repose on the fresh comfortable bed, whose whiteness was almost rivalled by her cheek, and Mrs. Halfpenny ordered off Alexis, who was watching her in great anxiety. However, when he came back after his afternoon's work, it was to find that she had eaten and slept, and now lay, with her eyes open, in quiet interested admiration of a spacious and pleasant bedroom, such as to be a great novelty to one whose life had been spent in cheap lodging houses. The rooms had been furnished twenty years before as a surprise intended for the wife who never returned to occupy them, and though there was nothing extraordinary in them, there was much to content the eyes accustomed to something very like squalidness, for had not Kalliope's lot always been the least desirable chamber in the family quarters?

At any rate, from that moment she began to recover, ate with appetite, slept and woke to be interested, and to enjoy Theodore's letter of description of St. Wulstan's, and even to ask questions. Alexis was ready to dance for joy when she first began really to talk to him; and could not forbear imparting his gladness to the Miss Mohuns that very evening, as well as to Mr. White, and running down after dinner with the good news to Maura, Mrs. Lee, and Lady Merrifield. Dinners with Mr. White had, on his first sojourn in that house, been a great penance, though there were no supercilious servants, for all the waiting was by the familiar housekeeper, Mrs. Osborne, who had merely added an underling to her establishment on her master's return; but Alexis then had been utterly miserable, feeling guilty and ashamed, as one only endured on sufferance out of compassion, because his brother cast him out, and fresh from the sight of his mother's dying bed; a terrible experience altogether, which had entirely burnt out and effaced his foolish fit of romantic calf-love, and rendered him much more of a man. Now, though not a month had passed, he seemed to be on a different footing. He was doing his work steadily, and the hope of his sister's recovery had brightened him. Mr. White had begun to talk to him, to ask him questions about the doings of the day, and to tell him in return some of his own experiences in Italy, and in the earlier days of the town. Maura came up to see her sister every day, and tranquillised her mind when the move was explained, and anxiety as to the transport of all their worldly goods began to set in. Mrs. Lee had found a house where she could place two bedrooms and a sitting-room at the disposal of the Whites if things were to continue as before, and no hint had been given of any change, or of what was to happen when the three months' notice given to Kalliope and Alexis should have expired.

By the Easter holidays Mrs. Halfpenny began to get rather restless as to the overlooking of the boys' wardrobes; and, indeed, she thought so well of her patient's progress as to suggest to Mr. White that the lassie would do very well if she had her sister to be with her in the holidays, and she herself would come up every day to help at the getting up, for Kalliope was now able to be dressed and to lie on a couch in the dressing-room, where she could look out over the bay, and she had even asked for some knitting.

'And really, Miss Gillian, you could not do her much harm if you came up to see her,' said the despot. 'So you may come this very afternoon, if ye'll be douce, and not fash her with any of your cantrips.'

Gillian did not feel at all in a mood for cantrips as she slowly walked up the broad staircase, and was ushered into the dressing-room, cheerful with bright fire and April sunshine, and with a large comfortable sofa covered with a bright rug, where Kalliope could enjoy both window and fire without glare. The beauty of her face so much depended on form and expression that her illness had not lessened it. Gillian had scarcely seen her since the autumn, and the first feeling was what an air of rest and peace had succeeded the worn, harassed look then almost perpetual. There was a calmness now that far better suited the noble forehead, dark pencilled eyebrows, and classical features in their clear paleness; and with a sort of reverence Gillian bent over her, to kiss her and give her a bunch of violets. Then, when the thanks had passed, Gillian relieved her own shyness by exclaiming with admiration at a beautiful water- coloured copy of an early Italian fresco, combining the Nativity and Adoration of the Magi, that hung over the mantelpiece.

'Is it not exquisite?' returned Kalliope. 'I do so much enjoy making out each head and dwelling on them! Look at that old shepherd's simple wonder and reverence, and the little child with the lamb, and the contrast with the Wise Man from the East, whose eyes look as if he saw so much by faith.'

'Can you see it from there?' asked Gillian, who had got up to look at these and further details dwelt on by Kalliope.

'Yes. Not at first; but they come out on me by degrees. It is such a pleasure, and so kind of Mr. White to have put it there. He had it hung there, Mrs. Halfpenny told me, instead of his own picture just before I came in here.'

'Well, he is not a bad-looking man, but it is no harm to him or his portrait to say that this is better to look at!'

'It quite does me good! And see,' pointing to a photograph of the Arch of Titus hung on the screen that shielded her from the door, 'he sends in a fresh one by Alexis every other day.

'How very nice! He really seems to be a dear old man. Don't you think so?'

'I am sure he is wonderfully kind, but I have only seen him that once when he came with Sir Jasper, and then I knew nothing but that when Sir Jasper was come things must go right.'

'Of course; but has he never been to see you now that you are up and dressed?'

'No, he lavishes anything on me that I can possibly want, but I have only seen him once—never here.'

'It is like Beauty and the Beast!'

'Oh no, no; don't say that!'

'Well, George Stebbing really taught Fergus to call him a beast, and you— Kally—I won't tease you with saying what you are.'

'I wish I wasn't, it would be all so much easier.'

'Never mind! I do believe the Stebbings are going away! Does Maura never see him?'

'She has met him on the stairs and in the garden, but she has her meals here. I trust by the time her Easter holidays are over I may be fit to go back with her. But I do hope I may be able to copy a bit of that picture first, though, any way, I can never forget it.'

'To go on as before?' exclaimed Gillian, with an interrogative sigh of wonder.

'If that notice of dismissal can be revoked,' said Kalliope.

But would you like it—must you?'

'I *should* like to go back to my girls,' said Kalliope; 'and things come into my head, now I am doing nothing, that I want to work out, if I might. So, you see, it is not at all a pity that I *must*.'

And why is it must?' said Gillian wistfully. 'You have to get well first.'

Yes, I know that; but, you see, there are Maura and Petros. They must not be thrown on Alexis, poor dear fellow! And if he could only be set free, he might go on with what he once hoped for, though he thinks it is his duty to give all that entirely up now and work obediently on. But I know the longing will revive, and if I only could improve myself, and be worth more, it might still be possible.'

'Only you must not begin too soon and work yourself to death.'

'Hardly after such a rest,' said Kalliope. 'It is not work I mind, but worry'— and then a sadder look crossed her for a moment, and she added, 'I am so thankful.'

'Thankful?' echoed Gillian.

'Yes, indeed! For Sir Jasper's coming and saving us at that dreadful moment, and my being able to keep up as long as dear mamma wanted me, and then Mrs. Halfpenny being spared by dear Lady Merrifield to give me such wonderful care and kindness, and little Theodore being so happily placed, and this rest—such a strange quiet rest as I never knew before. Oh! it is all so thankworthy'—and the great tears came to dim her eyes. 'It seems sent to help me to take strength and courage for the future. "He hath helped me hitherto."'

'And you are better?'

'Yes, much better. Quite comfortable as long as I am quite still.'

'And content to be still?'

'Yes, I'm very lazy.'

It was a tired voice, and Gillian feared her half-hour was nearly over, but she could not help saying—

'Do you know, I think it will be all nicer now. Mr. White is doing so much, and Mr. Stebbing hates it so, that Mrs. Stebbing says he is going to dissolve the partnership and go away.'

'Then it would all be easier. It seems too good to be true.'

'And that man Mr. White. He must do something for you! He ought.'

'Oh no! He has done a great deal already, and has not been well used. Don't talk of that.'

'I believe he is awfully rich. You know he is building an Institute for the workmen, and a whole row of model cottages.'

'Yes, Alexis told me. What a difference it will make! I hope he will build a room where the girls can dine and rest and read, or have a piano; it would be so good for them.'

'You had better talk to him about it.'

'I never see him, and I should not dare.'

'I'll tell my aunts. He always does what Aunt Ada tells him. Is that really all you wish?'

'Oh! I don't wish for anything much—I don't seem able to care now dear mamma is where they cease from troubling, and I have Alec again.'

'Well, I can't help having great hopes. I can't see why that man should not make a daughter of you! Then you would travel and see mountains and pictures and everything. Oh, should you not like that?'

'Like? Oh, one does not think about liking things impossible! And for the rest, it is nonsense. I should not like to be dependent, and I oughtnot.'

'You don't think what is to come next?'

'No, it would be taking thought for the morrow, would it not? I don't want to, while I can't do anything, it would only make me fret, and I am glad I am too stupid still to begin vexing myself over it. I suppose energy and power of considering will come when my heart does not flutter so. In the meantime, I only want to keep quiet, and I hope that's not all laziness, but some trust in Him who has helped me all this time.'

'Miss Gillian, you've clavered as long as is good for Miss White, and here are the whole clanjamfrie waiting in the road for you. Now be douce, my bairn, and mind you are not in the woods at home, and don't let the laddies play their tricks with Miss Primrose.'

'I must go,' said Gillian, hastily kissing Kalliope. 'The others were going to call for me. When Lady Phyllis was riding with her father she spied a wonderful field of daffodils and a valley full of moss at a place called Clipston, two miles off, and we are all going to get some for the decorations. I'll send you some. Good-bye.'

The clanjamfrie, as Mrs. Halfpenny called it, mustered strong, and Gillian's heart leapt at the resumption of the tumultuous family life, as she beheld the collection of girls, boys, dogs, and donkeys awaiting her in the approach; and, in spite of the two governesses' presence, her mind misgave her as to the likelihood of regard to the hint that her mother had given that she hoped the elder ones would try to be sober in their ways, and not quite forget what week it was. It was in their favour that Jasper, now in his last term at school, was much more of a man and less of a boy than hitherto, and was likely to be on the side of discretion, so that he might keep in order that always difficult element, Wilfred, whose two years of preparatory school as yet made him only more ingenious in the arts of teasing, and more determined to show his superiority to petticoat government. He had driven Fergus nearly distracted by threatening to use all his mineralogical specimens to make ducks and drakes, and actually confusing them together, so that Fergus repented of having exhibited them, and rejoiced that Aunt Jane had let them continue in her lumber-room till they could find a permanent home.

Wilfred had a shot for Mrs. Halfpenny, when she came down with Gillian and looked for Primrose to secure that there were no interstices between the silk handkerchief and fur collar.

'Ha, ha, old Small Change, don't you wish you may get it?'—as Primrose proved to be outside the drive on one of the donkeys. 'You've got nothing to do but gnaw your fists at us like old Giant Pope.'

'For shame, Wilfred!' said Jasper. 'My mother did Primrose's throat, nurse, so she is all right.'

'Bad form,' observed Lord Ivinghoe, shaking his head.

'I'm not going to Eton,' replied Wilfred audaciously.

'I should hope not!'—in a tone of ineffable contempt, not for Wilfred's person, but his manners, and therewith his Lordship exclaimed, 'Who's that?' as Maura came flying down with Gillian's forgotten basket.

'Oh, that's Maura White!' said Valetta.

'I say, isn't she going with us?'

'Oh no, she has to look after her sister!'

'Don't you think we might take her, Gill?' said Fly. 'She never gets any fun.'

'I don't think she ought to leave Kalliope to-day, Fly, for nurse is going down to Il Lido; and besides, Aunt Jane said we must not take *all* Rockquay with us.'

'No, they would not let us ask Kitty and Clement Varley, said Fergus disconsolately.

'I am sure she is five times as pretty as your Kitty!' returned Ivinghoe. 'She is a regular stunner.' Whereby it may be perceived that a year at Eton had considerably modified his Lordship's correctness of speech, if not of demeanour. Be it further observed that, in spite of the escort of the governesses, the young people were as free as if those ladies had been absent, for, as Jasper observed, the donkeys neutralised them. Miss Elbury, being a bad walker, rode one, and Miss Vincent felt bound to keep close to Primrose upon the other; and as neither animal could be prevailed on to moderate its pace, they kept far ahead of all except Valetta, who was mounted on the pony intended for Lady Phyllis, but disdained by her until she should be tired. Lord Ivinghoe's admiration of Maura was received contemptuously by Wilfred, who was half a year younger than his cousin, and being already, in his own estimation, a Wykehamist, had endless rivalries with him.

'She! She's nothing but a cad! Her sister is a shop-girl, and her brother is a quarryman.'

'She does not look like it,' observed Ivinghoe, while Mysie and Fly, with one voice, exclaimed that her father was an officer in the Royal Wardours.

'A private first,' said Wilfred, with boyhood's reiteration. 'Cads and quarrymen all of them—the whole boiling, old White and all, though he has got such a stuck-up house!'

'Nonsense, Will,' said Fly. 'Why, Mr. White has dined with us.'

'A patent of nobility, said Jasper, smiling.

'I don't care,' said Wilfred; 'if other people choose to chum with old stonemasons and convicts, I don't.'

'Wilfred, that is too bad,' said Gillian. 'It is very wrong to talk in that way.'

'Oh!' said the audacious Wilfred, 'we all know who is Gill's Jack!'

'Shut up, Will!' cried Fergus, flying at him. 'I told you not to—'

But Wilfred bounded up a steep bank, and from that place of vantage went on—

'Didn't she teach him Greek, and wasn't he spoony; and didn't she send back his valentine, so that—'

Fergus was scrambling up the bank after him, enraged at the betrayal of his confidence, and shouting inarticulately, while poor Gillian moved on, overwhelmed with confusion, and Fly uttered the cutting words, 'Perfectly disgusting!'

'Ay, so it was!' cried the unabashed Wilfred, keeping on at the top of the bank, and shaking the bushes at every pause. 'So he broke down the rocks, and ran away with the tin, and enlisted, and went to prison. Such a sweet young man for Gill!'

Poor Gillian! was her punishment never to end? That scrape of hers, hitherto so tenderly and delicately hinted at, and which she would have given worlds to have kept from her brothers, now shouted all over the country! Sympathy, however, she had, if that would do her any good. Mysie and Fly came on each side of Ivinghoe, assuring him, in low eager voices, of the utter nonsense of the charge, and explaining ardently; and Jasper, with one bound, laid hold of the tormentor, dragged him down, and, holding his stick over him, said—

'Now, Wilfred, if you don't hold your tongue, and not behave like a brute, I shall send you straight home.'

'It's quite true,' growled Wilfred. 'Ask her.'

'What does that signify? I'm ashamed of you! I've a great mind to thrash you this instant. If you speak another word of that sort, I shall. Now then, there are the governesses trying to stop to see what's the row. I shall give you up to Miss Vincent, if you choose to behave so like a spiteful girl.'

A sixth-form youth was far too great a man to be withstood by one who was not yet a public schoolboy at all; and Wilfred actually obeyed, while Jasper added to Fergus—

'How could you be such a little ass as to go and tell him all that rot?'

'It was true,' grumbled Fergus.

'The more reason not to go cackling about it like an old hen, or a girl! Your own sister! I'm ashamed of you both. Mind, I shall thrash you if you mention it again.'

Poor Fergus felt the accusation of cackling unjust, since he had only told Wilfred in confidence, and that had been betrayed, but he had got his lesson on family honour, and he subsided into his wonted look-out for curious stones, while Gillian was overtaken by Jasper—whether willingly or not, she hardly knew—but his first word was, 'Little beast!'

'You didn't hurt him, I hope,' said Gill, accepting the invitation to take his arm.

'Oh no! I only threatened to make him walk with the governesses and the donkeys.'

'Asses and savants to the centre,' said Gillian; 'like the orders to the French army in Egypt.'

'But what's all this about? You wanted me to look after you! Is it that Alexis?'

'Oh, Japs! Mamma knows all about it and papa. It was only that he was ridiculous because I was so silly as to think I could help him with his Greek.'

'You! With his Greek! I pity him!'

'Yes. I found he soon knew too much for me,' said Gillian meekly; 'but, indeed, Japs, it wasn't very bad! He only sent me a valentine, and Aunt Jane says I need not have been so angry.'

'A cat may look at a king,' said Jasper loftily. 'It is a horrid bad thing for a girl to be left to herself without a brother worth having.'

So Gillian got off pretty easily, and after all the walk was not greatly spoilt. They coalesced again with the other three, who were tolerably discreet, and found the debate on the White gentility had been resumed. Ivinghoe was philosophically declaring 'that in these days one must take up with everybody, so it did not matter if one was a little more of a cad than another; he himself was fag at Eton to a fellow whose father was an oilman, and who wasn't half a bad lot.'

'An oilman, Ivy,' said his sister; 'I thought he imported petroleum.'

'Well, it's all the same. I believe he began as an oilman.'

'We shall have Fergus reporting that he's a petroleuse,' put in Jasper.

'No, a petroleuse is a woman.'

'I like Mr. White,' said Fly; 'but, Gillian, you don't think it is true that he is going to marry your Aunt Jane?'

There was a great groan, and Japs observed—

'Some one told us Rockquay was a hotbed of gossip, and we seem to have got it strong.'

'Where did this choice specimen come from, Fly!' demanded Ivinghoe, in his manner most like his mother.

Fly nodded her head towards her governess in the advanced guard.

'She had a cousin to tea with her, and they thought I didn't know whom they meant, and they said that he was always up at Rockstone.'

'Well, he is; and Aunt Jane always stands up for him,' said Gillian; 'but that was because he is so good to the workpeople, and Aunt Ada took him for some grand political friend of Cousin Rotherwood's.'

'Aunt Jane!' said Jasper. 'Why, she is the very essence and epitome of old maids.'

'Yes,' said Gillian. 'If it came to that, she would quite as soon marry the postman.'

'That's lucky' said Ivinghoe. 'One can swallow a good deal, but not quite one's own connections.'

'In fact,' said Jasper, 'you had rather be an oilman's fag than a quarryman's —what is it?—first cousin once removed in law?'

'It is much more likely,' said Gillian, as they laughed over this, 'that Kalliope and Maura will be his adopted daughters, only he never comes near them.'

Wherewith there was a halt. Miss Elbury insisted that Phyllis should ride, the banks began to show promise of flowers, and, in the search for violets, dangerous topics were forgotten, and Wilfred was forgiven. They reached the spot marked by Fly, a field with a border of sloping broken ground and brushwood, which certainly fulfilled all their desires, steeply descending to a stream full of rocks, the ground white with wood anemones, long evergreen trails of periwinkles and blue flowers between, primroses clustering under the roots of the trees, daffodils gilding the grass above, and the banks verdant with exquisite feather-moss. Such a springtide wood was joy to all, especially as the first cuckoo of the season came to add to their delights and set them counting for the augury of happy years, which proved so many that Mysie said they would not know what to do with them.

'I should,' said Ivinghoe. 'I should like to live to be a great old statesman, as Lord Palmerston did, and have it all my own way. Wouldn't I bring things round again!'

'Perhaps they would have gone too far,' suggested Jasper, 'and then you would have to gnaw your hand like Giant Pope, as Wilfred says.'

'Catch me, while I could do something better.'

'If one only lived long enough,' speculated Fergus, 'one might find out what everything was made of, and how to do everything.'

'I wonder if the people did before the Flood, when they lived eight or nine hundred years,' said Fly.

'Perhaps that is the reason there is nothing new under the sun,' suggested Valetta, as many a child has before suggested.

'But then,' said Mysie, they got wicked.'

'And then after the Flood it had all to be begun over again,' said Ivinghoe. 'Let me see, Methuselah lived about as long as from William the Conqueror till now. I think he might have got to steam and electricity.'

'And dynamite,' said Gillian. 'Oh, I don't wonder they had to be swept away, if they were clever and wicked both!'

'And I suppose they were,' said Jasper. 'At least the giants, and that they handed on some of their ability through Ham, to the Egyptians, and all those queer primeval coons, whose works we are digging up.'

'From the Conquest till now,' repeated Gillian. 'I'm glad we don't live so long now. It tires one to think of it.'

'But we shall,' said Fly.

'Yes,' said Mysie, 'but then we shall be rid of this nasty old self that is always getting wrong.'

'That little lady's nasty old self does so as little as any one's,' Jasper could not help remarking to his sister; and Fly, pouncing on the first purple orchis spike amid its black-spotted leaves, cried—

'At any rate, these dear things go on the same, without any tiresome inventing.'

'Except God's just at first,' whispered Mysie.

'And the gardeners do invent new ones,' said Valetta.

'Invent! No; they only fuss them and spoil them, and make ridiculous names for them,' said Fly. These darling creatures are ever so much better. Look at Primrose there.'

'Yes,' said Gillian, as she saw her little sister in quiet ecstasy over the sparkling bells of the daffodils; 'one would not like to live eight hundred years away from that experience.'

'But mamma cares just as much still as Primrose does,' said Mysie. 'We must get some for her own self as well as for the church.'

'Mine are all for mamma,' proclaimed Primrose; and just then there was a shout that a bird's nest had been found—a ring-ousel's nest on the banks. Fly and her brother shared a collection of birds' eggs, and were so excited about robbing the ousels of a single egg, that Gillian hoped that Fergus would not catch the infection and abandon minerals for eggs, which would be ever so much worse—only a degree better than butterflies, towards which Wilfred showed a certain proclivity.

'I shall be thirteen before next holidays,' he observed, after making a vain dash with his hat at a sulphur butterfly, looking like a primrose flying away.

'Mamma won't allow any "killing collection" before thirteen years old,' explained Mysie.

'She says,' explained Gillian, 'by that time one ought to be old enough to discriminate between the lawfulness of killing the creatures for the sake of studying their beauty and learning them, and the mere wanton amusement of hunting them down under the excuse of collecting.'

'I say,' exclaimed Valetta, who had been exploring above, 'here is such a funny old house.'

There was a rush in that direction, and at the other end of the wide home-field was perceived a picturesque gray stone house, with large mullioned windows, a dilapidated low stone wall, with what had once been a handsome gateway, overgrown with ivy, and within big double daffodils and white narcissus growing wild.

'It's like the halls of Ivor,' said Mysie, awestruck by the loneliness; 'no dog, nor horse, nor cow, not even a goose,'

'And what a place to sketch!' cried Miss Vincent. 'Oh, Gillian, we must come here another day.'

'Oh, may we gather the flowers?' exclaimed the insatiable Primrose.

'Those poetic narcissuses would be delicious for the choir screen,' added Gillian.

'Poetic narcissus—poetic grandmother,' said Wilfred. 'It's old butter and eggs.'

'I say!' cried Mysie. 'Look, Ivy—I know that pair of fighting lions—ain't these some of your arms over the door?'

'By which you mean a quartering of our shield,' said Ivinghoe. 'Of course it is the Clipp bearing. Or, two lions azure, regardant combatant, their tails couped.'

'Two blue Kilkenny cats, who have begun with each other's tails,' commented Jasper.

'Ivinghoe glared a little, but respected the sixth form, and Gillian added—

'They clipped them! Then did this place belong to our ancestors?'

'Poetic grandmother, really!' said Mysie.

'Great grandmother,' corrected Ivinghoe. 'To be sure. It was from the Clipps that we got all this Rockstone estate!'

'And I suppose this was their house? What a shame to have deserted it!'

'Oh, it has been a farmhouse,' said Fly. 'I heard something about farms that wouldn't let.'

'Then is it yours?' cried Valetta, 'and may we gather the flowers?'

'And mayn't we explore?' asked Mysie. 'Oh, what fun!'

'Holloa!' exclaimed Wilfred, transfixed, as if he had seen the ghosts of all the Clipps. For just as Valetta and Mysie threw themselves on the big bunches of hepatica and the white narcissus, a roar, worthy of the clip-tailed lions, proceeded from the window, and the demand, 'Who is picking my roses?'

Primrose in terror threw herself on Gillian with a little scream. Wilfred crept behind the walls, but after the general start there was an equally universal laugh, for between the stout mullions of the oriel window Lord Rotherwood's face was seen, and Sir Jasper's behind him.

Great was the jubilation, and there was a rush to the tall door, up the dilapidated steps, where curls of fern were peeping out; but the gentlemen called out that only the back-door could be opened, and the intention of a 'real grand exploration' was cut short by Miss Elbury's declaring that she was bound not to let Phyllis stay out till six o'clock.

Fly, in her usual good-humoured way, suppressed her sighs and begged the others to explore without her, but the general vote declared this to be out of the question. Fly had too short a time to remain with her cousins to be forsaken even for the charms of 'the halls of Ivor,' or the rival Beast's Castle, as Gillian called it, which, after all, would not run away.

'But it might be let,' said Mysie.

'Yes, I've got a tenant in agitation,' said Lord Rotherwood mischievously. 'Never mind, I dare say he won't inquire what you have done with his butter and eggs.'

So with a parting salute to the ancestral halls, the cavalry was set in order, big panniers full of moss and flowers disposed on the donkeys, Fly placed on her pony, and every maiden taking her basket of flowers, Jasper and Ivinghoe alone being amiable, or perhaps trustworthy enough to assist in carrying. Fly's pony demurred to the extra burthen, so Jasper took hers; and when Gillian declared herself too fond of her flowers to part with them, Ivinghoe astonished Miss Vincent, on whom some stones of Fergus's, as well as her own share of flowers, had been bestowed, by taking one handle of her most cumbrous basket.

Sir Jasper and Lord Rotherwood rode together through the happy young troop on the homeward way. Perhaps Ivinghoe was conscious of a special nod of approval from his father.

On passing Rock House, the youthful public was rather amused at his pausing, and saying—

'Aren't you going to leave some flowers there?'

'Oh yes!' said Gillian. 'I have a basket on purpose.'

'And I have some for Maura,' said Valetta.

Valetta's was an untidy bunch; Gillian's a dainty basket, where white violets reposed on moss within a circle of larger blossoms.

'That's something like!' quoth Ivinghoe.

He lingered with them as if he wanted to see that vision again, but only the caretaker appeared, and promised to take the flowers upstairs.

Maura afterwards told how they were enjoyed, and they knew of Kalliope's calm restfulness in Holy Week thoughts and Paschal Joys.

It was on Easter Tuesday that Mr. White first sent a message asking to see his guest, now of nearly three weeks.

He came in very quietly and gently—perhaps the sight of the room he had prepared for his young wife was in itself a shock to him, and he had lived so long without womankind that he had all a lonely man's awe of an invalid. He took with a certain respect the hand that Kalliope held out, as she said, with a faint flush in her cheeks—

'I am glad to thank you, sir. You have been very good to me.'

'I am glad to see you better,' he said, with a little embarrassment.

'I ought to be, in this beautiful air, and with these lovely things to look at,' and she pointed to the reigning photograph on the stand—the facade of St. Mark's.

'You should see it as I did.' And he began to describe it to her, she putting in a question or two here and there, which showed her appreciation.

'You know something about it already,' he said.

'Yes; when I was quite a little girl one of the officers in the Royal Wardours brought some photographs to Malta, and told me about them.'

'But,' he said, recalling himself, that is not my object now. Your brother says he does not feel competent to decide without you.' And he laid before her two or three prospectuses of grammar schools. 'It is time to apply,' he added, 'if that little fellow—Peter, you call him, don't you?—is to begin next term.'

'Petros! Oh, sir, this is kindness!'

'I desired that the children's education should be attended to,' said Mr. White. 'I did not intend their being sent to an ordinary National school.'

'Indeed,' said Kalliope; 'I do not think much time has been lost, for they have learnt a good deal there; but I am particularly glad that Petros should go to a superior school just now that he has been left alone, for he is more lively and sociable than Theodore, and it might be less easy for him to keep from bad companions.'

The pros and cons of the several schools were discussed, and Hurstpierpoint finally fixed on.

'Never mind about his outfit,' added Mr. White. 'I'll give that fellow down in Bellevue an order to rig him out. He is a sharp little sturdy fellow, who will make his way in the world.'

'Indeed, I trust so, now that his education is secured. It is another load off my mind,' said Kalliope, with a smile of exceeding sweetness and gratitude, her hands clasped, and her eyes raised for a moment in higher thankfulness,— a look that so enhanced her beauty that Mr. White gazed for a moment in wonder. The next moment, however, the dark eyes turned on him with a little anxiety, and she said—

'One thing more, sir. Perhaps you will be so kind as to relieve my mind again. That notice of dismissal at the quarter's end. Was it not in some degree from a mistake?'

'An utter mistake, my dear,' he said hastily. 'Never trouble your head about it.'

'Then it does not hold?'

'Certainly not.'

'And I may go back to my office as soon as I am well enough?'

'Is that your wish?'

'Yes, sir. I love my work and my assistants, and I think I could do better if a little more scope could be allowed me.'

'Very well, we will see about that—you have to get well first of all.'

'I am so much better that I ought to go home. Mr. Lee is quite ready for me.'

Nonsense! You must be much stronger before Dagger would hear of your going.'

After this Mr. White came to sit with Kalliope for a time in the course of each day, bringing with him something that would interest her, and seeming gratified by her responsiveness, quiet as it was, for she was still very feeble, and exertion caused a failure of breath and fluttering of heart that were so distressing that ten days more passed before she was brought downstairs and drawn out in the garden in a chair, where she could sit on the sheltered terrace enjoying the delicious spring air and soft sea-breezes, sometimes alone, sometimes with the company of one friend or another. Gillian and Aunt Jane had, with the full connivance of Mr. White, arranged a temporary entrance from one garden to the other for the convenience of attending to Kalliope, and here one afternoon Miss Mohun was coming in when she heard through the laurels two voices speaking to the girl. As she moved forward she saw they were the elder and younger Stebbings, and that Kalliope had risen to her feet, and was leaning on the back of her chair. While she was considering whether to advance Kalliope heard her, and called in a breathless voice, 'Miss Mohun! oh, Miss Mohun, come!'

'Miss Mohun! You will do us the justice—' began Mr. Stebbing, speaking more to her indignant face and gesture than to any words.

'Miss White is not well,' she said. 'You had better leave her to me.'

And as they withdrew through the house, Kalliope sank back in her chair in one of those alarming attacks of deadly faintness that had been averted for many days past. Happily an electric bell was always at hand, and the housekeeper knew what remedies to bring. Kalliope did not attempt a word for many long minutes, though the colour came back gradually to her lips. Her first words were,

'Thank you! Oh, I did hope that persecution was over!'

'My poor child! Don't tell me unless you like! Only—it wasn't about your work?'

'Oh no, the old story! But he brought his father—to say he consented—and wished it—now.'

There was no letting her say any more at that time, but it was all plain enough. This had been one more attempt of the Stebbing family to recover their former power; Kalliope was assumed to be Mr. White's favoured niece; Frank could make capital of having loved her when poor and neglected, and his parents were ready to back his suit. The father and son had used their familiarity with the house to obtain admittance to the garden without announcement or preparation, and had pressed the siege, with a confidence that could only be inspired by their own self-opinion. Kalliope had been kept up by her native dignity and resolution, and had at first gently, then firmly, declined the arguments, persuasions, promises, and final reproaches with which they beset her—even threatening to disclose what they called encouragement, and assuring her that she need not reckon on Mr. White, for the general voice declared him likely to marry again, and then where would she be?'

'I don't know what would have become of me, if you had not come,' she said.

And when she had rested long enough, and crept into the house, and Alexis had come home to carry her upstairs, it was plain that she had been seriously thrown back, and she was not able to leave her room for two or three days.

Mr. White was necessarily told what had been the cause of the mischief. He smiled grimly. 'Ay! ay! Master Frank thought he would come round the old man, did he? He will find himself out. Ha, ha! a girl like that in the house is like a honey-pot near a wasps' nest, and the little sister will be as bad. Didn't I see the young lord, smart little prig as he looks, holding an umbrella over her with a smile on his face, as much as to say, "I know who is a pretty girl! No one to look after them either!" But maybe they will all find themselves mistaken,' and his grim smile relaxed into a highly amiable one.

Miss Mohun was not at all uneasy as to the young lord. An Eton boy's admiration of a pretty face did not amount to much, even if Ivinghoe had not understood 'Noblesse oblige' too well to leave a young girl unsheltered. Besides, he and all the rest were going away the next day. But what did that final hint mean?

CHAPTER XXII. — THE MAIDEN ALL FORLORN

One secret was soon out, even before the cruel parting of Fly and Mysie, which it greatly mitigated.

Clipston was to be repaired and put in order, to be rented by the Merrifields. It was really a fine old substantial squire's house, though neglected and consigned to farmers for four generations. It had great capabilities—a hall up to the roof, wainscoted rooms—at present happy hunting-grounds to boys and terriers—a choked fountain, numerous windows, walled up in the days of the 'tax on light,' and never reopened, and, moreover, a big stone barn, with a cross on the gable, and evident traces of having once been a chapel.

The place was actually in Rockstone Parish, and had a hamlet of six or seven houses, for which cottage services were held once a week, but the restoration of the chapel would provide a place for these, and it would become a province for Lady Merrifield's care, while Sir Jasper was absolutely entreated, both by Lord Rotherwood and the rector of Rockstone, to become the valuable layman of the parish, nor was he at all unwilling thus to bestow his enforced leisure.

It was a beautiful place. The valley of daffodils already visited narrowed into a ravine, where the rivulet rushed down from moorlands, through a ravine charmingly wooded, and interspersed with rock. It would give country delights to the children, and remove them from the gossip of the watering- place society, and yet not be too far off for those reading-room opportunities beloved of gentlemen.

The young people were in ecstasies, only mourning that they could not live there during the repairs, and that those experienced in the nature of workmen hesitated to promise that Clipston would be habitable by the summer vacation. In the meantime, most of the movables from Silverfold were transported thither, and there was a great deal of walking and driving to and fro, planning for the future, and revelling in the spring outburst of flowers.

Schoolroom work had begun again, and Lady Merrifield was hearing Mysie read the Geruasalemme Liberata, while Miss Vincent superintended Primrose's copies, and Gillian's chalks were striving to portray a bust of Sophocles, when the distant sounds of the piano in the drawing-room stopped, and Valetta came in with words always ominous—

'Aunt Jane wants to speak to you, mamma.'

Lady Merrifield gathered up her work and departed, while Valetta, addressing the public, said, 'Something's up.'

'Oh!' cried Primrose, 'Sofi hasn't run away again?'

'I hope Kalliope isn't worse,' said Mysie anxiously.

'I guess,' said Valetta, 'somebody said something the other day!'

'Something proving us the hotbeds of gossip,' muttered Gillian.

'You had better get your German exercise, Valetta,' said Miss Vincent. 'Mysie, you have not finished your sums.'

And a sigh went round; but Valetta added one after-clap.

'Aunt Jane looked—I don't know how!'

Whereat Gillian nodded her head, and looked up at Miss Vincent, who was as curious as the rest, but restrained the manifestation manfully.

Meantime Lady Merrifield found her sister standing at the window, and, without turning round, the words were uttered—

'Jasper was right, Lily.'

'You don't mean it?'

'Yes; he is after her!'—with a long breath.

'Mr. White!'

'Yes'—then sitting down. 'I did not think much of it before. They always are after Ada more or less—and she likes it; but it never has come to anything.'

'Why should it now?'

'It has! At least, it has gone further than ever anything did before, except Charlie Scott, that ridiculous boy at Beechcroft that William was so angry with, and who married somebody else.'

'You don't say that he has proposed to her?'

'Yes, he has—the man! By a letter this morning, and I could see she expected it—not that that's any wonder!'

'But, my dear, she can't possibly be thinking of it.'

'Well, I should have said it was impossible; but I see she has not made up her mind. Poor dear Ada! It is too bad to laugh; but she does like the having a real offer at last, and a great Italian castle laid at her feet.'

'But he isn't a gentleman! I don't mean only his birth—and I know he is a good man really—but Jasper said he could feel he was not a gentleman by the way he fell on Richard White before his sister.'

'I know! I know! I wonder if it would be for her happiness?'

'Then she has not answered him?'

'No; or, rather, I left her going to write. She won't accept him certainly now; but I believe she is telling him that she must have time to consider and consult her family.'

'She must know pretty well what her family will say. Fancy William! Fancy Emily! Fancy Reginald!'

'Yes, oh yes! But Ada—I must say it—she does like to prolong the situation.'

'It is not fair on the poor man.'

'Well, she will act as she chooses; but I think she really does want to see what amount of opposition—No, not that, but of estrangement it would cause.'

'Did you see the letter?'

'Yes; no doubt you will too. I told her I should come to you, and she did not object. I think she was glad to be saved broaching the subject, for she is half ashamed.'

'I should have thought she would have been as deeply offended at the presumption as poor Gillian was with the valentine.'

'Lily, my dear, forty-two is not all one with seventeen, especially when there's an estate with an Italian countship attached to it! Though I'm sure I'd rather marry Alexis than this man. *He* is a gentleman in grain!'

'Oh, Jenny, you are very severe!'

'I'm afraid it is bitterness, Lily; so I rushed down to have it all out with you, and make up my mind what part to take.'

'It is very hard on you, my dear, after you have nursed and waited on her all these years.'

'It is the little titillation of vanity—exactly like the Ada of sixteen, nay, of six, that worries me, and makes me naughty,' said Jane, dashing off a tear. 'Oh, Lily! how could I have borne it if you had not come home!'

'But what do you mean about the part to take?'

'Well, you see, Lily, I really do not know what I ought to do. I want to clear my mind by talking to you.'

'I am afraid it would make a great difference to you in the matter of means.'

'I don't mean about that; but I am not sure whether I ought to stand up for her. You see the man is really good at heart, and religious, and he is taking out this chaplain. The climate, mountains, and sea might really suit her health, and she could have all kinds of comforts and luxuries; and if she can get over his birth, and the want of fine edge of his manners, I don't know that we have any right to set ourselves against it.'

'I should have thought those objections would have weighed most of all with her.'

'And I do believe that if the whole family are unanimous in scouting the very idea, she will give it up. She *is* proud of Mohun blood, and the Rotherwood connection and all, and if there were a desperate opposition— well, she would be rather flattered, and give in; but I am not sure that she would not always regret it, and pine after what she might have had.'

'Rotherwood likes the man.'

'Like—but that's not liking him to marry his cousin.'

'Rotherwood will not be the person most shocked.'

'No. We shall have a terrible time, however it ends. Oh. I wish it was all over!'

'Do you think she really cares for the man—loves him, in fact?'

'My dear Lily, if Ada ever was in love with anybody, it was with Harry May, and that was all pure mistake. I never told anybody, but I believe it was that which upset her health. But they are both too old to concern themselves about such trifles. He does not expect it!'

'I have seen good strong love in a woman over forty.'

'Yes; but this is quite another thing. A lady of the house wanted! That's the motive. I should not wonder if he came home as much to look for a lady-wife as to set the Stebbings to rights; or, if not, he is driven to it by having the Whites on his hands.'

'I don't quite see that. I was going to ask you how it would affect them.'

'Well, you see, though she is perfectly willing and anxious to begin again, poor dear Kally really can't. She did try to arrange a design that had been running in her head for a long time, and she was so bad after it that Dr.

Dagger said she must not attempt it. Then, though she is discreet enough for anything, Mr. White is not really her uncle, and could not take her about with him alone or even with Maura; so I gather from some expressions in his letter that he would like to take her out with them, spend the summer at Rocca Marina, and let her have a winter's study at Florence. Then, I suppose she might come back and superintend on quite a different footing.

'So he wants Ada as a chaperon for Kalliope?'

'That is an element in the affair, and not a bad one, and I don't think Ada will object. She won't be left entirely to his companionship.'

'My dear Jane! Then I'm sure she ought not to marry him!' cried Lady Merrifield indignantly. 'Here comes Jasper. May I tell him?'

'You will, whether you may or not.'

And what Sir Jasper said was—

'"Who married the maiden all forlorn—"'

At which both sisters, though rather angry, could not help laughing, and Lady Merrifield explained that they had always said the events had gone on in a concatenation, like the house that Jack built, from Gillian's peep through the rails. However, he was of opinion that it was better not to make a strenuous opposition.

'Adeline is quite old enough to judge for herself whether the incongruities will interfere with her happiness,' he said; 'and this is really a worthy man who ought not to be contemned. Violent contradiction might leave memories that would make it difficult to be on affectionate terms afterwards.'

'Yes,' said Jane; 'that is what I feel. Thank you, Jasper. Now I must go to my district. Happily those things run on all the same for the present.'

But when she was gone Sir Jasper told his wife that he thought it ought to be seriously put before Adeline that Jane ought to be considered. She had devoted herself to the care of her sister for many years, and the division of their means would tell seriously upon her comfort.

'If it were a matter of affection, there would be nothing to say,' he observed; 'but nobody pretends that it is so, and surely Jane deserves consideration.'

'I should think her a much more comfortable companion than Mr. White,' said Lady Merrifield. 'I can't believe it will come to anything. Whatever the riches or the castle at Rocca Marina may be, Ada would, in a worldly point of view, give up a position of some consideration here, and I think that will weigh with her.'

As soon as possible, Lady Merrifield went up to see her sister, and found her writing letters in a great flutter of importance. It was quite plain that the affair was not to be quashed at once, and that, whether the suit were granted or not, all the family were to be aware that Adeline had had her choice. Warned by her husband, Lady Merrifield guarded the form of her remonstrances.

'Oh yes, dear Lily, I know! It is a sacrifice in many points of view, but think what a field is open to me! There are all those English workmen and their wives and families living out there, and Mr. White does so need a lady to influence them.'

'You have not done much work of that kind. Besides, I thought this chaplain was married.'

'Yes, but the moral support of a lady at the head must be needful,' said Ada. 'It is quite a work.'

'Perhaps so,' said her sister, who had scarcely been in the habit of looking on Ada as a great moral influence. 'But have you thought what this will be to Jane?'

'Really, Lily, it is a good deal for Jane's sake. She will be so much more free without being bound to poor me!'—and Ada's head went on one side. 'You know she would never have lived here but for me; and now she will be able to do what she pleases.'

'Not pecuniarily.'

'Oh, it will be quite possible to see to all that! Besides, think of the advantage to her schemes. Oh yes, dear Jenny, it will be a wrench to her, of course, and she will miss me; but, when that is once got over, she will feel that I have acted for the best. Nor will it be such a separation; he means always to spend the summer here, and the winter and spring at Florence or Rocca Marina.' It was grand to hear the Italian syllables roll from Adeline's tongue. 'You know he could take the title if he pleased.'

'I am sure I hope he will not do anything so ridiculous!'

'Oh no, of course not!' But it was plain that the secret consciousness of being Countess of Rocca Marina was an offset against being plain Mrs. White, and Adeline continued: 'There is another thing—I do not quite see how it can be managed about Kalliope otherwise, poor girl!'

It was quite true that the care of Kalliope would be greatly facilitated by Mr. White's marriage; but what was absurd was to suppose that Ada would have made any sacrifice for her sake, or any one else's, and there was something comical as well as provoking in this pose of devotion to the public good.

'You are decided, then?'

'Oh no! I am only showing you what inducements there are to give up so much as I should do here—if I make up my mind to it.'

'There's only one inducement, I should think, valid for a moment.' 'Yes'—

bridling a little. 'But, Lily, you always had your romance. We don't all meet with a Jasper at the right moment, and—and'—the Maid of Athens drooped her eyelids, and ingenuously curved her lips. 'I do think the poor man has it very much at heart.'

'Then you ought not to keep him in suspense.'

'And you—you really are not against it, Lily?' (rather in a disappointed tone), as if she expected to have her own value enhanced.

'I think you ought to do whatever is most right and just by him, and everybody else. If you really care for the man enough to overlook his origin, and his occasional betrayals of it, and think he will make you better and happier, take him at once; but don't pretend to call it a sacrifice, or for anybody's sake but for your own; and, any way, don't trifle with him and his suspense.'

Lady Merrifield spoke with unwonted severity, for she was really provoked.

'But, Lily, I must see what the others say—William and Emily. I told him that William was the head of our family.'

'If you mean to be guided by them, well and good; if not, I see no sense in asking them.'

After all, the family commotion fell short of what was expected by either of the sisters. The eldest brother, Mr. Mohun, of Beechcroft Court, wrote to the lady herself that she was quite old enough to know what was for her own happiness, and he had no desire to interfere with her choice if she preferred wealth to station. To Lady Merrifield his letter began: 'It is very well it is no worse, and as Jasper vouches for this being a worthy man, and of substantial means, there is no valid objection. I shall take care to overhaul the settlements, and, if possible, I must make up poor Jane's income.'

The sister, Lady Henry Grey, in her dowager seclusion at Brighton, contented herself with a general moan on the decadence of society, and the levelling up that made such an affair possible. She had been meditating a visit to Rockquay, to see her dear Lilias (who, by the bye, had run down to her at

Brighton for a day out of the stay in London), but now she would defer it till this matter was over. It would be too trying to have to accept this stonemason as one of the family.

As to Colonel Mohun, being one of the younger division of the family, there was no idea of consulting him, and he wrote a fairly civil little note to Adeline, hoping that she had decided for the best, and would be happy; while to the elder of the pair of sisters he said: 'So Ada has found her crooked stick at last. I always thought it inevitable. Keep up heart, old Jenny, and hold on till Her Majesty turns me off, and then we will see what is to be done.'

Perhaps this cool acquiescence was less pleasing to Adeline Mohun than a contest that would have proved her value and importance, and her brother William's observation that she was old enough to know her own mind was the cruellest cut of all. On the other hand, there was no doubt of her swain's devotion. If he had been influenced in his decision by convenience or calculation, he was certainly by this time heartily in love. Not only was Adeline a handsome, graceful woman, whose airs and affectations seemed far more absurd to those who had made merry over them from childhood than to a stranger of an inferior grade; but there was a great charm to a man, able to appreciate refinement, in his first familiar intercourse with thorough ladies. Jane began to be touched by the sight of his devotion, and convinced of his attachment, and sometimes wondered with Lady Merrifield whether Adeline would rise to her opportunities and responsibilities, or be satisfied to be a petted idol.

One difficulty in this time of suspense was, that the sisters had no right to take into their confidence the young folks, who were quite sharp-eyed enough to know that something was going on, and, not being put on honour, were not withheld from communicating their discoveries to one another in no measured words, though fortunately they had sense enough, especially under the awe of their father, not to let them go any further than Mysie, who was entertaining because she was shocked at their audacious jokes and speculations, all at first on the false scent of their elder aunt, who certainly was in a state of excitement and uncertainty enough to throw her off the even tenor of her way and excite some suspicion. When she actually brought down a number of the Contemporary Review instead of Friendly Work for the edification of her G.F.S., Gillian tried not to look too conscious when some of the girls actually tittered in the rear; and she absolutely blushed when Aunt Jane deliberately stated that Ascension Day would fall on a Tuesday. So Gillian averred as she walked up the hill with Jasper and Mysie. It seemed a climax to the diversion she and Jasper had extracted from it in private, both wearing Punch's spectacles for the nonce, and holding such aberrations as proof positive.

Mysie, on the other hand, was much exercised.

'Do you think she is in love, then?'

'Oh yes! People always do those things in love. Besides, the Sofi hasn't got a single white hair in her, and you know what that always means!'

'I can't make it out! I can't think how Aunt Jane can be in love with a great man like that. His voice isn't nice, you know—'

'Not even as sweet as Bully Bottom's,' suggested Gillian.

'You're a chit,' said Jasper, 'or you'd be superior to the notion of love being indispensable.'

'When people are so *very* old,' said Mysie in a meditative voice, 'perhaps they can't; but Aunt Jane is very good—and I thought it was only horrid worldly people that married without love.'

'Trust your good woman for looking to the main chance,' said Jasper, who was better read in Trollope and Mrs. Oliphant than his sisters.

''Tis not main chance,' said Gillian. 'Think of the lots of good she would do! What a recreation room for the girls, and what schools she would set up at Rocca Marina! Depend upon it, it's for that!'

'I suppose it is right if Aunt Jane does it,' said Mysie.

'Well done, Mysie! So, Aunt Jane is your Pope!'

'No; she's the King that can do no wrong,' said Gillian, laughing.

'Wrong—I didn't say wrong—but things aren't always real wrong that aren't somehow quite right, said Mysie, with the bewildered reasoning of perceptions that outran her powers of expression.

'Mysie's speeches, for instance,' said Jasper.

'Oh, Japs, what did I say wrong?'

'Don't tease her, Japs. He didn't mean morally, but correctly.'

The three were on their way up the hill when they met Primrose, who had accompanied Mrs. Halfpenny to see Kalliope, and who was evidently in a state of such great discomposure that they all stood round to ask what was the matter; but she hung down her head and would not say.

'Hoots! toots! I tell her she need not make such a work about it,' said Mrs. Halfpenny. 'The honest man did but kiss her, and no harm for her uncle that is to be.'

'He's a nasty man! And he snatched me up! And he is all scrubby and tobacco-ey, and I won't have him for an uncle,' cried Primrose.

'I hope he is not going to proceed in that way,' said Gillian sotto voce to Mysie.

'People always do snatch up primroses,' said Jasper.

'Don't, Japs! I don't like marble men. I wish they would stay marble.'

'You don't approve of the transformation?'

'Oh, Japs, is it true? Mysie, you know the statue at Rotherwood, where Pig-my-lion made a stone figure and it turned into a woman.'

'Yes; but it was a woman and this is a man.'

Mysie began an exposition of classic fable to her little sister, while Mrs. Halfpenny explained that this came of Christian folk setting up heathen idols in their houses as 'twas a shame for decent folk to look at, let alone puir bairnies; while Jasper and Gillian gasped in convulsions of laughter, and bandied queries whether their aunt were the statue 'Pig-my-lion' had animated, as nothing could be less statuesque than she, whether the reverse had taken place, as Primrose observed, and she had been the Pygmalion to awaken the soul in the man of marble. Here, however, Mrs. Halfpenny became scandalised at such laughter in the open street; and, perceiving some one in the distance, she carried off Primrose, and enjoined the others to walk on doucely and wiselike.

Gillian was on her way to visit Kalliope and make an appointment for her mother to take her out for a drive; but as they passed the gate at Beechcroft out burst Valetta and Fergus, quite breathless.

'Oh, Gill, Gill! Mr. White is in the drawing-room, and he has brought Aunt Ada the most beautiful box you ever saw, with all the stoppers made of gold!'

'And he says I may get all the specimens I like at Rocca Marina,' shouted Fergus.

'Ivory brushes, and such a ring—sparkling up to the ceiling!' added Valetta.

'But, Val, Ferg, whom did you say?' demanded the elders, coming within the shadow of the copper beeches.

'Aunt Ada,' said Valetta; 'there's a great A engraved on all those dear, lovely bottles, and—oh, they smell!'

'Aunt Ada! Oh, I thought—'

'What did you think, Gill?' said Aunt Jane, coming from the grass-plat suddenly on them.

'Oh, Aunt Jane, I am so glad!' cried Gillian. 'I thought'—and she blushed furiously.

'They made asses of themselves,' said Jasper.

'They said it was you,' added Mysie. 'Miss Mellon told Miss Elbury,' she added in excuse.

'Me? No, I thank you! So you are glad, Gillian?'

'Oh yes, aunt! I couldn't have borne for you to do anything—queer'—and there was a look in Gillian's face that went to Jane's heart, and under other circumstances would have produced a kiss, but she rallied to her line of defence.

'My dear, you must not call this queer. Mr. White is very much attached to your aunt Ada, and I think he will make her very happy, and give her great opportunities of doing good.'

'That's just what Gillian said when she was afraid it was you,' said Mysie. 'I suppose that's it? And that makes it real right.'

'And the golden stoppers!' said Valetta innocently, but almost choking Jasper with laughter, which must be suppressed before his aunt.

'May one know it now?' asked Gillian, sensible of the perilous ground.

'Yes, my dears; you must have been on tenter-hooks all this time, for, of course, you saw there was a crisis, and you behaved much better than I should have done at your age; but it was only a fait accompli this very day, and we couldn't tell you before.'

'When he brought down the golden stoppers,' Jasper could not help saying.

'No, no, you naughty boy! He would not have dared to bring it in before; he came before luncheon—all that came after. Oh, my dear, that dressing-case is perfectly awful! I wouldn't have such a burthen on my mind—for—for all the orphans in London! I hope there are no banditti at RoccaMarina.'

'Only accepted to-day! How did he get all his great A's engraved?' said Jasper practically.

'He could not have had many doubts,' said Gillian. 'Does Kalliope know?'

'I cannot tell; I think he has probably told her.'

'He must have met Primrose there,' said Jasper. 'Poor Prim!' And the offence and the Pig-my-lion story were duly related, much to Aunt Jane's amusement.

'But,' she said, 'I think that the soul in the marble man is very real, and very warm; and, dear children, don't get into the habit of contemning him. Laugh, I suppose you must; I am afraid it must look ridiculous at our age; but please don't despise. I am going down to your mother.

'May I come with you! said Gillian. 'I don't think I can go to Kally till I have digested this a little; and, if you are going to mamma, she won't drive her out.'

Jane was much gratified by this volunteer, though Jasper did suggest that Gill was afraid of Primrose's treatment. He went on with the other three to Clipston, while Gillian exclaimed—

'Oh, Aunt Jane, shall not you be very lonely?'

'Not nearly so much so as if you were not all here,' said her aunt cheerfully. 'When you bemoaned your sisters last year we did not think the same thing was coming on me.'

'Phyllis and Alethea! It was a very different thing,' said Gillian. 'Besides, though I hated it so much, I had got used to being without them.'

'And to tell you the truth, Gill, nothing in that way ever was so bad to me as your own mother going and marrying; and now, you see, I have got her back again—and more too.'

Aunt Jane's smile and softened eyes told that the young niece was included in the 'more too'; and Gillian felt a thrill of pleasure and affection in this proof that after all she was something to the aunt, towards whom her feelings had so entirely changed. She proceeded, however, to ask with considerable anxiety what would be done about the Whites, Kalliope especially; and in return she was told about the present plan of Kalliope's being taken to Italy to recover first, and then to pursue her studies at Florence, so as to return to her work more capable, and in a higher position.

'Oh, how exquisite!' cried Gillian. 'But how about all the others?'

'The very thing I want to see about, and talk over with your mother. I am sure she ought to go; and it will not even be wasting time, for she cannot earn anything.'

Talking over things with Lady Merrifield was, however, impeded, for, behold, there was a visitor in the drawing-room. Aunt and niece exchanged glances of consternation as they detected a stranger's voice through the open window, and Gillian uttered a vituperative whisper.

'I do believe it is that dreadful Fangs;' then, hoping her aunt had not heard —'Captain Henderson, I mean. He threatened to come down after us, and now he will always be in and out; and we shall have no peace. He has got nothing on earth to do.'

Gillian's guess was right. The neat, trim, soldierly figure, with a long fair moustache and pleasant gray eyes, was introduced to Miss Mohun as 'Captain Henderson, one of my brother officers,' by Sir Jasper, who stood on the rug talking to him. Looks and signs among the ladies were token enough that the crisis had come; and Lady Merrifield soon secured freedom of speech by proposing to drive her sister to Clipston, while Sir Jasper asked his visitor to walk with him.

'You will be in haste to sketch the place,' he said, 'before the workmen have done their best to demolish its beauty.'

As for Gillian, she saw her aunt hesitating on account of a parochial engagement for that afternoon; and, as it was happily not beyond her powers, she offered herself as a substitute, and was thankfully accepted. She felt quite glad to do anything obliging towards her aunt Jane, and in a mood very unlike last year's grudging service; it was only reading to the 'mothers' meeting,' since among the good ladies there prevailed such a strange incapacity of reading aloud, that this part of the business was left to so few that for one to fail, either in presence or in voice, was very inconvenient. All were settled down to their needlework, with their babies disposed of as best they might be. Mr. Hablot had finished his little lecture, and the one lady with a voice had nearly exhausted it, and there was a slight sensation at the absence of the unfailing Miss Mohun, when Gillian came in with the apologies about going to drive with her mother.

'And,' as she described it afterwards 'didn't those wretched beings all grin and titter, even the ladies, who ought to have had more manners, and that old Miss Mellon, who is a real growth of the hotbed of gossip, simpered and supposed we must look for such things now; and, though I pretended not to hear, my cheeks would go and flame up as red as—that tasconia, just with longing to tell them Aunt Jane was not so ridiculous; and so I took hold of For Half a Crown, and began to read it as if I could bite them all!'

She read herself into a state of pacification, but did not attempt to see Kalliope that day, being rather shy of all that might be encountered in that house, especially after working hours. The next day, however, Lady Merrifield's services were required to chaperon the coy betrothed in an inspection of Cliff House and furniture, which was to be renovated according to her taste, and Gillian was to take that time for a visit to Kalliope, whom she expected to find in the garden. The usual corner was, however, vacant; and Mr. White was heard making a growl of 'Foolish girl! Doesn't know which way her bread is buttered.'

Maura, however, came running up, and said to Gillian, 'Please come this way. She is here.'

'What has she hidden herself for?' demanded Mr. White. 'I thought she might have been here to welcome this—Miss Adeline.'

'She is not very well to-day,' faltered Maura.

'Oh! ay, fretting. Well, I thought she had more sense.'

Gillian followed Maura, who was no sooner out of hearing than she began: 'It is too bad of him to be so cross. Kally really is so upset! She did not sleep all night, and I thought she would have fainted quite away this morning!'

'Oh dear! has he been worrying her?'

'She is very glad and happy, of course, about Miss Ada! and he won't believe it, because he wants her to go out to Italy with them for all next winter.'

'And won't she? Oh, what a pity!'

'She said she really could not because of us; she could not leave us, Petros and all, without a home. She thought it her duty to stay and look after us. And then he got cross, and said that she was presuming on the hope of living in idleness here, and making him keep us all, but she would find herself mistaken, and went off very angry.'

'Oh, horrid! how could he?'

'I believe, if Kally could have walked so far, she would have gone down straight to Mr. Lee's. She wanted to, but she was all in a tremble, and I persuaded her not, though she did send me down to ask Mrs. Lee when she can be ready. Then when Alexis came home, Mr. White told him that he didn't in the least mean all that, and would not hear of her going away, though he was angry at her being so foolish, but he would give her another chance of not throwing away such advantages. And Alexis says she ought not. He wants her to go, and declares that he and I can very well manage with Mrs. Lee, and look after Petros, and that she must not think of rushing off in a huff for a few words said in a passion. So, between the two, she was quite upset and couldn't sleep, and, oh, if she were to be ill again!'

By this time they were in sight of Kalliope lying back in a basket-chair, shaded by the fence of the kitchen-garden, and her weary face and trembling hand showed how much this had shaken her in her weakness. She sent Maura away, and spoke out her troubles freely to Gillian. 'I thought at first my duty was quite clear, and that I ought not to go away and enjoy myself and leave the others to get on without me. Alec would find it so dreary; and though Mr.

and Mrs. Lee are very good and kind, they are not quite companions to him. Then Maura has come to think so much about people being ladies that I don't feel sure that she would attend to Mrs. Lee; and the same with Petros in the holidays. If I can't work at first, still I can make a home and look after them.'

'But it is only one winter, and Alexis thinks you ought; and, oh, what it would be, and how you would get on!'

'That is what puzzles me. Alexis thinks Mr. White has a right to expect me to improve myself, and not go on for ever making white jessamines with malachite leaves, and that he can look after Maura and Petros. I see, too, that I ought to try to recover, or I might be a burthen on Alexis for ever, and hinder all his better hopes. Then, there's the not liking to accept a favour after Mr. White said such things, though I ought not to think about it since he made that apology; but it is a horrid feeling that I ought not to affront him for the sake of the others. Altogether I do feel so tossed. I can't get back the feeling I had when I was ill that I need not worry, for that God will decide.'

And there were tears in her eyes.

'Can't you ask some one's advice?' said Gillian.

'If I were sure they quite understood! My head is quite tired with thinking about it.'

Not many moments had passed before there were steps that made Kalliope start painfully, and Maura appeared, piloting another visitor. It was Miss Mohun, who had escaped from the survey of the rooms,—so far uneasy at what she had gathered from Mr. White, that she was the more anxious to make the offer previously agreed to.

'My dear,' she said, 'I am afraid you look tired.'

'They have worried her and knocked her up,' said Gillian indignantly.

'I see! Kally, my dear, we are connections now, you know, and I have heard of Mr. White's plan. It made me think whether you would find the matter easier if you let me have Maura while you are away to cheer my solitude. Then I could see that she did her lessons, and, between all Gillian's brothers, we could see that Petros was happy in the holidays.'

'Oh, Miss Mohun! how can I be grateful enough? There is an end of all difficulties.'

And when the inspecting party came round, and Adeline bent to kiss the white, weary, but no longer distressed face, and kindly said, 'We shall see a great deal of each other, I hope,' she replied, with an earnest 'thank you,' and added to Mr. White, 'Miss Mohun has made it all easy to me, sir, and I am very grateful!'

'Ay, ay! You're a good girl at the bottom, and have some sense!'

CHAPTER XXIII. — FANGS

Events came on rapidly that spring. Mr. White was anxious that his marriage should take place quickly—afraid, perhaps, that his prize would escape him, and be daunted by the passive disapproval of her family, though this was only manifested to him in a want of cordiality. This, being sincere people, they could not help; and that outbreak to Kalliope had made the sisters so uneasy, that they would have willingly endured the ridicule of a broken engagement to secure Adeline from the risks of a rough temper where gentlemanly instincts were not inbred.

Adeline, however, knew she had gone too far to recede, though she would willingly have delayed, in enjoyment of the present homage and shrinking from the future plunge away from all her protectors. Though the strong, manly will overpowered hers, and made her submit to the necessities of the case and fix a day early in July, she clung the more closely to her sisters, and insisted on being accompanied by Jane on going to London to purchase the outfit that she had often seen in visions before. So Miss Mohun's affairs were put in commission, Gillian taking care of them, and the two sisters were to go to Mrs. Craydon, once, as Marianne Weston, their first friend out of their own family, and now a widow with a house in London, well pleased at any recall of old times, though inclined, like all the rest, to speak of 'poor Ada.'

Lord Rotherwood was, as his cousins had predicted, less disgusted than the rest, as in matters of business he had been able to test the true worth that lay beneath the blemishes of tone and of temper; and his wife thought the Italian residence and foreign tincture made the affair much more endurable than could have been expected. She chose an exquisite tea-service for their joint wedding present; but she would not consent to let Lady Phyllis be a bridesmaid; though the Marquis, discovering that her eldest brother hated the idea of giving her away to the stonemason, offered 'not to put too fine a point on it, but to act the part of Cousin Phoenix.'

Bridesmaids would have been rather a difficulty; but then the deep mourning of Kalliope and Maura made a decided reason for excluding them; and Miss Adeline, who knew that a quiet wedding would be in much the best taste, resolved to content herself with two tiny maidens, Primrose and the contemporary Hablot, her own goddaughter, who, being commonly known as Belle, made a reason for equipping each in the colour and with the flowers of her name, and the idea was carried out with great taste.

Valetta thought it hard that an outsider should be chosen. The young

Merrifields had the failing of large families in clannish exclusiveness up to the point of hating and despising more or less all who interfered with their enjoyment of one another, and of their own ways. The absence of society at Silverfold had intensified this farouche tone, and the dispersion, instead of curing it, had rendered them more bent on being alone together. Worst of all was Wilfred, who had been kept at home very inconveniently by some recurring delicacy of brain and eyes, and who, at twelve years old, was enough of an imp to be no small torment to his sisters. Valetta was unmercifully teased about her affection for Kitty Varley and Maura White, and, whenever he durst, there were attempts at stings about Alexis, until new game offered itself on whom no one had any mercy.

Captain Henderson was as much in the way as a man could be who knew but one family in the place, and had no resource but sketching. His yellow moustache was to be seen at all manner of unexpected and unwelcome times. If that great honour, a walk with papa, was granted, out he popped from Marine Hotel, or a seat in the public gardens, evidently lying in ambush to spoil their walk. Or he was found tete-a-tete with mamma before the five- o'clock tea, talking, no doubt, 'Raphaels, Correggios, and stuff,' as in the Royal Wardour days. Even at Clipston, or in the coves on the beach, he was only too apt to start up from some convenient post for sketching. He really did draw beautifully, and Mysie would have been thankful for his counsels if public opinion had not been so strong.

Moreover, Kitty Varley conveyed to Valetta the speculations of Rockstone whether Gillian was the attraction.

'Now, Val,' said Mysie, 'how can you listen to such nonsense!'

'You said so before, and it wasn't nonsense.'

'It wasn't Aunt Jane.'

'No, but it was somebody.'

'Everybody does marry somebody; but it is no use for us to think about it, for it always turns out just the contrary to all the books one ever read; so there's no going by anything, and I don't believe it right to talk about it.'

'Why not? Every one does.'

'All the good teachings say one should not talk of what one does not want one's grown-ups to hear.'

'Oh, but then one would never talk of anything!'

'Oh, Val! I won't be sure, but I don't believe I should mind mamma's hearing all I say.'

'Yes; but you've never been to school, and I heard Bee Varley say she never saw anybody so childishly simple for her age.'

This brought the colour into Mysie's face, but she said—

'I'd rather be simple than talk as mamma does not like; and, Val, do on no account tell Gillian.'

'I haven't.'

'And don't; don't tell Wilfred, or you know how horrid he would be.'

There was a tell-tale colour in Valetta's cheeks, by which Mysie might have discerned that Valetta had not resisted the charm of declaring 'that she knew something,' even though this was sure to lead to tortures of various kinds from Wilfred until it was extracted. Still the youth as yet was afraid to do much worse than look preternaturally knowing at his sister and give hints about Fangs' holding fast and the like, but quite enough to startle her into something between being flattered and indignant. She was scarcely civil to the Captain, and felt bound to express her dislike on every possible occasion, though only to provoke a grin from Wilfred and a giggle from Valetta.

Lady Merrifield's basket-carriage and little rough pony had been brought from Silverfold, and she took Kalliope out for quiet drives whenever it was possible; but a day of showers having prevented this, she was concerned to find herself hindered on a second afternoon. Gillian offered to be her substitute.

'You know I always drive you, mamma.'

'These are worse hills than at Silverfold, and I don't want you to come down by the sea-wall.'

'I am sure I would not go there for something, among all the stupid people.'

'If you keep to the turnpike you can't come to much harm with Bruno.'

'That is awfully—I mean horribly dusty! There's the cliff road towards Arnscombe.'

'That is safe enough. I don't think you could come to much real damage; but remember that for Kally a start or an alarm would be really as hurtful as an accident to a person in health.'

'Poor old Bruno could hardly frighten a mouse,' said Gillian.

'Only take care, and don't be enterprising.'

Gillian drove up to the door of Cliff House, and Kalliope took her seat. It

300

was an enjoyable afternoon, with the fresh clearness of June sunshine after showers, great purple shadows of clouds flitting over the sea, dimpled by white crests of wave that broke the golden path of sunshine into sparkling ripples, while on the other side of the cliff road lay the open moorland, full of furze, stunted in growth, but brilliant in colour, and relieved by the purple browns of blossoming grasses and the white stars of stitchwort.

'This is delicious!' murmured Kalliope, with a gesture of enjoyment.

'Much nicer than down below!'

'Oh yes; it seems to stretch one's very soul!'

'And the place is so big and wide that no one can worry with sketching.'

'Yes, it defies that!' said Kalliope, laughing.

'So, Fa—Captain Henderson won't crop up as he does at every sketchable place. Didn't you know he was here?'

'Yes, Alexis told me he had seen him.'

'Everybody has seen him, I should think; he is always about with nothing to do but that everlasting sketching.'

'He must have been very sorry to be obliged to retire.'

'Horrid! It was weak, and he might have been in Egypt, well out of the way. No, I didn't mean that'—as Kalliope looked shocked—'but he might have been getting distinction and promotion.'

'He used to be very kind,' said Kalliope, in a tone of regretful remonstrance. 'It was he who taught me first to draw.'

'He! What, Fa—Captain Henderson?'

'Yes; when I was quite a little girl, and he had only just joined. He found me out before our quarters at Gibraltar trying to draw an old Spaniard selling oranges, and he helped me, and showed me how to hold my pencil. I have got it still—the sketch. Then he used to lend me things to copy, and give me hints till—oh, till my father said I was too old for that sort of thing! Then, you know, my father got his commission, and I went to school at Belfast.'

'And you have never seen him since?'

'Scarcely. Sometimes he was on leave in my holidays, and you know we were at the depot afterwards, but I shall always feel that all that I have been able to do since has been owing to him.'

'And how you will enjoy studying at Florence!'

'Oh, think what it would be if I could ever do a reredos for a church! I keep on dreaming and fancying them, and now there really seems a hope. Is that Arnscombe Church?'

'Yes, you know it has been nicely restored.'

'We had the columns to do. The reredos is alabaster, I believe, and we had nobody fit to undertake that. I so longed for the power! I almost saw it.'

'Have you seen what it is?'

'No; I never had time.'

'I suppose it would be too tiring for you now; but we could see the outside.'

Gillian forgot that Arnscombe, whose blunt gray spire protruded through the young green elms, lay in a little valley through which a stream rushed to the sea. The lane was not very steep, but there were loose stones. Bruno stumbled, he was down; the carriage stood still, and the two girls were out on opposite sides in a moment, Gillian crying out—

'Don't be frightened—no harm done!'—as she ran to the pony's head. He lay quite still with heaving sides, and she felt utterly alone and helpless in the solitary road with an invalid companion whom she did not like to leave.

'I am afraid I cannot run for help,' said Kalliope quietly, though breathlessly; 'but I could sit by the horse and hold his head while you go for help.'

'I don't like. Oh, here's some one coming!'

'Can I be of any use?'

Most welcome sound!—though it was actually Captain Henderson the ubiquitous wheeling his bicycle up the hill, knapsack of sketching materials on his back.

'Miss Merrifield! Miss White! I trust no one is hurt!'

'Oh no, thank you, unless it is the poor pony! Kally, sit down on the bank, I insist! Oh, I am so glad you are come!'

'Can you sit on his head while I cut the traces?'

Gillian did that comfortable thing till released, when the pony scrambled up again, but with bleeding knees, hip, and side, though the Captain did not think any serious harm was done; but it was even more awkward at the moment that both the shafts were broken!

'What is to be done?' sighed Gillian. 'Miss White can't walk. Can I run down to the village to get something to take her home?'

'The place did not look likely to supply any conveyance better than a rough cart,' said their friend.

'It is quite impossible to put the poor pony in anyhow! I don't mind walking in the least; but you know how ill she has been.'

'I see. Only one thing to be done,' said the Captain, who had already turned the carriage round by the stumps of the shafts; 'you must accept me in lieu of your pony.'

'Oh yes, thank you!' cried Gillian eagerly. 'I can lead poor Bruno, and take care of your bicycle. Jump in, Kally!'

Kalliope, who had wisely abstained from adding a useless voice to the discussion, here demurred. She could not think of such a thing; they could very well wait in the carriage while Captain Henderson went on to the town on his bicycle and sent out a midge.

But there were showers about, and a damp feeling in the lane. Both the others thought this perilous; besides that, there might be rude passengers to laugh at their predicament; and Captain Henderson protested that the weight was nothing. He prevailed at last; and she allowed him to hand her into the basket, when she could hardly stand, and wrap the dust-cloth about her. Thus the procession set forth, Gillian with poor drooping Bruno's rein in one hand and the other on the bicycle, and the Captain gallantly drawing the carriage with Kalliope seated in the midst. He tramped on so vigorously as quite to justify his declaration that it was no burthen to him. It was not a frequented road, and they met no one in the least available to do more than stare or ask a question or two, until, as they approached the town and Rockstone Church was full in view, who should appear before their eyes but Sir Jasper, Wilfred carrying on his back a huge kite that had been for many evenings in course of construction, and Fergus acting as trainbearer.

Thus came on the first moment of Gillian's explanation, as Sir Jasper took the poor pony from her and held counsel over the damage, with many hearty thanks to Captain Henderson.

'I am sure, sir, no one could have shown greater presence of mind than the young ladies,' said that gentleman; and her father's 'I am glad to hear it!' would have gratified Gillian the more, but for the impish grimace with which Wilfred favoured her behind Kalliope's impassive back.

The kite-fliers turned, not without an entreaty from the boys that they might go on alone and fly their kite.

'No, no, boys,' said their father—'not here; we shall have the kite pulling you into the sea over the cliffs. I must take the pony home; but I will come if possible to-morrow.'

Much disappointed, they went dolefully in the rear, grumbling sotto voce their conviction that there would be no wind to-morrow, and that it was all 'Fangs's' fault in some incomprehensible manner.

At Cliff House Kalliope was carefully handed out by Sir Jasper, trying, but with failing voice, to thank Captain Henderson, and declaring herself not the worse, though her hand shook so much that the General was not content without giving her his arm up the stairs, and telling Maura that he should send Mrs. Halfpenny up to see after her. The maimed carriage was left in the yard, and Captain Henderson then took charge of his iron horse, and the whole male party proceeded to the livery stables; so that Gillian was able to be alone, when she humbly repeated to her mother the tale parents have so often to hear of semi-disobedience leading to disaster, but with the self-reproach and sorrow that drew the sting of displeasure. Pity for Bruno, grief for her mother's deprivation, and anxiety for Kalliope might be penance and rebuke sufficient for a bit of thoughtlessness. Lady Merrifield made no remark; but there was an odd expression in her face when she heard who had come so opportunely to the rescue.

Sir Jasper brought a reassuring account of the poor little steed, which would be usable again after a short rest, and the blemish was the less important as there was no intention of selling him. Mrs. Halfpenny, too, reported that her patient was as quiet as a lamb. 'She wasn't one to fash herself for nothing and go into screaming cries, but kenned better what was fitting for one born under Her Majesty's colours.'

So there was nothing to hinder amusement when at dinner Sir Jasper comically described the procession as he met it. Kalliope White, looking only too like Minerva, or some of those Greek goddess statues they used to draw about, sitting straight and upright in her triumphal car, drawn by her votary; while poor Gillian came behind with the pony on one side and the bicycle on the other, very much as if she were conducting the wheel on which she was to be broken, as an offering to the idol.

'I think,' said Mysie, 'Captain Henderson was like the two happy sons in Solon's story, who dragged their mother to the temple.'

'Only they died of it,' said Gillian.

'And nobody asked how the poor mother felt afterwards,' added Lady Merrifield.

'I thought they all had an apotheosis together,' said Sir Jasper. 'Let us hope that devotion may have its reward.'

There was a little lawn outside the drawing-room windows at Il Lido. Lady Merrifield was sitting just within, and her husband had just brought her a letter to read, when they heard Wilfred's impish voice.

'Jack—no, not Jack—Fangs!'

'But Fangs's name is Jack, so it will do as well,' said Valetta's voice.

'Hurrah—so it is! Jack—'

'Hush, Wilfred—this is too foolish!' came Gillian's tones in remonstrance.

```
'Jack and Jill went up the hill
        To draw—'
```

'To draw! Oh, that's lovely!' interrupted Valetta.

'He is always drawing,' said Gillian, with an odd laugh.

'He was brought up to it. First teeth, and then "picturs," and then—oh, my —ladies home from the wash!' went on Wilfred.

'But go on, Will!' entreated Valetta.

```
'Jack and Jill went up the hill
        To draw a piece of water—'
```

'No, no,' put in Wilfred—'that's wrong!

```
'To draw the sergeant's daughter;
        Fangs dragged down unto the town,
        And Jill came moaning after!'
```

'I didn't moan—'

'Oh, you don't know how disconsolate you looked! Moaning, you know, because her Fangs had to draw the other young woman—eh, Gill? Fangs always leave an aching void, you know.'

'You ridiculous boy! I'm sure I wish Fangs would leave a void. It wouldn't ache!'

The two parents had been exchanging glances of something very like consternation, and of the mute inquiry on one side, 'Were you aware of this sort of thing? and an emphatic shake of the head on the other. Then Sir Jasper's voice exclaimed aloud—

'Children, we hear every word you say, and are shocked at your impertinence and bad taste!'

There was a scatter. Wilfred and Valetta, who had been pinioning Gillian on either side by her dress, released her, and fled into the laurels that veiled the guinea-pigs; but their father's long strides pursued them, and he gravely said —

'I am very sorry to find this is your style of so-called wit!'

'It was only chaff,' said Valetta, the boldest in right of her girlhood.

'Very improper chaff! I am the last person to object to harmless merriment; but you are both old enough to know that on these subjects such merriment is not harmless.'

'Everybody does it,'whined Valetta, beginning one of her crying fits.

'I am sorry you have been among people who have led you to think so. No nicely-minded girl will do so, nor any brother who wishes to see his sisters refined, right-feeling women. Go in, Valetta—I can't suffer this howling! Go, I say! Your mother will talk to you. Now, Wilfred, do you wish to see your sisters like your mother?'

'They'll never be that, if they live to a hundred!'

'Do not you hinder it, then; and never let that insulting nickname pass your lips again.'

Wilfred's defence as to universal use in the family was inaudible, and he was allowed to slouch away.

Gillian had fled to her mother, entreating her to explain to her father that such jests were abhorrent to her.

'But you know, mamma, if I was cross and dignified, Wilfred would enjoy it all the more, and be ten times worse.'

'Quite true, my dear. Papa will understand; but we are sorry to hear that nickname.

'It was an old Royal Wardour name, mamma. Harry and Claude both used it, and—oh, lots of the young officers!'

'That does not make it more becoming in you.'

'N—no. But oh, mamma, he was very kind to-day! But I do wish it had been anybody else!'

And her colour rose so as to startle her mother.

'Why, my dear, I thought you would have been glad that a stranger did not find you in that plight!'

'But it makes it all the worse. He does beset us, mamma; and it is hard on me, after all the other nonsense!'

Lady Merrifield burst out laughing.

'My dear child, he thinks as much of you as of old Halfpenny!'

'Oh, mamma, are you sure?' said Gillian, still hiding her face. 'It was not silliness of my own; but Kitty Varley told Val that everybody said it—her sister, and Miss Mohun, and all. Why can't he go away, and not be always bothering about this horrid place with nothing to do?'

'How thankful I shall be to have you all safe at Clipston!'

'But, mamma, can't you keep him off us?'

Valetta's sobbing entrance here prevented more; but while explaining to her the causes of her father's displeasure, her mother extracted a good deal more of the gossip, to which she finally returned answer—

'There is no telling the harm that is done by chattering gossip in this way. You might have learnt by what happened before what mistakes are made. What am I to do, Valetta? I don't want to hinder you from having friends and companions; but if you bring home such mischievous stories, I shall have to keep you entirely among ourselves till you are older and wiser.'

'I never—never will believe—anybody who says anybody is going to marry anybody!' sobbed Valetta desperately and incoherently.

'Certainly no one who knows nothing about the matter. There is nothing papa and I dislike much more than such foolish talk; and to tease your sister about it is even worse; but I will say no more about that, as I believe it was chiefly Wilfred's doing.'

'I—told—Will,' murmured Valetta. 'Mysie begged me not, but I had done it.'

'How much you would have saved yourself and everybody else if you had let the foolish word die with you! Now, good-night, my dear. Bathe your eyes well, or they will be very uncomfortable to-morrow; and do try to cure yourself of roaring when you cry. It vexes papa so much more.'

Another small scene had to follow with the boy, who was quite willing to go off to bed, having no desire to face his father again, though his mother had her fears that he was not particularly penitent for 'what fellows always did when people were spooning.' He could only be assured that he would experience unpleasant consequences if he recurred to the practice; but Wilfred had always been the problem in the family.

The summer twilight was just darkening completely, and Lady Merrifield had returned to the drawing-room, and was about to ring for lights, when Sir Jasper came in through the window, saying—

'No question now about renewal. Angelic features, more than angelic calmness and dignity. Ha! you there, young ladies!' he added in some dismay as two white dresses struck his eye.

'There's no harm done,' said Lady Merrifield, laughing. 'I was thinking whether to relieve Gillian's mind by telling her the state of the case, and Mysie is to be trusted.'

'Oh, mamma, then it is Kalliope!' exclaimed Gillian, already relieved, for even love could not have perceived calmness and dignity in her sitting upon Bruno's head.

'Has she ever talked about him?' asked Lady Merrifield.

'No; except to-day, when I said I hoped she was safe from him on that road. She said he had always been very kind to her, and taught her to draw when she was quite a little girl.'

'Just so,' said Lady Merrifield. 'Well, when she was a little older, poor Mr. White, who was one of the most honourable and scrupulous of men, took alarm, and saw that it would never do to have the young officers running after her.'

'It was an uncommonly awkward position,' added Sir Jasper, 'with such a remarkable-looking girl, and a foolish unmanageable mother. It made poor White's retirement the more reasonable when the girl was growing too old to be kept at school any longer.'

'And has he been constant to her all these years? How nice!' cried Mysie.

'After a fashion,' said Lady Merrifield. 'He made me the receptacle of a good deal of youthful despair.'

'All the lads did,' said her husband.

'But he got over it, and it seemed to have passed out of his life. However, he asked after the Whites as soon as we met him in London; and now he tells me that he never forgot Kalliope—her face always came between him and any one whom his mother threw in his way; and he came down here, knowing her history, and with the object of seeing her again.'

'And he has not, till now?'

'No. Besides the absolute need of keeping her quiet, it would not exactly do for him to visit her while she is alone with Maura at Cliff House, and I wished him first to see her casually amongst us, for I dreaded her not fulfilling his ideal.'

'Oh!'

'When I think of her at fourteen or fifteen, with that exquisite bloom and the floating wavy hair, I see a very different creature from what she is now.'

'Peach or ivory carving,' said Sir Jasper.

'Yes; she is nobler, finer altogether, and has gained in countenance greatly; but he may not think so, and I should like her to be looking a little less ill.'

'Well, I can't help hoping he will be disappointed, and be too stupid to care for her!' exclaimed Gillian.

'Indeed?' said her father in a tone of displeased surprise.

'He is so insignificant; he does not seem to suit with her,' said Gillian in a tone of defence;' and there does not seem to be anything in him.'

'That only shows the effect of nursing prejudice by using foolish opprobrious nicknames. Henderson was a good officer, he has shown himself an excellent son, always sacrificing his own predilections for the sake of duty. He is a right-minded, religious, sensible man, his own master, and with no connections to take umbrage at Miss White's position. It is no commonplace man who knows how to honour her for it. Nothing could be a happier fate for her; and you will be no friend to her if you use any foolish terms of disparagement of him because he does not happen to please your fancy.'

'I am sure Gillian will do no such thing, now that she understands the case' said her mother.

'Oh no, indeed! said Gillian. 'It was only a first feeling.'

'And you will allow for a little annoyance, papa,' added Lady Merrifield. 'We really have had a great deal of him, and he does spoil the children's walks with you.'

Sir Jasper laughed.

'I agree that the sooner this is over the better. You need have no doubts as to the first view, now that Gillian has effected the introduction. No words can do justice to her beauty, though, by the bye, he must have contemplated her through the back of his head!'

'Well, won't that do! Can't he be sent off for the present, for as to love-making now, with all the doubts and scruples in the way, it would be the way to kill her outright.'

'You must take that in hand, my lady—it is past me! Come, girls, give us some music!'

The two girls went up at bed-time to their room, Mysie capering and declaring that here was real, true, nice love, like people in stories, and Gillian still bemoaning a little that, whatever papa might say, Fa—Captain Henderson would always be too poor a creature for Kalliope.

'If I was quite sure it was not only her beauty,' added Gillian philosophically.

Lady Merrifield went up to Cliff House as early as she could the next day. She found her patient there very white and shaken, but not so much by the adventure of yesterday as by a beautiful bouquet of the choicest roses which lay on the table before her sofa, left by Captain Henderson when he had called to inquire after her.

'What ought I to do, dear Lady Merrifield?' she asked. 'They came while I was dressing, and I did not know.'

'You mean about a message of thanks?'

'Yes; my dear father was so terribly displeased when I wore a rose that he gave me before the great review at Belfast that I feel as if I ought not to touch these; and yet it is so kind, and after all his wonderful kindness yesterday.'

The hand on the side and the trembling lip showed the painful fluttering of heart, and the voice died away.

'My dear, things are very different now. Take my word for it, your father could not be displeased for a moment at any kindness between you and Captain Henderson. Ten years ago he was a very young man, and his parents were living, and your father was bound in honour, and for your sake too, to prevent attentions from the young officers.'

'Oh yes, I know it would have been shocking to have got into that sort of thing!'

'But now he is entirely at his own disposal, and a man of four or five-and-thirty, who has gone through a great deal, and I do not think that to send him a friendly message of thanks for a bunch of flowers to his old fellow-soldier's daughter would be anything but what Captain White would think his due.'

'Oh,'—a sigh of relief,—'please tell him, dear Lady Merrifield!' And she stretched out her hand for the flowers, and lovingly cooled her cheek with their petals, and tenderly admired them singly, venturing now to enjoy them and even caress them.

Lady Merrifield ventured on no more; but she carried off ultimately hopeful auguries for the gentleman who had been watching for her, very anxious to hear her report. She was, however, determined on persuading him to patience, reinforcing her assurances with Dr. Dagger's opinion, that though Kalliope's constitution needed only quiet and rest entirely to shake off the effects of the overstrain of that terrible half-year, yet that renewed agitation would probably entail chronic heart-complaint; and she insisted that without making any sign the lover should go out of reach for several months, making, for instance, the expedition to Norway of which he had been talking. He could not understand at first that what he meant to propose would not be the best means of setting that anxious heart at rest; and Lady Merrifield had to dwell on the swarm of conscientious scruples and questions that would arise about saddling him with such a family, and should not be put to rest as easily as he imagined. At last, by the further representation that she would regard her mother's death as far too recent for such matters to occupy her, and by the assertion of the now fixed conviction that attentions from him at present could only agitate and distress her harmfully, and bring on her malicious remarks, the Captain was induced to believe that Rocca Marina or Florence would be a far better scene for his courtship, and to defer it till he could find her there in better health.

He was brought at last to promise to leave Rockquay at once, and dispose of himself in Norway, if only Lady Merrifield would procure him one meeting with Kalliope, in which he solemnly promised to do nothing that could startle her or betray his intentions.

Lady Merrifield managed it cunningly. It had been already fixed that Kalliope should come down to a brief twelve-o'clock service held at St. Kenelm's for invalids, there to return thanks for her recovery, in what she felt as her own church; and she was to come to Il Lido and rest there afterwards. Resolving to have no spectators, Lady Merrifield sent off the entire family for a picnic at Clipston, promising them with some confidence that they would not be haunted by Captain Henderson, and that she would come in the waggonette, bringing Fergus as soon as he was out of school, drink tea, and fetch home the tired.

Sir Jasper went too, telling her, with a smile, that he was far too shy to assist her in acting chaperon.

'Dragon, you had better say—I mean to put on all my teeth and claws.'

These were not, however, very visible at the church door when she met Kalliope, who had come down in a bath-chair, but was able afterwards to walk slowly to Il Lido. Perhaps Captain Henderson was, however, aware of them; for Kalliope had no knowledge of his presence in the church or in the street, somewhat in the rear, nor did he venture to present himself till there had been time for luncheon and for rest, and till Kalliope had been settled in the cool eastern window under the verandah, with an Indian cushion behind her that threw out her profile like a cameo.

Then, as if to call on Lady Merrifield, Captain Henderson appeared armed, according to a wise suggestion, with his portfolio; and there was a very quiet and natural overlooking of his drawings, which evidently gave Kalliope immense pleasure, quite unsuspiciously. Precautions had been taken against other visitors, and all went off so well and happily that Lady Merrifield felt quite triumphant when the waggonette came round, and, after picking up Fergus, she set Kalliope down at her own door, with something like a colour in her cheeks and lips, and thanks for a happy afternoon, and the great pleasure in seeing one of the dear old Royal Wardours again.

But, oh mamma,' said Gillian, feeling as if the thorn in her thoughts must be extracted, 'are you sure it is not all her beauty?'

'Her beauty, no doubt, began it, and gratifies the artist eye; but I am sure his perseverance is due to appreciation of her noble character,' said Lady Merrifield.

'Oh, mamma, would he if she had been ever so good, and no prettier than other people?'

'Don't pick motives so, my child; her beauty helps to make up the sum and substance of his adoration, and she would not have the countenance she has without the goodness. Let that satisfy you.'

CHAPTER XXIV. — CONCLUSION

The wedding was imminent by this time. The sisters returned from London, the younger looking brilliant and in unusual health, and the elder fagged and weary. Shopping, or rather looking on at shopping, had been a far more wearying occupation than all the schools and districts in Rockquay afforded.

And besides the being left alone, there was the need of considering her future. The family had certainly expected that a rich and open-handed man like Mr. White would bethink him that half what was sufficient for two was not enough for one to live in the same style, and would have resigned his bride's fortune to her sister, but, as a rule, he never did what was expected of him, and he had, perhaps, been somewhat annoyed by Mr. Mohun's pertinacity about settlements, showing a certain distrust of commercial wealth. At any rate, all he did was to insist on paying handsomely for Maura's board; but still Miss Mohun believed she should have to give up the pretty house built by themselves, and go into smaller quarters, more especially as it was universally agreed that Adeline must have Mrs. Mount with her, and Mrs. Mount would certainly be miserable in 'foreign parts' unless her daughter went with her. It was demonstrated that the remaining means would just suffice to keep up Beechcroft; but Jane knew that it could be only done at the cost of her subscriptions and charities, and she merely undertook to take no measures till winter—the Rockquay season.

Sir Jasper, who thought she behaved exceedingly well about it, authorised an earnest invitation to make her home at Clipston; but though she was much gratified, she knew she should be in his way, and, perhaps, in that of the boys, and it was too far from the work to which she meant to devote herself even more completely, when it would be no longer needful to be companionable to a semi-invalid fond of society.

However, just then her brother, the Colonel, came at last for his long leave. He knew that his retirement was only a matter of months, and declared his intention of joining forces with her, if she would have him, and, in the meantime, he was desirous of contributing his full share in keeping up the home. Nor did Jane feel it selfish to accept his offer, for she knew that Clipston would give him congenial society and shooting, and that there was plenty of useful layman work for him in the town; and that 'old Reggie' should wish to set up his staff with her raised her spirits, so that cheerfulness was no longer an effort.

The wedding was to be very quiet. Only just after the day was finally fixed,

Mrs. Merrifield's long decay ended unexpectedly, and Sir Jasper had to hasten to London, and thence to the funeral at Stokesley. She was a second wife, and he her only son, so that he inherited from her means that set him much more at his ease with regard to his large family than he had ever been before. The intention that Lady Merrifield should act mistress of the house at the wedding breakfast had, of course, to be given up, and only Primrose's extreme youth made it possible to let her still be a bridesmaid.

So the whole party, together with the Whites, were only spectators in the background, and the procession into church consisted of just the absolutely needful persons—the bride in a delicate nondescript coloured dress, such as none but a French dressmaker could describe, and covered with transparent lace, like, as Mysie averred, a hedgeback full of pig-nut flowers, the justice of the comparison being lost in the ugliness of the name; and as all Rockquay tried to squeeze into the church to see and admire, the beauty was not thrown away.

No tears were shed there; but afterwards, in her own familiar room, between her two sisters, Adeline White shed floods of tears, and, clinging to Jane's neck, asked how she could ever have consented to leave her, extracting a promise of coming to her in case of illness. Nothing but a knock at the door by Valetta, with a peremptory message that Mr. White said they should be late for the train, induced her to dry her tears and tear herself away.

Kalliope and Maura remained with Miss Mohun during the bridal journey to Scotland, and by the time it was ended the former had shaken off the invalid habits, and could hardly accept the doctor's assurance that she ought not to resume her work, though she was grateful for the delights before her, and the opportunities of improvement that she was promised at Florence. Her health had certainly been improved by Frank Stebbing's departure for America. Something oozed out that made Miss Mohun suspect that he had been tampering with the accounts, and then it proved that there had been a crisis and discovery, which Mr. White had consented to hush up for his partner's sake. Alexis had necessarily known of the investigation and disclosure, but had kept absolute silence until it had been brought to light in other ways, and the culprit was beyond seas. Mr. Stebbing was about to retire from the business, but for many reasons the dissolution of the partnership was deferred.

Alexis was now in a post of trust, with a larger salary. He lodged at Mrs. Lee's, and was, in a manner, free of Miss Mohun's house; but he spent much of his leisure time in study, being now able to pay regularly for instruction from the tutor who taught at Mrs. Edgar's school.

Maura asked him rather pertly what was the use of troubling himself about

Latin and Greek, if he held himself bound to the marble works.

'It is not trouble—it is rest,' he said; and at her gasp, 'Besides, marble works or no, one ought to make the best of one's self.'

By the time Mr. and Mrs. White came back from Scotland, the repairs at Clipston had been accomplished, and the Merrifields had taken possession. It all was most pleasant in that summer weather going backwards and forwards between the houses; the Sunday coming into church and lunching at Aunt Jane's, where Valetta and Primrose stayed for Mrs. Hablot's class, and were escorted home by Macrae in time for evening service at Clipston, where their mother, Gillian, and Mysie reigned over their little school. There was a kind of homely ease and family life, such that Adeline once betrayed that she sometimes felt as if she was going into banishment. However, there was no doubt that she enjoyed her husband's pride in and devotion to her, as well as all the command of money and choice of pretty things that she had obtained, and she looked well, handsome, and dignified.

Still it was evident that she was very glad of Kalliope's companionship, and that the pair were not on those exclusively intimate terms that would make a third person de trop.

By Sir Jasper's advice, Lady Merrifield did not mention the possibility of a visit from Captain Henderson, who would come upon Mr. White far better on his own merits, and had better not be expected either by Adeline or Kalliope.

Enthusiastic letters from both ladies described the delights of the journey, which was taken in a leisurely sight-seeing manner; and as to Rocca Marina, it seemed to be an absolute paradise. Mr. White had taken care to send out an English upholsterer, so that insular ideas of comfort might be fulfilled within. Without, the combination of mountain and sea, the vine-clad terraces, the chestnut slopes, the magical colours of the barer rocks, the coast-line trending far away, the azure Mediterranean, with the white-sailed feluccas skimming across it, filled Kalliope with the more transport because it satisfied the eyes that had unconsciously missed such colouring scenes ever since her early childhood.

The English workmen and their families hailed with delight an English lady. The chaplain and his wife were already at work among them, and their little church only waiting for the bride to lay the first stone.

The accounts of Kalliope's walks as Mrs. White's deputy among these people, of her scrambles and her sketching made her recovery evident. Adeline had just been writing that the girl was too valuable to both herself and Mr. White ever to be parted with, when Captain Henderson came back from Norway, and had free permission from Lady Merrifield to put his fate to the touch.

English tourists who know how to behave themselves were always welcome to enliven the seclusion of Rocca Marina, and admire all, of which Adeline was as proud as Mr. White himself. Recommendations to its hospitality did not fail, and the first of Adeline's long letters showed warm appreciation of this pleasant guest, who seemed enchanted with the spot.

Next, Mrs. White's sagacity began to suspect his object, and there ensued Kalliope's letter, full of doubts and scruples, unable to help being happy, but deferring her reply till she should hear from Lady Merrifield, whether it could be right to burthen any man with such a family as hers.

The old allegiance to her father's commanding officer, as well as the kindness she had received, seemed to make her turn to ask their approval as if they were her parents; and of course it was heartily given, Sir Jasper himself writing to set before her that John Henderson was no suddenly captivated youth unable to calculate consequences, but a man of long-tried affection and constancy, free from personal ties, and knowing all her concerns. The younger ones all gave promise of making their own way, and a wise elder brother was the best thing she could give them. Even Richard might be the better for the connection, and Sir Jasper had taken care that there should be some knowledge of what he was.

There was reason to think that all hesitation had been overcome even before the letters arrived. For it appeared that Captain Henderson had fraternised greatly with Mr. White, and that having much wished for an occupation, he had decided to become a partner in the marble works, bringing the art-knowledge and taste that had been desirable, and Kalliope hoped still to superintend the mosaic workers. It was agreed that the marriage had far better take place away from Rockquay, and it was resolved that it should be at Florence, and that the couple should remain there for the winter, studying art, and especially Florentine mosaic, and return in the spring, when the Stebbings would have concluded their arrangements and vacated their house.

Mr. White, in great delight, franked out Alexis and Maura to be present at the wedding, and a longing wish of Kalliope's that Mr. Flight would officiate was so far expressed that Lady Merrifield mentioned it to him. He was very much moved, for he had been feeling that his relations with the Whites had been chiefly harmful, though, as Alexis now assured him, his notice had been their first ray of comfort in their changed life at Rockquay. The experience had certainly made him older and wiser. Mrs. White—or, as her nieces could not help calling her among themselves, the Contessa di Rocca Marina—urged that her sister Jane should join the company, and bring Gillian to act as the other bridesmaid. This, after a little deliberation, was accepted, and the journey was the greatest treat to all concerned. Mr. Flight, the only one of the party who had travelled before in the sense of being a tourist, was amused by the keen and intense delight of Miss Mohun as well as the younger ones in all they beheld, and he steered them with full experience of hotels and of what ought to be visited, so as to be an excellent courier.

As to Rocca Marina, where they spent a few days, no words would describe their admiration, though they brought home a whole book of sketches to back their descriptions. They did not, however, bring back Maura. Mrs. White had declared that she must remain to supply the place of her sister. She was nearly fifteen years old, and already pretty well advanced in her studies, she would pick up foreign languages, the chaplain would teach her when at Rocca Marina, and music and drawing would be attainable in the spring at Florence. Moreover, Mr. White promised to regard her as a daughter.

Another point was settled. Alexis had worked in earnest for eight months, and had convinced himself that the marble works were not his vocation, though he had acquitted himself well enough to induce Mr. White to offer him a share in the business, and he would have accepted it if needful. He had, however, made up his mind to endeavour to obtain a scholarship at Oxford, and Captain Henderson promised that whether successful in this or not, he should be enabled to keep his terms there. Mr. White could not understand how a man could prefer being a poor curate to being a rich quarrymaster, but his wife and the two sisters had influence enough to prevent him from being offended, and this was the easier, because Theodore had tastes and abilities that made it likely that he would be thoroughly available at the works.

What shall be said of the return to Rockstone? Mr. Flight came home first, then, after many happy days of appreciative sightseeing, Aunt Jane and Gillian. They had not been ashamed of being British spinsters with guide- books in their hands; nor, on the other hand, had they been obliged to see what they did not care about, and Mr. White had put them in the way of the best mode of seeing what they cared about; and above all, the vicissitudes of travel, even in easy-going modern fashion, had made them one with each other according to Jane's best hopes. It was declared that the aunt looked five years younger for such recreation as she had never known before, and she set to work with double energy.

When, in May, Captain and Mrs. Henderson took possession of the pretty house that had been fitted up for them, though Miss Mellon might whisper to a few that she had only been one of the mosaic hands, there was not much inclination to attend to the story among the society to which Lady Merrifield introduced her. These acquaintances would gladly have seen more of her than she had time to give them, between family claims and home cares, her attention to the artistic side of the business, for which she had not studied in vain, and her personal and individual care for the young women concerned therein. For years to come, even, it was likely that visitors to Rockstone would ask one another if they had seen that remarkably beautiful Mrs. Henderson.

Mrs. White, reigning there in the summer, in her fine house and gardens, though handsome as ever, had the good sense to resign the palm of beauty, and be gratified with the admiration for one whom she accepted as a protegee and appendage, whose praise reflected upon herself. And Cliff House under the new regime was a power in Rockstone, with its garden-parties, drawing- room meetings on behalf of everything good and desirable, its general superintendence and promotion of all that could aid in the welfare of the place. There was general rejoicing when it was occupied.

Adeline, in better health than she had enjoyed since her early girlhood, and feeling her consequence both in Italy and at Rockstone, was often radiant, always kind and friendly and ready with patronage and assistance. Her sisters wondered at times how absolute her happiness was; they sometimes thought she said too much about it, and about her dear husband's indulgence, in her letters, to be quite satisfactory; and when she came to Rockstone there was an effusiveness of affection towards her family, an unwillingness to spare her sisters or nieces from her side, an earnest desire to take one back to Italy with her, that betrayed something lacking in companionship. Jane detected likewise such as the idolising husband felt this attachment a little over much.

It was not quite possible to feel him one with her family, or make him feel himself one. He would always be 'company' with them. He had indeed been invited to Beechcroft Court, but it was plain that the visit had been stiff and wearisome to both parties, even more so than that to Rotherwood, where there was no reason to look for much familiarity.

In the same way, to Reginald Mohun, who had been obliged to retire as full Colonel, Mr. White was so absolutely distasteful that it was his sister's continual fear that he would encourage the young people's surreptitious jokes about their marble uncle. Sir Jasper, always feeling accountable for having given the first sanction, did his best for the brother-in-law; but in spite of regard, there was no getting over the uncongeniality that would always be the drop in Adeline's cup. The perfect ease and confidence of family intercourse would alter on his entrance!

Nobody got on with him so well as Captain Harry May. For I do not speak to that dull elf who cannot figure to himself the great family meeting that came to pass when the colonists came home—how sweet and matronly 'Aunt Phyllis' looked, how fresh and bright her daughters were, and how surprised

Valetta was to find them as well instructed and civilised as herself, though she did not like Primrose, expect to see them tattooed. One of the party was no other than Dolores Mohun. She had been very happy with her father for three years. They had been at Kotorua at the time of the earthquake, and Dolores had acquired much credit for her reasonableness and self-possession, but there had been also a young lady, not much above her own age, who had needed protection and comfort, and the acquaintance there begun had ended in her father deciding on a marriage with a pretty gentle creature as unlike the wife of his youth as could be imagined.

Dolores had behaved very well, as her Aunt Phyllis warmly testified, but it was a relief to all parties when the proposal was made that, immediately after the wedding, she should go home under her aunt's escort to finish her education. She had learnt to love and trust Aunt Phyllis; but to be once more with Aunt Lily and Mysie was the greatest peace and bliss she could conceive. And she was a very different being from the angular defiant girl of those days which seemed so long ago.

There is no need to say more at present of these old friends. There is no material for narrative in describing how the 'calm decay' of Dr. May in old age was cheered by the presence of his sailor son, nor in the scenes where the brothers, sisters, and friends exchanged happy recollections, brightened each other's lives with affection and stimulated one another in serving God in their generation.

THE END

9 783732 618880